DEEP WITHIN A
Blueberry Sky

BY JEFFREY J. ANTONUCCI

Woodpecker Press, LLC
Livingston, New Jersey

Copyright © 2018 Jeffrey J. Antonucci

All rights reserved.

No part of this book may be used or reproduced by any means, graphic, electronic, or mechanical, including photocopying, recording, taping, or by any information storage retrieval system without the written permission of the author and publisher, except in the case of brief quotations embodied in articles and reviews.

This is a work of fiction. Names, characters, places, and events are products of the author's imagination and do not refer to any actual person, place, or event.

Published by
Woodpecker Press, LLC
www.WoodpeckerPress.com

ISBN: 978-1-937397-40-1

Printed in the United States of America

Environmental Characteristics of Paper:
• Sustainable Forestry Initiative® (SFI®) Certified Sourcing
• Made with Elemental Chlorine Free (ECF) virgin fiber content.
• Manufactured under alkaline (acid-free) conditions for increased longevity and performance.

Illustrations: Dan Burr Illustration, www.danburr.com
Author Photo: Rigoglioso Photography, www.paigerigoglioso.com
Title Design on Cover: Hannah Bischoff Design & Illustration
Cover and Book Design: Nu-Image Design, www.nu-imagedesign.com

TABLE OF CONTENTS

SARAH AT SEVEN

RISE AND SHINE

CHAPTER 1

"Oh, I hope everyone is as excited as I am to be on our way to visit Poppy Tom for a nice relaxing time in the country," Cecilia said to her family as they set out in the car on their summer getaway. "I love working with my clients, but sometimes I just need to take a break.

"Sarah, you should be especially excited this year because Poppy Tom has a special surprise in store for you now that you've turned seven."

"Do you know what this special surprise is, Mommy?" Sarah asked her mother from the back seat.

"Yes, I sure do. Poppy Tom had this very same special surprise for me when I turned seven."

"So that was what, about ten, twelve years ago?" Cecilia's husband, Justin, interrupted with a laugh.

"Don't I wish," Cecilia replied.

"Oh please, Mommy, tell me, what the surprise is. Please, oh please, Mommy. Tell me, tell me, tell me!"

"A team of wild horses couldn't drag it out of me, Sarah. I know Poppy Tom is really looking forward to telling you himself. You'll just have to be patient and wait 'til we arrive at Poppy's house."

"When will we get there? Will we be there soon, Mommy? How long 'til we get there?"

Cecilia's and Justin's rolling eyes conveyed their realization that this is going to be a long trip.

When they finally arrived at Poppy Tom's quaint and cozy country home, Sarah rushed from the car to the open arms of her grandfather and to the excited jumps and wiggles of his dog, Hollie the Collie, eagerly asking, "Poppy Tom, Poppy Tom, what's my surprise, what's my surprise?"

Cecilia and Justin looked on happily at the scene taking place before them while their two-year old, Justin Jr., anxiously kicked his legs and waved his arms to gain their attention and free him from the constraints of his car seat.

"You know there's a surprise?" Poppy Tom questioned Sarah as he glared at his daughter, Cecilia.

"I know you have a surprise for me, Poppy, but I don't know what it is. Is it a puppy? Did Hollie have puppies? A new video game? Maybe even my own pony?"

"Well Sarah, it's not any of those things or anything like them. The surprise I have for you isn't a thing at all but has to do with something we're going to do together. Something very special to do together. Oh, yes, there are wonderful adventures and discoveries in store for you if you are ready to take them on."

"Oh, what is it? What is this special surprise we're going to do together, Poppy?"

"Sarah, now that you're seven years old, Hollie and I will be guiding you to a special secret spot where we'll go fly-fishing for brook trout together. Just as I did with your mother when she was seven. You know Sarah, fly-fishing is a very grown-up thing to do, and by doing that you *will* find adventure and discovery."

"Fishing, you're taking me to a secret spot to go fishing? That *is* a very grown-up thing to do, Poppy. Sure, I'm big now so I can go. Sure, I can go! Are we going now? Let's go right now, Poppy. I can't wait to catch a giant river trout! I'm ready, I'm ready for *a'ventures* and *scoveries*."

"Okay, that sounds grand, but we can't go right now because there are some things we need to prepare for first. Besides, one of the best times to go fishing is early in the morning. So, we'll need to get up early tomorrow morning and, after a hearty breakfast, we'll head out to *try* and catch a brook trout. Not a river trout, Sarah. A brook trout. You know there are no guarantees that we'll catch one, let alone a giant one. But that doesn't matter. The most important thing is to go out there and try our best, enjoy the journey and our time together, and have *ad*ventures and make *dis*coveries along the way. So, I suggest we get you guys all settled in, have ourselves a bite to eat, and then Sarah, we can begin our preparations for tomorrow morning's expedition. Sound good?"

Sarah raised her two arms in the air, clenched her two fists, pumped them once, and said with conviction, "YES!"

After a satisfying lunch, Poppy Tom explained to Sarah in a loving, mentoring manner, "Granddaughter, please know that fishing is a privilege and a very responsible thing to do. We must respect the environment in which the brook trout and all wildlife live. Nature is their home and we're only visiting. The brook trout needs very clean, cold water to be happy. I noticed that there's a place where flooding has caused a washout, allowing dirt and rocks to enter the brook. If we expect there always to be many happy, healthy brook trout, then we must also always keep the brook in which they live healthy. So, Hollie and I would like you to help us make repairs to the bank of the brook. Doing that will earn us the right to venture into the brook trout's happy home. Are you with us, Sarah?"

"Yes, Poppy Tom! I sure am!"

As Poppy Tom and Sarah looked on admirably at the results of their efforts in repairing and restoring the bank of the brook with Hollie by their side, he said, "Well Sarah, I'd say together we did a great job. The brook trout and all the other creatures will stay happy and healthy living here. I'd say we've earned the privilege of entering the brook trout's home. So, now that we're finished up here, we'll head over to Nate's Baits, the next place on our agenda, to get you equipped with everything you'll need to go fly-fishing."

CHAPTER 2

"Hello, Mr. Nate," Poppy Tom called out.

"Well, hello there my friend, Tom," Mr. Nate replied from behind the counter of his rustic sporting goods store, adorned with various items depicting his noble, Native American culture. "If I didn't know better, I'd say that young lady joining you today was Cecilia accompanied by the pretty Polly."

"Well, I can understand you thinking so, but I'm proud to say this fine young lady is my granddaughter, Sarah, and that's pretty Polly's descendant, Hollie. We're hoping you can help equip Sarah with everything she needs for her first time going fly-fishing for brook trout."

"I remember doing that for Cecilia when you brought her here so many years ago, and I'd be honored to do that for Sarah today. So, come on, let's get started!"

As Mr. Nate was coming close to completely outfitting Sarah with all the necessities, she said with amazement, "Wow, you sure need a whole bunch of really fun, cool things to go fly-fishing."

"You're right, Sarah, but there's one more really fun, cool and important thing for you to get, and that's a hat." Mr. Nate explained. "And, we need to make that hat a lucky hat. So, I'm giving you this fine feather for your hat. This feather is representative of a feather from the tail of a red-tailed hawk. In my proud culture, this feather has great powers. It will give you luck, guidance, and the ability to see all the wonders of the beautiful world around you." To learn about this feather's powers, when you go outside hold your feather up to the sun. You'll be amazed at what you see and the secrets it will unfold."

"Okay, Sarah, now that Mr. Nate has you equipped, let's go visit a few of my friends over at the Farmer's Market," Poppy Tom said.

When they arrived, Poppy Tom proudly took Sarah to the farm stands where so many kind producers market their wares. "Sarah it's my pleasure to introduce you to my friends, Sherry and Jerry, owners of Sherry's and Jerry's Berries," he said with a smile. "The sweetest berries are grown on their fine, local, organic farm. They learned the secrets of how to do that, very expertly, from generations who tilled the rich soil of their native Japan."

"Nice to meet you both," Sarah said.

"It's our pleasure to meet you, Sarah," Sherry said, as Jerry looked on approvingly.

"Poppy, what does *organkick* mean?"

"Not *organkick*, Sarah, *organic*," he replied. "What organic means is that our friends grow all their crops without the use of any unhealthy chemicals or pesticides. So, when we eat those crops, we stay healthy and so does our environment. Mother Nature really likes it that way."

"And so do our brook trout friends, right Poppy?" Sarah asked confidently.

Poppy Tom's big smile and positive head nods conveyed to Sarah that he agreed with her statement and was impressed with her quick ability and enthusiasm to learn.

Next, Poppy Tom took Sarah to visit Mrs. T, who produces the finest maple syrup and honey and doles out extra portions of sugary warmth and sweet kindness to anyone who happens by. These are amazing qualities that were passed on to Mrs. T from her fine lineage while growing up in the deep south.

"Hello there, 'sugar.' My name is Mrs. T, of Mrs. T's Sugar from Trees and Honey from Bees," she said as she greeted Sarah. "I know this handsome gentleman escorting you here today, but I don't believe I've had the pleasure of meeting you."

Sarah replied excitedly, "My name is Sarah! Maybe you know my mommy?"

"Well, if I were to put two and two together, I'd say you're Cecilia's little girl. You're just as pretty and just as sweet."

"If you put two and two together, you get four. I know that from my math class. And you're right, Mrs. T., Cecilia is my mommy. Thank you very much!"

Poppy Tom, seeing Sarah and Mrs. T getting along fine, moved along, leaving the two ladies to chat.

Mrs. T looked on charmed by Sarah and said, "Well, honey child, if you're anything like your mama, you probably have a sweet tooth."

"Which one?" Sarah asked, while trying to taste her teeth. "My teeth don't taste sweet. They don't have any taste at all, not that I can tell."

"Oh no, sugar plum," Mrs. T said with a chuckle. "That's just an expression we use for someone who likes sweets."

"Oh, that's me because I do like sweets," Sarah replied. "But Mommy and Daddy say I can't have too many sweets because they can hurt my teeth."

"Yup, your mama and daddy are right, honey bunny. But I sure do hope they'll allow you to taste some of my good, wholesome sweets, proudly made by Mother Nature herself. Just make sure you brush your teeth afterward, that's all."

"I bet if I promise my mommy and daddy that I'll brush my teeth afterward, they'd be okay with me tasting your sweets. If Mother Nature made it, it will taste good and be good for me, too."

"Smart, just like your mama," Mrs. T confirmed.

With all the items on Poppy Tom's preps for the morning's outing complete, the whole family, including Hollie the Collie, was back at the cabin and it was time for bed. The blazing fire in the idyllic fieldstone fireplace cast a cozy, amber glow throughout the cottage and danced off the cabin's shiny, varnished wood beams and wrapped all its lodgers in a warm, cuddling embrace.

Poppy Tom, still at the helm said, "Sarah remember, we'll be needing to get up early in the morning to go fishing. So, I think you should be heading off to bed."

"Oh yes," said Sarah, "I'm on my way. What time are you setting the alarm clock for, Poppy?"

"Oh, there's no need for me to be setting any alarm clocks to wake us up," he answered.

"But how are we going to wake up on time?"

"Oh, don't worry about that, Sarah. We'll wake up on time. Brewster will see to that."

"Brewster? Who's Brewster?"

"Oh, you'll find out. Oh, yes, you'll find out alright," answered Poppy Tom, grinning. "Sarah would you say you had a good day today?"

"Oh, yes, I sure did!"

"Would you say that today you had adventures and made discoveries and some new friends, too?"

"Yes, I would say so."

"Well then, Sarah, that being the case, I'd say you had yourself a *great* day."

"You know, Poppy, I'd say you're right. I had a *great* day!"

"Good night, sleep tight, and may all your dreams be bright, my dearest granddaughter."

"Good night, don't fight, and sneeze with all your might, my dearest grandfather," Sarah replied, jokingly.

"Hey good one, Sarah," he responded, impressed with Sarah's spontaneity.

CHAPTER 3

"Well, good morning Sarah," said Poppy Tom. "I see Brewster the Rooster did his job and woke you up on time."

"He sure did," Sarah said groggily as she dragged herself from her bedroom toward the alluring aroma emanating from the kitchen. "I think I like waking up to music better."

"In the country, that is music," said Poppy Tom.

"Hey, look, I've prepared for us a hearty breakfast of pancakes hot off the griddle with fresh raspberries straight from Sherry's and Jerry's, smothered in good ol' Mrs. T's pure maple syrup."

"Yummy, they sure look good, Poppy, and they smell really good, too. Hey, there's a letter by my plate. Whose letter is this?"

"Can you read what it says on the envelope, Sarah?"

"Yes, I can. It says, 'To the Light of the World.' Who is that?"

"Why that's *you*, Granddaughter. Who else would it be?"

"Me? I'm the light of the world, Poppy?"

"Of course, you are. You didn't know that?"

"No, I didn't know that. How come I'm the light of the world?"

"Oh, that's easy, Sarah. Let me ask you, do you love your mother and father and your baby brother?"

"I sure do," she said, "a whole big bunch."

"And do you love me and Grandma Jennie, even though she's in heaven?"

"Oh, yes, a whole big bunch."

"Well, Sarah, when you love someone like that, that love is like a light shining on them and it makes them smile and feel happy.

"You make your mommy and daddy and little Justin smile. You make me smile, and you made Grandma Jennie smile, too. Yesterday, you made Mr. Nate, Sherry and Jerry, and Mrs. T all smile because they felt your love-light shining on them. You light up their world as you do for all of us."

"Hearing this makes me smile and feel happy too, Poppy."

"It should Sarah. That's because when your love-light shines on me, like it's doing right now, it gets reflected back on you. When love is given, it comes back to the giver in the same measure, and all are then smiling and happy. That's how love works, Sarah. And that's what makes you the light of the world."

"I love you, Poppy," she said, giving him a hug.

"I love you, too, Sarah. Now open your card and read what it says, please."

And so, she did.

To the Light of the World

Allow us to say with all of our hearts,
Treasure each day from the moment it starts.

Look for the good and never the bad,
Be the happy to those who are sad.

We know there are No Limits to what you can do,
So go out and discover worlds that are new.

"This is very pretty, Poppy. Did you write this just for me?"

"Actually, Sarah, Grandma Jennie and I worked on it together. Grandma wrote it out. She always had such beautiful handwriting. She made me promise to give this to you when the time was right. We want you to know how much we love you and how special you are to us, Sarah. It's for you to read now and to refer back to anytime you want to, as you get older. Allow it to act as a guide to live the wonderful life we know you have ahead of you, sweetheart."

"I will," Sarah said. "I'll keep this forever. It's so pretty, Poppy. Grandma Jennie writes very pretty. But remember, I'm a big girl already."

"Keep that poem and the lucky feather Mr. Nate gave you, and you can't go wrong," he told her. "And you're right. You are a big girl now; so, you'd better go ahead and eat like one, because your breakfast is getting cold."

CHAPTER 4

Now well fueled from their breakfast of pancakes oozing with sweet, generous toppings of love and devotion, Poppy Tom guided Sarah, with her lucky feathered hat, along with all her new equipment (expertly chosen for her by the wise Mr. Nate), and the glued-to-her-side Hollie, to the first stop on what would become a very eventful day for Sarah.

Sarah asked, "Poppy is this your secret fishing spot? It's really pretty here. Is this it? Are we here?"

"Oh, no Sarah, my secret fishing spot is more upstream. I'm taking you here first, so I can teach you the fine art of fly casting."

"Art? I have art in school, Poppy. I love art. I didn't know I'd be painting pictures and fishing all at the same time. This is really going to be a fun day."

"Well, Sarah, I don't mean to disappoint you, but we won't be doing any painting today. Although, heaven knows, the fence up by the house can sure use a little sprucing up.

"When I said art," he continued, "I didn't mean the art of painting pictures. Art, in this case, refers to a delicate way of fishing compared to other ways. But now that I know you take art in school, I can use your love and knowledge of painting pictures to help with your lesson."

"Do you think I can really do this, Poppy? I mean it sounds like maybe, I mean, I know I'm a big girl and all, but shouldn't I be a little more bigger? We can go paint the fence if you want Poppy. I wouldn't mind."

"Do I think you can do this? No, I don't *think* you can do this, Sarah, I *know* you can do this. You need to remember what's written in that poem I gave you this morning. You know, the part about, 'we know there are no limits to what you can do.' I believe in you Sarah, and so does Grandma Jennie looking down at you from heaven. We really do. You just have to believe in yourself. Don't worry, I'll be with you every step of the way. Hollie, too. Are you good with this now?"

"Yes, I'm good," she replied. "I'm good with this now, knowing you'll be with me every step of the way and Hollie girl, too."

"You can count on us, Sarah," he assured her.

"Okay, now back to our lesson. Let's pretend we were going to paint the fence up by the house. We would need to get big buckets of paint and big heavy brushes, and we'd have to work really, really hard for a long time to paint that big ol' fence. Right?"

She agreed with a quick, "Right!"

"So now, let's pretend we were going to paint something different. Let's say this beautiful landscape before us. See the blue water and the sky with all those puffy white clouds, the trees with all their green leaves, even the multicolored butterflies as they dance from flower to flower. Do you think we would paint this picture the same way using the same big ol' heavy brushes that we would have used painting that big ol' fence?"

"Oh no, Poppy. We'd have to use very thin brushes and all different colors of paint, and keep our hand real steady as we painted. We would have to become really, really, good artists."

"Sarah," said Poppy Tom, "that's why I'm *sooo* proud of you. You've just described the difference between taking a regular method of painting and bringing it to a whole other level. Bringing it to an art form. Good for you!

"So now, Sarah," Poppy Tom instructed, "take your fly rod in your hand. Close your eyes and using your imagination, pretend you are gently holding a very thin paint brush and you're about to paint the beautiful, delicate wing of a butterfly. Can you see the paint brush?

Can you see the beautiful colors on the wing of the butterfly as you're painting it?"

"Yes, Poppy, I see the paint brush, I see the beautiful colors on the butterfly's wing in my *magination* as I'm painting it. I can, I really can see it," Sarah said excitedly.

"Great Sarah, now move the paint brush—or what is now your fly rod—smoothly forward and backward and slowly open your eyes," Poppy Tom explained.

"Wow," Sarah said excitedly, "Am I doing it, am I doing it right?"

"So far, so good Sarah," he said, encouraging her. "Now here comes the important part. Slowly pull the fly line from the reel, see how the line goes out little by little as you keep moving your rod back and forth and forth and back?"

"Yes, Poppy, I see, I see!" Sarah said.

"Okay, keep the line floating in the air and let it out until it gets even with the middle of the brook. When it does, allow the fly to fall gently to the surface of the water."

"Is it there now, now? Should I let it come down now, Poppy?"

"No, it's not there yet. Let it go out a little bit more. Remember, you're painting a butterfly's wing, nice and smooth and gentle," he said with encouragement, keeping a watchful eye every time she cast her fly. "Okay, you're almost there. Alright, when you're ready, let the fly fall gently to the surface."

"Like that, like that, Poppy? Did I do it right? Did I do it the way I was supposed to, Poppy?"

"Yes, you sure did. Just like an expert. I knew you could do it, Sarah."

"I did it! I did it! I did it just like an expert!"

"You see, Sarah, there are no limits to what you can do. Just like your poem says. All you have to do is believe in yourself and you can do anything."

"Thank you, Poppy! Thank you for teaching me how to fly-cast."

"You're more than welcome, Granddaughter. Thank you for wanting to learn. We'll practice a little more, and then we'll head for the secret fishing hole. That's where your true test will be, Sarah. Are you up for it?"

"Yup, I sure am, Poppy, because I have you with me every step of the way. I have my poem in my pocket and my new lucky hat with my beautiful, red, lucky feather, and Hollie, too."

"You go girl!" Poppy Tom said encouragingly.

Feeling Sarah had practiced casting enough, he directed, "Sarah, it's time we head out. Follow me and I'll guide you to our secret spot. You must promise me that you'll keep its location a secret."

"Oh sure, Poppy, I promise to keep it a secret. I'm really good at keeping secrets."

"Okay, let's shake on it," Poppy Tom said, extending his right hand out toward her. "There, that makes it official. Now I can give you directions on how to get there, because when you're older, you might want to come here all by yourself."

Poppy Tom began with a question, "Sarah, do you know the first four letters of the alphabet?"

"Yup! *A*, *B*, *C*, and *D*," she replied.

"Okay, very good. Keep those letters in mind. Now, let's follow the path and when we get to that big apple tree over there, we're going to make a left."

"*A* is for…Apple," and they said the word apple together.

"So, we go left at the apple tree and when we get to that big old rock that looks like a bear, we're going to make a right," instructed Poppy Tom as they kept moving.

"*B* is for…Bear," and they said the word bear together.

"So, we go right," he added.

"Sarah, we're now going to take a shortcut through this corral, where these friendly horses, Lightning and Thunder, live. I have permission from Mr. and Mrs. Rivera, the owners of this farm, to cut through. I brought along some sweets that I'll describe to you how to share with these two beautiful animals. It's something I know you'll have fun doing and something Lightning and Thunder will appreciate and remember you by forever. Also, I'll explain how we must always remember to close the gates behind us and respect the landowner's property. Just so you know, these are all big, grown-up things to be doing, Sarah. When we go through the corral, we're going to make another left."

"*C* is for…Corral," and they said the word corral together.

"Well Sarah, so far, so good and we've now come to the last place before the secret fishing hole. It's called the Dark Woods."

"*D* is for…Dark Woods," and they said the words Dark Woods together.

"And all we have to do is go straight through and we'll be there," said Poppy Tom."

"So, remember Sarah, *A* is for…?" Poppy Tom asked.

"Apple tree," she quickly replied with a big smile on her face.

"And we go which way?"

"Left," she said.

"*B* is for…?" Poppy Tom asked.

"Bear," she blurted out.

"And we go where?" he asked.

"Right," she called out.

"*C* is for…?" Poppy Tom asked.

"Corral," Sarah responded.

"And we go which way?" he asked again.

"Left," she said.

"And *D* is for…?"

"Dark Woods," Sarah stated with certainty.

"And we go, where?"

"Straight through," she answered.

"One hundred percent correct there, smarty pants," Poppy Tom stated proudly.

"Sarah, you follow me through the Dark Woods, nice and slowly and quietly. We don't want to frighten or disturb the brook trout or any other wild creatures that might be nearby."

"Poppy, you go ahead. I'll go back through Lightning's and Thunder's corral and wait for you out there, okay?"

"What's that, Sarah? We're almost there. Don't you want to go fishing anymore? Are you alright?"

"Yes, I'm alright. I'm good. I just think I want to go back now."

"Tell me why, Sarah. Why do you want to go back?"

"I guess, I guess maybe I'm not as big a girl as I thought I was. I think I'm scared. I am. I'm really scared, Poppy. I want to go back."

"Scared? Tell me, what's making you so scared?"

"I'm scared of that big ol' mean-looking owl in that tree and those woods. Those woods are *sooo* dark and spooky. I really don't like it here anymore, Poppy. I really want to go back."

"Okay, okay, Sarah, if you really want to go back, we can. But can we take a moment to talk about this a little bit first, please? Remember, I'm right here with you. And remember what I said before, I would be with you every step of the way."

"Ah, ye, ye, ye, yes, Poppy. I, I, I, I remember," she replied very shakily. "We, we, we, we can take a mi, mi, mi, minute to talk, I guess."

"Okay, great. Thank you. Now, let's both take a couple of deep breaths as I share some thoughts.

"Please know, Granddaughter, I understand completely why you would feel frightened by the Dark Woods and want to turn back. And it has nothing to do with not being big enough. In fact, I know some folks that are my age who would have turned tail and run away a long time ago. But I feel if I help you look at things differently and have you face your fears, you won't be frightened by this place anymore. Are you up for us giving it a whirl?"

"Ah, okay," she said half-heartedly.

"If at any time you start to feel uncomfortable or afraid and feel it's time to leave, just say the word and we'll leave. No questions asked. Deal?"

"Deal," she said.

"Okay then, shake," Poppy Tom said, reaching out to her.

"How about we look again at Ol' Mister Scowl the Owl up there in that big ol' tree?" Poppy Tom asked. "You said he was mean."

"Do I have to, Poppy? I don't like him. He's an old meanie. I can tell. I can tell just by the way he looks that he's an old meanie. See, even his name is mean. Ol' Mister Scowl the Owl. He's an old meanie, alright."

"Well, okay, but think about this," Poppy Tom said. "Maybe it's not fair to judge poor Ol' Mister Scowl the Owl just by the way he looks or by his name. You see, Mother Nature made him look that way for a

reason. She made him with those big piercing eyes so he can see better in the low light of the dark forest. This is where he lives. This is his home. Where we see a scowl, maybe that's his way of smiling. Maybe he has the perfect owl smile. We wouldn't know for sure because we're people, but maybe all the other owls in the forest are jealous of Ol' Mister Scowl the Owl's perfect owl smile.

"And if you think about it, Sarah, he's really not making a fuss about us being here. If you ask me, he's saying to us, welcome to my home. Please come and enjoy passing through, but remember to leave my home as you found it. I'd do the same if I visited yours.

"What do you think now, Sarah? What do you think about your ol' meanie Scowl the Owl, now?"

"You know, Poppy, I think he *is* smiling! I think he *is* happy to see us. He's not an ol' meanie, after all."

"Good for you, Granddaughter."

"I wish he *could* come and visit our home someday, Poppy."

"Hey, you never know, he just might. But I bet ol' Brewster the Rooster would get jealous," Poppy Tom joked.

"I bet Ol' Mister Scowl the Owl would be a lot quieter in the mornings than ol' Brewster the Rooster," said Sarah.

Poppy Tom chuckled and asked, "So how are we doing so far, Sarah? Are you okay with hanging around here a little bit more and allowing me to continue?"

"Okay, Poppy, I'm okay."

"Great, let's shake on it again then.

"Now, Sarah, let's talk about these Dark Woods that have you so concerned. Sure Sarah, those woods are a dark place. And when places are dark, they can look spooky. But you know, there's really no difference between where we're standing now and the Dark Woods."

"Oh, yes there is, Poppy. It's dark and spooky-looking in there, and it's nice and bright and not spooky-looking out here."

"Well, that's true. But, the only reason why it's nice and bright out here is because we're standing in an open area where the sun can shine directly on us," he explained. "In there, these very grand, old growth trees live and their tops tower way up in the sky, making their branches act like an umbrella, preventing the sunlight from making its way down to the ground. That's the only reason it's dark in there. Think about it. It's just like the way your hat is now blocking the sun from shining on your face. Your face doesn't become spooky-looking just because it's shaded by your hat." And he quickly jokingly added, "Well, maybe a little bit."

"POPPY!" Sarah replied.

"What we have before us, Sarah, is not a spooky place at all, but a very special place. One that took Mother Nature many years of hard work to create. It is home to our new-found friend Ol' Mister Scowl the Owl, and red-tailed hawks who would recognize that lucky feather in your hat. Berries that Sherry and Jerry raise on their farm grow wild here and may even be sweeter. Some of these ancient trees can produce sugary maple syrup, and it's where bees weave their hives, which produce succulent honey, just like Mrs. T's. This forest also helps protect and clean the water in the stream, where brook trout, rare frogs, and so many other amazing creatures live.

"Yes, Sarah, this is a very special place. And if you chose to turn away just because you thought it was spooky, you would be missing out on a very wonderful experience. It offers a whole new world for you to discover. And if you remember the last line from your poem that says, 'so go out and discover, worlds that are new.' Well, this is one of those new worlds.

"My darling granddaughter, I promise you will find a bright, new, shiny world at the other end of these Dark Woods, and at the other end of any dark places you'll ever have to go through in your life as long as you look for the good and never the bad, are brave, and believe that there are no limits to what you can do. Remember your poem, Sarah. Always remember your poem and what it says.

"So, what are you thinking about doing my dear girl? Do we go through or do we go home?"

"You'll be with me every step of the way, right Poppy? Right?"

"I sure will be, Sarah, and so will Hollie. And don't forget you have your lucky feather that Mr. Nate says will give you luck, guidance, and the ability to see all the wonders of the beautiful world around you."

"Would you mind, I mean, it would be okay if you held my hand if you wanted to Poppy?" she asked. "You know, just in case you get a little scared, I can protect *you*. You can hold my hand nice and tight if you want to, Poppy. I mean, if it makes you feel better."

"Oh, okay, yes. Thank you, Sarah. I just might need some protecting. I guess this means we're going through," he said as they entered the Dark Woods.

"Oh, no, Poppy, there's a big ugly spider on that big ugly spider web," Sarah said, pointing in its direction. "Spiders bite and are poisonous. See it *is* spooky in here, and I'm getting scared again, Poppy."

"Okay, stay calm. That spider is minding his own business over there," he explained. "You're right, Sarah. Some spiders are poisonous, well, really venomous, but I know what you mean. This one might or might not be, but we'll respect his space and go around him just the same, so we don't disturb him."

"Ah, oh no, there's a creepy crawly thing hanging from that branch," Sarah said anxiously.

"That? That's just a fuzzy little caterpillar. She's not going to harm anybody, Sarah. That caterpillar will soon be changing into one of those beautiful butterflies you saw earlier and imagined you were painting."

"How can that happen, Poppy? How can that caterpillar change into one of those beautiful butterflies?"

"You're asking me?" he asked. "You need to be asking Mother Nature that question."

"How? How can I ask her, Poppy? Where is she so I can ask her?"

"Well, Sarah, Mother Nature is all around us. But she's not like a real person we can question about these things. She wants us to answer those kinds of questions and make those kinds of discoveries for ourselves. And when we do, we then realize how wondrous the many gifts are that she creates."

"Poppy, knowing Mother Nature is all around us helps me from not being too scared anymore. She's a really nice mother because she made all the great things that we see. She would never make anything that would be scary or spooky even though they sometimes look that way to me, uh, I mean to you. So, I'm not scared anymore. But if you want to keep holding my hand, you can. Just because I'm not scared anymore doesn't mean you're not."

"Sarah, I'd say your feather is working its magic by allowing you to see all the wonders of the beautiful world around you, and you just looked for the good and never the bad just like it says in your poem, which is great! Way to go, and if it's okay with you, I'd still like to hold your hand."

"Oh, sure, Poppy, you can. You can keep holding my hand. It's okay."

"Thank you, my dear Sarah. We're almost there. We're almost through the Dark Woods. Just a little bit more and we'll be at the special, secret fishing spot. Wait 'til you see it, Sarah. It's so, so beautiful."

CHAPTER 5

"Oh, wow, oh, wow, Poppy. You're right. It's so beautiful here. It is. It's so bright and shiny, just like you promised me it would be. A bright, shiny place at the other end of a dark place, just like you promised!"

"I knew it. I knew you'd love it here, Sarah. I was so looking forward to sharing this place with you, and now we're here together and you get to see it for yourself. But, you did it, Sarah. You had to work very hard to get here and overcome many tough challenges. I hope you're enjoying this journey and our time together. I hope you feel you're having adventures and making discoveries along the way. I hope you feel it's worth the very hard effort you're making, Sarah."

"Oh, yes, Poppy, I am. I'm really enjoying this, but the best part is being here with you, Poppy. You make me feel real special because you wanted to take me here, to your special, secret fishing spot. Thank you, Poppy. I love you. I love you so, so much! You too, Hollie."

"That's why you're the light of the world, Sarah. Your love makes me so very happy, my dear granddaughter, and I love you so, so very much too," he said lovingly.

"Now look, Sarah. Look at Hollie. While we've been chatting, she's been trying to remind us why we've come here in the first place. She knows we've come here to go fishing. Notice how she's creeping slowly toward the edge of the brook? She knows we need to be real quiet now," he said in a hushed voice. "Let's follow her to that bush at the water's edge and use that bush to hide behind."

"Why do we have to be quiet, and who are we hiding from, Poppy? I don't see anybody around," she said, using a louder voice than she should.

Poppy Tom motioned to Sarah to lower her voice as he answered, "We're hiding from the brook trout."

"From the brook trout? But they're underwater, how can they hear us and see us if they're way under the water and we're way up here?" asking, again, in a louder voice than she should.

"Whisper, Sarah. We need to whisper now. They can hear us and see us, even though they're underwater. They can even feel the vibrations from our movements. That's why we need to creep up to the brook very slowly and softly," he instructed. "If they see us or feel our vibrations, we'll spook them and then we'll never get them to bite, not today, anyway. Mother Nature gave the brook trout these defenses to help them survive."

Poppy Tom saw by Sarah's curious, squinting eyes and subtle head nods that she was beginning to realize that, in nature, there was much to be learned and discovered and how much fun this learning and discovering could be. He allowed her some time to ponder and then said, "Okay, Sarah, we've come all this way. We're in position, and it's now the moment of truth. Hollie and I are here to support you. You have your poem in your pocket, and you're wearing your lucky hat with your lucky feather. All you have to do now is cast your fly the same way you practiced earlier."

"Just like I'm painting the pretty wing of a butterfly, right, Poppy?" Sarah asked in a shaky whisper. "But it's like, like, a whole bunch of those butterflies are flying around in my tummy, and they're wearing backpacks filled with heavy rocks. I'm not holding the paintbrush very steady. I'm nervous, Poppy, and my hand is shaking."

"That's okay. It's only natural to be nervous. This is your first time doing this for real. You just have to try to control your nerves. Do like we did before and take a couple of deep breaths. That will help calm you down. And, remember what it says in your poem, 'there are no limits to what you can do.' Now, let's give it a try."

Sarah, hearing the understanding and confidence-building words of her devoted grandfather, shook off her apprehension and doubt, and began to cast.

"Perfect, Sarah! That's perfect! You're casting perfectly," Poppy Tom said in an excited whisper. "Just a little bit more, just feed out a little bit more line and then allow your fly to fall gently to the surface of the water, just like before."

"Okay, Poppy, a little bit more, a little bit…now, I'm letting my fly fall down now, Poppy," Sarah said in a more anxious whisper.

"Right on, Sarah! Perfect presentation! Now continue to let line out to allow the fly to float smoothly downstream. Get ready, there's no reason why a trout shouldn't strike."

"What happened, Poppy? How come no fish bited my fly?"

"That's okay, Sarah. Take up your line and repeat that same motion. You have to keep at it and not get discouraged. That was only your first cast."

Sarah continued casting and after a while asked, in a disappointing whisper, "What am I doing wrong, Poppy? How come I'm not catching any fishes? I keep casting and nothing's happening."

"You're not doing anything wrong, Sarah. Sometimes it takes a while for them to bite. Sometimes they don't bite at all. You never know. Fishing takes patience, a lot of patience. All you can do is keep trying your best, giving it your best, and hoping for the best. But we can make a little move. Nice and easy now, we'll move downstream a bit. Maybe we'll have better luck down there. I'll tie on a different fly for you to try."

After their move, Sarah asked, "Are you sure, Poppy? Are you sure I'm not doing anything wrong? How come I keep casting and no brook trout wants to eat my fly?"

"Sarah, I'm telling you, I'm not seeing you doing anything wrong. Maybe the trout just aren't hungry today." And then, things changed suddenly.

"Sarah that's a hit, you have a hit, a trout just took your fly! Now pull up, pull up sharply on your rod and set the hook, now, quickly, quickly!" Poppy Tom advised. "Yes, yes, you have one on! He's on, he's on!"

"Oh, Poppy, oh, Poppy, he bited my fly! He bited my fly, Poppy! I can feel him tugging, Poppy! I can feel him. He's really tugging. He's trying to eat my fly. I think he's eating it all up. What do I do now? What do I do now, Poppy?

"Here, Poppy, here take the rod. You know what to do. Here, you take it. Take it! Take the rod, Poppy, and catch the fish. But you're going to have to stop jumping up and down and stop shaking me so much first," Sarah said. "Maybe you should take a couple of deep breaths, Poppy."

"Oh, yes, right, I need to relax," Poppy Tom said excitedly. "I'm sorry, but this is all very, very exciting, Sarah! You have a fish on. Isn't that great? He looks like a nice one, too!"

"Come on, Poppy, take the rod, take the rod!"

"Oh, no you don't," Poppy Tom said. "You were successful in having a trout take your fly so now it's all up to you. Are you still feeling him fighting, is he still tugging?"

"Yes, he's tugging! He's tugging a lot. Oh, wow, he's tugging really hard, Poppy. What do I do now, Poppy?"

"Okay, listen very closely. You need to keep the pressure on him. You need to always keep a bend in the rod, but not too much and not too little. You need to tire him out now."

"Is this too much? Is this too little? How much of a bend? Oh, wow, he's really tugging, he's really tugging hard. Is the bend good? How's the bend, Poppy?"

"You feel him tugging? That's the fun part. Feeling him tugging is the fun part, Sarah. Just stay calm now and play him. Play him nicely. Keep taking nice deep breaths.

"You want to have a little bit more bend, it looks like to me," Poppy Tom suggested. "That tugging you're feeling is his wildness, Granddaughter. He doesn't like being hooked and wants to shake himself free. You need to put a little more tension on him," Poppy said urgently. "Sarah, listen, you need to put a little more bend in the rod or he'll get loose. Oh, no."

"Poppy, Poppy, how come he stopped tugging?" she asked in a state of confusion. "Why isn't he tugging anymore, Poppy? What happened?"

"Oh, Sarah…he got off. The trout threw your hook, and he's gone. I'm sorry, I'm sorry to say, sweetheart."

"He's gone? He's gone? Can we get him back? What can we do to get him to come back, Poppy?"

"Oh, no, honey, no. I'm sorry to say that there's nothing we can do now to get him to come back. But that's okay, you know. That happens a lot when fishing, especially fly-fishing," he explained. "The important thing is that you got him to take your fly. You made the perfect presentation, and you got him to take your fly. And you played him beautifully. While you had him on, you played him beautifully. That's a major accomplishment. You need to know that, Sarah. I'm very proud of you. Wasn't that exciting?"

"Oh, yes, it was. It sure was, Poppy! Wow, Poppy, you should have felt him tugging. He was really tugging hard. I had to hold on real tight. I thought he was going to pull me right into the brook. Right at the time when you were jumping up and down and shaking me, I thought he was going to pull me right in. He must have been a real big one, Poppy. Like a giant, a real big giant brook trout. Phew, I need to take a rest," she said as she wiped her brow. "Oh, boy, that was fun. That was *sooo* much fun, Poppy. I'm shaking. My whole body is shaking, but I don't need to take any deep breaths this time, because this is happy shaking. And those butterflies in my tummy aren't wearing heavy backpacks anymore. They're all light and *tick-a-ly*. They feel all tick-a-ly, wick-a-ly, Poppy."

"Sarah, let me hold your rod for a minute. How big do you think he was? Hold out your hands and show me how big you think your brook trout was."

"I'd say he was like this, Poppy," she said as she held her hands apart.

"How big, Sarah?" he asked again.

"This big," she said as she held her hands out wider than the first time.

"That big? Are you sure?"

"No, I think he was this big, Poppy," she said as she held her hands out as wide as she could. "He was like this, a real giant, a real big, giant brook trout, Poppy. He was tugging me so hard because he was so big that I thought he was going to pull me right into the brook. I didn't want to give you the rod because I didn't want him to pull you in either. So, I played him, Poppy, I played him really, really good, all by myself."

"Spoken like a true fisherperson. You learn very quickly my dear granddaughter," he said laughingly.

"I can't wait, I can't wait to tell Mommy and Daddy and baby Justin," she said excitedly. "Mr. Nate, too. Can we go back by Mr. Nate, so I can tell him about the giant trout I hooked? I want to tell him that he gave me a really good feather, a really, really good, lucky feather, Poppy."

"Oh, sure! we sure can! Mr. Nate will be thrilled to hear of your success. Sherry and Jerry, and Mrs. T, too, if you want."

"Oh, yes, let's. We should go now, Poppy. Let's leave. I can't wait to tell everybody!"

"Yup, you're right, Sarah. It's time we started heading back. But first, I'd like to mention that if we did end up landing that giant brook trout of yours, I would have allowed you to view him briefly and then we would have gently released him back into the brook, unharmed. Catch and release is a conservation-minded practice championed by a great fly fisherman by the name of Lee Wulff, many years ago. Then, you would have been able to see this beautiful creature up close and personal. The book trout is truly a sight to behold, Sarah. The brightness and colors of their spots are absolutely stunning.

"I can picture Mother Nature sitting at her easel with a fine paint brush in her steady hand and a palette full of incredibly bright colors as she delicately paints her gorgeous creation that is the brook trout. It's the same way you imagined painting the delicate wing of your butterfly as you practiced your casting. Only she can create such amazing things.

"You know, Sarah, there are a couple more things I'd like you to know."

"What, Poppy? What are they?"

"Well, I'll tell you if you promise to keep them a secret."

"Yes, I'll keep them a secret, Poppy. You can tell me. I promise, Poppy."

"Okay then, let's shake on it," he said with his hand outstretched.

"Okay, but we sure shake hands a lot, Poppy."

"You know, Sarah, the first time I took your mother here, when she was seven just like you, we didn't make it past the Dark Woods."

"You didn't? She didn't? *Noo*?" Sarah asked, surprised.

"No, we didn't, and it took your mom three seasons before she even got a trout to bite."

"Really, three seasons, Poppy, a whole three seasons?"

"Yup, that's right, Sarah. But realize your mom didn't quit. She worked through her fears and made it through the Dark Woods on her second try, and actually landed a brook trout, quite expertly, I might add, in her fourth season.

"By the way you performed today, Sarah, if all goes right, I think you just might be landing a trout next year. Remember, we can come back here again next year if you want."

"Oh, yes, please, Poppy, let's come back here next year. I'll land a trout. I'll land one for sure. A real big one, I know because there are no limits to what I can do," she said confidently.

"Hey, you're remembering what it says in your poem. That's terrific, Sarah. We'll come back here next year, for sure. You can count on that. So, let's start working our way back home now. When we pass Ol' Mister Scowl the Owl, you can let him know that we left his home just as we found it. And after that, I think you, Hollie, and I should take a break and have ourselves a little snack. I know just the place. What do you say?"

"I say, yes. How about you, Hollie?" Sarah asked. "Hollie says yes, too.

"Poppy, you can hold my hand if you want to when we go back through the Dark Woods, but I don't think you'll be afraid anymore. Just keep reminding yourself that it's just shady in there, just a bunch of big ol' shade. Okay, Poppy?"

"Okay, I will, Sarah. Thank you for reminding me."

"You're welcome, Poppy."

CHAPTER 6

"Sarah, let's take our break here at this lovely place and enjoy the beautiful view. I brought along some water and those delicious blueberries we picked up from Sherry's and Jerry's Berries to snack on. And I have a few treats for Hollie, too."

"Yes, Poppy, this is a real pretty place to rest. I can't wait to have some of those blueberries!"

"Okay, here you go, Sarah, enjoy."

"Yummy. These blueberries are delish…delishis…very good, Poppy. My sweet teeth really like them. Do you know I have sweet teeth, Poppy?"

"No, I had no idea, Sarah."

"Yup, Mrs. T told me so. She said it's a *spression*."

"Well, Mrs. T is the expert on everything sweet, and if she says you have sweet teeth, Sarah, then you have sweet teeth."

"I bet you have sweet teeth, too, Poppy, and don't even know it."

"Do you think so, Sarah? That sure sounds like a fun thing to have."

"Do you like to eat sweet things, Poppy?"

"I sure do, Sarah. In fact, Grandma Jennie used to scold me for eating too many sweet things."

"See, if you like sweet things, then you have sweet teeth, just like me. You should have told Grandma Jennie that you would promise to brush your teeth afterward, then she wouldn't have gotten mad. She just didn't want to see your teeth get hurt. Sweet things hurt your teeth if you don't brush after eating them."

"I'm happy to know that we both have sweet teeth, Sarah. I just wish I would have known that thing about brushing my teeth. Maybe then Grandma Jennie would have let me eat more sweets."

"Well, now you know, Poppy."

"Sarah, let me ask you. When you look up, what do you see?"

"I see the sky and the clouds."

"What color is the sky?"

"It's blue, Poppy."

"Sarah, do me a favor and hold up one of those blueberries for me. Hold it up against the sky, please."

"Like this, Poppy?" she says with her arm stretched out toward the sky.

"Yup, just like that. Can you see that today the sky is the same color as your blueberry?"

"Yes, it is, Poppy. It's the same color as my blueberry."

"Then, if you were to ask me, I'd say we're looking at not just a plain blue sky, but a deep blue, blueberry sky, and that's pretty special, Sarah. That makes today pretty special and a day you should treasure, just like every day."

"Just like my poem says to do, right, Poppy?"

"You got it, Sarah. What else do you see when you look up?"

"I see clouds, a bunch of white clouds. Why, Poppy? What do you see? Do you see something else?"

"Well, let me see now. Okay, okay. So up over there, I see something that looks like a big ice cream cone. And over there, I see a unicorn jumping over a white fence. And way up there, I see what looks like a spaceship."

"You do? Where? I don't see those things, Poppy. How come you can see those things, and I can't?"

"I'm using my imagination, Sarah. I can see a whole bunch of different things when I use my imagination, and you can, too. Just try it. Try using your imagination, just like you did when you imagined all the beautiful colors of the butterfly's wing as you were painting it before. Use that same imagination, Sarah, and tell me what you see up in those clouds."

"I don't know, Poppy. I think I'm using my *magination*, but I'm not seeing…Hey wait a second. I think, I think I see, I see a kitten. I see a kitten, Poppy! Right up there, I see a kitten! And over there, over there I see a snowman. He's big and round and has a carrot for his nose, just like the one me and Daddy made in the park the last time it snowed. And way up over there, that looks like one of Mrs. T's bees. I see its wings and everything, Poppy."

"Sure Sarah, that's what happens when you use your imagination. You get to see things that you never even knew were there. It opens up an endless world of possibility, adventure, and discovery, all your own. Don't ever stop using your imagination, Sarah. Don't ever, ever stop imagining."

"Up over there, over there I see a giraffe, a big giraffe," Sarah stated in awe. Then, in a complete change in mood, Sarah lowered her head and became sullen and said, "Poppy, I wish I can stay here with you forever. You can make me breakfast, and we can go fly-fishing. We can eat blueberries and use our *maginations* to find all kinds of fun things looking up at the clouds."

"That sure would be fun, Sarah. I would love having you here, but you know you have to be with your mommy and daddy and baby Justin, right?"

"Poppy, when our vacation is over and we get back home I have to go back to the...," she said, as she started to choke up and Poppy Tom interrupted.

"I know, sweetheart. I know where you have to go," he confirmed, also choking up. "It's very important that you go, Sarah. There are things that must be done to help you, my love. There are many wonderful people waiting for you to go so they can help you."

"I don't want to go, Poppy. I don't like going. I don't like going there, not one bit. It's a dark scary place. I want to stay here. I want to stay here with you and Hollie, Poppy."

"Sarah, let me ask you, if you were to stay here with me and Hollie, we would go fishing, right?"

"Oh, yes, we would, we sure would, Poppy."

"And, to get to our special secret fishing spot, we would have to go past that scary ol' meanie, Scowl the Owl, and go through the spooky Dark Woods, with all its creepy, crawly spiders and webs and everything, right?"

"Yes, Poppy, but you know, you know I'm not sacred of those things anymore. I was scared at first, but I'm not scared anymore."

"Oh Sarah, you're right, my beautiful, sweet, darling granddaughter. You are so, so right. Just think about how brave you are. Think about all the things we did together. Before yesterday, you never held a fly rod, let alone knew how to cast one. You didn't even know brook trout existed, let alone how to hook one. You struggled hard over a long, tough trail, never uttering a complaint. You were responsible enough to make sure you closed the gates of the corral behind us and found the time to give

Lightning and Thunder a sweet treat. As you say, you came to grips with your fears by making friends with Ol' Mister Scowl the Owl and saw the beauty and the good and never the bad in Mother Nature's handiwork in the Dark Woods. You were mature enough to be quiet and sneaky so not to spook any of those jittery trout. It would have been easy for you to give up after a few unanswered casts, but you kept at it and finally made the perfect presentation that completely fooled a very finicky fish. And in that short time you both shared together, that trout gave you a very special gift, one that I hope you will remember forever. He made you feel what it's like to be truly wild and free. And he made you know how to fight, fight with all your might, never give up, and to stay that way. Sarah, that trout is rooting for you. He wants to see you tug and shake as hard as he did, just as he showed you, to free yourself of your burden. He knows you can do it, Sarah, and so do all of us. You must remember what I promised you, sweetheart. That there will always be a bright, new, shiny world at the other end of any dark places that you'll ever have to go through, as long as you look for the good and never the bad and know that there are no limits to what you can do. You know that now, my sweet. Look how brave and strong you are. You wouldn't have accomplished all you did today if you weren't. Keep your poem and your lucky feather close, and they will help guide and protect you. And know that Mommy, Daddy, and baby Justin will be there with you, and so will I."

"You'll be there, too, Poppy?"

"Sarah, you know our deal, I'll be with you every step of the way. A team of wild horses wouldn't be able to keep me away."

"Poppy, what corral do these wild horses live in anyway?"

"I don't understand, Sarah. What? What wild horses?"

"The wild horses you and Mommy keep talking about, Poppy."

"Oh, a team of wild horses…right. That's just another one of those *spressions*, Sarah. I mean expressions."

"Like sweet teeth?" she asked.

"Yup, just like that."

"You know, Sarah, I'm a country boy. I'm not used to the big city. To me, that big ol' dark city is like the big ol' Dark Woods. I think I might be a little afraid being there. I'm hoping maybe, if it's okay with you, I'd like you to hold my hand when I'm there. Hold it really tight, Sarah. I wouldn't be afraid anymore if I knew you'd be holding my hand."

"You would need me to hold your hand? Oh sure, Poppy. I'll hold your hand. Don't worry, I'll hold it really tight. You won't have to be afraid at all. It's only dark in the city because the sun doesn't make it all the way to the ground. The big tall buildings block the sun the same way the big tall trees block the sun in the Dark Woods. It's like my hat, just extra shade. You remember, right, Poppy? Just big ol' extra shade."

"Thanks for the reminder, Sarah. It does help me to know that. But still, I would like you to hold my hand, just the same."

"Oh, I will, Poppy. That's a deal."

"Then let's shake on it, Sarah."

"You know, Poppy, my arms are really tired from all this shaking we keep doing and from fighting that big, huge, giant brook trout. Can't we just do a pinky swear instead?"

"Yup. Pinky swear it is, Sarah."

"Poppy, I'm going to keep my poem in my pocket and have my pretty red feather that gives me luck, guidance, and the *bility* to see all the wonders of this beautiful world around us, like the flowers and the butterflies and the blueberry sky and all the other beautiful things that Mother Nature works so hard to create for us. I now know because you promised and showed me that I will find a big, bright, new, shiny world at the other end of any dark places I ever have to go through because I'm always going to be looking for the good and never the bad and know that there are no limits to what I can do! There's a big, bright, new, shiny world out there where I can have *a'ventures* and make *scoveries*, a whole big bunch of *scoveries*, Poppy. And because I'm so strong and so brave, I'm not scared anymore. I was scared of going into the dark places, but I'm not scared anymore, not one bit. It's just shade. That's all it is, Poppy, just a bunch of big ol' shade. So I'm going to go, and I'm going to tug and shake and fight just like my big, giant, huge, humongous brook trout showed me. I'm going to tug real hard and shake real hard and break free, break free of my burden, just like he did.

Then I'm going to *magine* us—you, me, and Hollie—coming back here next year, and I'm going to catch that brook trout's daddy!"

"Hooray, Sarah! Hip, hip hooray! Hip, hip, hooray! It makes me so very happy and proud to hear you say that, Sarah. I knew it. I knew you'd feel this way. So brave, so brave and so strong. That's you, alright. The light of the world. That's you my darling granddaughter, the light of the whole wide world!"

"Oh, no Poppy, you're jumping up and down again. Does this mean you're going to be shaking me some more? It's okay to jump up and down if you want to, Poppy, but no shaking this time, please."

"Oh, sure, don't worry, Sarah. No, no more shaking. Just a lot of jumping up and down. Hooray!"

"Deep breaths, Poppy. Take some deep breaths. They'll calm you down."

Okay, you're right. I need to rest a spell, Sarah. All this excitement and jumping has plumb tuckered me out. Let's rest a little and finish eating our blueberries, then we'll head for home. We'll be making one quick stop along the way. We have some carving to do."

"Carving? What's carving, Poppy?"

"Don't worry, Sarah. You'll see. You'll see soon enough."

SARAH AT EIGHT

LIGHTING THE DARK

CHAPTER 7

"Welcome, welcome, everyone," Poppy Tom, accompanied by Hollie the Collie, said excitedly, as he walked toward his just-arrived family, "I'm so happy to see everyone."

"Well, well, look at this big guy running so fast. Oh, you're getting so big, Justin, my boy. Looks to me like we have a future linebacker on our hands," he said as he raised baby Justin up in his arms, hugging and kissing him.

"Sarah, hi…uh, is everything okay, sweetheart?" asked Poppy Tom, as he quickened his pace after realizing that she was still sitting in the car with her door closed. Cecilia and Justin looked on with all-knowing smiles on their faces.

"Stay right there, Poppy. Stop, stop, don't come any closer," Sarah shouted out through the open car window.

"What do you mean, Sarah?"

"Stop, please, Poppy. Don't come any closer."

"Okay, okay I'm stopping. I'm stopped. See, Sarah, I stopped, but tell me, are you okay? Cecilia, is Sarah okay?"

"I'm fine, Poppy. I'm very, very, fine. Don't worry," she said giggling. "Poppy, do you remember the big surprise you had for me when I got here last year, you know, you remember right?"

"Yes, I do. Of course, I do, Sarah. Why? What's going on? Cecilia, Justin, can anyone tell me what's going on here?"

Grinning, Cecilia said, "Dad, put your grandson down."

"Come to mama, sweetie. Dad, listen to Sarah, she has something…"

"No, Mommy. I'm doing it. I'm supposed to do it, Mommy."

"Okay, Sarah, go on, go on. I wasn't going to say anything. Go ahead before Poppy Tom pops a fuse right here in the driveway."

"Poppy, listen. You had a surprise for me last year, so I have a surprise for you this year, just as big a surprise that you had for me. Maybe even bigger. You're going to think even bigger, Poppy. Wait, wait 'til you see."

"Okay, wonderful. So, what's the surprise? I'm ready and waiting with bells on, Sarah."

"No, Poppy, you must close your eyes first. Bells, what bells do you…? Close them real tight and don't open them 'til I tell you, okay?"

"Okay, my eyes are closed."

"Are you sure they're closed, Poppy?"

"Yup, I'm sure."

"Alright, Poppy, no peeking now. Promise no peeking," she said with a slight strain in her voice.

"I promise, Sarah."

"Wait Poppy. You're not peeking, are you?" she asked with more of a strain in her voice.

"Nope, no peeking going on here."

"Almost ready, Poppy, but not yet," she said, breathing heavily and again with sounds of strain and exertion in her voice. "Okay Poppy, now! Open your eyes. Open them real, real wide, Poppy!"

Sucking in air and in an utterly amazed and disbelieving whisper, Poppy Tom said, "GLORY BE!" as tears began to stream down from his eyes, and he stood frozen by the glorious sight before him.

Sarah, standing upright and proud, her hands clutching the shimmering handles of her walker, began her strenuous but undaunted advance toward her overjoyed grandfather. Poppy Tom fell to his knees. He raised and opened his arms to receive what appeared to him to be make-believe. He commanded his senses to confirm that the vision before him was real. It wasn't until Sarah trekked closer that he was able to hear and almost feel her labored but victorious breaths pumping from her proud, dedicated lungs that he realized that what he was witnessing was real.

"See, Poppy? Look at me! I'm walking," she said huffing and puffing. "Wait right there, Poppy. I'm coming to you! Aren't you surprised? Look how tall I am. Isn't this a big surprise, Poppy?"

"This is a glorious surprise," Poppy Tom said in a crackly voice, "the most glorious surprise ever! My eyes, my eyes have never witnessed a more amazing sight," he said, as Sarah now reached him and they embraced.

Tears continued to fall from Poppy Tom's eyes as he asked stammering, "When did this happen? How did you ever…? I had no idea. No one let me know."

"I did it, Poppy! I did it! I keep my poem in my pocket, the poem that Grandma Jennie and you made for me, and I always remember what it says. Just like you told me to do. I keep my pretty, red feather that Mr. Nate gave me real close, too. I know it gives me luck, protection, and guidance. And I fought, Poppy. I fought and tugged and shook real hard, just like my big, huge, giant brook trout friend showed me. I didn't forget, Poppy. I didn't forget what you said and what my brook trout taught me either," Sarah assured him.

"Poppy, you know where I go, the halls are real long and dark, very dark, Poppy. But I'm brave. I'm brave and I'm strong. I don't ever feel scared, because you promised me and I know that there's always a big, bright, new, shiny world at the end of those long dark halls, just like when we get through the Dark Woods, Poppy, a beautiful, bright shiny world that I can now walk to!"

"Oh, Sarah, I am so, so thrilled for you," he said, still fighting back tears. "If only Grandma Jennie could see you now. She would be so very, very proud. She would know that the poem we wrote together is helping you. That was the idea of us wanting to write it for you in the first place. So you could keep it and read it whenever you needed, and it would always be there to help you in life."

"Oh, don't worry, Pops. Grandma Jennie sees. She knows. She knows I can walk," Sarah said with certainty.

"What do you mean? What are you saying, Sarah? I don't understand."

Cecilia interjected and asked, "Sarah, did I just hear you refer to your grandfather as Pops? That's not very respectful, my dear. You need to apologize."

"Oh, no Cecilia, thank you, but I kind of like the sound of that," said Poppy Tom.

"Sarah, it's okay if you want to call me Pops. It reminds me of what I called my father as he got older. He liked it then, and I like it now. That's your great grandfather, I'm referring to, Sarah. My father is your great grandfather. He was a wonderful man just as my mother, your great grandmother, was a wonderful woman. It was from your great grandfather that I learned to fly-fish. He taught me, and I was able to teach your mom and now you. I intend to teach baby Justin when he turns seven, too. Then we all can go fly-fishing together."

"Poppy, I mean Pops. Uh, can I use both? I think I'd like to say whatever name comes out at the time I say it and not be too worried."

"Sure, Sarah, that's a deal. Should we shake on it, pinky swear, or how about a thumbs-up for this one?" he added.

"Thumbs-up it is, Pops!" she replied as she let go of her walker and balanced herself to give her grandfather a big thumbs-up with both hands.

"Now, Sarah, I'd like to hear more about what you mean when you say that Grandma Jennie knows you can walk, but we've been out here in the driveway long enough. Let's all go into the house. I have a nice warm boysenberry pie waiting. The boysenberries are fresh from Sherry's and Jerry's, and the pie recipe is your grandmother's. Let's all sit and have a nice piece of pie while it's still warm, and you can help us understand. We can unload the car afterward."

"Well, Pops," Justin said, "we know all about it, but we'll be happy to enjoy a nice, warm piece of boysenberry pie while Sarah explains all of this to you."

Poppy Tom replied jokingly, "Hey, I remember saying it was alright for Sarah to call me Pops, but I don't ever remember saying it was okay for anyone else to call me Pops." All got a good chuckle.

As the family was seated at the table each enjoying their piece of freshly baked boysenberry pie, Poppy Tom questioned Sarah. "Sarah, please tell me what you meant when you said that Grandma Jennie sees and knows you can walk? Do you see her? Help me understand what you are saying, sweetheart."

"No, Pops. I don't see her. I never get to see her. But I know she's by me. She comes by me and hugs me. It's when I'm away at the place I have to go to and it's nighttime and I'm all alone. She hugs me and holds my hand when Mommy and Daddy and you aren't there at night."

"But you say you don't see her, Sarah. So, how do you know she comes? How do you know it's your Grandma Jennie?"

"It's a feeling, Poppy. It's like when you're cold and your mommy puts a fuzzy blanket over you and everything gets nice and warm and cuddly. Then, I see lines from my poem. Not like the real poem that I keep in my pocket, but one that's behind my eyes when I have them closed. You know how you can see things even though you have your eyes closed, right? Just like how you taught me to see things using my *magination*. When I close my eyes, I can see the lines and they're written so very pretty and fancy, just like Grandma Jennie wrote. That's how I know it's her. Nobody writes as pretty as Grandma Jennie. When she's by me, a very pretty smell comes, too, Pops. It's kind of like the way your bright, shiny, secret fishing spot smells all light and breezy."

"Sarah, please smell these roses. Tell me if they smell like the smell you are talking about."

"Yes, they are, Pops. That's the smell."

"Mommy, Daddy, these roses smell just like it does when Grandma Jennie comes to hug me."

"Sarah, these roses were your grandmother's favorite," Poppy Tom responded. "She's the one who planted them all along the fence and tended to them for many years. She loved their aroma. Mother Nature's perfume, she called it." Poppy Tom rested his head in his hands, and the tears came again. Then, he looked up and pointed his finger up in the air, swallowed hard, and said proudly, "That's my Jennie."

Cecilia jumped in to change the subject. "Sarah, I don't believe Poppy Tom knows you have a nickname. Why not tell him about that?"

"Nickname, you have a nickname, Sarah?"

"I sure do, Pops."

"I think you're the youngest girl around that has herself her very own nickname. What is it?"

"My nickname is Sarah Night in the Gale. All the smiling people where I have to go call me that."

"Okay, so now I have two questions," said Poppy Tom. "How did you get that nickname, and who are the smiling people?"

"Well, Pops, the smiling people are all the kind people that help me—and all the other boys and girls—to get better at the place we have to go. So, okay Pops, say you're asleep and someone comes to wake you up. When you open your eyes, the first thing you see is a happy smiling face. Sometimes, after they wake you up, they take you to another place where you have to fall back to sleep again. You see their smiling face as you fall asleep and then again when you wake back up. That's why we call them the smiling people. Smiling faces on the smiling people are fun to see, Poppy, and make us feel happy.

"I'm not really sure why I have this nickname, but the smiling people call me this when I'm *the happy* at night."

"What do you mean, when you're *the happy* at night? Poppy Tom asked, shaking his head and with a confused look on his face.

"You know, Pops," Sarah replied, "you know the line in my poem that says, *be the happy to those who are sad.*"

"Yes, Sarah, I do, but what does that…?"

"Well, Pops, I have to go by my poem and do what it says, right?"

"I suppose, if you can."

"So, sometimes at night, Poppy, sometimes I hear a friend crying. And, if they're crying, I know they're sad. So, I go and be their happy."

"Sarah? Cecilia, am I understanding Sarah correctly here?" Poppy Tom asked. "Sarah gets up in the middle of the night and…?"

"Yes, Dad, you're correct," Cecilia interrupted. "Her nickname is actually, Sarah Nightingale," she whispered to her father. Then saying aloud, "Now, allow Sarah to continue."

"Thank you, Mommy.

"So, when I go to visit my friends that are sad, the smiling people call me Sarah Night in the Gale. They say, there goes Sarah Night in the Gale, spreading her happy. I guess they call me that because it's nighttime when I go. I'm not really sure."

"Wow," Poppy Tom said. "That's a lot to take in all in one afternoon. I'm glad I'm sitting down. Sarah dear, what do you do? What do you say to make your friends that are sad, feel happy?"

"Well, Pops, when I hear a friend crying I get up and visit them. I sit by their bed and we talk."

Choking back tears, Poppy Tom asked, "What do you and your friends talk about my dearest?"

"Oh, we talk about a lot of things, Pops. But I need to be their happy. So, I do for them things that make me happy when I'm sad. Things that make their bad shaking into happy shaking, so they don't have to take deep breaths anymore. Things that turn butterflies that fly around in their bellies with big heavy backpacks on, into the tick-a-ly, wick-a-ly kind. Tick-a-ly, wick-a-ly, pretty colored butterflies tickle inside their bellies and turn their frowns into smiles. And smiles chase away their tears."

"What things are these? What wonderful things are these that turn your friends' frowns into smiles, my sweetest granddaughter?"

"Well, Poppy, my friends didn't have a grandma and poppy give them a poem that they can keep in their pocket, like me," Sarah said. "So, I make one for them so they can keep it in their pocket and read it anytime they want. I can't write them as pretty as Grandma Jennie, but my friends like them anyway. I tell them all the things that the poem says and then we hold our poems up together and say, we're 'The Lights of the Whole Wide World,' and their frowns and tears run away."

"Cecilia, Justin, you both know about all this?" he asked.

"We sure do," replied Cecilia. "We cannot be more proud of our little girl."

"MOM," Sarah corrected, "I'm not little anymore! I'm a big…"

"You're right, you're right, Sarah," her mom confirmed. "You are a big girl now."

Cecilia turned to her father and said, "You know, Dad, we have you to thank for this. You and Momma. That poem you wrote together has done so much."

Cecilia, turning back to Sarah, said, "Honey, tell Poppy Tom what else you do."

"There's more? Poppy Tom asked. "What more can you possibly do, Sarah? Wait a minute. I have to have another piece of pie. I need my strength...Okay, go ahead sweetheart."

"Well, Pops, my friends don't have a nice man like Mr. Nate to give them a pretty red feather like I have. So, I color one for them so they have one of their very own. I make their feather look just like it does when you hold it up to the sun. You know, I learned to color really good in art class. I tell them that their feather has great powers. It gives them luck, guidance, and the *bility* to see all the wonders of the beautiful world around them. Sometimes, this makes them frown again because they think they can't see the beautiful world around them. My friends wish they could go outside and run around and play, but right now they can't. But I tell them they can. Anytime they want, they can.

"See, Pops, they don't know about using their *maginations*. So, I teach them. Just like you taught me, Poppy. We put our poems in our pockets and hold our feathers real tight and close our eyes. And I tell them to think about doing something very fun. Like my friend Emily, she has fun sliding around on ice with skates on. So, I tell Emily to look behind her eyes and picture herself sliding around and tell me what she sees. When she tells me what she sees, the frown goes away and a smile comes. Then I tell her she is using her *magination* and that she can use her *magination* anytime she wants to see all kinds of fun things and smile some more. I also tell her that she is making me smile, too. Because I could never go sliding around on ice with skates on before, but now that she told me what it's like, I use my *magination* and do it just like Emily says and that makes me happy, too. So, Emily and I use our *maginations* and skate together. We hold hands and slip and slide around real fast. We do spins that make us dizzy and sometimes we fall on our fannies, but it's all so much fun. We get cold. So, we have hot chocolate and that warms us up from the inside of our bellies out, all by using our *maginations*.

"My friend, Manuel, and I have fun playing soccer together. Jasmine and I have fun doing gymnastics. So, I tell all my friends to keep their poems in their pockets to remind them that they are the lights of the whole wide world and that there are no limits to what they can do. To squeeze their pretty red feathers and close their eyes and their feather will let their *maginations* see all the secrets of the beautiful world around them, whenever they want."

"Granddaughter, you are one amazing girl. I now understand how you got your nickname."

"There's more yet, Dad," Cecilia said to her father.

"I'm all ears," said Poppy Tom.

"No, you're not, Pops," said Sarah. "You're not all ears. You have a nose and a mouth and eyes and a head and a whole body."

"Oh, that's just a *spression*," he replied.

"You mean an expression, Pops," Sarah corrected. "You said it wrong. The correct way to say it is expression."

"Well, okay then. Thank you for correcting me."

"You're welcome, Pops."

Justin, interjected, "Sarah, tell Pops, I mean Poppy Tom, the part about the Dark Woods."

"Do you mean the Dark Woods at the place I go, Daddy?" asked Sarah.

"Yes, Sarah, I know Poppy Tom will like hearing this."

"I'm liking everything I'm hearing from this child," Poppy Tom chimed in. "I'm sure this will be no different. Tell me, dear. Tell me about the Dark Woods."

"Well, Poppy, sometimes one of the nice, smiling people come to me saying that there's a really sad friend they think I should spread my happy to. See Pops, sometimes a friend is so sad that they can't cry. It's like their eyes don't want to make any more tears. I don't hear them because they don't cry. So, I don't know. That's why one of the smiling people have to come and tell me. I go because they're really, very sad and I want to be their really, big happy."

"What does my Sarah Night in the Gale do to help these friends of hers?" he asked as tears welled up in his eyes again.

"I give them our poem and their pretty, red feather picture and tell them all about them. But it's like, it's like, it's dark where they are Poppy, even though the lights are on," Sarah explained. "It's like they're lost in the Dark Woods and it's very scary looking and there's no bright, new, shiny world at the other end. So, I tell them, Poppy. I tell them what your bright, new shiny world looks like at the end of the Dark Woods. I tell them how so, so beautiful it is there, Pops, and how very pretty it smells. How the water where the brook trout live is all bubbly and how each bubble shines like glittery rainbows from the sun that lives up in the blueberry sky. How colorful butterflies play hide-and-go-seek with flowers and never get caught, and how frogs sing a happy tune and bluebirds fly all around you just like little kites.

"I tell them what it looks like, Pops, but I also tell them what it feels like. I tell them when you walk from the dark place to the bright, your eyes hurt from the beautiful sunshine, but it's a happy hurt. I let them know how the air is warm and fuzzy, not all cold and goose-bumpy like in the dark place. I tell them all about how those butterflies with the heavy backpacks that make your tummy all achy fly away, and only the good butterflies that tickle your tummy stay and make you all giggly. I tell them how strong the brook trout are that live in the bubbly water and what it feels like to have them fight and tug and shake real hard to free themselves of their burden. And, I explain to my friends that's how they have to be to shake themselves free of *their* own burdens. They have to be just like those strong, brave brook trout that live in the bubbly, glittery brook.

"Then, I let them know that the best feeling they'll have is knowing that they made it to a beautiful place that is safe and happy. A place of *a'ventures* and *scoveries*. I tell them, 'You made it through the dark to a place where hope grows on the trees like big green leaves and anything is possible,' and I have them squeeze their feathers real tight and close their eyes and *magine* that this bright, new, shiny world is right outside their door. Then I make them a promise, the same promise you made me, Pops.

"I promise them that there will always be a bright, new, shiny place at the other end of any of the dark places they'll ever have to go through in life as long as they look for the good and never the bad, are brave, and believe that there are no limits to what they can do. Then we do a pinky swear, just because. I tell them to always remember their poem and what it says. Then together we hold our poems up in the air and say, 'We're the Lights of the Whole Wide World!' Then, Pops, they become really big happy."

For a little while, Poppy Tom sat motionless and speechless with tears flowing from his eyes, as the greatness of the words just spoken by his benevolent, spirited granddaughter sank in. He looked deep into her loving compassionate eyes, raised his hands, and gave her two solid, thumbs-up.

Justin, broke the silence, saying, "Hey, I think I'm ready for another piece of that pie."

Poppy Tom said, "Go right ahead and help yourself. I don't mean to be an old fuddy-duddy, but I think I'm going to lie down for a bit."

"But Pops, aren't we going to do things to get ready to go fly-fishing in the morning?" Sarah asked.

"Are you okay, Dad?" asked Cecilia.

"Cecilia, I'm just fine, thank you. You're looking at one proud grandfather who wishes to close his eyes and rest, knowing he is one of the luckiest Pops alive. You all get settled in and, Sarah, when I wake up, we'll talk about going fishing. Oh wait, I need to help with unloading your…"

Cecilia interrupted her father and said, "No Dad, you go rest. We'll get ourselves situated."

Justin's head nods between the chomps and swallows of his fast-disappearing piece of boysenberry pie confirmed his agreement with Cecilia.

CHAPTER 8

"Mommy, when is Poppy waking up?" asked Sarah. "He wants to talk about going…"

Cecilia interrupted, "I think I hear him now, sweetie."

"Yes, yes, I'm up, I'm up," said Poppy Tom. "Oh, that power nap sure felt good. Everyone all settled in, I hope?"

"Yes, yes, we're all squared away, Dad," said Cecilia. "JJ likes having his own room this year. It makes him feel like a big boy."

"Poppy, Poppy, I go fithin', too?" Baby Justin asked his grandfather.

"JJ, so that's what we're calling our big guy now?" asked Poppy Tom. "I like that. Come here, JJ. Come sit on Poppy's lap. So you want to go fithin', do ya? You're going to have to wait a few more years, my boy. But don't worry, son. Your time will come, and you'll be great, just like your momma and sister. I'll make sure of that."

"How 'bout us, Poppy? How 'bout us?" asked Sarah. "We're going fithin', I mean fishing, right? Early in the morning, right, Pops?"

"Oh, well, uh, let's talk about that a little bit, Sarah," he replied. "There are two things."

"What two things, Poppy? We have to go, Pops. I have to hook the daddy of my trout from last year. You know, Poppy. You remember. Then I need to get a line. Another line."

"I remember. Of course, I remember about you hooking your trout's daddy, Sarah, and I know you can do it. But what line are you talking about? What line do you have to get?"

"You know. The line! The line you carve in the post. I need to get another line carved in the post. I need to catch up to Mommy."

"Ohhh, of course, the line," said Poppy Tom. "I've never known such a determined girl. Or a more competitive one. You know? I take that back. I did know another girl like that, and I married her."

"What two things, anyway, Poppy?" Sarah asked again.

"Well, first, I think we have to talk about…Cecilia, you know it's a long, tough trek to get to where we have to go. Wouldn't it be hard for Sarah…?"

Sarah interrupted, as she began to get upset, "Poppy, you think I can't do it? You think I can't go?"

"Please, please Sarah, don't get upset, sweetheart," said Poppy Tom. "But I'm concerned. It's a very long way over some very rough ground. Last year you had your…"

"Poppy, I can do it," Sarah proclaimed! "I have to do it. I have it all planned. I *magined* myself going there, Pops. I have my walker that I lean on. I have you and Hollie with me every step of the way. I have my poem in my pocket and my lucky feather in my hat. I'm already there, Pops. In my *magination*, I'm already there, fighting my trout's daddy."

"Dad," Cecilia said, "we talked to Sarah's caregivers, you know her smiling people. We explained the situation to them."

Cecilia turned toward her daughter, saying, "Sarah, you know what they said you have to do."

"Yes, Mommy," Sarah agreed. "If I get tired, I have to stop and rest. If I get too tired and start to feel funny, I need to quit and come back home. I'll rest if I have to. We'll stop and rest. But I won't quit, Mommy. I won't ever quit. Never, ever. I believe in myself and know that there are no limits to what I can do. I'm there already. I'm standing at Poppy's special, secret fishing spot, and I'm fighting my brook trout's daddy."

"Well," Poppy Tom said, "the score stands at, Sarah one, Poppy zero. Sarah, I have another concern, and this one has nothing to do with your condition but rather the condition of Mother Nature."

"Mother Nature, Poppy? What's happened to Mother Nature?"

"Well, it's not what's happened to Mother Nature, but more what's not happened," Poppy Tom responded. "See Sarah, we haven't had rain in quite some time. The weather's been hot, very hot with no rain at all. We know about burdens, right? Well, hot weather with no rain puts a burden on Mother Nature and all her plants and animals. You know how the brook trout need clean, cold water to be happy and healthy. I'm afraid that this year the brook is low, making the water very warm."

"Poppy are my brook trout sick?" Sarah asked, concerned. "They can't be sick. They have to be strong so they can fight to stay free. They have to stay happy and healthy."

"See that's just the thing," replied Poppy Tom. "We know how smart and wise Mother Nature is. She makes it so all her creatures know how to adapt to these kinds of conditions. The way she makes the brook trout adapt is kind of like making them nap a lot. Like I just did a little while ago. That way, they don't use up all their energy. We would say Mother Nature makes them know how to conserve their energy. That way, when the rains come and the water gets all nice and cold and bubbly again, they have the energy to be happy and healthy."

"I understand, Pops. That's what I do, too. Before I have to do my exercises, one of the smiling people has me rest and stretch first."

"That's exactly right. Good example, Sarah. So, we need to think about the effect we would have on our brook trout friends if we were to hook one when they aren't feeling their strongest," he explained. "Maybe it would be too much for them. It could make them use up too much of their precious energy."

"Oh, no, Poppy, we wouldn't want them to use up all their energy. They might get sick. We have to let them take their naps like Mother Nature wants them to. But, Poppy, I really wanted to hook my brook trout's daddy and get another line. Otherwise, I have to wait 'til next year. Will there be rain next year, Poppy? Will the brook be all nice and cold and bubbly next year like it was last year?"

"I hope so, dear. Who knows? The way things go, maybe next year they'll be flooding and that's another whole set of concerns for our brook trout friends. Let's hope not, but you never know.

"Sarah, you can see that Mother Nature has a big job keeping all her creations happy and healthy. That's why people have to help her.

Remember how we worked to repair the brook before we went fishing last year? We helped her there. Remember how Sherry and Jerry grow their crops organically? Mrs. T, too. I'll be taking you and JJ—he's old enough now—back to the farmer's market to meet Mr. Reggie, of Reggie's Veggies and Miss Mary of Miss Mary's Eggs and Dairy. They, too, do everything organically. So, they all help Mother Nature. We need to remember that we're a part of nature, just like the brook trout. Just like the trees and the flowers and the butterflies and the owls. We all need a clean, heathy environment, just like Mother Nature wants, so we all can stay happy and healthy."

"Does Mr. Reggie sell carrots?" Sarah asked. "I like carrots. Broccoli not so much, but if he sells it we should buy some. We don't want to make the broccoli feel left out. How about Miss Mary, does she sell yogurt? We can mix some sweet berries from Sherry's and Jerry's in our yogurt, topped with some of Mrs. T's honey from the bees. Since everything is organic, it would make a nice healthy treat for everybody."

"Organic, you said organic," Poppy Tom said.

"Of course, I did," Sarah agreed. "How else would I say it, Pops?"

"No, no, no other way. You're right. It's just that last year…uh, never mind. So Sarah, are you thinking we won't be heading out fishing in the morning because of this year's conditions?"

"I suppose not," Sarah said reluctantly. "But I really wanted to go. I *magined* it all, Pops. Everything behind my eyes. Hiking there, holding onto my walker together with you and Hollie. Resting if we had to but not quitting Pops, never quitting."

Sarah now saying in a whisper and winking to Poppy Tom, "Going by the secret path, *A, B, C,* and *D.*"

Then saying aloud again, "Giving Lightning and Thunder their sweet treats and making sure we closed the gates behind us. Seeing my friend Ol' Mister Scowl the Owl, with his perfect owl smile. Then going through the special Dark Woods holding your hand if you needed me to. And then, having the bright sunshine do a 'good hurt' to my eyes when getting through the dark to the light and seeing everything all shiny and smelling pretty. Seeing Hollie show us how to sneak up to the brook and hiding behind a bush. Then holding my fly rod nice and gentle, just like I was holding a fine paint brush and painting the beautiful wing of a butterfly all pretty colors. Nice and smooth, moving my fly rod back and forth and forth and back 'til the fly got to the middle of the brook. Then allowing it to fall gently to the surface of the water making the perfect cast. Just like you taught me, Poppsey.

"And, seeing the bubbly water, all clear, glittery and rainbowy, get all foamy when my brook trout's daddy jumps to gobble up my fly. He's big Poppy, huge. My arms can't open up wide enough to show you how big he is. And he's fighting. He's fighting really hard. You start jumping up, too, Poppy, jumping up and down and all around. But you're not shaking me this time, and that's a good thing. I keep the bend just right. The bend in my rod is just right, Pops. He tries pulling me into the brook, but I hold on. I fight him, and he fights me back. He's strong, really strong. He's tugging and shaking a lot. He's tugging really hard. He's shaking really hard. I have to tire him out. I keep the bend just right.

"You stop jumping, Poppy, because you get tired, but you're still coaching me. It's the same way my smiling-people friends coach me when I'm doing my workouts, and we feel the great fun we're having together. Even Hollie knows. She's excited and so are you and me. I think I'm starting to feel my brook trout's daddy getting tired. Yes, he's getting tired. He's not fighting as hard. Not tugging and shaking as hard either. I feel I'm beginning to win this fight. He was strong, but I must be stronger. I'm tired, but he must be more tired. But wait, that last tug and last shake felt a little strong again. How could that be? He is, he's starting to pull and shake and tug harder now. He's fighting me hard. Even harder than before. How come? I had him. I thought he was done but now it feels like I have two huge, giant brook trout on. Maybe my brook trout from last year's daddy went and got his daddy, and now I'm fighting both of them. My arm hurts. I have to take deep breaths because my whole body is shaking bad shakes, not happy ones. Big, heavy backpack butterflies are crashing around in my tummy. No tickles going on there at all. My brook trout's daddy and granddaddy stop tugging. They stop shaking. All they are doing now is pulling. Just a hard, hard pulling. I think they might pull me right into the brook.

I can't hold onto my rod and my walker much longer. My arm aches, my back and legs ache. My whole body aches. The bend gets too much. There's way too much of a bend, Poppy. I'm afraid my rod will break. Then, like in slow motion, I see my fly floating back to me. How could my fly be loose in the air and yet there's all this heavy pulling? Then I realize there's no more heavy pulling. There's no more heavy pulling at all. My brook trout's daddy and granddaddy are gone, and there's no getting them back. They won and I lost. They fought real hard to stay wild and free themselves of their burden. So, they won and I lost, and now they're back in their brook trout home being all happy, wild, and free."

Poppy Tom said, shaking his head, "I'm going to need another nap. Sarah. I was really enjoying your story until the part where you lose your trout…or two. I'm not understanding how you would work so hard to imagine yourself doing all this to lose the fight in the end. Why wouldn't you want to see yourself landing those trout? Wouldn't you want to land those trout?"

"Poppy," Sarah began, "remember last year after my brook trout got loose? Remember what you said he gave me?"

"Go ahead and refresh my memory please, Granddaughter."

"You said he's rooting for me and that he gave me a very special gift. One I should remember forever. So, I'm remembering it, Poppy. I'm remembering his very special gift."

"Okay, yes, I do remember, dear. Go ahead and tell me more, please."

"His very special gift to me was to make me feel what it's like to be truly wild and free, Poppy. He made me know how to fight, fight with all my might, never give up, and to stay that way. He wants to see *me* tug and shake, the same way he did, to free myself of my burden. So that's what I did, and that's what I tell my friends to do when they're sad. That's why I don't need my wheel…I walk instead. I use my walker, and now I can walk because of his gift, my poem and my feather, and all you teach me, too, Poppy. Because of all the love I'm given by you and Grandma Jennie, Mommy, Daddy, JJ, and all my smiling-people friends is why I can walk now.

"But I have more fighting to do, Pops. A lot more fighting to do. See, Pops, when these trout take my fly, that fly becomes their burden. That's what they're tugging and shaking and fighting so hard to free themselves from. They were all happy, wild, and free before, but that fly—my fly—gives them a burden. So really, it's me, Poppy. I become their burden, and yet, they give me a gift. That trout's daddy and granddaddy had to be so much stronger to fight to free themselves of their burden because their burden—me—is so much stronger. But they gave me a special gift, too. They showed me you can fight even harder. When your burden gets stronger, then you must get stronger. If I landed them, Poppsey, that would mean I won. If I won, then that would mean their burden won. And, all the hard fighting and all the tugging and shaking that they were showing me how to do wouldn't have been enough. Their burden would be stronger, and it would beat them. If I fight just as strong as they showed me, my burden would be stronger and it would beat me, too. I can't let my burden be stronger than me, Pops. I can never and I will never let my burden be stronger than me, because I believe in myself and there are no limits to what I can do. I will fight the way my brook trout friends showed me to fight. That way made them beat their burden no matter how strong, and that way will allow me to beat mine."

"Sarah, you are wise beyond your years. I don't know what else to say."

"Poppy, all this is in my *magination*. When something is in my *magination* and gets behind my eyes, it falls down and ends up in my heart. I can feel it end up there, Pops. So, I know what it feels like for those trout to fight so hard, and I know what I have to do to fight like them. But that doesn't get me my line. I still need to get a real line—not a *magined* one—on that post."

"We could just go and carve another line on the post, Sarah."

"You mean carve another line that means I went fly-fishing without really going fly-fishing?" Sarah asked, surprised. "That wouldn't count."

"I had a feeling that wasn't going to fly," said Poppy Tom. "Alright, here's what we can do. We'll get up early, have breakfast, and go. We'll take our time and rest as much as we have to. We'll let Hollie show us how we need to sneak up and hide behind a bush. Then you cast."

"No, Poppy, no," Sarah said excitedly. "A trout might bite my fly and get hooked. Then he would have to fight and get all tired and get sick. We can't do that. I don't want to do that, Poppy."

"Hold on, you didn't let me finish, Sarah. You don't realize it, but the fly you use is a fly tied onto what's called a barbless hook. You know how we said if you landed a trout I would let you view it briefly so you could see his beautiful, bright spots. Then we would gently release your trout back into the brook, unharmed. A fly with a barbless hook allows us to do that much more easily and safely. But what I'll do this time is cut off the hook entirely so there's nothing but the fly itself left. There will be nothing for a trout to even come close to getting hooked on. Here's the deal. You make one cast and one cast only. That allows you to 'wet your line' as we say in fly-fishing. If a trout happens to take your fly, you pull up sharply on your rod as you would, and because the hook has been cut off, the fly will easily pull free from the trout's mouth. It won't hurt the trout one bit, and he'll go back to his home with hardly any of his precious energy being spent. Then we're done. You can say you officially went fly-fishing this year and that officially gets you another line on your post. And I will say, by you choosing to forgo hooking a trout because you know of the stress they're under this year and your concern for their well-being, you would be doing the best sportsperson-like thing possible. I would expect nothing less from my amazing granddaughter, of whom I and Mother Nature are so very proud. So, do we have ourselves a deal, Sarah?"

"Deal," she replied, making a thumbs-up with both hands.

Cecilia said, "Now that you two are done negotiating world peace, I have a question for my darling daughter. Did I hear a Poppsey or two come from you in this recent conversation? I mean, we went from Poppy Tom to Pops to Poppsey. What's next?"

"Cecilia, really that's okay," said Poppy Tom. "Thank you, but it's fine."

"Sarah, you can call me anyone of those names. Just don't call me late for supper."

"Why would I do that Poppsey? Why would I call you late for supper?"

"That's just an expression, my dear."

"Oh, Poppsey Woppsey," said Sarah.

"Sarah!" Cecilia said loudly.

"Just one more thing, Pops," Sarah said.

"Yes, Sarah. What is it?"

"Will Brewster the Rooster be up to his old tricks again so early tomorrow morning?" she asked.

"He sure will be. You can bet on that, Sarah. Why do you ask?"

"Well, a line in my poem says, I have to treasure each day from the moment it starts. It's very hard to treasure them when they start out with Brewster making all that noise."

Chuckling, Poppy Tom said, "Mark my words dear granddaughter. Someday, not tomorrow or the next day, but someday, Brewster's noise will be music to your ears."

Turning toward her mother, Sarah said, "Mommy, with Brewster waking me up at the crack of dawn I better get to bed. I have a big hike in the morning. Do you have any of those ear plugs you say you use when Daddy snores? I'd like to borrow them if you do."

"No, sorry sweetie, I don't," Cecilia said, chuckling. "I left them home. Now, kiss everybody good night."

"Off to bed are we, Granddaughter?" asked Poppy Tom. "Well then, good night, sleep tight, and dream with all your might."

"Good night, wash right, and don't forget to fly a kite, Poppser Woppser," Sarah said kiddingly.

"You always outdo me on those, Sarhie Warhie," joked Poppy Tom. "Sarah two, Poppy zero," he said as he gave her a two-handed thumbs-up.

CHAPTER 9

"Sarah, I have to say, when you set your mind to doing something, my goodness, you do it. You made it all the way to the special secret fishing spot, as you said you would. You took a few brief rests along the way, mostly because I insisted you do. The thought of quitting never even entered your mind. When we make it back to the post, I'll be carving another line for you because of your one perfect cast. You earned it, fair and square.

"Sarah, do you remember stopping here and resting last year? This is the place where we ate blueberries and looked up at the clouds."

"Yes, Poppy, I do," Sarah replied. "I think that cloud looks like…"

"Well, if you don't mind," interrupted Poppy Tom, "I'd like us to go to a different place this year to rest. Seeing your strength and determination has inspired me to do something that I have been putting off for far too long. It won't take us long to get there. It's just a little ways away."

"Oh, sure, Pops," said Sarah. "You lead, and me and Hollie will follow. Did you bring blueberries again for us to snack on when we get there, and how about treats for Hollie?"

"Thank you for being flexible, Sarah. And, I sure did. I have our blueberries and Hollie's treats and some nice cool spring water for us to drink. I just wish I had remembered to bring those sweet treats for Lightning and Thunder. I thought I packed them. I could have sworn I did. Lightning and Thunder sure looked disappointed when we left without giving them any sweets. We'll have to see if we'll have time to swing back another day to make it up to them. You know, I think Lightning and Thunder have sweet teeth just like you and me," Poppy Tom said kiddingly.

"Big sweet teeth, Poppy," Sarah said, laughing. "They need big toothbrushes and a lot of toothpaste to clean those big sweet teeth of theirs," she said, laughing harder.

Poppy Tom led Sarah and Hollie further along the trail. "Okay, Sarah, here we are. We made it," said Poppy Tom with a slight sound of relief in his voice. "Please go easy. The path is all overgrown. No one's been here in years. Why don't you sit down and rest on one of those old tree stumps over there? Nice and easy now.

"Hollie, show Sarah where to go.

"Sarah, Hollie can show you. She remembers this place. We used to come here a lot, years back."

After sitting to rest, Sarah asked, "What is this place, Poppy? Why did you and Hollie come here a lot?"

"Well," Poppy Tom said, "Hollie and I used to come here a lot, but it was always with your grandmother. See, this was a special place to her. The same way my secret fishing spot is special to me. This was always special to her, Sarah. She loved it so very much here."

"But why, Poppy?" asked Sarah. "I mean, it's pretty, but there's no bright, shiny spot at the end of the dark place like your spot. It's kind of dark and shady. Not as dark and shady as being in the Dark Woods, but almost. There's no brook, so there's no brook trout or frogs or anything. It's just like a place like other places around here. It's nice but why did Grandma Jennie love it here so much?"

"For me to answer that question, I'm going to have to get you to use your imagination again," said Poppy Tom. "I-magination," Sarah. "Not *magination*. I'll have you look at this place in a different way and then you might be able to understand why your grandmother loved it here so much."

"Imagination, not *magination*?" Sarah asked.

"Yes, sweetie, imagination."

"Why didn't you tell me? I thought it was…I didn't know. All this time I was…"

"That's okay," assured Poppy Tom. "Now you know. So, to answer your question, if you look down to your left through the trees and brush, you might be able to see a stone wall. Do you see it, dear?"

"Yes, I see it, Poppy," Sarah confirmed. "I can make it out."

"Okay, good. Now, look to your right," Poppy Tom directed. "You should be able see through the trees and all that brush and see another stone wall."

"Yup, I can, Poppy."

"And right here in front of where we're sitting is a big gap in that wall. Right? Do you see that, too, Sarah?"

"Yes, Pops. Hollie took me right here. Right here, in front of the gap, to rest on this stump."

"I think Hollie may have done that for a reason," said Poppy Tom. "The stone wall and this gap will play a big role in the story I'm about to tell you. Let me ask you, Sarah, do the trees on the other side of the wall look familiar to you?"

"Ah…yes…Poppy, they're like the trees in the Dark Woods. They're just as big and make just as much shade."

"Right! You're very observant, Sarah. And do you see that all the trees on this side of the stone wall are so much smaller? Some really can't even be called trees. They're just considered heavy brush."

"Yes, Poppy, how come?"

"To answer that question, I'll need you to use your imagination now," he instructed. "Imagine there's no stone wall at all. Just make it disappear in your mind. Then, imagine all the big Dark Woods trees are growing up all around you. You are surrounded by all these giant Dark Woods trees. As far as you can see in all directions there's nothing but these majestic old trees. Are you seeing that? More important, are you feeling that? Are you letting the picture that is behind your eyes drop down into your heart so you can really see and feel what you are imagining?"

"Yes, Poppy, it is. It's in my heart,' she assured him. "I can see the trees all around, and I can feel them, too."

"Well, Sarah, there was a time when what you're imagining was real.

There was that kind of forest here, Sarah, right where we're sitting. It was made up of all these magnificent trees, and they went on forever. Can you imagine what a glorious sight that must have been?"

"Yes, Pops, I can. But what happened? What happened to all those giant trees? Where did they go?"

"I'm sorry to say, sweetheart, they were cut down. The stump you're sitting on was most likely one of those trees."

"That's sad, Poppy. That makes me very sad to hear. It must have made Mother Nature sad, too."

"Yes, that made Mother Nature very sad. And you say you're sad, too. So, if you're sad, then you need someone to be your happy. I know just who that someone is."

"Who, Pops, who?"

"Your happy is the hero of this story. None other than your Grandma Jennie," he stated proudly.

"Grandma Jennie is already my happy, Pops. She comes and hugs me at night. When I'm at the place...I smell her pretty roses. She's my happy already."

"Well, she's going to be your happy some more. I'll give you a little history lesson and at the same time tie you back to your ancestors. Just so you know, ancestors are family members from a long time ago. You see, Sarah, many years back, people came to this country to, what they called, settle the land. They were the ones who cut down the trees to make way for their homes and fields. Before that, Mr. Nate's ancestors lived here. Their culture lived in harmony with Mother Nature. They felt these beautiful trees were Mother Nature's children, just like themselves. So, cutting the trees down would be like cutting down their own brothers and sisters."

"That wouldn't be very nice, Poppy. JJ's my brother. I wouldn't cut him down if he was a tree."

"I'm sure you wouldn't, Sarah. It's hard to understand, even for an old guy, I mean, someone my age. But basically, it was two cultures seeing and doing things differently. If there could have been more of an understanding between the two, maybe things could have been better.

"Sarah, look at Hollie there, she's trying to remind us about our treats. We're lucky we have Hollie to keep us on track."

"Here you go, lady, here are your treats," Poppy Tom said as he gave Hollie her treats.

"Sarah, open up this container and enjoy some blueberries."

"Thank you, Poppy. They look so good. Oh, Poppy, look. Inside this bowl are the sweet treats for Lightning and Thunder. We had them all the time. They're here with the blueberries. No wonder we couldn't find them before."

"Gee, that's funny, Sarah. How did they get in there? I don't remember sticking them in with the blueberries. Oh, well. While you enjoy snacking and having some water, I'll continue with the story.

"These people that came here were settlers, and they worked very hard to clear the land. Think about it. They didn't have modern equipment like we have today. They had to do everything by hand. Cut the trees. Remove all the stumps. And plow all the fields. The soil here is rocky. So, when they plowed the ground, all the rocks would get unearthed. Meaning they would come to the top of the ground. The people would have to go around and pick up all the rocks. That's how stone walls like this one were built. The people would pick the rocks up off the ground and make these walls. It was very, hard work, Sarah. However, this wall was built for a special reason. The people back then realized they shouldn't cut down all the big trees. Some should be left to help protect the waterways and keep a place for owls and other animals to live. So, they made a pact among themselves. A pact is like a deal. The pact said no big trees would be cut down on the other side of this stone wall. Everything would be left as it is. And that's how it was for many years. But then, about, maybe fifteen...no, more like twenty years ago, a group of people decided they were going to come here and knock down this wall and cut down all the trees. They thought they could build something better than what it took Mother Nature so many years to build on her own.

"The gap you see here is where they began to knock the wall down. But this was as far as they got, thanks to your grandmother."

"Grandmother? My grandmother, Jennie? What did she do, Poppy?"

"She stopped them, Sarah, plain and simple. She would not allow these beautiful trees and this beautiful environment to be destroyed. Oh, you should have seen her, Sarah. She worked so hard. She worked just as hard to protect these trees as the people did so many years ago to cut them down. But she did it in such a way, not forceful, not loud. It was like the way you paint the wing of a butterfly or like the way you hold your fly rod and make the perfect cast, nice and smooth and gentle. It got the job done.

"With, kind, gentle persuasion, she was able to allow people to see things differently. She made them realize that the value of what was here already was worth way more than what they could ever hope to replace it with. She said she used Mother Nature's example on how to get a job done. Like these giant trees, the ones she protected didn't get to be giants overnight. They started out as little, tiny seeds or acorns, and over time with gentle, steady determination, they became giants. That's nature's way. And that's how she won. Also, it was her ancestors—now your ancestors—that made that pact. Your grandmother was honoring that pact and, by doing so, honoring her ancestors. She fought so these trees would be here forever, just as your ancestors intended. So, they can be enjoyed by her child, her child's children, and by generations to come. She saved all these trees, as far as you can see to your right, all the way up to that mountain in the distance, and all the way down to your left. All those trees would have been gone. So too, would have been the brook trout, the frogs, butterflies, owls, and countless others of Mother Nature's amazing creations. She's a hero, alright. She's my hero, and she's Mother Nature's hero, too."

"Mine, too, Pops!"

"Grandma Jennie, you're the best," Sarah said proudly, giving a double thumbs-up while looking up at the sky.

"So, that's why this was a place of special meaning to your grandmother, Sarah. She used to sit here, maybe on that same stump, and imagine just like you did, what it was like when Mr. Nate's ancestors lived here, before the trees were cut down. But she was happy in knowing she helped save the ones that are left."

CHAPTER 10

"Sarah, see that big, high mountain way up there?"

"Yes, Pops, I see it."

"That mountain was special to Grandma Jennie, too."

"It was? How come?"

"Well, as I mentioned before, the area your grandmother helped preserve goes all the way to that mountain and beyond. There is a hiking trail that leads to its summit. It's a long, tough trail. Many people tried to make it to the top, but very few have. The name of the mountain is 'The Mountain of Singing Trees.'"

"That's a pretty name, Poppsey. How did it get that name?"

"Well, here's what I can tell you about that, Sarah. A legend, which is like a story, was passed down through the generations and told of a young Indian girl just about your age. She loved her family and friends and her home here among the giant trees. She saw the beauty in Mother Nature and all her handiwork. She loved to play among the wild flowers, whose bright colors hurt her eyes but with a good hurt and whose fragrances made her nose all tick-a-ly, wick-a-ly.

"She learned from her mother how to weave pretty baskets and sew fine beadwork onto her family's clothes. Her mother also taught her how to grow corn, beans, and squash. Her people called these vegetables, 'The Three Sisters.' They were a very important food source for this young girl and her people. But this young girl had no sisters of her own, so when she tended her crops, she would pretend these crops were actually her three sisters. She would imagine singing and dancing with them, playing jokes, and having all kinds of fun together. The more she sang and the more she danced, the bigger her crops would grow. They grew bigger than anyone else's crops in the whole village. It was as if her crops were having fun, too, and grew real big because they were so happy.

"Then one summer, Sarah, there was a bad drought. It was much worse than the one we're having now. All the people's crops were dying from the lack of rain. If the people's crops were dying, so could the people. The crops were dying except those of this young girl. As long as she imagined singing and dancing and playing with her three sisters, her crops grew big and plenty. She tried sharing her crops with the other villagers, but there wasn't enough to go around. She even tried pretending that the other crops were her sisters', too, hoping she could make them happy, but the other crops continued to die. Only her crops grew. The drought went on. Every day the hot sun baked and scorched the land. The brooks and streams were drying up. The trees and grasses were withering.

"With the ground being so dry, this girl saw that when she sang and danced with her sisters, clouds of dust would rise up toward the sky. She thought if only she could make bigger dust clouds. Big, huge, dust clouds that would go way up into the sky. Those clouds would block out the hot sun and trick the lightning and thunder and rain into thinking a storm, a big storm was coming, allowing life-giving rains to finally come down. So, she went to her three sisters and told them they were going to play a fun game, a big fun game with lots of singing and dancing—the most singing and dancing they had ever done before. Her sisters were so excited and began to sing and dance more than they had ever done before. Then she went to all the villagers and told them to sing and dance more than *they* had ever done before, too, and they all joined in. Soon giant clouds of dust rose high into the sky and blocked the hot sun. The lightning thought a big storm was coming and started shooting jagged lightning bolts across the cloud-filled sky. The thunder, seeing the storm coming and the lightning bolts shooting, began to slap and bang mighty booms of thunder back at the lightning. The shooting lightning bolts and the mighty booms of the thunder woke up the sleeping rain, which then poured down precious, life-giving moisture.

"The brooks and streams were now flowing with clear, cold, bubbly water, making the brook trout and frogs happy. The trees and grasses drank in the cooling rains, making the owls and butterflies happy. And all the crops began to grow again, bigger and more abundant than they had ever been before, making the people of the village very happy. There was a great celebration. The people sang and danced, honoring this girl and her three sisters for saving the people and the land. While they were celebrating, a beautiful, vibrant rainbow appeared above the mountaintop. The people stopped singing and dancing to view such an amazing sight. Then, they heard the singing. It started out soft and serenely at first. Then became louder and louder until the entire valley echoed with its wondrous sound. It was coming from all the giant trees on top of the mountain. Mother Nature was leading a choir of singing trees to honor this young girl and her three sisters with a beautiful, inspiring song. From then on, the people of the village called that mountain, 'The Mountain of Singing Trees.' They made this young girl the princess of their village and gave her the name 'Dancing Cloud.'"

"That was a very good, legend story, Pops. Dancing Cloud and I like to pretend and use our imaginations."

"Imaginations, right Sarah? I think you and Dancing Cloud have a lot of things in common. It's as if she had a poem and feather just like you. You both look for the good and never the bad. You are the happy to those who are sad and know there are no limits to what you can do, making you both the lights of the whole wide world. I'm glad I got to tell you this story, Sarah. Maybe someday you can share it with your children."

"Poppy, did you ever climb to the top of The Mountain of Singing Trees?"

"Yes, I did, Sarah. Only because your grandmother made me do it, and Hollie, too."

"What do you mean, Poppsey?"

"You know, Sarah, you take after your grandmother in so many ways. You're strong, brave, and determined. You may not realize it, Sarah, but your Grandma Jennie had a burden, too."

"She did? She didn't have a wheel...or a walker. She didn't have anything to help her walk."

"No, Sarah, she didn't. You see, there are all different kinds of burdens a person can have. Sometimes they're burdens you can see. Sometimes they're burdens you can't see. Your grandmother had a different burden, one you couldn't see but a burden just the same. But, like you, she didn't let her burden stand in her way from doing what she needed to do. Her fight to save these trees took place at a time when her burden was at its strongest. As you say, when your burden gets stronger, then *you* must get stronger. She did just that and saved the trees. She set a goal for herself to climb to the top of The Mountain of Singing Trees. She needed to see the view from up there. It was a view that allowed her to see all she fought to protect, and she needed to hear the trees sing. Climbers much more skilled than her couldn't make it. But she did. In spite of her burden, she got there."

"So, you went, too, Pops? You and Hollie?"

"We sure did, Sarah."

"Did you hear the trees sing?"

"We didn't, but your grandmother did."

"She did?" Sarah asked, with a sound of awe in her voice.

"Yes, she did. It was a tough climb, Sarah. Experienced mountain climbers can make it in about a day and a half. It took us more than three. We set up camp at the end of the third day and planned to wake up early the next morning and make the summit just as the sun was starting to rise. The weather had turned colder, and we woke to a few inches of fresh fallen snow. The chill had set right into your grandmother's bones. The cold and the exertion of the last three days had really taken its toll. She could hardly move. Just getting out of her sleeping bag was a struggle. Someone else, anyone else in her condition would have quit. But just like you, for her, quitting was not an option. The climb to the summit from where we were should have taken about forty-five minutes. It took us more than three hours. During the last half hour, she crawled on her hands and knees. I tried to help her, Sarah, but she wouldn't let me. By the time we got to the summit, the sun had already risen. She labored to pull herself up using the branches from an old dead hollow tree. Then, slowly, courageously, she stood straight and tall, looking out at the stunning view before her. Looking out at all she fought to protect. The warmth of the sun had started to melt the snow that covered every branch and every pine needle. All these droplets of melting snow, infinite in number, fell like rain, each one glistening like countless rainbows until they all blended into one. We stood hypnotized at the sight of one solid, glistening wall of countless rainbows. That's when I saw it. That's when I saw it on her face, and I knew. I knew she was hearing the singing, Sarah. Mother Nature, just like she did for Dancing Cloud and her three sisters, was leading a choir of her singing trees in wondrous, inspiring song, to honor your fearless, spirted grandmother for saving her forest. But it was for her ears only. Hollie and I didn't hear a thing.

"Sarah, if you were to ever go up there, you would see, carved into that old, dead, hollow tree the letter "J" and under that letter, is one single line. Your Grandmother Jennie met her goal of climbing to the top of The Mountain of Singing Trees, in spite of her burden, and heard their glorious song."

"Way up there? Grandma Jennie has a line way up on the top of The Mountain of Singing Trees? Someday, so will I, Poppsey. I'll have a line and I'll hear their song, just like my Grandma Jennie did."

"I believe you will, Sarah. I believe you will."

"Poppy, what is Hollie trying to do? It looks like she's trying to pick up rocks and fix the wall."

"I swear, sometimes I think dogs are smarter than people," Poppy Tom said. "That's why I had us come here, Sarah. Hollie is reminding me why I took us here in the first place. I would have plumb forgotten. It was the gap in this wall, Sarah. I have been wanting to fill in the gap in this wall for years now, for Grandma Jennie. I should have done it while she was still here. This stone wall needs to be rejoined. It needs to be back to how it was before they tried to knock it down. I kept putting it off and putting it off, but hearing how Grandma Jennie comes and hugs you, how you smell her roses, and how much you remind me of her has inspired me to do it now. I know when I get this wall reconnected, I will be reconnected with my Jennie. Today, I just want to begin. It will take me a long time to do this. But today I will begin because of your inspiration, Sarah, because of you. I'll work on it just for a little while, and then we'll head for home. Oh, yeah, remind me to stop at the post on the way so I can carve you another line."

"Oh, don't worry, Pops, I won't let you forget. That other line is already carved on that post in my imagination."

"I bet it is," he replied, laughing. "Now, what do you think you're doing?"

"I'm helping you build back the wall, Poppy."

"Sarah, no, that's too hard for you to do. The stones are too heavy."

"Pops, I'm just sitting here on this stump picking up the stones right here in front of me and putting them back in the wall. I'm resting all my walking-back-home muscles. I'm just using my picking-up-some-little-ol'-stone muscles. I'm fine."

"Okay, Jennie," he replied.

"Pops, you just called me Jennie."

"I know I did," he said, smiling.

SARAH AT NINE

RIDING RAINBOWS

CHAPTER 11

"Dad, you had us worried," Cecilia said with distress and fatigue in her voice. "We expected you here over an hour ago. Was there traffic?"

"I'm sorry, Cecilia," he replied, also with distress and fatigue in his voice. "I didn't mean to cause you more anxiety. No, no traffic. Just the normal congestion. I don't know what happened. Maybe because I was rushing to get here and with all the stress, I must have made a wrong turn or something. I got completely turned around. Tell me, how's Sarah doing? Tell me, is she okay?"

"Well, Dad, our little girl has another respiratory infection," Cecilia said regrettably. "But this one is quite severe. They have her on heavy doses of antibiotics. Her caregivers are so wonderful, Dad. You know how wonderful they are," she said as she began to cry.

"They are," he agreed as he choked back the tears and hugged his daughter. "They're the best there are. They'll get her better, Cecilia. She'll be fine. There's no question about it."

"They feel, they feel," Cecilia repeated while softly crying, "she'll be back...back to needing her wheelchair. Oh, Dad, Sarah will be so upset. She worked so, so hard to...You know how hard she worked. And how proud she is...I'm afraid, Dad. I don't know how much more fight she has left in her. I'm afraid she's going to quit fighting and..."

"Quit fighting? Sarah quit?" Poppy Tom asked his distraught daughter. "There's no way that's going to happen. Not your Sarah. She doesn't know the meaning of the word. Listen, Cecilia, you know she's had these setbacks before. And every time, she's come back stronger. This time is going to be no different. She's strong and she's a fighter. You know that. You'll sec.

"Can I go see…? Poppy Tom asked.

Cecilia interrupted, "Oh, here comes Justin. He was just in with her."

"Justin, how is my granddaughter? Can I go see her?"

"You know your granddaughter," said Justin. "She's a fighter."

"Yes, yes, I do," Poppy Tom confirmed. "See Cecilia, what did I just say? What did I just tell you?"

"Why, Justin? What's making you say that?" asked Cecilia with a sign of hope in her voice. "What's happened? What did you see?"

"I saw her fighting," Justin answered with confidence. "Just like always. You know her challenge with coughing. You know, the nurses have to get her to cough. Her smiling people, they're coaching her with that. They got her going, and you know Sarah, she took right off. They had to tell her to slow down. They didn't want her overdoing it."

"See, that's Sarah. That's your daughter, Cecilia. I told you so," Poppy Tom said proudly.

"She never ceases to amaze," confirmed Justin. "She wore herself right out though. She fell fast asleep. So, Dad, I'm afraid you'll have to wait a while before paying her a visit. While she's resting, how about we all go grab a bite to eat? You can visit your grand-fighter granddaughter afterward."

"Sounds good to me," he replied.

Then he turned to his daughter and asked, "You feeling better, Cecilia?"

"Yes, a little," she replied. "But I'm still concerned about her reaction when she finds out about the chair. I hope it doesn't…"

"When do they plan on letting her know?" asked Poppy Tom.

"Not for a few more days," said Cecilia. "They want her to get stronger."

"Pops, you're like the smiling people," Sarah said groggily. "When I open my eyes, I see your smiling face. Happy, smiling-face medicine."

"That's a nice compliment. You're putting me in some good company there, Sarah. Tell me, how's my darling granddaughter, the light of the world, feeling this morning?"

"I'm okay. I'm fine, Pops."

"Which one is it, okay or fine?"

"Poppy," Sarah began, "last night when Mommy and Daddy and JJ were here, Doctor Miss Nicole came to visit me." As tears welled up in Sarah's eyes, she continued, "Doctor Miss Nicole told me…She said when I go home. When I leave to go home, I'll need my…"

"Yes, Sarah, I know. I know what Doctor Nicole told you."

"I can't use my walker. My lungs got…my lungs got hurt and weak. Why did my lungs have to go and get hurt and weak again, Poppy?"

"Well, Sarah, that darn bug got you. It affected your lungs. Your lungs couldn't help it, and neither could you. It was that darn bug. We have to be thankful for all the wonderful smiling people here that are getting you all better. But tell me. What else did Doctor Miss Nicole tell you? I'm very interested in having you tell me what else Doctor Nicole said."

"She said all the smiling people are going to make my lungs get better. Then I can make my lungs get strong again. Just like I did before. And when they get back to being strong again, I can go back to using my walker."

"Well, there you go, Sarah. That's very good news. Doctor Nicole would not have said that if she didn't think it was so. She knows, just like all of us, what a strong fighter you are. We all know there are no limits to what you can do. Right?"

"I think so, Pops, but I'm not so sure," Sarah admitted. "I feel sleepy a lot, Poppy. I don't know if I can be strong and fight like I did, like all my brook trout friends showed me. I think I want to sleep some more, Pops."

"Sure, Sarah, you sleep. You need to get your rest. Don't worry about all this business of being strong and fighting and everything right now. There will be plenty of time for that. You sleep, and when you wake up, I'll tell you about Paula Jean."

"Who's Paula Jean, Pops?"

"Shush, sleep now and we'll talk later," he said.

Awaking from a nap while sitting in Sarah's hospital room, Poppy Tom said, "Sarah, now I know what it's like to open my eyes to the smiling people. Seeing such a pretty smiling face looking back at me when I opened my eyes does make me feel happy, just like you said."

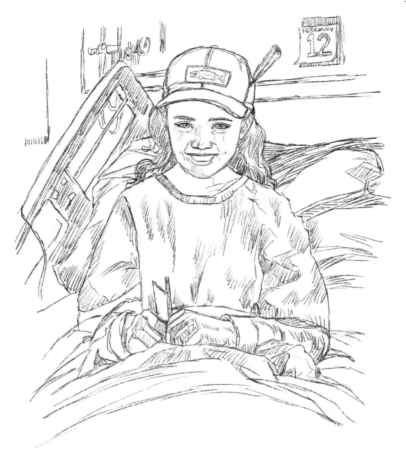

"Happy, smiling medicine, right, Pops? What's in that bag, Pop...?"

"That it is," he interrupted her, "but I'm supposed to be the one smiling when you wake up. You're the patient here."

"Hey, Pops, that's how it was when you were here the other day. I woke up to see your smiling face. So, it was your turn to wake up and see my smiling face today. That's how it is when you're a team, and we're a team, right, Poppser? Now, what's in that bag?"

Poppy Tom interrupted again, "That we are, Granddaughter. We're there for each other every step of the way. How's my hero granddaughter feeling today?"

"I feel fine, Pops. Thank you. But not so much like a hero. Poppy, what's in the...?"

"What's that you say," Poppy Tom asked, interrupting? "That doesn't sound like the confident, never-say-quit granddaughter I know."

Sarah doesn't answer Poppy Tom's question directly but asks instead, "Poppy, did you hear the news? Did you hear I get to go home tomorrow?"

"I sure did, Sarah! I'm very happy about that. How about you?"

"I guess I am, Pops. That bag, Pops, what's…?"

"You guess you are?" he asked, interrupting again.

"No, I am. I'm happy, pretty much, Pops. But you know what Dr. Miss Nicole said? I have to go back to using my chair again, Pops. That makes me sad. A hero wouldn't need to go back to using a chair again."

"Well, we knew about the chair, right, sweetheart? It's just a matter of time before you get back to using your walker. And this business about not being a hero, heck, you wrote the book on how to be a hero."

"I wrote a book…? Is that another one of those expressions, Pops? And, that bag, Pops, what's…?"

"Yes, my dear," confirmed Poppy Tom as he interrupted her once again. "It is an *expression*. Good for you."

"It's just that I…I don't know, Pops. I don't know if I have the energy to fight to get my lungs strong again. I really feel sleepy a lot, Poppsey. Heroes don't feel sleepy."

"Well, now, of course you feel that way, Sarah. That's totally understandable. Come on. Look at what you just went…no, not went through, are going through. Just the fact that you get to go home tomorrow is a major victory on your part. You're fighting this thing, Sarah, and you're beating it. Just like always. It will take time, but you'll be back to using your walker again. There's no doubt about that."

"Poppy, I want to fight, but I don't think I can fight very good, feeling so sleepy all the time."

"Well, Sarah, do you see this bag…?"

Now Sarah interrupted Poppy Tom and said, "Yes, I've been trying to ask you about that bag all morn…"

Again, Poppy Tom interrupted her. "I'm *sooo* surprised you haven't noticed it."

"I did. I have been trying to…," Sarah began to say when, again, Poppy Tom interrupted.

"So, let me tell you all about it. I have some special things in this bag that will help raise your energy level a whole big bunch, Sarah. I just hope…I mean, it's pretty powerful stuff. I just hope they don't make you too strong. Maybe I shouldn't show you. Maybe I shouldn't give you any…"

"What Poppy, what's in the bag?" Sarah asked excitedly. "Tell me. That's a big bag, Pops. You can show me. It's a big bag, and it looks really heavy. Tell me, Pops. Whatever's in the bag, I can have some."

"Well, okay, if you really want to know. But before I open it up, I have to warn you. This big, heavy-looking bag is filled with the most special, top secret, super-turbocharged, rocket-boostered, off-the-charts, whipped, dipped, flipped, zipped, bang, zoomed, wished, washed, washed, wished, highly engineered, completely versatile, triple-your-money-back-guaranteed, energy-enhancement products ever assembled in the history of triple-your-money-back-guaranteed energy-enhancement products."

"Wow, wee, wee, wow, Poppy, can I…?" Sarah began, but Poppy Tom interrupted once again.

"Shhh, shhh, not *sooo* loud, Sarah," he whispered, as he looked around suspiciously. "No one can know what's in this bag. It's just between you and me. Are you sure you want to see what's inside?"

"Yes, I…," Sarah began, but Poppy Tom interrupted again.

"You need to answer questions just by nodding your head yes or no, Sarah. No talking. Now, do you want to see what's inside?" he again asked, whispering.

Sarah, looked around suspiciously, too, and then nodded her head.

"Okay then, let's do this," he said quietly, as he slowly unzipped the bag. The first thing he pulled from the bag was a small dark brown bottle. "Sarah, see this here bottle? This bottle was given to me by a person who has keen knowledge of ancient Native American customs. Secret, ancient Native American customs. He goes by the code name, Mr. N."

"I bet ya I know who," Sarah started to say excitedly when Poppy Tom cut her off.

"Hey, hey, hey, no talking, Sarah. Remember? These potions can lose their powers if it gets too noisy around here," he said as he raised his pointer finger up to his lips and glanced back and forth again to confirm no one was around. "This bottle contains the very thing that gives the eagle its regal and the bear its roar. Take a sip from this bottle and you'll be able to soar," Poppy Tom whispered as he offered Sarah a sip from the bottle.

Sarah looked around to first confirm no one was looking and then took a sip from the small dark brown bottle. "Tastes like apple ju…," she began to say but then quickly put her hand over her mouth.

"That's enough, that's plenty," Poppy Tom said quietly. "It's good your lying in bed for all of this, because when the powers kick in, believe you me, you'll want to take off for the moon."

"I think I'm feeling stron…," Sarah began to say but again quickly put her hand over her mouth.

Then Poppy Tom asked in a hushed voice, "Feeling better already, right?"

Sarah enthusiastically nodded her head.

Poppy Tom gave Sarah a thumbs-up. He returned the small dark brown bottle back into the bag and carefully pulled out a small dark blue bottle. "This bottle was given to me by people who have a keen knowledge of the secret energy powers of special berries. They go by the code names, Mrs. S and Mr. J. This bottle contains the very thing that gives the straw to strawberries and the blueberries their blue. Take a sip from this bottle and you'll feel just like new," as he offered Sarah a sip from the blue bottle.

Sarah took her sip and then quietly began to flex her muscles and do fist pumps. Again, Poppy Tom approvingly gave Sarah another thumbs-up and returned the small dark blue bottle back into the bag and pulled a small dark green bottle from it.

"This dark green bottle was given to me by a person who has the wizardry to talk to trees and bees and knows of their super, secret tricks. She goes by the code name, Mrs. T-rific. This bottle contains the very thing that gives syrup its sugar and honey its sweet. Take a sip from this bottle and feel the power from your head down to your feet."

Sarah took her sip and quickly began to do hip-hop dance moves while giving a thumbs-up with each hand.

"Looks like you're feeling the energy and getting your groove back, Sarah," Poppy Tom said quietly.

Sarah sent the message that she was, by continuing to hip-hop and wave her arms with a giant smile on her face.

Poppy Tom returned the small dark green bottle back into the bag and pulled a small dark red bottle from it. "This dark red bottle was given to me by a person who has the mystical ability to speak to vegetables and learn of their enchanting secrets. He goes by the code name Mr. Reg the Veg. This bottle contains the very thing that puts the *cauli* in flower and the *brussels* in sprouts. Take a sip from this bottle and your powers will never be in doubt."

Sarah took her sip and quickly mimicked the moves of a one-person baseball team. She pretended to swing a bat and hit the ball. Then, she pretended to run and catch the ball and throw the imaginary runner out, then celebrated as her pretend throw got the runner out at the plate.

Poppy Tom said in a whisper, "I have one more bottle of secret potion left in this bag, but I'm thinking maybe you've had enough of this most special, top secret, super…"

Sarah shook her head and pointed down to the bag, signaling she wanted Poppy Tom to bring out the last bottle.

Poppy Tom signaled back, okay, then returned the small dark red bottle back into the bag and pulled a small white bottle from it. "This bottle was given to me by a person who has the supernatural ability to communicate with chickens and cows. She goes by the code name Miss Mar-aculous. This bottle contains the very thing that makes yolks so yellow and milk so mellow. Take a sip of this final bottle, and you'll be the strongest of any lady or fellow."

Sarah took her sip and went right into pretending she just caught a football and was dodging players as she raced down the field, then made the end zone, spiking the ball and celebrating her touchdown.

Poppy Tom said in a whisper, "As soon I place this bottle back into the bag, we can talk normal again. Okay, it's back in the bag. So, tell me, how is my thumbs-up–giving, hip-hop–dancing, baseball-bat–swinging, touchdown-making granddaughter feeling?"

"I'm feeling wonderful, Poppsey Woppsey," Sarah said loudly and excitedly. "All these special potions from all your secret friends have really helped me not to feel sleepy anymore. I know I have the strength to fight to get my lungs strong again. I have the strength to fight just like my brook trout friends showed me. Thank you, Poppy, and please tell all your secret friends that I thank them, too. Wow wee, those secret potions really work."

"You're welcome," said Poppy Tom. "I'll be sure to tell my secret friends you said thank you. They'll be thrilled to know that all their secret energy potions did the trick. It might be a good idea for you to lie down a little bit now and allow all the powers of the secret potions to really sink in. It would be like a really good power nap. What do you say?"

"Sure, Pops! Good idea. A power nap will allow all the super, turbo, wish, wash stuff to really sink in. Wait until I wake up. All this stuff will be really sinked in good by then, and I'll be even more super-stronger."

"I'm sure you will, Sarah. Rest and we'll see who wakes up to whose face smiling back at them."

"Maybe this time we'll wake up at the exact same time, Poppy, and see both our smiling faces together."

"That would be something alright, Sarah."

CHAPTER 12

"Hollie," Sarah said excitedly, "come to me, lady!" Hollie went straight to Sarah, and Sarah hugged and kissed her. Hollie, with her tail wagging rapidly, licked Sarah's face to return the affection.

"Hi, Poppy. What a nice surprise. You brought Hollie to visit me."

"Hi, Sarah. Hollie couldn't wait until summer to see you. She kept dragging out your fishing boots from the garage. That was her way of saying she missed you and wanted to visit you."

"You missed me, Hollie? I missed you too, so, so much girl. Hollie, you've never been to my house before, pretty lady."

"Mommy, can I show Hollie my room? I want her to see the picture of her and me when we went fly-fishing for the first time."

"Of course, you can," Cecilia replied.

"That was the year we were talking, and Hollie reminded us to be quiet and sneak up to the brook. You remember that, right Pops?"

"You have a picture of you two fly-fishing?" Poppy Tom asked.

"Sure, Pops. You took it. You gave it to me. Don't you remember?"

"Gee, I don't recall."

"Come on, Pops. You come, too. You'll remember the picture once you see it."

"Hollie, Sarah's going to show us her room," said Poppy Tom. "How special is that?"

"We'll follow you, Sarah. Let's go see that picture."

"See, guys, here it is. Look at this great picture," said Sarah. "Look at you, Hollie. Look how pretty you look."

"Hey, what a great shot, Sarah. Oh, sure, I remember taking that now. We had just finished with your instruction on how to cast and were ready to head to our secret fishing spot. I remember now. What a nice room you have, Sarah.

"Hollie, doesn't Sarah have a nice room?

"You have a lot of great pictures here, Sarah. Who's this pretty young lady with you in this picture?"

"Oh, that's my friend Emily, Pops. She came and visited me last week, and we went ice skating together. You know, Pops, in our imaginations. Emily came with her mom to visit me, just like I visited her when we were in the hospital. She said I came to her and made her happy and that made her feel better. So, she came to me to get me happy and make me feel better. And just before she left, we held up our poems and said, 'We're the lights of the whole, wide world.' We had fun, Poppy."

"Sarah, I'm so happy to hear that Emily came to make you happy and that you had fun together. And I'm thrilled to know she's feeling better. What wonderful news. That's exactly why you both truly are the lights of the world. You went to her and shined your love-light and made her happy and then she returned the favor and shined her love-light on you and made you happy. How great is that?"

"Yup, Pops, I got to go skating with Emily and we didn't even get tired. And now that I'm home, we're going to call each other up and go ice skating together over the phone, and we won't even get tired either."

"Sounds like you two have a great plan there, Sarah. Very, very good. You know this is reminding me. I'm hoping you can help me with something when you're out by me this summer."

"What, Pops? What can I help you with?"

"You'll need to wear your Sarah-Night-in-the-Gale hat for this one, Sarah."

"It's Nightingale, Pops. Sarah Nightingale is my nickname," she said, correcting her grandfather. "Florence Nightingale was the name of a famous nurse lady from a long time ago. Dr. Miss Nicole told me all about her. That's why the smiling people gave me that name. They said I was like this famous nurse lady. At first, I thought it was because I went to visit my friends at night, but Dr. Miss Nicole taught me the real reason why they gave me that nickname. You know, Pops, I like this part about growing up. You get to learn new stuff all the time. There's a lot of new stuff to learn about, Poppy, and I like learning about it."

"Sarah, it's great that you feel that way. Learning new things and making discoveries opens up even more things to learn about and discover. Allow that to happen now as you're growing up and for always. Never stop learning or discovering worlds that are new, my sweet granddaughter, please. Take me, for instance. I stopped growing a long time ago, but I keep learning new things from you. And I love it!"

"Poppy, do you think I can discover...I mean, maybe, someday, discover a cure so other kids wouldn't get born with what I was born with?"

"Sarah, I'll answer your very noble question the same way I've answered other questions like this in the past. I don't *think* you can do anything you set your mind to. I *know* you can do anything you set your mind to. There are no limits. No limits to what you can do. There are, as we speak, many wonderful people working very hard to find a cure for what kids like you are born with, Sarah. We're thankful for all they are doing, and I believe they will find a cure long before you're at that stage. But please know, unfortunately, there are plenty of other cures that need to be discovered—cures to help children and people of all ages. I believe you and, thankfully, others like you, of your generation, will go out there and make those discoveries. That would be the ultimate happy to so many who are longing to be. Can you imagine what a wonderful gift that would be, Sarah?"

"I did imagine it, Pops. I imagined myself doing that, at nighttime, after you let me have all those sips of secret potions. In my imagination, behind my eyes and falling down into my heart, I saw and felt myself being all grown up and making discovery cures."

"When you believe it, see it, and feel it, you will be it for sure, Sarah. And what a great thing it will be."

"Poppy, what's Hollie doing? How come she keeps pushing my wheelchair?"

"Oh, yeah, I know, Sarah. She's doing it again. Thank goodness for Hollie. When I forget things, which seems to be more and more lately, she's there to remind me. Remember how you went to visit your friend Emily because she was sad. Well, there's a young girl that lives near me that is sad, too. I'm hoping when you're out by me this summer, you can visit her and spread your happy. That's why I brought up your Sarah Nightingale nickname."

"Oh, sure, Pops. I'd be happy to be her happy. How old is she? What's her name? How come she's sad?"

"Well, her name is Paula Jean, and I think she's five. I meant to talk to you about her when you were in the hospital. Hollie was just pushing your wheelchair to remind me to tell you now."

"Thank you. Hollie," he said.

"Is Paula Jean in a chair like me, Pops?"

"No, Sarah, she's not in a chair like you. But Paula Jean's mommy is."

"How come, Poppy? How come Paula Jean's mommy's in a wheelchair? Is her mommy sad, too?"

"Well, I'd say, seeing her daughter sad makes her sad, but she doesn't show it. She's trying to be strong for her daughter. Paula Jean is having a tough time seeing her mom in a wheelchair. It's almost like she's afraid of the chair. Helping Paula Jean to be happy, Sarah, will help Paula Jean's mommy to be happy too, I'm sure."

"But Poppy, I'm in a wheelchair, too. If I was using my walker, maybe then...I mean, Paula Jean might be afraid of seeing me in my chair. She might be too afraid and too sad for me to make her happy. What if I can't...?"

"Sarah, I would say Paula Jean *will* be afraid when she sees you in your chair, at first. But I know, Sarah Nightingale, the light of the world, the happy-to-the-sad, no-limits-to-what-she-can-do, future-discoverer-of-cures granddaughter of mine will come up with a way to help Paula Jean and her mommy be happy."

"Is that a freshly baked cherry pie I see sitting on the counter?" asked Justin, as he and JJ walked into Sarah's room.

"Yes, it certainly is, ohhh...," Poppy Tom said, just as JJ rushed toward him and tried to jump into his grandfather's arms. "JJ," Poppy said groaning, "pretty soon, you're going to be too heavy for me to be picking you up.

"Cecilia, Justin, what are you feeding this boy, anyway?"

CHAPTER 13

"Come on, quick, come in, before you all get drenched," Poppy Tom called out anxiously from the open door of his cabin to his just-arrived family as the rain came pouring down.

"Hollie, stay. No sense you going out there. Hollie, come back. You're gonna get soaked. Oh, too late."

"She's running to help Sarah," Cecilia called to her father in a voice almost being drowned out by the sound of the pouring rain. "Hurry, JJ, run to Poppy."

"Dad, his boots are all wet."

"JJ take your boots off when...Hollie, Justin's helping Sarah. You don't have to go. Come on, girl, come in," Cecilia rattled off in a flurry.

"Okay, girl, good girl, you want to help Sarah, don't you," Justin said as he held an umbrella over Sarah and they rushed as fast as they could to the open door.

"Hello, lady, how's my girl," Sarah asked as she stopped to hug Hollie even though it was raining heavily. "In all this rain, you still came out to help me, didn't you? You're such a good girl."

"Sarah, come on, we're getting soaked," Justin said urgently. "Let's get in the house.

"Phew, we made it," he said with relief, closing the door. "Sarah, I hope you didn't get too wet?"

"No, not bad. I was under the umbrella, Dad. You were the one getting wet."

"Here," said Poppy Tom. "Here are some towels. Dry yourselves off. It's been like this all week. It comes down in buckets and the next thing you know the sun's out."

"That's how it was on the drive up here, too," said Justin. "One minute you needed the wipers going full blast, the next, you needed sunglasses."

"We've made it here safe and sound. That's the main thing," Cecilia said thankfully. "Justin, honey, dry Sarah and her wheelchair off for me please. I'll get JJ."

"JJ, come here sweetheart. Oh, don't step in the water," she added. Your socks are gonna get all wet. Uh oh, too late. Alright, come on."

"I'll get us a good fire going, while you get yourselves squared away," said Poppy Tom. "Wait, you'll need your luggage...Hey, we'll unload the car later.

"Listen," he added as he built a fire. "I have a nice lunch prepared. Cecilia, I'm eager for you to taste my zucchini pie. I want to know how it compares to your mother's."

"Zucchini pie?" Cecilia asked with a surprised look on her face. "Somebody's getting quite daring on what they're baking around here. I'm impressed."

"Don't be too impressed until you try it," said Poppy Tom laughingly. "Yeah, I keep raiding your mother's recipe file. She had all her great recipes written out all neat and orderly. So, I like experimenting, especially when I know you guys are coming."

"Good for you, Dad. Mom would be very proud."

"I like the sound of zucchini pie for lunch," said Justin. "But I'm more interested to know what you made for dessert. Maybe a cherry pie like you brought down with you when you visited back in April?"

"That was delicious, remember, JJ? We devoured that pie, you and me."

"Well, now we know where Sarah got her sweet tooth from," said Poppy Tom. "No, Justin, no cherry pie. Actually, lemon meringue pie is on the dessert menu for today, I'm proud to say."

"Oh, JJ, did you hear that, son?" Justin asked excitedly. "We have lemon meringue pie for dessert. Wait until you taste that. Scrumptious. Oh, I can't wait."

"Well, we'll see how scrumptious it is when we have it, Justin. There's a trick to making that pie that I hope I gleaned from momma's recipe. We'll see."

"Sweet tooth, not sweet teeth?" Sarah asked. "Hmm...Okay, I got it."

Before we dig into dessert, Cecilia interjected, "I have to say, Dad, you did a good job on that zucchini pie. Maybe add a little bit more Parmesan cheese the next time and I think it would be right on."

"Okay, thank you for that advice, Cecilia. I'll try to remember that next time. You know, I better jot that down on the recipe card right now; otherwise, I'll forget. I'm finding that if I don't write things down anymore..."

As Poppy Tom turned away, Cecilia and Justin looked at each other, concerned.

"So, is everybody ready for some dessert?" asked Poppy Tom.

"I don't know about everybody, but I know I am," said Justin.

"Me, too!" said JJ.

"Me, three," said Sarah.

"Well, I don't want to be the party pooper here," said Cecilia, "so I guess I'm in, too. Me and my diet are being outnumbered by the sweet tooth quartet here. What's a girl to do?"

"Okay, here goes," said Poppy Tom with anticipation as he cut into the pie. "Oh, my goodness. What happened here? It didn't set. Oh, it's running all over. The lemon filling never set."

"Oh, Dad, too bad," said Cecilia. "It looked so beautiful, too. These pies are hard to bake. Don't feel bad, Daddy."

"I do feel bad, Cecilia. I don't know...I don't understand. I went by the recipe. See, all the ingredients are listed right here. Oh, no, didn't I add the cornstarch? Look here, the cornstarch. I never added the cornstarch. I had it all measured out and everything but never added it. No wonder. Oh, what a shame."

"That's okay, Dad," said Cecilia. "That's an easy mistake to make. It happens to the best of chefs."

"That's right, Poppy, don't feel bad. It's okay," Sarah said, encouraging her grandfather. "The main thing is you tried."

"I want pie," said JJ.

"Me, t…," Justin began to say, before Cecilia and Sarah glared at him, sending the message that he needed to rethink saying anything at all.

"Oh, well, the best I can offer everyone is some ice cream," said Poppy Tom.

"Yay, ice cream! I want ice cream," said JJ, happily.

"Ice cream sounds good, too…," Justin said as Cecilia and Sarah glared at him once again, this time even more intensely, sending the message, loud and clear, that he needed to zip it.

As he was serving the ice cream, Poppy Tom said, "Sarah, when we're all cleaned up from lunch, I'd like to have you and JJ help me finish up a few projects I've been working on out in my woodshop."

"Oh, that sounds like fun, Pops."

"JJ, you and I are going to help Poppy. What kind of projects, Poppy?"

"Well, for one, I have some birdhouses that need to be finished. So you guys can help me with that, and I've been working on a larger project that's almost complete. Just a few more finishing touches and that'll be ready to go. I can have you both help with that too, if you'd like."

"Yes, we'd like to very much, right JJ?" asked Sarah.

"I like to hammer a hammer. Can I hammer, Poppy?" asked JJ.

"Yup, you sure can, JJ. Let's get cleaned up here…"

Cecilia interrupted her father and said, "You go ahead, Dad. Take the kids to the shop and start. Justin and I will clean up."

"I can help with your projects too, Dad," Justin added.

"No, dear. You're going to help me, and Dad will take the kids," Cecilia corrected Justin, in a directing tone. "Go on, Dad, you go."

Cecilia said under her breath to Justin, "I want to talk to you about something. Besides, we have the whole car to unload."

"Maybe that's a good idea," said Poppy Tom. "We'll shoot out there now before we get another deluge. I don't want to see these kids get all wet again."

"Come on, JJ, we're going with Poppy to his woodshop," Sarah called out. "We have projects to help Poppy finish."

"You too, Hollie," she added.

"Yay," said JJ excitedly, as he was about to run out the door without his boots on until Poppy Tom lassoed him with his arms and booted his eager feet.

Now that Cecilia and Justin were alone, Cecilia took the opportunity to ask, "Justin, are you seeing what I was talking to you about? Does it seem to you my father is getting forgetful?"

"Maybe a little, but I don't think it's anything to be worried about."

"That's what I'm wondering," she said, concerned. "Am I making more of this than I need to? I don't know. I mean, he's all alone here. I don't know what we'd do if he…," Cecilia stopped talking and just gazed forlornly down at the floor.

"Hey, come on now, Ce. So, he forgot to add some cornstarch to the pie. You said it yourself, the best of chefs do things like that. He's a guy full of energy. He's always hopping. We'll keep an eye on him. You're always calling, always checking in on him. Let's see how things go. If you ask me, he's more on the ball than me."

They both laughed because what Justin told his wife helped relieve her of her worry.

"I think I'll do some research when we get home," Cecilia said. With that she opened the refrigerator door to return the milk and noticed a set of keys sitting on the shelf inside the refrigerator.

Just then Poppy Tom entered the house calling out in a frustrated voice, "Did anybody see my keys? I have the door to my woodshop locked and can't find the keys. I have the kids waiting, and it looks like it's about to rain again."

Cecilia interrupted her father and with an upbeat voice said, "Oh, here they are, Dad, sitting right here on the kitchen counter. Here you go."

"Oh, good. I usually keep the keys…," he said, confused. "I don't know how they ended up there. Thanks. Alright, let me get out there and get those kids in before it rains."

"Sure, Dad, don't mention it," Cecilia said as she glanced out into space, pondering the implications of what just occurred.

"Okay, kids, I have the keys. Let's get inside that shop before the rains come again," said Poppy Tom. "I'm hearing thunder."

"I've never been in your shop before," Sarah said. "Oh, my, it's really nice in here, Pops. It smells really good, too."

"Oh, yeah, there's nothing like the smell of newly cut wood, Sarah. I love that smell, myself. I always have. Oh, hear that, its pouring again. We made it in just in time.

"Ahhh, we're nice and warm and dry in here," Poppy Tom said, rubbing his hands together contentedly. "So, tell me, are you guys ready to help with some of these projects?"

"Oh, yes, we sure are," Sarah and JJ said in unison.

"Okay, then, the very first thing we have to do is to get on your PPE. House rules. In this case, you need to wear these gloves and safety glasses. No excuses. Don't ever think you're going to work in this shop and not wear your PPE, which stands for personal protective equipment. Okay, do you guys promise?"

"We promise, we promise, Pops," Sarah and JJ agreed.

"You had me wear this stuff when we worked fixing the bank of the brook that time, Poppy," Sarah added.

"Sure, anytime you do work, you need your PPE. You never want to take a chance of something getting in your eye and doing damage. Your vision is far too valuable to risk. The safety glasses protect your eyes, and the gloves protect your hands. There are a lot of sharp tools in here that can cause nasty cuts. When working in a shop like this or any other place, we always want to think safety first. Is that a deal, grandchildren?"

"Yes, Poppy, that's a deal."

"Okay, what do you say? Can we high-five each other with gloved hands to make it official?"

"Deal, deal, deal!" they all said, as they gave each other high fives.

"JJ, I think I'm going to get you over here to paint this sign I made. How do you guys like what it says?"

"'Pop's Shop,' hey that's really great. I like it," said Sarah.

"Glad you think so, Sarah."

"You go ahead and paint it any colors you want, JJ. I've got all different color paints and brushes here for you. When it's all dry, we'll tack on this little brass plaque I had made that says, 'Painted by JJ,' and then we'll hang it out over the door of the shop for all to see. Oh, yeah, I almost forgot. Here are a couple of aprons for both you and Sarah to put on.

"Put them over your heads, and I'll tie them for you. Okay, there we go. You both look like professional woodshop workers now. Very good."

"I'm going to paint it, red and blue and green and yello…," JJ said.

Sarah interrupted JJ and said, "Oh, no JJ, that's way too many colors."

Then Poppy Tom interrupted Sarah and said, "Let him go, Sarah. Let JJ be free to use his imagination to paint that sign any way he wishes. We know how important it is to use our imaginations any way we want, right?"

"Yup, now that you say so, you're right, Pops.

"I'm sorry, JJ. Poppy's right. Paint the sign any colors you want."

"Yeah, I'm gonna to paint it purple and orange and…," JJ said, excitedly.

"What's *my* job, Poppy? What project do you have for me to do?"

"Right over here, Granddaughter. I have your project waiting for you right over here. I mentioned those birdhouses. Sitting on this workbench are all the pieces of wood, already precut and predrilled to build those houses. They just need to be assembled. Your job is to be the assembler, Sarah."

"Birdhouses, I'm going to be building birdhouses, JJ."

"I want to build birdhouses, too," said JJ. "I want to hammer a hammer."

"JJ, when you finish your painting project, then you can come over and help Sarah with the birdhouses," Poppy Tom said. "You never want to start a project and not finish it. There will be plenty of birdhouses to build. JJ, just so you know, you use a hammer to drive nails not a hammer to hammer a hammer. Got that, boy?"

"Yup, Poppy, I use a hammer to do hammering to hammer nails with a hammer. That's what I do with my toy hammer I have at home."

"Uhhh, yeah, I think that's right, JJ," Poppy Tom said, confused.

"Uh, anyway. Sarah, I'm going to have you use screws instead of nails. Let me show you. Each birdhouse consists of seven pieces, a bottom, four sides, and two pieces for the roof. Watch me, I'll assemble the first one and then you'll be on your own.

"The back piece of the birdhouse is the pointed one with no hole. We lay it flat on the table with the point facing out. We get one of the side pieces, they're both the same. Now we align the bottom of the side piece with the bottom of the back piece, Sarah. See, we make like an 'L.' We're now ready to screw these pieces together. They have power screwdrivers nowadays, but I like using a good old-fashioned Phillips-head screwdriver powered by me. It gives me a better feel for things. It's more hands on. I hope you don't mind, Sarah.

"Let me show you something. See this block? This is a block of beeswax. I get it from Mrs. T. A little trick is to rub the screw through the beeswax first. Like this. Then I place the screw in the hole and turn it. The beeswax helps the screw cut through the wood more easily and smoothly. It kind of makes it glide. Okay, you do one, Sarah."

"Okay, Pops. I get the screw, rub it in the beeswax, put it in the hole, and turn the screw."

"Yup, perfect, Sarah. You'll want to just snug the screw. Sometimes people have a tendency to overtighten. Just make it tight enough. Okay, good job, Sarah."

"Yeah, good job, Sarah," said JJ.

"Thank you, JJ. Wow, that's some colorful sign you're painting there. You're doing a good job, too."

"I know," JJ said confidently.

"Okay, Sarah, we're ready for the other side."

"Hey, Pops, I think I have the idea."

"Already?" he asked.

"Sure, I'll put the other side piece on, Pops, then the front with the hole, then the bottom, and then the last two pieces for the roof. I'll use the beeswax for each screw to help them glide in more easily, and I'll make sure I just snug them in. Then, we'll have ourselves a brand-new birdhouse that will just need to be painted."

"That's it, Sarah. You do that, and we'll have a brand-new birdhouse. But we're not going to be painting them. The idea is to keep everything natural. We're using wood that I've collected from dead, fallen trees. It's like a way of recycling this material. We'll be putting it to good use. And we save a live tree from getting cut down in the bargain. Besides, this wood is already dried out and weathered, making it perfect for birdhouses. This wood allows the air to circulate through. It's like the wood breathes. This makes for a healthier home for the birds to lay their eggs and raise their young.

"If we were to paint everything, the paint would seal the wood and prevent it from breathing. That would make the inside space of the house very humid. Humid space allows all kinds of bad molds and fungi to grow making for an unhealthy place. Also, if you see on the front panel, I have this thing called a hinge. This hinge allows us to open the hatch, remove the old nest, and clean the house out after each season. So, the birds can come back to a nice clean, healthy home the following year. When you get all the pieces screwed together, we're pretty much done. We'll just need to get JJ to hammer a nail a little way in on the front, just below the entrance hole, so the birds have a place to rest before entering their new home. He's our using-a-hammer-to-do-hammering-to-hammer-nails-with-a-hammer guy."

"I'm the hammer guy, Sarah, not you," said JJ.

"I know. I know," she said, laughing.

"Now that I have you both working away on your assignments, I can get going on mine."

"What are you working on, Poppser?" Sarah asked.

"I mentioned a larger project, Sarah. You see all this lumber piled up here?"

"Yes, that's a lot of wood, I'd say, Pops."

"Well, we're about to turn this wood into an access ramp at the home of a very wonderful person, and I'm proud to say, friend of mine," he explained.

"Poppy, you built a ramp for me at my house, and you built a ramp for me at this house," Sarah informed. "Does your friend need a ramp for the same reason I need a ramp?"

"Yes, exactly, Sarah. You remember me telling you about a young girl by the name of Paula Jean? She's the one…"

Sarah interrupted, "She's the one who's sad and I need to be her happy, Pops. Sure, I remember you telling me about her back in April. I want to go and be her happy. When should we go, Pops?"

"So, we'll see when we can work that in," Poppy Tom said. "I'm thinking either tomorrow afternoon or the next day. We'll see how things go. I want our time with Paula Jean to coincide with another event that's going to be taking place. Anyway, this ramp is for her."

Sarah interrupted again to say, "Oh, Paula Jean's mommy needs the ramp. Her mommy is in a wheelchair like me. I remember now. But I don't know why she's in a wheelchair. You never told me."

"I wasn't sure if I did or I didn't, Sarah."

"No, Poppy, you didn't. Was she born with something like I was born with or did…?"

Poppy Tom interrupted and said in a lower, more subdued tone, "No, Sarah, Paula Jean's mommy wasn't born with something like you have. She was a perfectly healthy, whole young woman…," Poppy Tom paused so he could think about how best to discuss a topic of such a stark nature with his young, impressionable granddaughter. "Paula Jean's mommy is one of our country's…uh, her name is Grace. When you meet her, I'm thinking you can call her Mrs. Gracie. She likes being called Gracie. I'll tell you, she's one amazing young lady, Sarah. Wait until you meet her. You're going to love her, and she's going to love you. I told her all about you, and she's very eager to meet you. She thinks you're wonderful for being willing to spread your happy to Paula Jean."

"Poppy, was Mrs. Gracie in the army?" Sarah asked directly.

Poppy Tom stood dumbfounded by his granddaughter's question, then answered, "Yes, she was, Sarah. How did you know that? How would you ever have known that," he asked, shaking his head from side to side and holding out his hands and shrugging his shoulders, questioningly.

"She got hurt in the army, huh, Pops?" Sarah asked softly so as not to let JJ hear the conversation.

Poppy Tom silently nodded his head as he glanced over at JJ finishing up with his painting project. Then asked, "JJ, you all done there, lad?"

"Yup, Poppy, all done," JJ replied. "How do you like all my colors? I got a lot of paint on the board and a lot on me, too," he said giggling.

"I love what you did there, Grandson. That's one unique-looking sign, I'll tell you that. That's why you have that apron on. Paint on the board, paint on you, it's all good. Come on over here by Sarah now, and we'll get you hammering on these birdhouses."

Then Poppy Tom turned to Sarah, still in a state of amazement by the level of maturity just displayed by his youthful granddaughter and said softly, "We'll talk more about Mrs. Gracie later on, after JJ goes to bed."

Sarah nodded.

"You guys hear that thunder out there?" asked Poppy Tom.

"Yeah, a lot of loud thunder out there, Poppy," JJ agreed. "Hammering sounds just like all that loud thunder. Boom, boom, boom."

"Poppy, what are we going to do with all these birdhouses anyway?" Sarah asked.

"Well, I was thinking we'll mount them on the posts of the fence up by the house."

"Oh, they would look great there, Pops," Sarah agreed.

"I was thinking this would be our way of helping out Mother Nature this year," said Poppy Tom. "She would like knowing her birds have a few nice, new, happy, healthy houses in which to raise another generation of feathered friends. And because of their location, we can view all the birds' activities right from the den window. Also, I like giving away a birdhouse or two to friends of mine. Mr. Nate, Mr. Reggie, Mrs. T, all those folks have one. I was thinking we'll bring one over when we visit Paula Jean. I think she would like to have one, too. Don't you?"

"Oh, I'm sure she would, Pops," said Sarah.

"JJ, let's make that one, the one you're hammering on now, be Paula Jean's."

"Can that one be Paula Jean's, Poppy?"

"Sure, that's a real nice one," said Poppy Tom. "Paula Jean should love it."

"Can't we paint her name on it, Poppy?" asked Sarah. "That way she can see we made it just for her. She would feel real special if she knew that. Would painting her name on the birdhouse make it bad, like unhealthy, Pops?"

"Not really," answered Poppy Tom. "But how about I carve her name in it, instead? I can carve, 'From Sarah and JJ, to Paula Jean.'"

"Oh boy, that would be great," said Sarah excitedly.

JJ stuck his hammer under his arm and clapped his hands, then he and Sarah high-fived each other.

"Let me get back to my project now, Grandchildren. I want to finish predrilling the decking, and I have a few more posts and rails to cut. When I have everything ready to go, I'll get your dad to help me load my pickup. Your mom and dad are going to help me build this ramp for Mrs. Gracie. They just don't know it yet. You both will, too. I have some things you both can help out with. I'd like to do this as a family. Mrs. Gracie did so much for us and our entire country. This is the least we can do for her."

"Oh boy, JJ, we're going to build a ramp, a whole big ramp for Mrs. Gracie. Isn't that great?"

"I want to do the hammering, Poppy, not Sarah. She don't know how to hammer. I'm the best hammerer. Not her."

"I know how to…," Sarah began as Poppy Tom interrupted.

"Alright, JJ, you can do all the hammering you want, but I wouldn't count your sister out. She's pretty good at everything she does, and I would think hammering, too."

"But I'm better, Poppy," JJ said. "Way better."

"Okay, lad, you're better," Poppy Tom agreed as he glanced over at Sarah and winked.

Sarah winked back at Poppy Tom, and they both chuckled. Then Sarah asked, "Poppy, how did you get so good at making stuff out of wood? You know how to build ramps and birdhouses and carve things."

"Oh," Poppy Tom said with a slight laugh in his voice. "I worked with wood all my life. I was what you call a carpenter by trade. That was my occupation. A carpenter builds things out of wood."

"Did you like doing that, Pops?" Sarah asked with interest.

"I sure did, Sarah. I can actually say I loved it. I loved working with wood. I loved the feel of it and the smell, too. I got a lot of satisfaction and gratification from seeing things get built from the ground up and knowing I had a hand in making it happen. It was honest work for honest pay, and I was proud to do it."

"Did you hammer things a lot, Poppy?" JJ asked.

"Oh, yeah, I sure did, JJ. That's all I did. Back then, it was all hammer and nails. Today, they have screw guns and nail guns, you name it. Oh, yeah, the trade is very different today. Still good though. It's still a good way for someone to earn a good honest living."

"What are some things that you built, Pops?" asked Sarah.

"Oh, my goodness, Sarah, I built homes and buildings, all kinds of things. Hey, now that I think about it, I made the bed you sleep in when you're here. I made the table and chairs we just ate lunch on, and even the kitchen cabinets, too. Grandma Jennie loved those cabinets. Oh, yeah, I made all kinds of things."

"I want to be a *hammenter* when I go up, just like you Poppy," said JJ. "I want to *hammenter* all kinds of beds and chairs and birdhouses and things."

"Carpenter, JJ, not *hammenter*," Poppy Tom said laughing. "I could see you being a carpenter, and a good one at that. That would be something alright. Well, we ought to try to get finished up here soon. That way, when the rain stops, we'll be able to run back to the house."

CHAPTER 14

"Mommy, Poppy made this table and chairs. Did you know that?" Sarah asked.

"Of course, honey," Cecilia replied. "Poppy made many pieces of furniture here, like the bed you're sleeping in. That was my bed. Poppy made that for me when I became old enough to sleep in a big girl's bed. Notice the "C" carved in the headboard. I'll tell you what else Poppy made. He made a beautiful cradle for me when I was born. We used that same cradle for you and JJ. Someday, you and JJ will have that for your children to use. That beautiful cradle needs to get passed down to future generations. It will be something very special to remember Poppy Tom by."

"Did I hear my name mentioned?" asked Poppy Tom. "JJ went out like a light. All that *hammentering* he did today wore him right out."

"Hamm...what?" Cecilia asked.

"Oh, JJ's our official hammer operator," said Poppy Tom. "He created a whole new occupation for himself in the process. Ce, you and Justin are doing a great job raising your kids. I love spending time with them. What fun! Makes an old grandpa like me proud."

"Thank you, Dad. That's a very nice thing to say. Justin and I had good parents that taught us wonderful parenting skills."

"That's good to hear, but you were supposed to say, 'Ah, Dad, you're not an old grandpa. You're a young one,'" Poppy Tom said jokingly.

"You are," Cecilia laughed and added, "they love spending time with you, too, Dad. We all do."

"Yup, we sure do, Poppser Woppser," Sarah chimed in.

Poppy Tom chuckled and then asked, "Where's Justin?"

"He's outside, Dad," Cecilia answered. "He loves taking a walk at this time of night, just before the sun goes down. He likes the peace and serenity."

"Oh, I do the same thing," said Poppy Tom. "He's right. Very peaceful. We'll wait until he comes in. I want to talk to all of you about a few things."

"Is everything alright, Dad?"

"Oh, yeah, everything's fine. There's just some things I'd like you guys to help me with. That's all. I'll fill you in when your husband gets back."

"Okay, I'll put the water on in the meantime. We can have ourselves a nice, hot cup of tea while we talk."

"I hear Daddy coming in now," said Sarah.

"Justin, how was your walk?" Poppy Tom asked.

"Oh, just great," answered Justin. "I can't tell you how beautiful it is out there this time of night. The sun was going down behind the mountains, the clouds were all breaking up, and everything was wet from the rain. There was this lazy mist rising up from the trees. The sky, wow, what colors. Pinks and reds and purples. The more the sun went down, the more vibrant the colors became. And the quiet, not a sound could be heard. Complete opposite from all the thunder before. It was so peaceful, so relaxing, and serene. A real soul-restoring experience. I didn't want it to end."

"Oh, I know," Poppy Tom said nodding. "I like to do the same thing. I love taking those walks just before dark. I'm glad to know you appreciate that too, Justin."

"Come and have a seat, Hon," Cecilia called out to her husband. "My father wants to talk to us about some things. Do you want tea? Who would like a cup of tea?"

"Okay, sure, Ce, I'll have a cup of tea, if it's decaffeinated," Justin replied. "I'll be up all night if it's not."

"What's up, Dad? Is everything alright?" Justin asked.

"I want tea, too, Mommy," Sarah said.

"I'll take a cup, Cecilia," Poppy Tom said. "Decaffeinated, too, if we have it. I don't even know if I have decaffeinated in the cabinet."

"Yes, you do, Dad. It will be decaffeinated all around except for you, Sarah. It's time you head to bed."

"Cecilia, I need Sarah to be part of our conversation," said Poppy Tom. "Would it be okay if she stayed up a little past her bedtime tonight, please?"

"Oh, sure Pops, I can stay…," Sarah said.

"For a little while, Dad, okay," Cecilia interjected as she gazed at her daughter.

"Okay, good," he replied. "No, everything's fine, to answer your question, Justin.

"I'll be brief. I think I told you both about a little girl that I would like Sarah to talk to. Her name is Paula Jean."

"Sure, Dad, we know," confirmed Cecilia.

"You're both okay with that, right?"

"Yes, Dad, of course," Cecilia answered. "If Sarah's okay with that, then we're okay with that."

"I'm okay," Sarah quickly replied. I'm good. I want to visit her…"

Poppy Tom interrupted Sarah and said, "Okay, so here's what I'd like you to know. Paula Jean's mom is in a wheelchair."

"Oh, that's too bad. Why, Dad?" Cecilia asked with much concern in her voice.

"I'll get to that in a minute. That's what I needed Sarah to stay up for. Anyway, I volunteered to build Gracie—that's her name—a ramp at her house. She doesn't have a ramp. Well, she has one, but it was just put together quickly. She needs a good, well-built ramp. I have all the material ready to go. The kids helped me finish up the loose ends today. I would like you, Justin, to help me load the pickup with everything I have to do the job. Then I'd like it if we all went together as a family and built that ramp for Gracie."

"Absolutely, Dad! I'm in," Justin said enthusiastically.

"Yes, that would be terrific," Cecilia said, just as enthusiastically as

Justin. "What a wonderful thing, Dad. We'd love to help."

"JJ and me, we're helping, too, Mommy. JJ is going to hammer, and I'm going to...What am I going to do, Pops?"

"Well, Sarah, you're going to have a lot to do. First and foremost, I'd say you'll be talking to Paula Jean. Sarah Nightingale, you'll be spreading your happy like your smiling people say. There will be plenty of chores for you to do on the ramp after you spend some time with her."

"Cecilia, Justin, here's the deal. Gracie is...," then he became choked up. "This is very hard." He took a moment to compose himself, then began again. "Gracie is a wounded veteran. I really don't want to go into the details of her wounds, but she needs this ramp and we're going to build it for her.

"Sarah, I have to ask you. Before in the shop when I started to talk to you about Mrs. Gracie, how did you know? I hardly said anything and yet you knew she was in the army. How did you know that?"

"My math teacher, Pops," said Sarah, "Mrs. Bari. Her son was in the army and he got hurt, so he needs a wheelchair. He came to visit us one day at school, him and his friends. They were in wheelchairs because they all got hurt. They came to thank us for sending them boxes of candy and stuff. They said they really liked getting all those goodies, even baby wipes. I guess they have to wipe babies sometimes. When you said, 'Mrs. Gracie wasn't born with something like I was, she was whole, but now she needs a wheelchair,' that was like Sergeant. That's Mrs. Bari's son's name, Sergeant Bari. He showed us a picture before he got hurt. He had everything good. But when he got hurt, his legs got really hurt, so he doesn't have them anymore. He said someday soon, he's going to have new legs, so he won't need his wheelchair so much. Sergeant Bari's friend, Sergeant Sanchez—they both have the same first name—he showed us his new legs. He showed us how he puts them on and then he can walk so he doesn't need his wheelchair so much. They wanted to know why I needed a wheelchair. So, I told them. I showed them my poem and my lucky hat and feather, too. They all said they wished they had a poem and lucky hat and feather like mine. They said maybe they wouldn't have gotten hurt so much if they had those things.

"Did Mrs. Gracie's legs get real hurt, Pops? She can get new legs. They really work good."

"Oh, my goodness," said Poppy Tom sullenly. "That's some story. Yes, Sarah, I'm afraid Mrs. Gracie's legs were hurt very badly. But you're right, she'll be getting new legs someday. It's a long process, but someday she'll have new legs, too.

"Sarah, just think, think about how strong and brave you are and how hard you must fight to free yourself of your burden. Can you imagine how strong and brave Mrs. Gracie and all those amazing veterans that came to visit your class are? How brave all our military service people are to choose to go to a very dangerous place to fight for us to keep us free? Can you imagine how brave a person needs to be to do that, Sarah? And they have to continue to be strong and brave to fight to free themselves of the burdens they now have as a result of their wounds, both physical and mental, as a result of their service to us and our country. We need to help them, Sarah.

"Cecilia, Justin, we need to help them anyway we can. We owe them so much," Poppy Tom said as tears welled up in his eyes.

"Poppy, I have an idea," said Sarah. "I can write more poems and give them one. The poems will help them to keep being strong and brave and know that there are no limits to what they can do. Just like for me. Can we get more feathers from Mr. Nate? Do you think he has more feathers, Poppsey? We can give the vets feathers; they can put them in their hats. Those feathers will give them luck, guidance, and the ability to see all the wonders of the beautiful world around them."

"That's a fantastic idea, Granddaughter," said Poppy Tom excitedly. "By the way, I like the way you said the word, ability. I bet Mr. Nate has more feathers. How about this idea? Over the next few days, you make up a couple of poems and we'll visit Mr. Nate to see if he has more feathers. When we visit Paula Jean and her mommy, you can give them each a poem and a feather, and then we'll arrange to send your veteran friends theirs. You can sit at your grandmother's desk, where she sat to write your poem. You can use her fine stationery and even her fountain pen. I'll show you how. Sound good?"

"Great, Poppsey. That would be great," Sarah said enthusiastically, giving her grandfather two thumbs-up and then, all joined in, giving each other high fives.

"Okay, now that you two have solved the ills of the world," Cecilia said, "how about you getting yourself off to bed, my dear daughter?"

"Okay, I'm off," said Sarah. Turning to Poppy Tom, she said, "Good night, sleep right, and don't forget to turn off the light."

"Hey, another good one, you," said Poppy Tom. "Okay, let me see... Gee, I can't seem...Uh, sleep tight...good night...Hmmm, I must be having one of those, what they call, senior moments. Don't let...Nope, I'm drawing a blank. You got me, Granddaughter," he said with a tinge of embarrassment in his voice.

"That's okay, Poppy. You can share mine," said Sarah. "We're a team and team people always share. Remember?"

"Oh, good, I feel better now," said Poppy Tom. "Oh, hey, are we going fishing in the morning?"

"Of course, we are, Pops. Got to get another line. Can't not get another line, Pops."

"Well, okay," said Poppy Tom. "But with all this rain, the brook is really high and the trail is quite muddy."

"Are my brook trout friends okay, Poppsey?"

"They're okay, Sarah. I'll just get you using a different tactic because of the high water. I've had you dry fly-fishing all along. You know, having the fly float on the surface of the water. We'll switch it up, and I'll show you how to wet fly-fish tomorrow instead. We'll use different flies that sink below the surface. The high water makes for tough conditions, so I don't know how successful we'll be, but you'll wet your fly line and qualify for another carved line. I guess this is the perfect time to use the expression, come heck or high water, Sarah's going fishing."

"I don't want you getting wet Sarah," Cecilia said sternly. "Your lungs are still not fully recovered, and you can't afford to get sick again. I don't know, Dad. What if it rains?"

"Your mom is right, Sarah. I didn't even think of that...the way these storms have been coming."

"Poppy, you got me rain clothes," said Sarah. "By Mr. Nate that time, you got me clothes to put on if it rains. I'll put those clothes on.

"Hollie knows where they are, right Hollie? They're by my boots. We can bring an umbrella, too."

"Yeah, the rain gear, we bought you rain gear," confirmed Poppy Tom. "We can bring an umbrella. Well, how about we see what the weather is like in the morning and go from there."

"Justin, you said the sky was red before, right?"

"Yes, a beautiful red," Justin confirms.

"Well," Poppy Tom began, "there's an old seafaring rhyme that goes, 'Red sky at night, sailor's delight. Red sky in the morning, sailor's take warning.' Let's hope this holds true for us fisher people tomorrow, Sarah. Hit the hay, and we'll see what the weather is like after Brewster the Rooster personally provides you with his wake-up call."

"Oh, yeah, Brewster the Rooster, my buddy," Sarah said sarcastically. "Hit the hay. I know, don't tell me. Expression, right?"

Poppy Tom, Cecilia, and Justin got a good chuckle as Sarah moved off to bed, while shaking her head and mumbling..."Brewster the Rooster..."

Then, Cecilia said, "I can't even imagine what poor Gracie is going through. How hard that must be."

"She is something, Ce," said Poppy Tom. "So strong. The thing is, Gracie doesn't worry about herself at all. All she worries about is her daughter. She sees that this has really affected her. Paula Jean, she's only, like five, five and a half, maybe."

"Just a little older than JJ," Cecilia said. "Honestly, I can't imagine it. How is this affecting this poor little girl?" Cecilia asked, as her eyes filled with tears.

"Paula Jean's very distant," Poppy Tom said. "She really doesn't want to talk much. Gracie said she was a lively, full-of-fun kid, until, you know, seeing her mother come home...Her mother was fine... before. Then all the time in the hospitals. All the operations. Seeing her come home without...It's a very tough thing. I told Gracie about Sarah. She's so thankful to you all for being willing to have Sarah talk, just try and talk to Paula Jean. They've tried all different kinds of counseling. Nothing has helped. Let's hope and pray Sarah can help her. If anybody needs Sarah's happy, it's poor little Paula Jean."

"Of course, Dad, we'll pray," said Cecilia.

"Yes, of course," Justin said, agreeing.

CHAPTER 15

"Good morning, Poppy," Sarah said while rubbing the sleep from her eyes. "Are you giving Brewster the Rooster any of that secret energy potion? He seems to crow louder and louder every year."

"Good morning, Sarah. No, he said chuckling. "Ol' Brewster the Rooster doesn't need any secret energy potion. I think he just gets better with age."

"Can't we get him to trade places with Ol' Mister Scowl the Owl?" Sarah asked. "Mister Scowl the Owl would be nice and quiet sitting outside my window, and I would wake up to see his perfect owl smile. That would be treasuring each day from the moment it starts, alright. Ol' Brewster the Rooster could crow as loud as he would like to and wake up all the big, giant trees way over by the Dark Woods."

"Well, Sarah," Poppy Tom said laughing. "If you know of a way to make that happen, then I'd say go for it. But I'd think you'd have to learn how to speak rooster and owl first. Sarah, did you happen to notice that the sun is shining this morning?"

"Oh my, it is, Poppy. What a beautiful morning. I won't need to wear my rain clothes or bring an umbrella when we go fly-fishing this morning, Pops."

"Well, the sun is shining now, but I think we want to be prepared just in case it does rain while we're out there. The weather's been quite changeable lately. I'd say you should wear your rain gear pants over your jeans, and we can pack your jacket and umbrella. So, we'll have everything handy if it starts to rain. We don't want to chance you getting wet."

"Okay, Poppy, that sounds like a plan. Wow, Pops, you picked some of Grandma Jennie's roses."

"Ah, you noticed. I couldn't resist, Sarah. When I looked outside this morning, the sun was just coming up and shining directly on these roses, making all the water droplets that were on them sparkle and shine. It was like the roses were saying, 'Hey there, look at…'"

"Oh, Poppy," Sarah, interrupted. "I just remembered my dream. Smelling Grandma Jennie's roses is making me remember my dream."

"What dream, Sarah?"

"Grandma Jennie came to me in a dream, Pops."

"She did? Tell me about it, please."

"I felt all warm and cuddly," Sarah began, "but I was sleeping. You know dreaming. I felt all warm and cuddly and smelled the roses, Grandma Jennie's roses. That's why I know it was her. Then, in the dream I saw writing on a note. All pretty writing."

"What did the note say, Sarah?"

"It said, let me think," Sarah said, then paused. "Oh, what did the note say? Something about Paula Jean."

"Paula Jean?" Poppy Tom asked surprised as he looked over at Hollie, who had a questioning look on her face, too.

"Yes, Pops, I'm trying to remember," said Sarah. "Have Paula Jean… do something. Wait, it's coming…Have Paula Jean…ride…ride rainbow! That's it, Pops. The note said, 'Have Paula Jean ride rainbow!'"

"Have Paula Jean ride rainbow?" Poppy Tom questioned. "That's what the note said? Are you sure, Granddaughter? Do you mean, the rainbow? Have Paula Jean ride the rainbow. But that wouldn't make any sense either. I wonder…?"

"I'm pretty sure it said, have Paula Jean ride rainbow," Sarah said. "Maybe, on the day we visit Paula Jean, maybe there will be a rainbow outside. Maybe, we can pretend, like imagine we're riding the rainbow up in the sky and that would make Paula Jean smile and then be happy. Maybe that's what Grandma Jennie is trying to tell me."

"Maybe. Hey, you never know," said Poppy Tom. "If we see a rainbow at the same time we're visiting Paula Jean, that would be a sign to do something, that's for sure. Okay, let's be on the lookout for rainbows. We'll make that our own private little project, you, me, and Hollie. Come on, we have waffles with fresh strawberries for breakfast this morning. Let's eat up and head out. It's getting late."

After breakfast, Sarah, Poppy Tom, and Hollie made their way to the secret fishing spot for Sarah's third time. While pausing at the rock that looks like a bear, Sarah said, "Pops, come on, this way," as Poppy Tom stood staring at the rock.

"That way, Sarah, are you sure?"

"Sure I'm sure," Sarah said with confidence. "We go right at the rock that looks like a bear. I know, Pops. You're just trying to test me. I know, you just wanted to see if I remembered."

"Oh, yes, right, I was just testing you," Poppy Tom said with a hint of insecurity in his voice. "You remembered. Good girl."

Approaching the corral, Sarah asked, "Did we remember to bring sweet treats for Lightning and...Hey, Pops, where are Lightning and Thunder?"

"They're not in the corral today, Sarah. They're in the barn. I want to wait to explain to you why that is. You'll be seeing them soon. That's all I'll say for now."

"Oh, okay, Poppsey. As long as they're happy in the barn, I'm happy for them."

"Oh, they're happy alright, Sarah. And they'll be even happier in another day or two. You'll see."

Now at the secret fishing spot, Sarah said, "Wow, Poppy, the brook is real high. I've never seen it this way before. It was very low last year, but this year it's all high and making a lot of noise."

"Yes, it is. All this rain we've been having has caused the brook to rise. Total opposite from last year. I had a feeling this was going to happen. One year it's low, the next it's high. Mother Nature has a way of equaling things out that way. So, there are a couple of things to go over with you on our approach." Whispering, Poppy added, "Even though the brook is making a lot of noise, as a result of the rushing water, we still want to be quiet and walk softly. The brook trout can still hear us and feel our vibrations. That's how sensitive their survival skills are. I figured I'd mention this so Hollie wouldn't have to remind us," Poppy Tom said as he smiled at Hollie, and she looked back at him approvingly. "Also, and I really should have said this first, we don't want to get too close to the bank of the brook. The bank could easily give way. We wouldn't want to fall in and get swept away by the fast current. You should always make it a point, no matter what you're doing or where you are, to look over the conditions and situations you find yourself in to determine if any dangerous circumstances exist. Then, make good judgments on how best to safely go about whatever business you have to do. Make sense, Granddaughter?"

"Makes sense, Grandpoppser," Sarah agreed, whispering too.

"So now, let's go over our tactics for this morning's fly-fishing mission, Sarah. As I mentioned last night, the high-water levels will have us wet fly-fishing today, as opposed to dry fly-fishing. You're going to be handling your fly rod with the same delicate, gentle motion as always. You know, like painting the…"

"Yes, Pops, I know, like painting the delicate wing of a butterfly."

"Good. Good. Okay, so the difference with wet fly-fishing is, for one, the fly and line are weighted. Right from the get go, you'll feel that extra weight as you cast. Then, when you're casting and letting out line, you can allow the fly to fall to the surface with each cast. You're not going to have to keep the fly floating in the air as you did when casting a dry fly. You cast, strip out line, and cast again until you get the fly out to where you want it to be. Once it's out there, the fly will sink as it moves downstream. I've tied on a fly, referred to as a Tunghead Muddler. See, the head is weighted and brassy looking. Our hope is that the weight will get the fly down to where the brook trout are, and the shiny brass will allow them to see it through the murky water and then want to strike. One more thing, as the fly works its way downstream, the line will form a loop until it gets fully extended in the water. At that point, you'll need to hold the line with your right pointer finger, because you're righty, and use your left hand and pull the line up to where we are here, and then repeat the same process again, making another cast. You follow, Sarah?"

"You lost me at, so the difference with," Sarah replied softly while giggling. "But let me try casting and we'll see how I do. Delicately hold the rod, gentle motion. Feeling the weight. Cast. Allow the fly to fall. Strip out more line. How we looking, Pops?"

"Did we go over this before?" Poppy Tom asks surprised.

"No, no, first time. It's just that you're such a good teacher, Pops."

"I think it's because you're such a good student," he replied with such admiration for his quick-learning granddaughter. "Okay, so see how the fly worked itself downstream?"

"Yup, I see, Pops."

"Now is when you want to bring the line back in, using short, pulling motions, and sometimes, if you can, give the rod a slight twitching action."

"Sort of like this, Poppy?"

"That's alright, but maybe ease up just a bit on the twitching motion. Just a slight movement. Doing it that way makes the lure resemble what's called a sculpin, swimming upstream. Our hope is the brook trout will think so too and want to have it as a snack."

"Better, Poppser?"

"Yes, much better, Sarah. Try and think of anything to do with fly casting as less is more. The same theory applies to swinging a golf club, but that's a whole other sport that you don't want me to do any teaching on."

"Why, Pops, aren't you good at golf?"

"I'd be great at golf, if the person with the highest score wins," Poppy Tom said jokingly. "But that's not how it works, unfortunately. So, no, I'm not good. Anyway, back to the sport at hand. Just to refresh your memory, if you get a strike, pull up sharply on the rod to set the hook. Then you'll be fighting your fish, and this year you'll be fighting the swift current, too. I must say, Granddaughter, we're up against some tough conditions this year. So, don't feel bad if you're not successful."

"That's okay, Poppsey. I treasure our time together, catching a brook trout or not. You know, Pops, I thought I'd be walking here this year without even needing my walker. Like maybe just using arm crutches, I thought. But you know, that bug got me and hurt my lungs."

"Yes, Sarah, that bug got you. But you shouldn't feel…"

"Oh, no Pops," Sarah interrupted. "I'm okay. It just means I have more fighting to do. If my burden gets stronger, then I have to fight even more stronger. It just means that I'm still in like a Dark Woods place. But there's always a bright, shiny place at the other end, just like where we are right now. Sergeant Sanchez, Sergeant Bari, and even Mrs. Gracie, their legs got hurt much more than my lungs. Sergeant Sanchez, he can walk already. Sergeant Bari and Mrs. Gracie, they'll have new legs and they'll be able to walk, too. If they can be strong and fight to walk with their really hurt legs, I can be strong and fight with my not-so-hurt lungs. So, I do what my poem tells me to do. I treasure today, Pops, right from the moment it started. We had good waffles with good berries. Even ol' Brewster I treasure. He's not so bad, really. He's just doing his job. Today, I learned a new way to fly cast and even a little something about golf. And I'll get another carved line. But the most, best thing I treasure is being here with you, Pops, you and Hollie. You are the best Poppy ever, and I love you very much."

"Looking for the good and never the bad, and I love you, too, Sarah. See, you, the light of the world, your love-light is getting reflected back to you. You should be wearing sunglasses."

Both Sarah and Poppy Tom laughed as they hugged each other and hugged Hollie, too.

As their fly-fishing efforts came to a close, Poppy Tom said, "Well, Sarah, you gave it another gallant effort to try and hook a trout. I believe we'll find the conditions better next year. I believe it will all come together for you next season, and you'll land your brook trout. I'm so very eager for you to see one up close."

"We'll see, Pops. I know we're going to try. You, me, and Hollie. We make the best team ever. Don't forget to carve another line for me later."

"I won't. Line number three, this one will be."

"I like that, Poppser. Line number three, this one will be. Line number three, this one will be…," Sarah sang in a rap music style, while using rap dance moves.

Poppy Tom picked up on Sarah's lead and together they sang and danced while trekking to the gap in the stone wall, as Hollie joined them, wagging her tail and howling as best she could to mimic their singing.

Arriving at the stone wall, Sarah said, surprised, "Wow, Poppy, you got a lot of the wall back together."

"Not bad, right, Sarah? You'd be surprised how much can get done by just working at something at a nice steady pace. Nothing crazy. I get a lot of satisfaction being out here, Sarah. It's peaceful and quiet, and I feel it brings me closer to my...your grandmother."

"I'm going to pull up to this spot and help you fix the wall...," Sarah said.

Then, Poppy Tom interrupted her to say, "Please, Sarah, I would prefer it if you just sat and looked up at the sky and clouds and used your imagination today. Please, I wouldn't want you straining to pick up any stones. That would be much too strenuous for you to do right now. Besides, we're not going to be staying here too long. Look up at The Mountain of Singing Trees. Its summit is all covered in clouds. I'm afraid there's more rain on the way."

"Okay, Poppy. I'll sit here with Hollie while you work. I can snack on blueberries while Hollie has her treats. We have them right, Pops? You remembered to bring our blueberries, right?"

"In my backpack, Sarah," Poppy Tom said with a tinge of hesitation in his voice. "I have our snacks and our water. But I brought us raspberries not blueberries. Don't we usually have rasp...?"

"Oh, that's a good change," Sarah interrupted. "I like Mrs. Sherry's and Mr. Jerry's raspberries as much as I like their blueberries. It's not a blueberry sky today, anyway, Pops. Here are your treats, Hollie. We'll snack while Poppy works."

Poppy Tom went back to his task of repairing the stone wall with a forlorn look of concern on his face regarding his apparent forgetfulness. He concealed this look from Sarah.

After a few moments passed, Sarah asked, "Hey, Poppy, do you think the trees sing when its cloudy?"

"I think Mother Nature has her trees sing their glorious song whenever she feels there's someone worthy enough to hear them, no matter the weather conditions. However, rainbows seem to play a roll. But I think Mother Nature can make a rainbow anytime she wants."

"It must be nice to be able to make trees sing and make rainbows anytime you want, Poppy. Mother Nature is one lucky lady. Remember when you and Hollie came to visit me at my house, Poppy?"

"Oh, yes, Sarah. I remember."

"Do you remember us talking about me making discovery cures, Pops?"

"Yes, I do."

"I don't know, Pops. I don't know if I should make discovery cures to help children and people or if I should make discovery cures that help Mother Nature. You know, Poppy, I have a goal to someday climb to the top of The Mountain of Singing Trees and hear their song, just like Grandma Jennie did and get a carved line right next to hers. And I'm going to get there on my own two feet."

"Yes, I know your goal, Sarah. And there's no doubt in my mind that someday you'll accomplish that goal."

"But Poppy, I think Mother Nature only has her trees sing for people that help her creations. Dancing Cloud made it rain, and that rain helped all the crops and trees and owls, and everything was happy again. So, Mother Nature had her trees sing to honor Dancing Cloud. Grandma Jennie saved all of Mother Nature's giant trees that we see here. So, Mother Nature had her trees sing to honor Grandma Jennie, too. I have to do something that helps Mother Nature—something big—so when I climb up to the top of the mountain, Mother Nature will have her trees sing for me, too."

"Okay, now I understand the basis of your question, Sarah. How about considering this idea? Go out there and make discoveries that help children and people and Mother Nature. After all, in the big picture, we're all interconnected."

"Do you think I can do that?" Sarah asked when she realized Poppy Tom was glaring back at her with a look on his face as if to say, "Do you really have to ask me that question?"

"Oh, you're right, Pops. I can make all those discovery cures. There are no limits to what I can do. That's right! I'll go out there and make discovery cures that help children, people, and Mother Nature, too. Thank you, Pops. But what big picture?"

"You don't have to thank me, Sarah. I didn't say anything. You figured it out all by yourself. That poem of yours—its message will be there to inspire and guide you forever. Hey, the wind is picking up. That could mean rain is on the way. Let's get headed back."

"Okay, Pops, you lead, and Hollie and I will follow as always," she replied with a proud, confident voice.

Cecilia, feeling relieved knowing her troop returned home safe and sound from their outing, said, "Oh, I'm happy to see you all made it back before the rain. We didn't want to see anybody get wet. I was also concerned about, God forbid, lightning. How was the fishing?"

"The fishing was good, Mommy, but the catching wasn't. We don't worry about the catching part though. We all like being together and learning new stuff. Right, Poppsey? Right, Hollie?"

Hollie barked her agreement, and Poppy Tom said, "Right, Granddaughter. We're glad we're back, too. We didn't need to get caught in any rain storms. By the looks of things, I bet it will be raining within half an hour."

"Oh, Dad, while you were out, Mrs. Rivera called. She said she wants to let you know that things are getting close. Tomorrow should be the day. What's that all about, Dad?"

"Okay, good to know, Cecilia. That could not have worked out better. Thank you for telling me. Mrs. Rivera is letting me know about something that I'd like to keep under my hat for now."

"Under your hat?" Sarah asked. "But you took off your hat. Oh, I know, it's another expression. You sure know a lot of expressions, Poppy. Mrs. Rivera, don't Lightning and Thunder live in the corral by Mrs. Rivera? But they weren't in their corral today. You said they were in the barn."

"Yes, you're right there, Sarah."

"Hmmm, I think I might know what's going on," Cecilia said.

"What, Mommy, what do you think…?" Sarah asked.

Cecilia interrupted her to say, "No, I won't say. We'll let Poppy Tom tell us when he feels it's right."

"Thank you, Daughter," he said with a sly smile on his face. "I'm going to call my friend Gracie to see if tomorrow is a good day for us to go there and work on the ramp. If so, Sarah, you can plan on talking to Paula Jean. You'll need a couple of poems ready to go, and we'll have to get over by Mr. Nate's to pick up a few feathers. I'll need Justin to help me load the truck."

"The birdhouse, too, Pops. We can't forget to bring Paula Jean's birdhouse," Sarah reminded him.

"Yes, right. Good for you for remembering that, Sarah. I'll put that birdhouse in the truck right now, while it's fresh on my mind."

"Where's Justin, Ce? We might as well load the truck now, too."

"He was out playing catch with JJ, Dad."

"Okay, I'll look for him outside. Cecilia, I'd like to pack us a cooler with drinks and sandwiches for tomorrow. I'll call Gracie from the shop and confirm for tomorrow. Once we know tomorrow is good for her, we can detail out what we have to do on our end."

"Okay, Dad. I like that idea. We're all looking forward to meeting Mrs. Gracie and Paula Jean and building them that ramp. So, anything we need to do, we'll do."

"Perfect, Jen," said Poppy Tom. "I'm headed to the shop."

After Poppy Tom left the house, Sarah said, "Mommy, Poppy Tom just called you Jen."

"He just meant that as, well, you know, I remind him of her," said Cecilia.

"Oh, yeah, he said that to me one time for the same reason. Poppy Tom thinks we're just like Grandma Jennie. I like knowing we're like her, Mommy."

"Uhh, me too, Sarah. Me, too," said Cecilia as she gazes into space reflecting on her concerns with Poppy Tom's memory.

CHAPTER 16

"Hello, Gracie," Poppy Tom shouted out as he and Hollie exited from his truck loaded down with materials to build the ramp. "We picked a good day. Looks like the weather's cooperating. Maybe just a few spotty storms working through later this afternoon, they say."

"Hello Tom," Gracie shouted back excitedly, as she wheeled herself out onto the small front stoop of her neat, modest home. "It is a beautiful morning!"

Hollie, eager to greet Gracie, ran up to just before the stoop, then slowed to walk the rest of the way to her, displaying her respect for Gracie's condition. It was something Hollie learned from years of interacting with Sarah.

"Hey Hollie, good to see you girl," Gracie said affectionately while hugging Hollie.

Poppy Tom followed Hollie, then both Gracie and Poppy Tom hugged, too.

Then Gracie said, "I can't believe this is happening. You and your family are so wonderful for doing this. I could never thank you all enough or ever be able to repay you."

"No. No thanks needed, none whatsoever…," said Poppy Tom. "We're the ones that could never thank you enough or repay you for all you did, for all your service and sacrifice to me and my family and our entire country. What we're about to do is nothing compared to what you have done for all of us. But I'm not kidding about having a family, Gracie. I do have one. They were right behind me," Poppy Tom added as he peered down the street. "Oh, good, here they come now."

The moment the car stopped, all four doors opened up and Justin and JJ exited the car and walked quickly toward Gracie, smiling, waving, and calling out greetings. Cecilia helped Sarah into her wheelchair. Then they moved, but at a much gentler pace, toward Gracie with caring smiles on their faces.

Warm introductions and hugs were exchanged between Gracie, Justin, and JJ, after which they, along with Poppy Tom and Hollie, moved down from the stoop to allow room for Cecilia's approach to Gracie. All were quiet as Cecilia's and Gracie's eyes, each now filling with tears, met. Then, instantly and without ever uttering a sound between them, volumes of words were telepathically being related and understood. Words that spoke to the deep sorrow and feelings of guilt in Cecilia's heart for seeing Gracie, a beautiful, dynamic, fellow woman, wife, and mother seemingly shackled by her condition. A condition Cecilia, for reasons hard to fathom, felt she caused. A condition she wished she could somehow remove from Gracie, so to be burdened with it herself. If that were to happen, then perhaps the weighty mountain of debt, a debt Cecilia felt she could never repay, would be removed from her hunching back and shoulders. But, it's a debt Cecilia would not be seeking repayment of from anyone else.

At the same time, Gracie's valiant, watery eyes spoke volumes back to Cecilia, as if to say, there's no need for your heart to hurt with sorrow for me. No feelings of guilt either. I am proud to be considered by you a fellow woman, wife, and mother. Sisters, bound together by our life's calling and faithful never to point a crooked finger of fault or blame upon the other. Whole, spirited, and free, we are and must always remain so. No matter our condition. No matter our circumstances. Shake off this imaginary weight of debt that has you slumped and troubled. It does not exist. It never did. Allow yourself to stand straight and tall, free of sorrow, guilt, and burden and gaze out at the land before you. A land of freedom and liberty that I, my sisters, and brothers in arms, past, present, and future, gave and will give, our blood, bones, and lives to protect and preserve. A simple, sincere thank you to us will do.

Cecilia and Gracie, with eyes still moist and locked in this trancelike stare, nodded their heads in unison, as soft smiles creased their cheeks signaling the understanding, respect, and love that was just secured between the two by their silent, intimate exchange. Cecilia bent down to Gracie, allowing their arms to wrap together in a warm, lingering embrace, cementing the bond between them. Then, as they slowly released their hug, Cecilia straightened and turned aside to allow Gracie to see Sarah sitting patiently in her wheelchair at the lower level of the stoop.

"Sarah. You are Sarah. You're every bit as pretty as your grandfather said you were," Gracie confided in a soft, admiring voice. "I am so very happy to meet you, sweetheart."

"You are very pretty, too, Mrs. Gracie," Sarah said happily. "Thank you for saying I'm pretty, too. I couldn't, we all couldn't wait to meet you, and I can't wait to meet Paula Jean. I want to be friends with Paula Jean and be her happy."

"I want to be friends with Jeanie Paul, too," JJ said excitedly. "I want to *hammenter*, too."

"Paula Jean, JJ," Cecilia corrected her son, laughing. "Paula Jean, not Jeanie Paul, is Mrs. Gracie's little girl's name."

"Is Paula Jean home?" Sarah asked. "I have something for her and you, too."

"You do?" Gracie replied. "Well, Paula Jean is...well, she's become somewhat shy. I saw her peeking out the window when you were all pulling up, but I think she might've gone back to her room. That's where she spends...She stays in her room a lot. What kinds of things do you have Sarah? Wait a second, we don't need to be hanging out here? Why don't we go inside the house where we all can…?"

Then Poppy Tom interrupted Gracie and said, "Hey, everybody, let's not forget we have a ramp to build. We want to take advantage of the good weather."

"Gracie, how about you have Sarah meet you in the house where you guys can talk? I'll try and get my crew of vastly ham-fisted, highly overpaid, immeasurably underutilized, and exceedingly overfed, ramp constructers working," Poppy Tom said chuckling.

"Hey, Captain Bligh, keep that up and you're going to have a mutiny on your hands before your ship even leaves the dock," Cecilia said kiddingly so to keep Poppy Tom's jocularity going.

All get a good laugh, as Gracie said, "Honey, the only way for you to get in the house is to go around the back. That'll change once this wonderful ramp gets built. I can't tell you all how much that's going to help."

"Hollie, can you show Sarah the way please?" she added.

Sarah said, "Okay, Mrs. Gracie, we'll see you at the back of the house."

"Come on Hollie, you show me the way, sweetie lady."

Then she whispered, "Poppy, can you get me Paula Jean's birdhouse please?"

"Sure can," Poppy Tom whispered back. "I put it in a box, wrapped it in paper, and tied it with a pretty pink ribbon, so when you give it to Paula Jean, she can open it like a present."

"Oh, that's great, Poppy. Thanks!"

Then, Poppy Tom said, "Come on over by the truck everybody. Let's get on our PPE and then Justin and I can start unloading the truck. Let's get this show on the road."

"Show? Road?" Sarah looked at Poppy Tom confused.

Then they said in unison, "Expression," while pointing an oh-I-got-it finger at each other.

Hollie successfully guided Sarah to the back door of Gracie's home, allowing Gracie to instruct, "Come right in, Sarah, the door will open up for you."

"Hey, that's cool," Sarah stated. "That's just like the doors at the hospital. Mrs. Gracie, can Hollie come in too? She's…"

"Of course, she can," Gracie confirmed.

"Come right in, Hollie girl." She wasn't going to come in until she was told. "How cute is that? What a good girl you are, Hollie. Let me get you some water."

"Sarah, what can I get you, honey? A glass of milk? Some cookies?"

"Some milk and cookies, yes please, Mrs. Gracie, but no honey, thank you. I like honey, especially if it's Mrs. T's, but milk and cookies will be fine."

"No honey…? Oh, okay, no honey, sure. Milk and cookies it is. Coming right up," said Gracie, gazing at Sarah with a warmhearted smile as she realized all the wonderful things Poppy Tom told her about Sarah are true. She could see, but even more important, she could feel down deep in her heart that this young girl—full of innocent love and kindness—was truly special and will, by the grace of God, be able to help her disenchanted Paula Jean. "Please come to the table, hon, uh… sweetie, where we can sit and talk. That's a pretty wrapped package you have there. You can set that on the table if you want. And, Sarah, I have to tell you; I love your hat and my goodness, what a beautiful feather."

"You see my feather? Thank you for loving my hat, Mrs. Gracie. You see my feather? I have one for…Mrs. Gracie, Paula Jean, can she come and sit, and we can have some milk and cookies all together?"

"You know, Sarah, thank you for asking. I don't know…Let me ask her. Excuse me for a moment while I go and see."

Gracie moved down the hall to Paula Jean's closed bedroom door and called, "Paula, precious, come on out. I have someone very nice here that I'd like you to meet. A very nice girl named, Sarah, and her dog, Hollie. They're here visiting. We're having milk and cookies." No sound was heard from the room. "Come on out, sweetie, please."

Then they heard the words, "NO, I DON'T WANT TO!"

"Uhh, come on now, please Paula. It's not polite…"

"NO! GO AWAY!"

Gracie moved back to the table where Sarah sat and said sadly, "I'm so sorry, Sarah. Paula Jean…She doesn't want to come out. She wants to stay in her room."

"Oh, that's okay, Mrs. Gracie. I understand. Paula Jean is sad. Sad is happier being alone. Mrs. Gracie, is this milk from Miss Mary's Dairy?"

"Yes, it is, Sarah. You know about Miss Mary? You can tell?"

"Yup, I can tell, Mrs. Gracie. It tastes real good because it's organic. My Poppy Tom took me there, and I got to meet Miss Mary. She's a very nice lady, like you. Anything organic tastes real good and is good for you and is good for Mother Nature, too. Did you know that, Mrs. Gracie?"

"I never really thought of it that way, Sarah. I'm glad you made me aware. Miss Mary *is* a very nice lady. You're so right. I'm going to tell you just how nice she is. She…," Gracie started to choke up a bit, then said, "she gives us this wonderful milk for free. Yogurt, too. She, your Poppy Tom, you, so many people help us, give me and my family so much, Sarah. We are truly blessed."

"I have some things to give…My feather, you said how beautiful my feather is, Mrs. Gracie. I have some things to give you. Paula Jean, too. But I'll give Paula…"

"Oh, yes, you said you have some things, Sarah. I can't believe this. You're here to help with Paula Jean, and you're bringing me gifts, too."

Sarah, with slightly shaky fingers, took a few deep breaths, then reached into her pocket and pulled from it, four neatly sealed small envelopes. She laid them on the table and separated them into two piles. Then, by looking closely at each pile, she determined which envelope she wished to pick up first. She chose one of the envelopes and handed it to Gracie saying, "Mrs. Gracie, I have two envelopes for you, but open this one up first, please."

Gracie graciously accepted the envelope and said, "I'd be honored to." She gingerly began to open the envelope and said, "What beautiful stationery." Then she removed the brightly colored red-tailed hawk feather from the envelope. She looked in awe at this beautiful object and immediately realized it was something very special. Gracie gasped and said, "Oh my goodness, Sarah, a feather, a beautiful feather. For me? This is for me?"

"Yes, Mrs. Gracie. That's a feather, just like mine. Me and my Poppy went by Mr. Nate to get them. Mr. Nate, he's a very nice man and has feathers and a whole bunch of other real cool stuff."

"Oh, Sarah, how wonderful. How very nice. I thank you so much."

"No, wait," Sarah said. "Wait, I have to tell you all about these feathers. You don't know. Wait 'til you know," Sarah said eagerly.

"What can you tell me…?" Gracie asked excitedly. "I can't wait to hear. I want you to tell me all about our feathers."

"Well, so, first, this feather makes hats lucky. But you need a hat. Do you have a hat, Mrs. Gracie?"

"I sure do, Sarah. I have my army hat. Hold on, let me go get it. I'll be right back."

"Oh, neat, that's a really neat hat, Mrs. Gracie. Put the feather on your hat. Can it go?"

"Sure, I'll pin it on, Sarah. I have pins right here in the drawer. There we go. Nice. Here, I'll put it on. How's it look, Sarah?"

"It looks great, Mrs. Gracie. You look so pretty with that pretty feather in your pretty hat. So now your hat is lucky and so are you. But, there is a whole lot of other stuff our feathers can do, too. See, Mr. Nate, all his family from a long time ago, his ancestors, were sisters and brothers with all of Mother Nature's creations. We are too, but we kind of forget. They knew all about their secret secrets. Mother Nature, she's a good mother like you and my mommy. And she makes a lot of beautiful creations, and they all have a bunch of secret secrets. Like trees and brook trout, butterflies and owls, and hawks and their feathers. Oh yeah, potions, too, but that's a secret I have to keep a secret. Unless someday you get sleepy a lot and don't want to be sleepy anymore. Then I think we can tell you. So anyway, Mr. Nate's ancestors told him about the secrets of the feather and Mr. Nate told me and my Poppy, and now I can tell you."

"Oh, I can't wait. This is so exciting, Sarah!"

"That feather," Sarah said, then paused to look around to see if anyone else was nearby. Confirming there wasn't, she whispered, "That feather has *greaaat* powers. It will give you luck, guidance, and the bil... bil...the ability to see *allll* the wonders of the beautiful world around you. Mrs. Gracie, quick, hold the feather up to the light. See, aren't you amazed at what you see? And wait, wait 'til you see all the secrets it will be unfolding on you."

"Oh, would you look at that? Honestly, Sarah, it's so beautiful," Gracie said, awestruck. "What a precious gift. I will treasure this always and know it will do just what you say it will do. Thank you *sooo* very, very much."

"You're welcome, but there's more, Mrs. Gracie. This next one is real cool, too," as she hands Gracie the second envelope.

"Another one, this is so...Where did you find such nice stationery, Sarah?"

"My Grandma Jennie," Sarah answered proudly. "She writes so pretty and she has this desk with all this nice paper and fancy pens and ribbons and stuff. My Poppy Tom let me sit right in her chair, right at her desk and use all her really fancy stuff."

"I feel so...You're making me feel so special, Sarah," Gracie said with appreciation as her eyes started to water. "Your grandmother's stationery. I heard so many wonderful things about her. Oh...so very special." Gracie, again, carefully unsealed the envelope so as not to cause any uneven tears. She removed the note, looked back at Sarah with a soft smile, and then began to read the words, words written with such care and diligence by Sarah, who Gracie already considered to be her new, albeit young, comrade for life. Here's what it said,

To the Light of the World

Allow me to say with all of my heart,
Treasure each day from the moment it starts.

Look for the good and never the bad,
Be the happy to those who are sad.

I know there are No Limits to what you can do,
So go out and discover worlds that are new.

Gracie sat frozen, as these inspiring words flowed into the deep crevices of her wounded body, mind, and soul. What wasn't frozen, however, were the tears flowing from her eyes and chasing each other down the rounded slopes of her cheeks. She felt obligated to give Sarah thanks and praise for this amazing offering of kindness and support. She didn't want Sarah to think she wasn't appreciative. Heaven forbid. But no words came.

To Gracie, no words of gratitude seemed worthy enough to speak. She was also perplexed. Perplexed by this young girl who carried upon her small, fragile shoulders such a heavy, cumbersome burden of her own, and yet had the ability to deliver such a heavy, powerful message of hope, inspiration, and love, with such selfless joy and ease. Not only to deliver the message, but to be able to understand its true value, to fully understand the immense good that it could do. Gracie was the adult here. She was the one that should be supplying the support and setting the example for Sarah. Things were supposed to be the other way around. Gracie, still feeling ill-prepared to address Sarah, forced her resistant, moist eyes up from the comfort zone of the note to align with Sarah's.

Instantly she saw, in the exact same manner in which Gracie and Cecilia communicated without words just a short time ago, Gracie and Sarah were communicating now. Sarah's warm eyes and inviting, mature beyond her years' smile, sent the message that no thanks were needed.

Sarah's eyes conveyed messages of happy stuff, "Right, Mrs. Gracie? And hey, no biggie. I do this for my friends all the time. You're my friend now, Mrs. Gracie, my really good, new friend."

Gracie and Sarah nodded their heads in similar fashion as Gracie and Cecilia, acknowledging their understanding and love just created by their wordless heart-to-heart. Then, Gracie pulled herself back from the table and wheeled herself alongside Sarah. The metallic sound of their wheelchairs merging, heralded the bond that had just been made between the two. And their silent, absorbing hug welded this bond together making them, as Gracie thought earlier, comrades for life.

The tranquil silence of the moment suddenly broke by the sound of a slamming door, startling Sarah, Gracie, and Hollie. All heads turned in the direction of Paula Jean's room.

Then Gracie said sullenly, "Oh, that was Paula Jean. She must have been peeking out of her room and saw us hugging. Oh, Sarah," Gracie confided, "I don't know what to do. My poor little girl. She's having such a...This is all so very difficult for her. I can deal with what I have to deal with. But seeing how this is affecting my poor little Paula Jean. I want to make things better. I want to make this all go away so I can get my happy-go-lucky little girl back. But I can't. I don't know...What do you think, Sarah? Can you help? Do you think there's something, anything, you can do to help?"

Sarah responded confidently, "No, I don't *think* there's something I can do to help, Mrs. Gracie. I *know* there's something I can do to help. I know I can help and so will you and my Poppy Tom, my mommy, everybody. We're all going to become Paula Jean's happy so she's not going to be sad anymore. Just like our poems say. Just like our feathers, too. I *know* we can, Mrs. Gracie."

"Oh Sarah, I believe you and I believe in the power of our poems and feathers," Gracie stated with moist attentive eyes. "I feel it way down deep in my heart."

"Yup, Mrs. Gracie. There are no limits to what we can do," Sarah said assuredly. "When something gets behind your eyes and falls down into your heart and you feel it there, it always comes out and happens. I think it's the heartbeats that pump them out. Mrs. Gracie, did Paula Jean...? Does she like rainbows?" Both Sarah and Hollie waited in anticipation of Gracie's answer.

"Does she like rainbows?" Gracie asked with some confusion. "I...I guess."

"I mean did she see rainbows and say she liked them? Did rainbows make her happy?"

"Gee, not that I can say," Gracie answered. "She would maybe, when she colored, you know, draw rainbows. But she would draw other things, too. I'd say the things she liked to draw and color the most were horses. Not sure why. But most of her pictures were of horses."

"Oh, Paula Jean liked to color?" Sarah asked.

"Oh, she sure did," Gracie confirmed. "We used to sit and color together for hours. There are a few of her pictures on the refrigerator. See how some of them are of horses. All her pictures back then were of such happy scenes. So colorful. Then they turned…She doesn't color anymore."

"I like to color too, Mrs. Gracie," stated Sarah. "I learn all kinds of ways to color and paint in my art class at school. I'm going to look forward to coloring with Paula Jean and you, too, Mrs. Gracie. We're all going to color some really good pictures. You just wait and see."

"You'd be the answer to my prayers," said Gracie. "Those are the things I miss. We would sit right at this table and color. We played that patty-cake game too, you know, Miss Mary Mack. You reminded me of that when you mentioned Miss Mary's Dairy before. How I long to have those days back."

"So, okay, Mrs. Gracie, you guys colored. You guys played Miss Mary Mack, Mack, Mack. What else did you and Paula Jean like to do? What else made Paula Jean happy, Mrs. Gracie?"

"Oh, there was this game…," Gracie started to say, then paused as she choked up. After a few moments, she continued with a shaky voice, "There was this game we used to play. We kind of made it up. We called it 'Supergirl Fly!' I would sit on the floor and Paula Jean would come up to my bent…legs. Together, we'd do a countdown from ten, you know, like when a rocket ship blasts off, ten, nine, eight. When we'd yell BLASTOFF, we'd make all kinds of blastoff noises. Then I'd lie down real fast while raising Paula up and balancing her on my legs saying together real loud, SUPERGIRL FLY! She'd hold her arms out and I would move my legs around to make her feel like she was soaring through the air.

"We'd pretend she was flying over…say New York City. I'd tell her about the Empire State Building and have her use her imagination to wave at all the people on the top floor waving back at her. Then we'd fly down to Washington, D.C. and pretend she was soaring by all the monuments and wave to all the people there. Or maybe we'd be flying by the Grand Canyon, the Rocky Mountains, the Mississippi River, or even way out to Mars and Jupiter and Saturn. We'd pretend to see all kinds of different places. She loved playing that game. That made her happy, Sarah. That made us both very happy. I'm afraid she sees me like I am now and knows I can't play that game with her anymore. That's the tough thing. She sees me like I am now, sitting in this chair. I think Paula Jean feels cheated. I think she feels scared. She thinks I'm not the mother…"

Gracie started to cry.

"Oh, Mrs. Gracie, don't cry. You can play that game," Sarah said strongly. "Paula Jean and you are going to play that game, and it's going to be even more funner than it was before. All the fun things you did together you will do again, and even more new things. Things Paula Jean and you never even thought possible. I promise, Mrs. Gracie. I promise you, and I promise Paula Jean, too."

"But how, Sarah, darling? How can you make…? I know you mean well, but how can you make me a promise like that?"

"Because I know, Mrs. Gracie. I know that Paula Jean is sad and scared because she's looking at everything bad. We're going to have her see things good instead. Just like our poems say. Paula Jean doesn't have a poem yet. A feather either. But that's okay, she will. She's stuck in a Dark Woods place. Sad makes kids get stuck there. Mrs. Gracie, you and me, we're the lights of the whole wide world. Paula Jean will be, too. You want to shine your love-light on Paula Jean. But it's like she has a hat on, and her hat blocks your love-light from shining on her and makes things look all dark, and dark looks scary. The hat shades her. But it's really only shade, just plain ol' shade, and plain ol' shade isn't scary. We can make Paula Jean see things differently, and when we do, she'll see the good instead of the bad. And then, she'll see the dark turn to light, really bright, shiny light all around her. There's always a beautiful, bright, new, shiny place at the other end of any dark places you ever have to go through, Mrs. Gracie, as long as you look for the good and never the bad, are brave and know that there are no limits to what you, uhh, we can do. My Poppy Tom promised me that and then he showed me. And it's true. I saw it. So, I can make you that same promise and show you it will be true, too. I promise, Mrs. Gracie. I promise I will."

"You've convinced me, Sarah. What do we have to do? What's your plan?"

"We're going to play games, Mrs. Gracie. We're going to play the same games you and Paula Jean played before you got hurt. But this time, we're going to play them really, really, happy, happy. We're going to talk louder and laugh louder and make all kinds of having-a-whole-bunch-of-fun-together noises. More louder noises than you've ever made before with Paula Jean. A girl a long time ago, by the name of Dancing Cloud, made her sisters play and dance and sing real loud to make dust look like clouds and go way up in the sky to make it rain. We're going to play and laugh real loud so our happy sounds will go through Paula Jean's door and walls of her room and knock the hat that shades your love-light right off her head. Then, your love-light can shine real bright on her and she won't be in the Dark Woods place anymore and won't be scared anymore. Can you get us all crayons and paper, so we can color? Then we can play Miss Mary Mack, Mack, Mack," Sarah added. "Then, we'll play Supergirl Fly, real loud, real happy."

"You think? You think we can?" Gracie asked. "You think this will work?"

Sarah gazed at Gracie with a "do you really have to ask me that question, Mrs. Gracie" look on her face.

Gracie looked back at Sarah sheepishly and, in another wordless communication between the two, implied, "Oh, right, Sarah, of course you know you can." After that telling look, she added, "Okay, Sarah, I'll go get the crayons and paper and be right back."

When Gracie returned with the goods, Sarah and Gracie began coloring. As they did, in loud, tickled voices that they knew Paula Jean would hear, they complimented each other on the great job they were doing. They made up jokes and then laughed exaggeratedly at the punchlines. Even Hollie joined in on the fun by barking and prancing around the table with her tail wagging joyfully. After a short while of this happy deception, they saw from the corner of their eyes, the door to Paula Jean's room opening slowly and from this slender gap in her cocoon of despair, Paula Jean peered a probing eye. Sarah and Gracie concealed their acknowledging winks from Paula Jean's welcomed curiosity.

Gracie, thinking she was keeping the merriment going, said to Sarah, "I'm going to tape some of these beautifully colored pictures we did up on the fridge." When boom, Paula Jean's door slammed shut. "Oh, I shouldn't have said that, Sarah. Why did I go and say that? That's what I used to do with her pictures. Now she sees me wanting to hang our pictures up there instead. I think I just made my little girl jealous. With all the issues already, I've just added another one."

Sarah raised a calming hand to Gracie and said, "That's okay, Mrs. Gracie, that was only our first cast. Nice and smooth and gentle now, we'll make another cast." Then, she said in a loud, excited voice, "COME ON, MRS. GRACIE, LET'S PLAY MISS MARY MACK, MACK, MACK!"

Gracie, convinced by Sarah's confident coaching, engaged with her in this simple pleasure that had them soon laughing, genuine laughs, especially when one of them missed a beat or missed the other's hand. Hollie timed her lively barks to the gleeful, hopeful cadence being generated by the team of Sarah and Gracie Nightingale. It was a gleeful, hopeful cadence that seemed to be breaching the walled barrier to Paula Jean's heart, for the door to her room opened again. Gracie could see this occurring but didn't want to do anything this time to disrupt its progress, so she kept her eyes transfixed on Sarah's. Sarah, who actually had a better view of this positive development, also felt that it's safer for them to act as if they and Hollie were the only living things around and that playing this game, even more robustly, was the only thing in the world to be doing.

Paula Jean peered out from her door so she could directly see and hear the fun her mother was having with this strange girl and her dog who seemed to have taken up residence in her kitchen. She had a strong urge to slam her door again, even harder than she did before, but for some odd reason she felt an even stronger urge to get a closer view of their fun play. She knelt down and began to crawl from her doorway across the hall to the closest corner of the open archway to the kitchen.

Sarah, Gracie, and Hollie were aware of this development but stayed completely involved in their game. Hollie turned away from Paula Jean. Sarah and Gracie saw this and followed Hollie's lead and did the same thing but kept her partially in view.

Paula Jean, thinking her movements had gone unnoticed thus far, ventured sneakily from the open archway to what she saw as a hideout under the kitchen table. Except for the slight scuffing sounds from the rough undersides of the toes of her feety pajamas rubbing against the floor, she felt she made it there undetected.

Gracie could hardly contain herself. This was the closest Paula Jean had come to her in a very long time. She wanted to turn and call out to her. She wanted to reach down and grab her little girl from under the table and raise her up into her arms. But she resisted. It took all of her might, but she resisted.

"Just keep staring at Sarah, just keep playing the game," Gracie told herself, "with silver buttons, buttons, buttons, all down her back, back, back." But before Gracie had a chance to even think about having things back to how they used to be, Paula Jean darted from under the table, back to her room, and slammed the door once again.

Gracie's arms fell to her lap and her head drooped down in disappointment. "What happened now?" she asked in a voice tinged with despair. Still looking down in desperation, she said, "She was so close. What made her run?" But she sensed Sarah's optimistic gaze pouring over her. She turned to Sarah to see an acknowledging smile on her face and a "we've got this thing, don't worry Mrs. Gracie" look in her eyes.

Sarah whispered, "I know why she ran, Mrs. Gracie. I knew she would be scared. When Paula Jean went under the table, she saw I was in a wheelchair. She didn't know I was in a wheelchair, too. My wheelchair scared her.

"You said Paula Jean was peeking out the window when we pulled up to your house before. She went back to her room before I got out of the car. She didn't see me get into my chair. Looking from her room now, she couldn't see my chair either. I was sitting behind the table. She thought I was just sitting in a regular ol' chair. It wasn't 'til she got under the table that she saw it. My wheelchair, our wheelchairs scared her, Mrs. Gracie. That's why she ran away. When something's scary, it makes kids not want to be by it; so, they run away. I bet there's a whole bunch of reasons why Paula Jean is afraid of our chairs and thinks they're all bad. We'll make her see our wheelchairs differently. We'll make her see the good in our chairs and that will make her happy and her happy will make her big ol' scary go away. That's when you'll see big happy smiles on Paula Jean's face."

"That's what I long for Sarah, sweetheart," said Gracie. "Big happy smiles on my precious little girl's face. How do we do that Sarah? What can we do to make that be?"

"We make another cast," Sarah said confidently. "We're going to play "SUPERGIRL FLY," Mrs. Gracie. We're going to play "SUPERGIRL FLY" bigger and louder and noisier and happier than we ever could have before. Paula Jean thinks our wheelchairs are scary, ol', mean, metal-ly things that stop her from playing Supergirl Fly with you. We're going to show her differently."

Sarah, still whispering so Paula Jean couldn't hear her, said, "Mrs. Gracie, Hollie, let's get ready. We're going to countdown like a big rocket ship is getting ready to blast off. We'll yell blastoff real loud and make lots of big blastoff noises and yell, Supergirl Fly. Then, we'll spin and zip in our wheelchairs around the kitchen table imagining we're flying to lots of special places around the whole wide world and hooting and hollering and waving to the people we see and that see us, along the way. Let's take a couple of deep breaths first. Okay, ready? Together, real loud, TEN, NINE, EIGHT, SEVEN, SIX, FIVE, FOUR, THREE, TWO, ONE, BLASTOFF!!! BERSWISHISSHOWISHPOWWEE-WISHSWISH!!! SUPERGIRL FLY!"

"I'm soaring over the Grand Canyon and waving at the people riding mules along the Colorado River, and they're all waving back at me," Gracie said blaringly.

"I'm soaring all the way up in the sky and around the clouds that look like ice cream cones and snowmen and unicorns and waving at all the people in the planes that are passing by," Sarah said exuberantly as she and Gracie swirled and whizzed around the kitchen table with Hollie in tow, barking cheerily.

They would be happy to know that Paula Jean had been drawn from under the covers of her bed to the closed door of her room by all this raucous noise and merriment that was penetrating her walls. Once there, this miniature ninja followed her now covert routine of opening the door, doing the customary peering, kneeling, and crawling to her next checkpoint at the kitchen's open archway.

Sarah, Gracie, and Hollie kept up with their jubilant sport and, while making one of their many gamely laps around the kitchen table, happily noticed Paula Jean watching. Sarah led the group to the far side of the kitchen to allow for an unobstructed route to Paula Jean's under-the-table hideout in the hopes she would take it once again.

Which she did!

Sarah, seeing this, led the group back to their original flight pattern of circling around the kitchen table for the purpose of ringing Paula Jean inside the circle.

Paula Jean found herself sitting cross-legged in the eye of a storm of thunderous joy and laughter. She used the legs of the table that surrounded her as imaginary bars meant not to keep her in, but to keep others out, just like the door and walls of her room did. These imaginary bars of hers may stop *people* from coming in but couldn't stop *sounds* from coming in. And in this case, the sounds that were now twirling around her and pouring through the gaps of her feeble facade and into her young, hurting heart and soul, were beautiful.

These lovely sounds of joy, happiness, and laughter came at Paula Jean from all sides and wrapped around her like so many soft blankets warmed in a glowing oven. These soft, warm blankets began to weaken the hardened layers of rust encrusting so many of her thought-to-be-gone-forever feelings of love and laughter. Paula Jean began to realize that she loved and laughed like this with her mother, just like this, when they played this very same game and soared all around the world. But that was before—before her mother went away, when her mother had all her parts.

Paula Jean felt that when her mommy went away, so did the love, so did the laughter, and when her mommy came back, the love and laughter stayed away. Gloom and sadness took their place. But how could Paula Jean ever love and laugh like this with her mother ever again if her mother was so different? The chair proved it. The chair proved her mother was different. The chair caused this problem. Before the chair came, there was love and laughter. Now that the chair was here, there was no love or laughter. It was that chair's fault. It was that chair's fault Paula Jean's mother came back different, without legs. The chair took her mother's legs because it wanted to come home and be close to her mother and take her place. The chair didn't want her mommy to have legs. If her mommy had legs she wouldn't need the chair, so the chair could go away. But the chair didn't want to go way. It wanted to stay and be her little girl instead of Paula Jean. The chair was bad, and her mother didn't even know it.

To Paula Jean one chair was bad enough. Now there were two, and they were both swirling and whirling around her like the ugly, spindly legs of some giant, gray metal centipede, all dangly and creepy feeling, without a beginning or an end. Round and round they went. Her eyes tried to follow them, but they couldn't keep up. They tired and wanted to close but she resisted. Paula Jean couldn't take a chance on closing her eyes. This thing was so scary, if she closed her eyes, it could easily breach what she now knew were meager defenses and gobble her up for lunch. So, she fought to keep her eyes open, but she knew she was losing the fight.

Paula Jean allowed them to close, just for a second, she thought. But when she tried to reopen them, she couldn't. They were way too heavy. It was like they'd been glued shut. Paula Jean thought maybe the chair came in when she closed her eyes for that one second and glued them shut. Or maybe it was this girl's chair that glued them. Why not? She thought both chairs were bad, all chairs were bad. She felt this girl's chair and her mommy's chair were working together on keeping her mommy different, keeping her mommy away. It could even be that dog. Maybe it was that dog's job to come in here when it had the chance and glue Paula Jean's eyes shut. Whoever, whatever it was, it really didn't matter to her anymore. She was much too tired to fight anyway. Paula Jean knew it was time to surrender. She gave up trying to open her eyes, she gave up on thinking she was safe inside her hideout.

Let whoever, whatever wants to come and get me, let them come and get me. I give up, she thought to herself. With her eyes closed and back slumped in her waiting-for-the-end position, instead of hearing growls and hisses and other monster-getting-ready-to-eat-their-victim noises, Paula Jean heard those sounds again. Those happy, joyous sounds of love and laughter. Those same sounds that wrapped around her, like so many soft warm blankets were back. Paula Jean realized they never really left. These beautiful sounds never left and neither did the blankets. They were there the whole time. But now she really heard them, and more important, she really felt them.

These beautiful sounds blended into music and songs. Music and songs of joy and love, of hope and love, and of love and love were passing right through and behind Paula Jean's closed eyes. The warm blankets were even warmer now and following the music and song through and behind her closed eyes, too, and together they descended to do a delightful, delicate ballet of restoration around Paula Jean's, oh, so-in-need-of-restoration heart and soul.

She heard the music and song and felt the music and song tickling and renewing her very being. She felt the warmth of the blankets warming her up from the inside out and could feel them melting away the feelings of sadness, badness, and darkness.

Did Paula Jean dare open her eyes? They didn't seem to be glued shut anymore. She thought they would open easily now, but what if this was all just a trick? What if that ugly, spindly legged monster was still there and even closer now and ready to gobble her up for lunch, she thought? But Paula Jean sensed it wasn't.

Even though her eyes were closed, she caught flashes of light shining on her. The music and song of love, the soft warm blankets, and the flashes of light beckoned her to open her eyes. She couldn't resist anymore, and slowly, squinting, she allowed her eyes to open. To Paula Jean, the vision before her was amazing. The music and song and warmth of the blankets that caressed and danced around her heart and soul on the inside were now playing right before her eyes on the outside. The ugly, creepy legs of the monster were replaced by so many playful legs of beautiful, prancing ballerinas whose pure white lace tutus and silky-ribboned shoes followed the graceful leaping of their delicate dance. This same delicate dance that was tickling and renewing Paula

Jean's soul on the inside was now playing out before her eyes on the outside, and it was wonderful. She saw that the light she sensed when her eyes were closed was real, too, and it would shine on her fully if not for being interrupted by the shooting and darting legs of the ballerinas. But what a light. She'd never seen a light so bright, so vibrant. She could see and feel this ever-so-bright, intense light shining on every deep, dark, sad feeling she ever had, and it made them disappear.

A light this bright should be hurting Paula Jean's eyes, and it was. But, it was a good hurt. She saw more and more of the light taking over. It became harder for her to see the ballerinas. The ballerinas eventually faded away, but the music and song stayed and the light continued to flash. What caused the light to flash now? With the ballerinas gone, what caused the light to flash? Paula Jean squinted to see. There, that thing. What is that? There went another one. Her head turned to try and get a better glimpse, but they zipped by so fast. Like jets, they zipped by. All this head turning and jets zipping was making her dizzy. Any more of this and Paula Jean could pass out. Just then, luckily for her, things began to ease.

The music and song slowed down, and their sounds began to fade, but the happy feelings they brought to the show remained. These jetlike objects slowed, too, and Paula Jean was able to regain her bearings. It was then that she saw what she thought were jets weren't jets at all, but were chairs! And these chairs were not interrupting the light. No, in fact, they were adding to it. Bright, white, happy light was glinting and twinkling from the chairs and gently falling upon Paula Jean like glittery fairy dust. All the light combined and shrouded her and bathed her in a pool of shimmering, luminescent liquid. Now, all Paula Jean saw and felt was luscious, blissful light.

It was then that she saw it. From out in the distance, out from this light, she saw a glimmering form slowly approaching. Paula Jean struggled to make out what it was. It wasn't until the form got closer that she realized it was her mother, whose face glowed with a wondrous, loving smile and who glided smoothly and happily toward her on the wheels of her luxurious thronelike, chair. It was then that it hit Paula Jean, and she thought to herself, "It's the chair that's bringing my mommy to me, not keeping her away! It came here to help my mommy and take the place of her legs, not take my mommy's legs away. The chair came to help. All the while the chair was here to help, not to hurt. It's strong, too, and can take my mommy anywhere she needs to go. That's its noble job. It made my mommy play our game, better and stronger and faster than when she had her legs and better than we ever did.

"The chair is strong. It can take my mommy's weight, and it can take mine, too. The chair is so strong and good that it can and wants to carry both of us. Me and Mommy together can play our games and go wherever we want to go and laugh and be happy together, forever. The chair loves my mommy, and the chair loves me, too. It wants to be here for as long as it needs to be here to help us and love us and be our friend. We love the chair, too. I love the chair. The chair is like the sister I never had. How could I have ever thought otherwise? The chair made me realize my mommy isn't different. She's the same loving, warm, happy, laughing mommy I always had. Just because she lost her legs doesn't change that. Nothing can or ever will change that. Besides, my beautiful sister chair takes the place of Mommy's legs so it's like she never lost her legs, ever. I love you chair, and I thank you my sister chair for bringing my beautiful, loving, happy mommy back home to me."

Pure, plain, and simple, Gracie's love-light was shining bright and beautiful on Paula Jean, and Paula Jean wasn't wearing a hat anymore! There's no more shade. There's nothing stopping her mother's beyond-limit, forever-glowing (like only a mother can) light of love from shining on Paula Jean and penetrating every fiber of her being. Paula Jean was seeing things differently. She was seeing and feeling the good and not the bad. She was seeing and feeling the happy and not the sad. The good was making Paula Jean be and feel happy, and the happy took away all her sadness, fear, and despair. Love was doing its job the only way love knows how. There were no limits to the good love could do. And it was beautiful and restorative and amazing. Paula Jean had just come through a Dark Woods place and was now basking in the bright, white, happy glow of her new, shiny world at the other end. Just as Sarah promised Gracie she would! Sarah Nightingale's plan had worked!

All this love, joy, and happiness flowing into Paula Jean's mind, body, and soul allowed words that she kept locked away inside of her for so long to begin to churn, stir, and shake free of the chains that bound them. When suddenly, miraculously, like pressurized, red rock candy lava spewing out from a sweet, icing-coated, chocolate-cake volcano, Paula Jean uttered the words, "MOMMY, MOMMY, I WANT TO PLAY, TOO!"

BOOM! These glorious words from out of the mouth of her newly restored little girl hit Gracie so hard that it halted her assigned route around the kitchen table dead in its tracks. Within a split second, she was drenched by a tidal wave of countless, wondrous thoughts and emotions that filled every pore of her being and washed upon her refreshing, life-giving moisture that triggered a torrent of wet, fat, salty tears of joy to cascade from her eyes and inundate the parched soil of her wounded heart, body, and soul with a beneficial washing-away-the-pain rain.

She struggled to take in enough air to speak a few words from the in-between pantings of her overexcited lungs. She thought, "Here's a little air, here's a little more I can steal, a little more…" Then pow, out pumped the words, "COME TO MOMMY MY BEAUTIFUL BABY GIRL!!!"

Upon hearing those incredible words, Paula Jean dashed out from under the kitchen table toward her mother, who sat spellbound by this dream-come-true vision before her. For Gracie, all was in slow motion as she was able to peer long and deeply into the now clear, dazzling eyes of her daughter. She was able to fully absorb every curve of her daughter's adorable, happy face. And she was able to savor it fully, basking in the glow radiating from Paula Jean's shining smile, for which she had ached so long to see. This radiating glow was Gracie's love-light reflecting back to Gracie from Paula Jean. When love is given, it comes back to the giver in the same measure and all are happy and smile. That comes straight out of the "What Happens When You Shine Your Love-Light" manual of Poppy Tom, Grandma Jennie, and Sarah Nightingale. Gracie and Paula Jean's successful completion of this elegant exercise earned them the rare, envious title of lights of the whole wide world, and Paula Jean hadn't even received her poem yet, again, proving the limitless, glorious power of love.

Paula Jean jumped into the open arms of her mother, where their warm, unifying embrace melded the two together as one, where their happy tears blended together to shower them both with liquid glee and where their generous offerings of love-light radiated throughout the entire room, allowing all to frolic in its glistening glow.

Sarah turned to Hollie and gave her two rambunctious thumbs-up, and Hollie barked and wagged her tail in celebration.

Gracie, still squeezing her daughter as tight as she could, slowly and gently turned her head to look appreciatively at Sarah. She knew, if no words of gratitude were worthy enough to speak when she first received Sarah's gift of her poem before, for sure there were no words of gratitude worthy enough to speak for this tremendous gift Sarah had just given her now. But once again, no words were needed. Gracie's eyes reached deep into Sarah's and sang out the message, "Sweet child, you gave me my daughter back and in so doing, you gave me my life back! I am forever indebted to you."

Sarah's nonchalant smile and cavalier eyes responded, "Hey, Mrs. Gracie, me and Hollie, we just played some games. You were the one that did all the work. It was you shining your love-light that did the trick. It was all you, Mrs. Gracie."

Gracie's soft acknowledging smile and happily tearful eyes let Sarah know she received her good-natured message loud and clear.

"Paula Jean, baby girl," Gracie said in a gentle, whispering voice, "I'd like to introduce you to our beautiful new friend, Sarah, and her lovely dog, Hollie."

Paula Jean pulled back slowly from her mother's hug and turned her head to gaze at Sarah. Again, no words needed to be spoken. Paula Jean raised her arms to Sarah.

Sarah moved her chair closer, and the two embraced. The coming together of these two sweet young children, one just newly arrived at her bright, new, shiny place and the other, in her bright, shiny place, too, but knowing she has other dark places she'll need to go through but doesn't let on, was truly a sight to behold. Hollie came in close, too, allowing Paula Jean to wrap an arm around her. Gracie, Paula Jean, Sarah, and Hollie sat draped together in a pod of quiet bliss. Today, within the walls of Gracie's humble kitchen, platters overflowing with love were being served.

Paula Jean was the first to move from their conjoined embrace. She looked in the direction of the kitchen table and pointed a tender finger. This caused Gracie, Sarah, and Hollie to stir and look in the direction of Paula Jean's interest. They realized the neatly wrapped package sitting on the table was the object of her attention.

Sarah said, "Yes, Paula Jean, that present is for you. Come on, open it up. I can't wait for you to see what's inside."

Gracie moved in closer to the table with Paula Jean on her lap. Sarah and Hollie moved in, too. Sarah grabbed the present and offered it over to the eager hands of Paula Jean.

Paula Jean excitedly pulled at the pretty pink ribbon, ripped off the paper wrapping, and opened the box. A huge smile came across her face as she saw the special gift. Gracie helped her remove the gift from the box and said, "Oh, Paula honey, look what you have here. Look how beautiful," as they placed the birdhouse on the table for all to see.

"See, Paula Jean," said Sarah, "that's a birdhouse. Me and my brother JJ made it just for you. See what it says. See what my Poppy Tom carved right on the front, 'From Sarah and JJ to Paula Jean.' JJ's outside hammering stuff, and my Poppy Tom is outside building a new ramp with my mommy and daddy."

Paula Jean's smile couldn't get any bigger as her head darted all around, looking at everyone's happy smiles, and they all looked back at hers.

Gracie whispered in Paula Jean's ear, "Say thank you to Sarah, sweetie."

Paula Jean turned to Sarah and shyly whispered, "Thank you," then grabbed the birdhouse and, with a slight struggle because of its weight, took it in her arms and hugged it.

Sarah said, "Oh, you're welcome, Paula Jean. Wait, I bet my Poppy Tom will put that up outside in a spot where you can look at it through the window and watch the birds going in and out. The birds will love laying their eggs and living in their new, healthy house right outside yours."

Paula Jean turned to look at her mother, smiling, and nodded in agreement.

"Mrs. Gracie, does Paula Jean have a hat?" Sarah asked.

"Yes, she does. She has a hat just like mine, and I know why you're asking. I think I have it tucked away in either my bedroom closet or dresser. We'll go and find it. Paula honey, let's set the birdhouse on the table."

"We'll be right back, Sarah, sweetheart."

After a short time, Gracie and Paula Jean returned to the kitchen. Paula Jean held her miniature version of her mother's hat in her hands, signaling that their search mission was successful. Gracie pulled up to the drawer that held the pins, pulled one out, and then moved over to the kitchen table where Sarah and Hollie sat, and where Sarah had Paula Jean's two envelopes waiting for her.

"Paula Jean," Sarah said happily, "I have two more things to give you. Open this one first, please."

Paula Jean opened the envelope with a little more vigor than her mother and quickly and excitedly pulled the feather from it. Her face beamed as she raised it up in the air, moved it all around, and even smelled it. Then without Sarah even having to tell her, Paula Jean held it up to the light and was instantly captivated by its luminescence.

"See, Paula Jean, isn't that beautiful?" Sarah asked.

Paula Jean nodded.

"Mrs. Gracie, can you pin it on Paula Jean's hat, please?"

"Roger that," Gracie replied, saluting.

"Here you go, Paula Jean, your feather is pinned on your hat just like mine. Let's see you put it on."

Paula Jean proudly placed her feather-adorned hat on her head.

A combination of claps, yays, and barks from the gallery of Gracie, Sarah, and Hollie confirmed their approval.

"You look so pretty with that hat on, Paula Jean," Sarah said admiringly, "just as pretty as your mommy. Guess what? That feather is just like mine and your mommy's, and it's very special. It makes our hats lucky and makes us lucky, too. Our feathers have great powers and give us guidance and the ability to see all the wonders of the beautiful world around us. See how it was all glowy when you held it up to the light? There are secrets unfolding on you in all that glowy."

Gracie whispered to Paula Jean, "What do we say?"

"Thank you very much," Paula Jean whispered to Sarah, as she prettied up the hat on her head and looked over at the other envelope.

"Yup, this one is for you, too, Paula Jean," Sarah confirmed. "Go ahead and open it," she said as she slid it over to Paula Jean.

Paula Jean opened the envelope, again with vigor, saw the note with the writing and gave it to her mother to read.

Gracie asked Paula Jean, "Isn't this such pretty paper? Sarah wrote these for us on her grandmother's pretty paper. One for you and one for me. This is very special, sweetie, and so gracious of Sarah. Doesn't Sarah write beautifully?"

Paula Jean, with wide-eyed wonderment nodded her head.

"I'll read it to you and then we'll let Sarah tell us all about this wonderful poem," Gracie told Paula Jean.

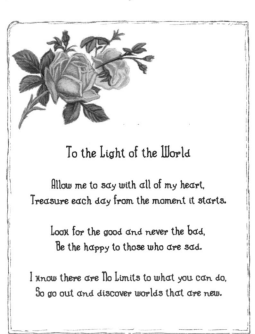

To the Light of the World

Allow me to say with all of my heart,
Treasure each day from the moment it starts.

Look for the good and never the bad,
Be the happy to those who are sad.

I know there are No Limits to what you can do,
So go out and discover worlds that are new.

Sarah began, "Paula Jean, I'm giving you this poem because I love you and you are my new special friend. Your mommy, too. Hollie, my mommy and daddy, my Poppy Tom, and JJ, too. We all love you and make you and your mommy our new special friends."

"I love you, too," whispered Paula Jean.

"Thank you for saying you love me, too, Paula Jean. See, that's what our poem says we are, the lights of the world. I love you and you love me. And, all that love back and forth and forth and back shines light and makes us smile, and that's what makes us the lights of the world. We always want to keep our poems close to us forever, Paula Jean."

"Yours, too, Mrs. Gracie, and do what it says. It will keep us brave and strong and will guide us to the wonderful life we know we have ahead of us. Because of the love we have for each other, there are no limits to what us girls can do!"

Gracie and Paula Jean clapped and high-fived each other, and Sarah joined in, too, while Hollie raised her front paws to the table, allowing all to grab a paw doing an original version of hands-to-dog-paws high fives.

It was during this feel-good, mission-accomplished celebration that they heard Cecilia calling out to them from the front stoop saying, "Excuse me, ladies, we're about to have lunch. You able to come out and join us?"

"Yes, Cecilia, we sure are," Gracie replied.

"How many should we be expecting?" Cecilia asked with anticipation.

"Three, plus Hollie," answered Gracie, victoriously!

"Hallelujah!" Cecilia stated joyously and then turned to the rest of her fellow ramp construction crew to share the good news, and all cheered.

"Sarah, would you and Hollie want to swing around to the front yard?" Gracie asked. "I'll get Paula Jean dressed and then we'll meet you out there as soon as we're done."

"Okay, Mrs. Gracie, sure. We'll be waiting for you guys outside."

"Everybody's looking forward to meeting you, Paula Jean."

Paula Jean smiled at Sarah then hugged her mother tightly around her neck, implying she was ready to take a ride on her mother's wheelchair express to the now open-door policy of her bedroom.

"Let's go, Paula Jean, my darling daughter," Gracie said happily as she began wheeling. Then in a singing voice said, "I'm taking my little girl to get her dressed, la, la...la, la. I'm taking my little girl to get her dressed, la, la...la, la."

Then Gracie halted and said to Sarah, "This is a wonderful simple pleasure that I now get to enjoy because of you, Sarah. I didn't start out treasuring today, but I sure treasure it now and I know I'll treasure each and every day from the moment it starts, forever. I'm in heaven. Thank you, sweet child!"

Sarah just waved her hands back to Gracie, signaling, ah, don't mention it, and then headed out with Hollie saying, "We'll be out front. Let's go, Hollie."

CHAPTER 17

After a short while, Gracie and Paula Jean wheeled out of the back of their house wearing their newly feathered U.S. Army hats and camouflage T-shirts. Paula Jean's T-shirt had a U.S. Army emblem and the words, "Loved and Protected by My Soldier Mommy," on the front of hers, and Gracie's T-shirt had the words "Our Love is Army Strong" on the front of hers. Then they turned the corner to the front yard riding their wheelchair in the manner in which a victorious Roman General entered the eternal city in triumph on his four-horse-led chariot to the cheering throng of Cecilia, Justin, JJ, Poppy Tom, Sarah, and Hollie.

Overjoyed, Cecilia, Justin, JJ, and Poppy Tom ran up to Paula Jean, hugging and kissing and introducing themselves to her. Then Cecilia, Justin, and Poppy Tom took turns going up to Sarah Nightingale and Hollie, hugging and kissing them as a means of recognizing them for a job well done, while JJ hung around Paula Jean, showing her his morning's hammering accomplishments.

Cecilia broke up this lovefest by saying, "Come on everybody, let's eat!"

"My goodness, what a table you've prepared for us, Cecilia," said Gracie, and then in disbelief, added, "Wow, look how far you've gotten with the ramp. It looks like it's almost finished."

Justin replied, "Good, I'm starving. Come on, JJ, let's have at it, son. We'll just have to make sure we save some room for those chocolate chip cookies Poppy Tom made for dessert."

"As long as I didn't forget to add in the chocolate chips," Poppy Tom said, half-jokingly. "Yes, come on everybody. There's nothing more satisfying than bellying up to a good, hearty lunch served on a sheet of plywood supported by a couple of sawhorses with a view of our morning's labor.

"Gracie, Paula Jean, lovely ladies, please help yourselves. We made a few different types of sandwiches. We hope you like them. These are potato, pepper, and egg sandwiches. Those are asparagus, wild mushrooms, melted mozzarella cheese, and egg. With a little ketchup, they make good moist sandwiches. I'm not sure if you had anything like them before, but this is a platter of the delicate flowers of the zucchini plant that were dipped in egg with a little added Parmesan cheese and then fried. They're so tender and delicious. All of them are my Jennie's recipes. We have a nice, fresh tomato salad, and the iced tea has been steeping in the morning sun with fresh sprigs of mint and a touch of Mrs. T's honey. It makes for a wonderful, refreshing drink. Please everyone, enjoy."

Gracie's eyes moistened as she peered into the eyes of this group of amazingly kind and generous people before her. "I can't thank…There's no way I could ever…" She held her hands out to them and said in a crackle-ly voice, "You are angels. You are gifts from God, and I'm so very thankful."

They all smiled back as Cecilia walked up to Gracie, bent down to hug her, and said, "You're welcome, sister. You know, Gracie, my father mentioned that your husband, Louis, is a police officer. We pray that God keeps him safe and continues to bless you all."

Then, taking the conversation in another direction, Cecilia said, "All you ladies look so pretty with those feathers in your hats. I'm getting kind of jealous, you know. I have to see if I can locate mine. It's been a while since good ol' Mr. Nate gave me mine. Well, come on now, eat, let's all eat."

Gracie whispered out the words, "Thank you, thank you," and then proceeded to squeeze Paula Jean tightly, enforcing all she had to be thankful for on this amazingly miraculous day.

Then this band of merry revelers bellied up to the seemingly crude workbench-converted plywood table—one that any king and queen would be envious of because of all the fine food and drink painstakingly prepared by following a neatly written recipe calling for generous portions of love, caring, and compassion that were set upon it. And as they partook of this soul-replenishing banquet, some ketchup merrily dripped here and some iced tea cheerily spilled over there, adding to the layers of legacy imparted onto this table's humble surface from years of noble service and quiet dedication to duty.

For right next to the newly dripped ketchup was a ring of sun-dance yellow paint. This is the same paint that the then-young daddy-to-be, Thomas, lovingly applied to the expertly crafted cradle of his soon-to-be-born child—a color picked by the youthful apple of his eye and oh-so-pregnant wife, Jennifer. Jennifer intuitively knew she was having a girl and wanted to go with pink, but at the last minute went with the safer bet of sun-dance yellow. Turns out, pink would have worked, because she went full term and delivered a healthy baby girl. However, this pregnancy would leave her with a condition that she would have to deal with for the rest of her life, which she did bravely and courageously, never looking for sympathy or assigning blame. These were strong traits that would get passed onto her daughter and granddaughter. These were strong traits that they would need themselves.

Over by the spilled iced tea were small shavings of white oak ensconced in the now-darkened varnish used to seal the headboard Thomas carved for his quickly growing daughter's big-girl bed. He had the time to spend building that bed because then, work as a journeyman carpenter was slow. He took a job at the local plumbing supply house, Sal's and Al's Pipes and Valves, stocking shelves and delivering materials, while Jennifer baked pies and cakes, selling them out of her kitchen to help make ends meet. It was then that he was forced to sell his father's precious and rare bamboo fly rods. Rods that his father cherished and used to teach Thomas how to cast when he was a boy. To this day, he regrets selling those rods. In time, work opportunities improved and thankfully so did Thomas's and Jennifer's financial situation.

Under the platter of potato, pepper, and egg sandwiches, remnants of the Antique Maple stain that, at that time, the growing-older Tom used to finish the cabinets he made to replace the basic stock cabinets in Jennie's kitchen. Jennie absolutely loved those cabinets. She said that Mother Nature must have been guiding Tom's hands as he applied his craft, for only she could help create something so beautiful and precise out of something she originally created in the form of her majestic maple trees. Tom told her that no tradesman could ever ask for a better compliment.

Over at the far corner, there was dried glue left from the fabrication of the dining room table and chairs. And lastly, there are a few dried blood stains from cuts Tom received when building Jennie's desk and chair that have become harder to notice, especially since JJ added every color of the rainbow to the archives when he painted the "Pop's Shop" sign on this very surface just the other day. But he learned a lot from this experience and vowed never to allow himself or anyone else to work in the shop or anywhere else with tools, without the proper protective equipment—a vow he's kept to this very day.

So, it can be said that this workbench/banquet table/keeper-of-the-family-history sheet of plywood has witnessed a lot. If asked, it would say it was lucky to have been picked decades ago from a stack of four-foot by eight-foot, three-quarter-inch plywood sheathing by an honest, hardworking, aspiring, young carpenter. Heck, its fate could've consisted of being stuck under layers of roof shingles or rolls of carpeting, never to have seen the light of day. Instead, it witnessed, firsthand, what transpired when skilled, prideful hands applied themselves in worthy, honorable effort for good principled pursuits. And it felt the more ketchup, iced tea, paint, varnish, and stain that continued to shellac, splatter, and spill upon its very capable platform shoulders, the merrier. For it wears these benevolent blemishes as badges of honor.

Then Poppy Tom heard Justin say, "Phew, I'm stuffed," as he leaned back from the table. "After a lunch like that, I could go for a nap."

"Never mind nap," Poppy Tom said laughing as he rose from his chair and headed briskly back in the direction of the ramp. "We have miles to go before we sleep. Yes, children, as the great poet, Robert Frost, wrote,

The woods are lovely, dark, and deep,
But I have promises to keep,
And miles to go before I sleep,
And miles to go before I sleep."

"Very apropos, there, Father-in-law," said Justin.

"Yes, that did fit in there rather nicely, Justin. I must say so myself," Poppy Tom replied, kiddingly.

"Oh, Gracie, you said before that the ramp looked almost finished. I'd say we're just about halfway done. We're doing good and right about where I'd hoped we'd be at this point. Nice going crew."

Cecilia, Justin, and JJ responded happily to Poppy Tom's compliment by patting each other on their backs and giving a thumbs-up.

Gracie, Sarah, and Paula Jean clapped their congratulations. Then Gracie asked, "How can we help?"

"It's not often a crew doubles in size after a lunch break," said Poppy Tom. "So, okay, good. Here's what I think we can do. Gracie, Paula Jean, Sarah, we can have you ladies get started installing the spindles on the upper end. I'll get with you and go over that. Cecilia, Justin, and JJ, you guys keep working on the decking, and I'll stay…," when JJ interrupted.

"I want to work by…what's her name again, Mommy?" JJ asked.

"Paula Jean, why is that so…," Cecilia said, when JJ cut in again and said, "I want to work by Paula Jean. I want to show her how to hammer."

"Well okay, lad. That's fine," Poppy Tom confirmed, and then added, "Now, where was I? Oh, yeah, so Cecilia and Justin, you keep working on the decking and I'll stay ahead of you with the posts and rails on the lower sections. I do have something to mention to everybody though. I'm realizing I miscalculated the quantity of decking and spindles."

"Over or under, Dad?" Cecilia asked.

"Under," Poppy Tom replied.

"Is that going to be a problem, Dad?"

"Whoa, now, let me say," Poppy Tom began, "there's never a problem. Something might be a challenge, something might be an issue, but never is something a problem. Got that everybody? So how about you ask your question again, Ce."

"Okay, fine," Cecilia said while rolling her eyes. "How's this? So dearest Father, will the underestimating of the quantity of decking and spindles pose a challenge for us in the completion of the ramp?"

"Ah, now wasn't that better?" Poppy Tom asked. "So, no I don't believe we have a challenge here, dearest Daughter, but thank you for asking. By the way it looks, I left the platform section out of my calculations. Don't ask me how. I think we'll be alright though. I believe I have enough material back at the shop. I'll just need to run it through the table saw. Let's put in another hour or so. That should get us to where we need to be for today. I can make all the cuts back at Pop's Shop later on."

"Then, Justin, we'll load up the truck and have everything ready to go for tomorrow morning."

"We're okay to come back in the morning, right Gracie?"

"Oh, absolutely," Gracie confirmed.

"Fabulous," said Poppy Tom. "You know, I'm looking up and seeing some clouds building in the western sky. We just might be having some of those showers coming through. Let's keep an eye out. Oh, one more thing gang. I'm thinking if all goes well tomorrow and we get finished up early enough, I'd like us all to head over to the Rivera's farm. There's something there that I think the kids would like to see."

All voiced their approval to Poppy Tom's plan, when Sarah asked, "Did anybody see any rainbows today?" Everyone, except for Poppy Tom and Hollie, looked quizzically at Sarah, then at each other because of her question. Then all answered, "No." Sarah and Poppy Tom looked at each other with questioning expressions on their faces, scanned the sky, then seeing no rainbow, shrugged their shoulders and shook their heads.

"Hey, Dad, no harm, no foul on the miscalculation of the materials," said Cecilia as work on the ramp resumed the next day.

"Yes, Daughter, no challenges or issues and we're coming down the old home stretch now," stated Poppy Tom as he rubbed his hands together in satisfaction. "Just a few more finishing touches and our ramp will be complete."

"And what a ramp it is," said Gracie. "Louis and I could never thank you enough for this amazing gift. What we'd like to do is invite you all over for dinner on Saturday night. It's the least we can do."

"Gracie, that's not necessary. Come on," said Poppy Tom. "You don't have to do that."

"No, honest, we'd love for you all to come, please," Gracie said sincerely.

"We'd love to come," said Cecilia, graciously accepting Gracie's invitation. "Tell us what time, and we'll be here with bells on."

Paula Jean and JJ looked at each other puzzled and asked, "Bells on?"

"Don't worry," Sarah said to them while waving her hand in

dismissal. "There are no bells. It's just a funny way big people like to talk. They're called expressions. They use them all the time."

Sarah's explanation satisfied Paula Jean's and JJ's curiosity and allowed them to get back to their assigned task of picking up any nails and screws left scattered on the ground.

"Excellent!" said Gracie. "Let's say six o'clock. Be there or be square."

Sarah, Paula Jean, and JJ looked at each other again and said, "Expressions," then shook their heads.

"Six o'clock it is," confirmed Cecilia. "What can we bring?"

"Well, now that you ask," said Gracie. "Would you be able to get your hands on any more of those zucchini flowers?"

Both Cecilia and Poppy Tom excitedly said, "Yes!"

"You liked those?" asked Poppy Tom.

"Oh, they were absolutely delicious," said Gracie. "I told Louis how delicious they were. Hey, let me tell you, everything was delicious. That entire lunch was amazing. But those fried zucchini flowers, incredible! Louis is a pretty good cook. He would like to try frying them in a hush puppy batter. We would like to serve those and a few dishes from Louis' West-African heritage. Do you think you'd like that?"

"We'd love it," Cecilia, Poppy Tom, and Justin answered happily.

Then Justin said excitedly, "Oh, I bet zucchini flowers fried in hush puppy batter will be fantastic! Nice and sweet."

"We'll bring a lot of them, Gracie," Cecilia said as she gazed at Justin. "Don't you worry," as all got a good chuckle.

Poppy Tom said, "I think now's a good time for me to take a run over to Percy's and Mercy's Nursery. I need to pick up a few things from there really quickly. Are you guys okay if I leave you to finish things up here while I go?"

All agree, then Cecilia asks, "Dad, why don't you let Justin take the ride with you? We can finish up here."

"I was actually going to ask Justin if he could do something for me while I was gone, Cecilia."

"Sure, Dad, what do you need me to do?" Justin asked.

"I have a little digging for you to do," Poppy Tom said. "Just three holes."

"Okay, you got it," said Justin. "Just show me where."

"Grab the shovel and follow me," Poppy Tom directed. "One here... one here...and one over...there. Listen, Justin, the holes don't need to be too big. I'd say about a foot and a half wide and about a foot and half deep would be plenty."

"Comin' right up there, Poppser," Justin joked.

"Gracie, do you guys have a hose?" asked Poppy Tom.

"Yes, we do," Gracie confirmed.

"Would it reach out to the front of the ramp?"

"I believe so. I'll roll it out and see."

"I'll help you," Cecilia said.

"Oh, Gracie, there's another thing I'm thinking of," said Poppy Tom. "Can you have Paula Jean's birdhouse handy, too, for when I get back please?"

Paula Jean's head popped up by the mention of her new prized possession and she smiled, anticipating what Poppy Tom would be doing with it upon his return, as she looked over at Sarah, who was giving a two-handed thumbs-up. Gracie smiled, too, knowing what was behind Poppy Tom's request, and said, "Hoorah," while saluting respectfully.

"Alright, good. Let me run," said Poppy Tom. "When I get back, we'll take care of a few formalities here and then we'll head over to the Rivera's. Remember, we need to get over there today, too. Hey, another thing, keep an eye to the sky. More storms are predicted.

"Come on, Hollie, let's go girl."

"Yes, everybody, look at the sky and let me know if you see any rainbows," Sarah said.

Again, everyone glanced at Sarah with curious looks on their faces due to what they think is Sarah's apparent growing obsession with rainbows.

CHAPTER 18

Beep...beep, beep...beep...beep...Poppy Tom sounded the horn of his truck as he pulled into Gracie's driveway, returning from his trip to Percy's and Mercy's Nursery. "Looking good guys," he said as he opened the tailgate of his truck, and Hollie ran toward the proud group of accomplished ramp builders.

"What do ya have there, Dad?" Justin asked as he and Cecilia walked toward the truck.

"Here, I'll show you," Poppy Tom said in a quiet voice as he lifted a tarp, revealing three small fruit trees.

"Oh, Dad, how cute," said Cecilia.

"Yeah, I have a little ceremony planned for us. Cecilia, can you go in the glove box and grab the spool of ribbon and scissors that's in there please, and you'll see a bag of bird seed on the floor, grab that too, if you will?

"Justin, can you grab one of these trees and meet me over by the ramp, please?"

"Here, let me take two, Dad. You take the other one."

"Okay, thanks. I can take this box then."

"Good, Cecilia. Tie the ribbon across the entrance to the ramp," Poppy Tom said in a voice more mouthing the words than actually saying them.

Then, in a louder, jovial voice, he said, "Hey, everybody, gather around," as he placed the tree he was carrying next to one of the holes Justin dug. Justin followed suit and placed the two trees he was carrying next to the other two holes.

All met in a semi-circle around Poppy Tom, who used the newly completed ramp as a backdrop. He then said, "I thought it was only fitting we celebrate the successful completion of the ramp and recognize everyone's hard efforts by having our very own ceremony."

All voiced their approval verbally and by clapping their hands and Gracie added, "You think of everything. As if you haven't done enough. What an amazing man."

"First on the agenda," Poppy Tom began, "is our tree-planting event. As you can see, we have three holes for three trees. I'm looking for three strong volunteers to help with the planting of these fine specimens."

No sooner did Poppy Tom get the words out, Sarah, Paula Jean, and JJ waved their arms and shouted out their acceptances. "Ah, I love it when my audience is quick to participate. Okay, let's have Paula Jean go first. Pick a tree, any tree, my dear," Poppy Tom said in a voice trying to mimic W.C. Fields, and continued with that same fun, saying, "Ah, the young lady picks the apple tree. Great choice. Great choice."

"May I ask this strapping fellow here to assist this young lady with the planting of her tree please?" Poppy Tom asked Justin. "When planting trees, remember this saying: Plant them high, never die, plant them low, never know. So, the higher the better. There you go. Wonderful, wonderful. Okay, who's next?"

Sarah and JJ both signaled they wanted to go next, when Paula Jean said to JJ, "Let your sister go next."

JJ looked at Paula Jean, studying her face for a moment and then said to Sarah, reluctantly, "Okay, Sarah, you can go."

Cecilia almost fell over in disbelief by JJ's agreeing so easily to Paula Jean's instruction as Gracie whispered to Cecilia, "Interesting. You seeing what I'm seeing?"

"I think I am," Cecilia whispered back.

Sarah picked the peach tree, and Justin helped her plant her tree, leaving the pear tree for JJ to plant with Justin assisting him, following

Poppy Tom's wise instruction.

"Okay, excellent job, I must say," Poppy Tom confirmed. "Now we need to give these trees a drink. Can someone turn the water on, please?"

"I got it Dad," said Justin.

"Okay, kids, you can each take turns watering your trees," said Poppy Tom. "Not too much water and not too little."

"Like the bend in the rod, Pops, right?" Sarah asked.

"You got it, Granddaughter."

"Okay we have one more thing to do here and then we'll move on to the next item on the agenda. I had these three bronze plaques made up in anticipation of today's event. Paula Jean, this is your plaque honey. It says, 'This Tree Planted by Paula Jean.' Can you take it please and stick it in the ground in front of your tree?"

Paula Jean, with a huge smile on her face, proudly did as she was asked, while getting a rousing round of applause from her group of highly supportive onlookers. As did Sarah and JJ when they placed their personalized bronze signs in front of their respective trees.

Poppy Tom announced, "These signs will stand forever in testament to these three wonderful children who, on this day, so caringly planted these three fine trees. I know because of the terrific job they did, there will be no limits to how tall these trees will grow and no limits to how much fruit they will bear.

"And to this team of young aspiring arborists, I say, there will be no limits to how deep your roots will grow and no limits to how far and wide your fruit-laden branches will spread.

"Let's give them all a loud round of applause!"

Loud applause, hoots, hollers, whistles, and yelps surrounded this group of three lovely children, making them feel special, like heroes, like they were sitting on top of the world. As well they should, Poppy Tom thought, and as well as all children should be made to feel, no matter what their condition or lot in life. For all children are special. For all children are precious. Each and every one of them holds in their precious little hands and deep down in their young but mighty hearts, a life force and a light force so great, so powerful that, when planted and nurtured and loved in the same manner in which these three children planted their trees today, there will truly be no limits to the good that will be done by each and every one of them and for the benefit of our entire world. Give power, love, and light to the children and power, love, and light will be reflected back. They can be trusted to do that.

"Okay folks," Poppy Tom said, "next on the agenda is the official presentation and placement of a very special item that will make the ramp one hundred percent complete. This activity will be representative of what is referred to in the building trades, when a project is completed, as a *topping-out ceremony*."

He then whispered over to Gracie asking, "Where's the birdhouse?"

Gracie turned to her right side, reached down, and picked up the birdhouse that was sitting on the ground next to her. Then, JJ walked toward her, took the birdhouse, and brought it over to Poppy Tom to the oohs and ahs of the duo of Cecilia and Justin as Paula Jean, Sarah, and Hollie looked on in happy anticipation and joy.

"Thank you, sir," Poppy Tom said to JJ.

Then, holding the birdhouse high in the air, he addressed the group by saying, "What we have here is a super unique, highly customized, one-of-a-kind, made of the finest materials Mother Nature ever created for her fine-feathered friends, residential birdhouse abode, made with love and care by the extremely talented and ever so expert, PPE-protected hands of Sarah, the Assembler of Devonshire, and JJ, the Duke of Hammenter. May I ask my Lady Fair, Paula Jean, Princess of the Army Ball, to come up and accept her royal bequest?"

Paula Jean gracefully promenaded to Poppy Tom, like the princess she was being made to imagine she was, wearing a dazzling court dress complete with an endless, elegant train. She graciously accepted her endowment, and then cradling this stately scepter in her arms, bowed to her court of loyal cheering subjects.

Poppy Tom said, "If you'll allow me, my Duchess of All She Touches, I'll place your fine birdy abode upon this royal ramp so you can view it anytime you wish from your palace window."

Paula Jean looked up at Poppy Tom smiling, turned to her mother, Gracie, who smiled back and nodded. Then Paula Jean looked back up at Poppy Tom and said, "Okay," and then handed over her treasured possession to his trusting hands.

Poppy Tom placed the birdhouse in a good, strategic location on the ramp, took a few steps back to eye it up, went back to make an adjustment, then turned to the audience and asked, "How's that look, gang?"

All sent their approvals by combinations of claps, yells, whistles, and yaps.

Poppy Tom said, "I'll come back later and fasten it down. Okay, if I may ask everyone to proceed to the front of the ramp, where we'll take care of our third and final item on today's agenda."

As Gracie worked her way to the front of the ramp, she saw the ribbon tied across the opening and asked, "Oh my, is this what I think it is?"

Poppy Tom, Cecilia, and Justin got a laugh out of Gracie's reaction, then Cecilia said, "It sure is, sister."

Poppy Tom said, "Okay everyone, here's what I'd like us to do.

"I'm happy to see you're still wearing your gloves, Gracie. Take the scissors, being careful with them please, and position yourself right in front of the ramp entrance with Paula Jean on your lap. We'd like it if you can cut the ribbon, officially dedicating your new ramp.

"But first, I'm going to ask everybody else to reach into that bag of birdseed, where you'll see some cups. Fill your cups with birdseed and station yourselves along the sides of the ramp. Now, the way I'd like us to do this is, all together real loud, we count down from ten to one and then say, 'blast off' real loud and make all kinds of blast-off noises.

"And, Paula Jean, honey, you shout out the words, Supergirl Fly, okay?"

Paula Jean clapped her hands happily.

"Gracie, that's when you cut the ribbon and take your maiden voyage on your ramp with your darling daughter on your lap while we shower you both with birdseed. I'm thinking all that birdseed will attract birds that might want to occupy Paula Jean's new birdhouse."

Everyone was thrilled with Poppy Tom's plan and excitedly scurried to their designated positions.

Gracie and Paula Jean, readied themselves at the entrance to the ramp by waving their feathered hats and giving the thumbs-up. Then, Poppy Tom took the reins by saying, "Alright everybody, here we go!

"All sound off, TEN, NINE, EIGHT, SEVEN, SIX, FIVE, FOUR, THREE, TWO, ONE, BLASTOFF!!!

"BERSWISHISSHOWISHPOWWEEWISHSWISH!!!"

Gracie reverently sliced the ribbon as Paula Jean, holding her arms out in front of her, shouted out loudly, "SUPERGIRL FLY!!!"

Gracie tossed the scissors aside, grasped the push ring of her wheelchair like she was grasping the controls of her mothership, USS Restoration, and with afterburner fuel-thrusted strokes, propelled herself and her copilot daughter from their launch pad of compassion and goodwill into the exhilarating sensation of flight. They could hear and feel the rocket's fiery blasts shooting out from behind them as they jettisoned through a congratulatory meteor shower of birdseed coming from the dedicated hands of their ground crew. The craft shivered and shook as it achieved speeds beyond those for which it was designed. Then suddenly, without warning, the external fuel tanks jarred loose from their bonds to the mothership and went into free fall. Seeing this, the service module baled to take its chances in the infinite unknowns of space. This left the crew of mother, child, and faithful navigator chair safe and sound within their command module, Love One, on a smooth, quiet descent to their final destination within their very own sea of tranquility. Mission control announced, "Love One, we have touchdown, repeat, we have touchdown. Congratulations on a job well done, Love One."

And as the glittery pixie dust stirred up by their descent settled around these intrepid voyagers, it revealed to them a bright, shiny, Shangri-la of a world—a world where love, laughter, and contentment were the orders of the day. It is one so completely different from the brooding dark side of an alien world they were catapulted from just the day before—a world they thought was only to become even more brooding and even more dark with each passing day were it not for the heroic efforts of a kind, gentle titan of a man, Poppy Tom, and his extraordinary, always-putting-others-before-herself, miracle-making-machine granddaughter, Sarah, and their energetic, always-willing-to-do-right and good support staff of Cecilia, Justin, JJ, and Hollie to help the heroines of their world, Gracie and her daughter, Paula Jean. Written in this mission's after-action report, all objectives met. Mission accomplished!

Poppy Tom waited for the cheers to decrease and the hugs to subside to say, "Okay, all, let's wrap up here and head over to the Riveras'.

"Justin, you can drive with me and Hollie.

"Gracie, you and Paula Jean can go with Cecilia and the kids if you'd like. We can put the chairs right in the back of the pickup."

Gracie said, "We'd love to."

JJ called out to Paula Jean, "Come on Jubee Jean, sit by me in my car."

Cecilia and Gracie looked at each other with questioning smiles on their faces, then Cecilia asked JJ, "Jubee Jean? Where did that come from?"

Paula Jean answered her by saying, "Oh that's what Jubee Jay calls me, Mrs. Cecilia."

Gracie turns to Paula Jean and asked, "Jubee Jay?"

Then JJ answered her by saying, "Oh, that's what Jubee Jean calls me," as the two clasped hands and walked nonchalantly over to the car.

Gracie and Cecilia looked back at each other grinning, shook their heads, and opened their hands gesturing, well, okay, whatever.

Just then, there was a flash of lightning across the western sky followed by a loud boom of thunder, which startled everyone.

Poppy Tom said, "Oh boy, here we go again," and then called out to Cecilia, "Follow close and take care driving. We'll probably hit rain on the way. Lightning and thunder make raindrops."

Sarah said, "Lightning and thunder make raindrops. Maybe those raindrops will make a rainbow."

All looked at Sarah for bringing up the subject of rainbows again. Poppy Tom then looked to the sky and said, "Maybe so, Sarah," as Hollie barked in agreement.

CHAPTER 19

A heavy downpour obscured the quaint look and feel of the Riveras' horse farm from Poppy Tom's happy group of visitors until they pulled up under the protection of the farmhouse's bluestone-columned portico. It was there that they were greeted by the friendly, welcoming faces of Victoria and Miguel Rivera.

"Hello everybody," Victoria called out, "My name is Victoria, and this is my husband, Miguel."

Then both said together, "Welcome to Happy Horizons Horse Farm."

Victoria then added, "We're so thrilled you're here. We've heard so many wonderful things about each and every one of you from Mr. Tom."

Poppy Tom took the lead to proudly introduce his family and who he now felt were his newly adopted daughter, Gracie, and granddaughter, Paula Jean, to the Riveras.

As the introductions wound down, Victoria asked in an excited voice, "Who likes horses?"

Everyone responded to her question in the positive, but Paula Jean nearly jumped out of her skin in excitement, saying, "Me, me, I love horses. Can we see the horses? Please, Mrs. nice farm lady, can we see the horses? Sarah told me she gave some horses some treats. Can we do that, too, please?"

"Oh, it looks like we have a real horse lover here," Victoria said. "Reminds me of when I was that age. Yes, I know Sarah has already met a couple of our horses named, Lightning and Thunder, on her travels through their corral with her Poppy Tom and has given them some treats. Sweetheart, we would be elated to have you and all your friends see Lightning and Thunder and our other horses and give them some treats. I can tell you something else. Lightning and Thunder have a special treat for all of you, too."

"They do?" asked Paula Jean. She, Sarah, and JJ look at each other in wide-eyed wonderment as Gracie relished taking in the joy and excitement on her daughter's face.

Poppy Tom's reason for wanting to bring the children to this charming place with its delightful people and magnificent horses was already paying dividends.

Victoria said, "Follow us everybody. Since it's raining, we'll go through the house and out the backdoor to the covered walkway that will lead us to the stables. The stables are where the horses spend much of their time, especially when it's raining. We'll spend some time there, and when were done, we'll come back to the house for some of Mr. Miguel's hot cocoa. Does that sound like fun?"

Yays, claps, and nodding heads signaled everyone's approval, as Justin said excitedly, "Oh, hot cocoa. I love hot cocoa."

Cecilia said, "Oh, please," as everyone of Poppy Tom's group laughed.

Victoria said, "Come on everybody, let's go."

She then realized Hollie remained sitting, thinking she was not permitted to enter the house. Victoria said, "Hollie, when I say everybody, I mean everybody. Come on girl, we have some treats for you, too."

Hollie sprung up from her sitting position and followed Victoria's lead, as all got a charge out of Hollie's good manners. As the group entered the stable, Sarah immediately recognized Lightning, who peeked her head out of the opening of her stall.

"Hi, lady," Sarah said, greeting Lightning. "Everybody, that's Lightning. Isn't she beautiful?" Sarah asked as they walked toward

Lightning's stall at the front, left side of the stable.

Everyone voiced their agreement to the beauty of Lightning and her pure white coat.

Victoria said, "Here you are children, here are some sugar cubes. You can take turns feeding Lightning.

"And, here's a treat for you, Hollie."

"Sarah, your Poppy Tom showed you how to hold your hand out. Why don't you show Paula Jean and your brother how to do it?"

"Oh, sure, Mrs. Victoria."

"Like this. Watch me, guys. See, I hold out my hand and keep it real flat, and Lightning will...See, she gobbled her treats right up. It tickles your hand. It's really tickily when she eats them. It's so much fun."

"Can I try?" asked JJ.

"You should let Paula Jean go next, JJ," Justin said. "Ladies first is the gentlemanly thing to do, son."

"Okay, Jubee Jean, you can go next."

"Good boy, JJ," said his dad.

Paula Jean politely approached Lightning with a look of reverence on her face, held out her hand, following Sarah's example perfectly, then giggled softly as Lightning ever so delicately partook of her treat. Paula Jean's now empty hand rose to pet the top of Lightning's nose as she wrapped her other hand under the horse's throat. Lightning responded by nuzzling Paula Jean's face, allowing the two to quietly embrace. After a time, Paula Jean raised her head, looked deeply into Lightning's eyes, then stepped back, turned to her mother and said, "I love Lightning, Mommy."

Then added, "Your turn, Jubee Jay."

Victoria said to all in a calm, quiet voice, "I don't think I've ever witnessed anything more beautiful than that."

Gracie, with a serene look on her face, responded, "There's been a lot of that going on lately."

As JJ happily and successfully completed his turn feeding Lightning her treats, Victoria said, "Well children, you all just made a friend for life. Lightning will always fondly remember each of you for giving her those goodies.

"Sarah, she already had you imprinted in her memory from the time you first met her up in the corral. That's why she was looking out of her stable. She heard you coming and was eager to see you again. Horses are like that. She can feel the genuine love coming from each of you and would now like to give you something to show you her love. Please move back just a little and off to the side. Miguel will open the door to Lightning's stall. Then you all can take a look inside while I stand here holding her."

Everyone moved as instructed with questioning looks on their faces, except for Poppy Tom, Cecilia, and Hollie.

Miguel slowly swung open the stall door as the three children moved back to the front of the stall with the adults following close beyond. It was there and then that the treasure within was revealed. For sitting before them, nestled on a bed of freshly cut hay was a wonderfully beautiful newborn foal. Lightning, the proud mother, whinnied gleefully, as if to say, "Say hello to my magnificent baby girl!"

Not to go unrecognized, Thunder, with his jet-black coat shimmering in the low light of the stable, whinnied loudly from the open door of his stall at the rear right side of the stable. Miquel said, "Oh that's Thunder. He wants to let you all know that he's the proud poppa."

The children and adults alike displayed every expression of surprise, awe, and admiration when they saw the incredible sight before them.

Then, Paula Jean asked Victoria in a breathy whisper, "Can we pet her?"

Victoria said calmly, "Yes, but you'll need to approach her slowly and pet her gently."

"Sarah and JJ, too?" Paula Jean asked.

"Yes, but please go in one at a time. Nice and easy."

Paula Jean said, "Sarah, you go in first."

Sarah, with a huge smile on her face, gave Thunder two thumbs-ups and said, "You're a good daddy."

Then she moved on and petted Lightning, saying, "Pretty baby you have here. And, you're a good mommy, too," as she wheeled past her on her way to the newborn foal. The foal willingly accepted Sarah's gentle petting and hugs.

As Sarah moved away from the foal, Paula Jean motioned for JJ to take his turn. JJ followed the example of his sister as he took his turn greeting this amazing creation. He then quietly moved away to allow Paula Jean to take her turn.

Paula Jean looked eagerly at everyone standing around her, then turned to her mother and said, "It's my turn, Mommy," as she hugged and kissed her, as if she was leaving on a long journey.

To Paula Jean, it just might be. It just might be a journey of discovery of a whole new world for her. Just like her poem instructs. A whole new world that she will explore and enjoy for the rest of her life. It just might be the wisdom and foresight of a gentle giant of a man and his family, shining their light on a young innocent child, giving her the ability to love and laugh and to discover again. And it might be what happens when love-light can shine unbridled from the heart and soul of an amazing, and now happy, young girl, getting reflected back to her unbridled and in the same measure, for all to see. Paula Jean's quiet, gentle, loving embrace of this new-to-a-new-world foal confirmed that it was all of the above.

More dividends.

Paula Jean loosened her hug and, as she backed away from the foal, asked, "Mrs. Victoria, what's the baby horse's name?"

Victoria answered, "She doesn't have a name yet, honey. Mr. Miguel and I would love it if you children would name her for us."

Paula Jean, JJ, and Sarah looked at each other, thrilled by what they just heard. Sarah said excitedly, "Come here you two, let's pick a name." The adults looked on as the three children huddled together, intently discussing their options. Gracie blew Victoria and Miguel a kiss as a means of thanking them for their grand gesture, as did Cecilia, Justin, and Poppy Tom. Then finally, the huddle broke up and Sarah said enthusiastically, "We have a name!"

Victoria asked, "What is it? We can't wait to hear."

Sarah said, "The name for Lightning and Thunder's new baby is... RAINDROP! Right Poppy? Just like you said before, lightning and thunder make raindrops. Dancing Cloud made the lightning and thunder come and then came the raindrops. Lightning and Thunder are the mommy and daddy, so we say their baby's name is RAINDROP!"

"That's an absolutely perfect name," said Victoria excitedly.

"Raindrop, that is ideal," Miguel shouted happily. "I love it! Great job, kids!"

Gracie, Cecilia, Justin, and Poppy Tom, clapped their hands and moved over to the children, patting them on their backs and congratulating them on a great pick, as Hollie excitedly barked her approval.

Then Victoria said, "You don't know how perfect a name Raindrop is. We have a pony named Rainbow, and now we have a foal named Raindrop! Lightning, Thunder, Raindrop, Rainbow, they all tie together just perfectly!"

Sarah and Poppy Tom turned to each other with astonished looks on their faces while Hollie barked enthusiastically. Then Poppy Tom asked Victoria with urgency in his voice, "Victoria, what did you just say about a rainbow?"

"No, not *a* rainbow, Mr. Tom," said Victoria. "Rainbow. We have a pony named Rainbow. He's right down there in the stall next to Thunder. He's a beautiful little pony. Here, I'll call him.

"Hey, Rainbow, whatcha doin' boy?" When out from the opening of the stall next to Thunder pokes the handsome face of a Quarter Pony named Rainbow.

Sarah asked with just as much urgency, "That's Rainbow? Rainbow's a pony?

"Poppy, Rainbow's a pony!

"Mrs. Victoria, can we have…? Would you allow…? Would it be possible to have Paula Jean ride Rainbow?"

"Of course, if she would like to," answered Victoria.

Poppy Tom ran over to Sarah, hooting and hollering as the two embraced and then together sang out, "We're going to have Paula Jean ride Rainbow, la, la, la! We're going to have Paula Jean ride Rainbow, la, la, la! We're going to have Paula Jean ride Rainbow, la, la, la," as Hollie joined them, prancing about in celebration.

With the exception of Hollie, everyone, including Lightning, Thunder, Raindrop, and now Rainbow because he heard his name being called so often, stared at Sarah and Poppy Tom wondering what this was all about.

Poppy Tom separated himself from his hug with Sarah, turned to Cecilia, and said joyously, "Cecilia, your mother just did it again!"

Then he said, looking up with watery eyes and pointing, "Jennie, Jennie, Jennie! My amazing Jennie!"

Cecilia looked at her father, then around to everyone else, then back to her father and questioned, "What do you mean, Dad?"

"Don't worry about it, Ce. Just know your mother is working her magic once again."

Then, he and Sarah high-fived each other a whole bunch of joyous times and petted and hugged Hollie happily.

Miguel asked, "Gracie, are you okay with Paula Jean riding Rainbow?"

Paula Jean looked at her mother in anxious anticipation of her answer and so did everyone else.

Gracie answered, "You know, Mr. Miguel, two days ago, Paula Jean...well let's just say, Paula Jean nor I couldn't ever have imagined in our wildest dreams that she could be riding a pony today. Something it looks like she would love to do and something I would love to see her do. Thanks to the love and goodwill of all you wonderful people, she has that...no, we have that opportunity. How could I ever say no? She'll go easy though, right?"

"Oh, yes," assured Miguel. "I'll be holding Rainbow the whole time, and we'll ride nice and easy. Rainbow is a calm, gentle pony and loves children. And children love him. It'll be fine."

Paula Jean ran over to her mother, hugging and kissing her, thanking her for letting her ride. Gracie savored their embrace.

And Victoria said, "I take back what I said before, this is the most beautiful thing I've ever witnessed in my life."

Cecilia said, "The day's not over yet."

Even more dividends.

Miguel said, "I'll get Rainbow saddled up."

"Victoria, please take Paula Jean over and have her try on a few riding helmets. We always want to use the proper personal protective equipment."

"A man after my own heart," said Poppy Tom. "Look outside, the rain has stopped and it looks like the sun's starting to peek through. Perfect timing."

All gathered around as Paula Jean is lifted onto the saddle, and JJ shouted out, "Ride him good, Jubee Jean."

"I will, Jubee Jay," Paula Jean called back confidently. As she settled herself upon the trusty back of Rainbow and began her ride, guided and protected by the secure, capable hands of Mr. Miguel, she raised her arms high up in the air and shouted, "Look at me, Mommy, SUPERGIRL FLY!"

Tears of joy streamed down Gracie's face as a beautiful, vibrant rainbow appeared in the western, blueberry-speckled sky, framing all in a glorious, heavenlike scene.

Sarah turned to Poppy Tom and said, "Lightning and thunder made raindrops and the raindrops made a rainbow and everybody gets to see

it. Today is really a day to be treasured, Pops," while giving him a rousing double thumbs-up.

This doesn't qualify for Mother Nature to conduct her choir of trees in song. But it's close enough to get an honorable mention at their next practice session. Grandma Jennie will see to that.

Dividends, dividends, and more dividends.

SARAH AT TEN

BRIGHT SPOTS

CHAPTER 20

"Come on, everyone, it's time for dessert," Poppy Tom called out to his family from the kitchen. "Justin, you'll be happy to know that tonight's sweet tooth satisfying item is strawberry shortcake."

"Oh, Dad," Justin said, "I need to let you know that I'm watching what I'm eating nowadays."

"You are?" asked Poppy Tom with some disappointment in his voice.

"Yup, I sure am," confirmed Justin. "I'm watching what I'm eating go from my plate to my fork and right into my mouth," he said, as he let out a loud laugh.

Then Cecilia said half-kiddingly, "Yeah, Dad, I'm watching what he's eating, too. I'm watching it go from his plate, to his fork, into his mouth, and right to his waistline," she said, as she gazed at Justin with a smirk on her face.

"I'll eat daddy's piece of short-berry straw-cake if you want me to, Mommy," said JJ.

"TRAITOR," Justin said to JJ, as all had a really good chuckle.

Sarah said, "Poppo, while they're trying to figure out who gets what, I'll take my piece, please."

"You got it, Sarah. What would you like yours topped with? I have vanilla ice cream or whipped cream."

"I'll take both, please," Sarah said without hesitation.

"That's my granddaughter, no limits," said Poppy Tom. "Good choice."

"Figure mine the same way please, there, Daddo," said Justin.

"Me too, please," said JJ.

"I'll just take some strawberries please, Dad, hold everything else," Cecilia stated proudly.

"I don't know what you're worried about, Ce," said Justin. "What you eat doesn't end up on your waist, or anywhere else, for that matter. You're lucky like that."

"Well, thank you for saying so, Hon," Cecilia said appreciatively. "I suppose I'd like to keep it that way," acknowledging it takes more than luck to achieve that end.

"Yup, just strawberries, you got it," said Poppy Tom, supporting Cecilia's effort to eat healthy and recognizing Justin's sincere compliment to his daughter.

"You know, guys," Cecilia said laughing. "It may not be apparent now, but I was the original sweet tooth girl."

All looked at Cecilia confused, as Justin asked, "What do you mean by that, Ce?"

"Oh, yeah," said Cecilia, "you guys think you own the title of sweet tooth champion, but I ascended to that position a long time ago. Yup, I was given that title by the official sweet tooth title giver, none other than Mrs. T."

All looked at Cecilia, impressed, as Sarah said, "Oh, hey, I think I remember Mrs. T saying…Yes, when I first met her. When you took me, Poppy. She said if I was like you, Mommy, I'd have a sweet tooth, too."

"Anyway, Poppy," Sarah said, thinking it was time to move the conversation on to a subject more important to her, "we're wetting a line tomorrow morning, right?"

As Cecilia said, shrugging her shoulders, "Oh, well, so much for my reign as the sweet tooth originator."

As Sarah continued, "Wet a line, get a line, right, Poppsey? This will be line number four, you know!"

"Will it be line number four, already?" asked Poppy Tom.

"It sure will be, Poppy."

"I'm catching up to you, Mommy."

"Wow, time sure flies," said Poppy Tom. "My goodness. Hey, you're going to be running out of room on that post before you know it there, Sarah-O."

"Four lines represent four seasons," said Cecilia. "Wow, you're taking me back. Memories of Mrs. T, going fishing. You know, I think I landed my first trout in my fourth season, if I'm not mistaken."

"You sure did, Daughter," assured Poppy Tom. "I don't remember a lot, but I do remember that. Your perseverance paid off. You landed a beauty. I know we have a picture of you and that trout around here somewhere. Your mother would have known where that picture is."

"But, Dad, if I remember correctly, it wasn't in the morning when I caught that trout. I'm thinking it was more toward evening. Wasn't that the case?"

"That was the case, Ce. You're correct."

"But I thought you said the morning is the best time to go fly-fishing, Poppy?" Sarah asked.

"What I think you heard me say, fisher girl, is that the morning is *one* of the best times to go fly-fishing. The early evening is another one of those best times, Sarah.

"You know it's funny, Ce, I was going to talk to you all about allowing me to take Sarah fishing tomorrow evening instead of in the morning."

"Well, I don't know, Dad," Cecilia said with a degree of apprehension in her voice. "I mean, I can remember it was a different experience going fly-fishing at that time of day. I mean, you know, a pleasant one. And I remember the fish were really biting. But, I also remember getting home past dark. I don't know if it's a good idea to have Sarah out there that late. You know, this year she'll be walking…using her walk…coming back in the dark. I don't know."

"But, why, Mommy? What's the big…"

Then Poppy Tom interrupted, "No, I know what you're thinking. Listen, let me lay out my reasons for wanting to do this, then you can let me know what you guys think. For the last two seasons, we've had to…well actually Sarah, had to face some tough fishing conditions. Low water levels one year, high water levels the next."

"Yes, Mommy, they were tough, real tough," Sarah chimed in to say in support.

Then Poppy Tom continued, "This year, I'm happy to say, the conditions are perfect."

"Yes, perfect conditions!" Sarah said as she pumped her two fists.

"Yup, perfect water and temperature levels," Poppy Tom reported. "These perfect conditions create high insect activity. You said the fish were really biting the night you caught your trout, Ce. Do you remember the hatch? Do you remember the trout rising?"

"Yes, Dad, I do. I'll always remember those things," she confirmed, reminiscing. "They were beautiful things to experience."

"Well, that's what I'm thinking," said Poppy Tom. "I would love to have Sarah experience going fly-fishing at that time, too."

"What do you mean, Dad, when you asked Cecilia if she remembered the hatch?" Justin asked. "What's hatching? And what about the trout rising? What's that about?"

"Ah, two beautiful things to behold," said Poppy Tom with admiration in his voice. "A *hatch* and a *trout rising* are terms we use for particular occurrences in nature. Basically, very basically, a hatch occurs when insects that live on the bottom of the brook rise to the surface and change into a winged type of insect and then fly away, sort of like the way a caterpillar changes into a butterfly. It all has to do with the different stages of an insect's lifecycle. Well, you can imagine all these insects—or what we call flies—floating with the current offer up a great food source for the brook trout. So, a trout will *rise* to the surface to feed on these flies. This is a perfect example of Mother Nature's intricate design and cycle of life and can only happen when the brook and surrounding environment are in a pristine state. Thankfully, ours is."

"We have Grandma Jennie to thank for that," Sarah proudly informed everyone.

"Right, Sarah. Thank you for saying so," said Poppy Tom. "And you, too, don't forget. You helped restore a section of the brook a few years back."

Cecilia smiled at Sarah and nodded her head, letting her know that she too was thankful to Sarah for recognizing her mother's efforts and for being a good steward of the environment herself.

"So, if we were to allow Sarah the opportunity to 'catch the hatch,' she would be experiencing the ultimate in dry fly-fishing," stated Poppy Tom. "Still no guarantees that she'll land a trout. We'll have to 'match the hatch,' which is tying on the right type and size fly, and Sarah will have to make some of the best casts of her life to get a trout to 'take.' And all that's assuming we'll have things timed out right. We're just going by assumptions that there will be a hatch in the first place. Mother Nature makes the ultimate decision on that."

"Sarah, sweetie, I'd love for you to go," Cecilia said, "but it will be pitch dark by the time you get back. I mean, you know, the stars will be shining bright by then. I don't know."

"Oh, come on, Mom," Sarah began.

Poppy Tom interrupted her and said, "Stars, that's something else I'd like to mention."

"What about stars, Dad?" Cecilia asked.

"Well, there's another reason why I'd like to be out past dark tomorrow night," said Poppy Tom, "and this one involves the whole family."

"What's this all about, Dad?" questioned Cecilia.

"Yeah, I'm curious, too," said Justin.

"Okay, so here's what I'm thinking," Poppy Tom began. "There just so happens to be a meteor shower occurring, and it will be viewable from our area. Cecilia, you know how Sarah and Hollie and I have been swinging by the wall, you know, Mommy's wall, to do a little work when we'd finish up fishing. I'd like it if we went there after fly-fishing tomorrow night and you guys met us there. We're supposed to have clear skies, and there's no moon. It's real dark out there. No lights from any houses or anything. It'll be a perfect night and a perfect place to view the stars and that rare meteor shower. I think it will be a great thing for us to experience together. But, I understand it's asking a lot. What do you guys think?"

"Oh, I don't know, Dad," Cecilia said.

"Oh, come on, Ce," Justin interjected. "That sounds like a really nice thing to do."

"It sure does, Mommy," said Sarah.

"That's a long way out there, Dad," Cecilia stated. "Do you think you'll know? ...I mean...I don't know if I'll remember how to get there."

"Oh, you'll remember," Poppy Tom encouraged. "Just continue past the entrance to the Dark Woods and the place I used to take you to look at the clouds. I'm sure you'll remember how to get to those places."

"Yes, I remember how to get to those places," Cecilia realized. "I think I remember, anyway. It's sure been a while."

"You'll just have to keep going," stated Poppy Tom. "When you get to the place where we looked at the clouds, continue on. Keep the tall trees to your left, and you'll come to it. Remember, it won't be dark when you guys get there. It won't be that dark when we get there, either. It'll be the return trip when we'll be dealing with the dark. We'll all be together for that. I'm thinking of heading over to Nate's Baits in the morning to pick up some of those headlamps for us. They attach to our hats and will light our way home. Hollie will be the only one of us that won't need a lamp. She sees great in the dark. I'll bet she takes the lead and guides us home. We'll just have to remember to bring some warm jackets. Its gets chilly at night. It'll be a great adventure and a perfect opportunity for the kids to make some discoveries. Looking up at stars tends to do that. What do you say, Ce?"

"Ah, okay, Dad, you convinced me. Mrs. T, fishing, Mommy's wall...Yeah, I'll look forward to going back out to those places that I haven't been to in a while and where I have such fond memories. And this sounds like it will be a great way to make some new ones. Besides, it'll be a good way for us to get some much-needed exercise.

"And, especially you, Justin. You'll have some strawberry shortcake to walk off."

All celebrated Cecilia's approval of Poppy Tom's plan as Justin said, "So, this means I'll need another piece of cake."

"How does this mean that?" Cecilia asked, confused.

"Here's how," Justin said confidently. "The piece I just had, I'll walk off on the way out there, and the piece I'm going to have now, I'll walk off on the way back."

Cecilia raised her hands in the air and shook her head and said, "I guess I'm not the sweet tooth champ I thought I was." All got a good laugh.

Then Sarah said, "Come on JJ, we'll let the adults figure all this stuff out. Let's head to bed. It sounds like we have a busy day ahead of us."

"So, Pops, goodnight, don't sleep upright, and we'll look forward to staying out late tomorrow night."

"Okay, Sarah, another good one there," said Poppy Tom. "I have one, too, but I cheated and wrote it down ahead of time. I'll read it to you if I can remember where I put it."

"Here it is, Dad," said Cecilia. "I found it in the refri...I found it sitting on Mom's desk. Right where you must have left it."

"That's funny, I don't remember leaving it there...I wrote it out here, at the table. Anyway, thank you for finding it.

"Sarah, is it okay I use it, I mean, will it count, even though I made it up ahead of time?"

"Oh, sure. No rules between us team players, Poppo."

"Okay, good. Here goes," said Poppy Tom in a somewhat sheepish voice. "Goodnight, sleep tight, and know I love you all with all my might."

"Ah, Pops, I think that's the best one of them all. I love you too, Poppy."

Cecilia said, "I'd say Sarah's right, Dad. That's beautiful. We all love you so very much."

"Very interesting about the hatch and trout rising thing, Dad," said Justin as he gobbled up another piece of strawberry shortcake.

Poppy Tom smiled contentedly and said, "On that note, I think I'll head to bed myself. What a great way to end a very treasured day. Night all."

CHAPTER 21

"Sarah, look, do you see what I see? Poppy Tom asked with a hushed voice.

"What Pops? I don't see anything."

"The fact that you're not able to see something very special that's right out in front of you," said Poppy Tom softly, "is a testament to Mother Nature's perfect design."

Sarah raised her hands up from her walker and held them out in a questioning gesture. She looked intently in the direction of Poppy Tom's stare while shaking her head.

Poppy Tom stood Sarah's fly rod upright against a sapling, freeing his hands, and crouched while stepping slowly next to Sarah as Hollie laid down in the cool grass at the edge of the entrance to the Dark Woods. He placed a gentle arm over Sarah's shoulder, pointed a wise, guiding finger and said, "Right there, Sarah, lying among those ferns is a fawn. A baby deer. See it?"

"Where Poppy? I don't see any…," Sarah asked in an inquiring whisper just as the inconspicuous outline of the fawn appeared to her. "Oh, how beautiful, Poppy. I see it. I can see it now, Pops. It's so cute. Look, it's just lying there sleeping. Oh, how pretty. She's sleeping, Pops, right? I mean, she's okay, right? She's all alone. Where's her mommy, Poppy?"

"Well, I can't tell if it's a she or a he, Sarah, but we can call it a she if you'd like. I can tell you that she's one hundred percent fine. I can tell you, too, that her mommy is somewhere nearby. Besides, she has Ol' Mister Scowl the Owl keeping a watchful eye over her as she rests. See, look up there. There he is," Poppy said, as Sarah and Hollie looked up to see their old friend watching over them, and the newest arrival to the forest, from his lofty perch. "Let's move on now. Nice and easy. We don't want to get our new fawn friend or her mommy nervous."

"Oh, Poppy, I'm so glad you showed her to me. I would've walked right by her without noticing she was even there if you didn't tell me."

"I'm happy you got to see her, but I'd say it was Mother Nature that put her there. I just happened to spot her. See how she blended right into her surroundings?"

"I did, but it took me a while to make her out."

"That's the whole idea, Sarah. Mother Nature designed that special coat for all her newborn fawns, to help them blend in and keep them safe from harm. Those bright white spots on her coat are made to resemble dappled sunlight as it filters through the vegetation that surrounds her, acting as a form of camouflage. Mother Nature thinks of everything, doesn't she?"

"What's that noise, Poppsey? asked Sarah as her and Hollie's heads turned in the direction of the sound.

"Okay, yeah. You hear that? That's her mother bleating. That's her mother calling her baby home," confirmed Poppy Tom. "It's best we go now."

Just then Ol' Mister Scowl the Owl let out a few sharp howls.

Poppy Tom said, "Alright Scowl, we're going. Don't worry. Come on guys, time to go."

Now, well into the realm of the Dark Woods, Poppy Tom directed, "Sarah, let's pause here for a few minutes."

"How come, Pops? We're not at the secret fishing spot yet. We're still in the Dark Woods. We can't fish from here."

"No, you're right, we can't. We're pausing here because I'd like to take care of a few things while we're still under the cover of the Dark Woods. First, let me help you put on your jacket. Feel how cool it's getting?"

"Yes, I do, Poppy. Okay, thank you. I can feel it getting cooler, and I can feel, I don't know, I can feel it getting quieter, too, Pops. I mean, I can hear it getting quieter, but I can feel it, too."

"See, Sarah, that's why I enjoy spending time with you and witnessing you experiencing new things. You have a way of using all your senses to not only see but to feel things. It's great that you do that, because it allows you to fully benefit from the experience. What you're feeling is the calm surrender that takes place in nature at this time of day. Everything becomes hushed and still."

"Yes, Poppy, it makes you think you should whisper whether you have to or not. In the morning, you can feel everything waking up and stretching and getting ready for a brand-new day. Like when ol'

Brewster the Rooster wakes everything up. Now, it's like everything is slowing down and getting ready for bed, you know like for the night."

"Yes, I do know, Sarah. So right you are. We now have to get ourselves into that same rhythm. If we're not, nature or, in our case, the brook trout will sense something's not right. I'm going to ask that you stay here with Hollie for a few minutes. I'm going to get myself, or at least try to get myself, in nature's rhythm and work my way over to the brook. I want to see, for one, if there's a hatch taking place; two, what flies are hatching; and three, if the trout are rising for them. Then I'll work my way back to you and Hollie and make my report. Sound good?"

"It sure does, Poppy," Sarah agreed as Hollie let out a slight yelp in agreement, too.

"Are you okay, staying here for a few minutes, Sarah? You won't be afraid, will you?"

"Oh, no Pops. I have Hollie with me and Hollie has me with her. We'll be waiting for you to come back and tell us what you see. These good ol' Dark Woods are like my good ol' friends now, Poppy."

Poppy Tom gave Sarah and Hollie a thumbs-up and headed ever so slowly and quietly out to the brook.

After a while, Sarah and Hollie saw Poppy Tom returning from his scouting mission. The upbeat look on his face let them know that he had some good news.

"Poppy, how's it looking out there?" Sarah asked as she smiled, knowing Poppy Tom's report would be positive.

"Oh, Sarah," Poppy Tom said in an excited but whispered voice, "what a great hatch we have going on! And you wanna see the trout rising! I'd say our timing is just perfect this season. It looks like we have insects called Pale Evening Duns hatching. I know Mr. Nate stocked your fly boxes with some good flies. Let's see if he has a fly called a Light Cahill in a size...oh, I'd say in a size sixteen. That would make a good match to the hatch. Sure enough, he has a few of them here. Wise Mr. Nate sure knows how to equip a young fly-fisher girl with the best flies. I'll tie this one on for you. You know, I need to teach you how to tie on your own flies. But we'll do that another time back at Pop's Shop.

Maybe the next rainy day. Oh, I'm trying to rush too much. See, look, my hands are shaking."

"Breathe, Poppy. Take deep breaths. We have to be like nature and stay hushed and calm."

"Oh, right, I know. I'm getting overanxious. Okay, hold on a second, let me relax a bit. Breathe...breathe...Okay, okay, that's better."

"That's a little fly, Poppy," Sarah observed. "Is that tied on one of those barbie hooks?"

"Barbie hooks, barbie hooks?" Poppy Tom questioned. "Oh, you mean a *barbless* hook. Yes. Yes, it is."

"So, it won't hurt my brook trout friend too much, right Pops? I mean, if I get to land a trout, the hook will…"

"Right, the hook will come out easily and we'll send your friend on his or her merry way. You know, I was wondering if you wanted to land a trout if you are fortunate enough to hook one this year. You know, last year, you had this thing about you being the trout's burden and if you landed a trout then…"

Sarah interrupted and said, "Oh, no, Pops, that wasn't last year."

"It wasn't? Poppy Tom asked with a confused look on his face. "When was it then?"

"No, it was like two years ago. But I know what you mean, Poppy. I'm okay. If I land a trout, I mean, if I get to hook one, I'm going to try and land him. You see, that was back then. My brook trout friends were teaching me to fight and be strong and when my burden gets stronger, then I have to get stronger. So, I listened to them, Pops. And I remembered what they taught me to do. That's how come I got to walk out here this year. I'm back to using my walker because of what they taught me. When my lungs got weak, I fought real hard and got them real strong again. So, I don't need my chair anymore, Poppy. I won't ever, ever, never forget what they taught me.

"So, if I hook a trout, I'll try and land him this season, as long as I won't hurt him. I don't want to hurt him at all, Poppy. Besides, I really want to see one up close. You always said how pretty a brook trout is, and that was what Mommy was saying to me just before. She's hoping I get to see a hatch and see the trout rising and then get to land one to see how beautiful it is. Mommy wants me to have the same happy time like she had. She said she can close her eyes and see her first trout with all its bright spots, just like she landed it yesterday. The picture of her beautiful trout is still right behind her eyes, and Mommy can see it anytime she wants. I'd like to have a picture of my first trout, my pretty first trout, right behind my eyes, too, Poppy."

"Good, Granddaughter. Even though my timing was off, I'm happy to know yours is right on. That's a wonderful way to think of things," confided Poppy Tom. "So, let's do what we have to do to make that happen. Listen, there's one thing I need to let you know. There's going to be a difference in the way you fly-fished in the past to how you'll be fly-fishing tonight. In the past, you cast your fly in the hopes that a trout was in the general area and decided to come up and take your offering, as one did, during, I think, your very first season. Tonight, however, you're going to actually see the particular trout you're casting to. You just have to make sure that he doesn't see you. It's still about a smooth, gentle way of casting, which you do so well. But tonight, to succeed, the timing and precision of your casting will play an important role. It's the art of dry fly-fishing in its purest form and such great fun. But understand, it's a great challenge, too. I think it's one of the greatest one-on-one challenges in sport. But, just like any great challenge, great satisfaction comes when you succeed. I know you will take on this challenge the same way you take on any great challenge, and you *will* succeed. And I know you know that too, sweetheart."

Sarah took in the sage advice and confidence-building pep talk just offered by her doting grandfather. She pat the pocket that holds her trusty poem, removed her hat to do a ceremonious kissing of her faithful feather, and then grabbed the handles of her walker and strode bravely and stealthily toward her next waiting-to-be-won victory, while the coaching team of Poppy Tom and Hollie followed quietly behind.

With the use of hand signals, Poppy Tom directed Sarah on a path downstream, wisely keeping a sharp rise in the ground between them and the brook. After a while, he signaled for Sarah to make a ninety-degree turn at the location he wished her to begin her direct approach to the brook.

Sarah knew that, with this signaling, H-hour had arrived. She knew when she managed to get to the top of the rise before her—an effort she knew wouldn't be easy—a whole new scene would be revealed and a whole new world of discovery awaited her. She struggled to contain her excitement and, at the same time, her nervousness and apprehension; so, a few deep breaths were needed. She balanced herself to wipe her sweaty palms on her jacket, then grasped her walker again, leaned forward, and began her uphill climb.

Each step took her triple the effort due to the degree of rise. Poppy Tom attempted to assist his granddaughter, but her no-shaking head and stoic glare told him she'd have none of that. At about halfway up the incline, she took a reluctant break. She stretched her neck to try and gain a view of the event taking place down by the brook, but the setting sun, low in the western sky, hit her squinting eyes with a wall of silvery light. Her head dropped down like a prizefighter to shield her eyes and to buttress and battle the onslaught of negative pressure from the slope she again began to spar with, a slope now slick with evening dew. She too battled the hurt from the chilled air rushing into her easily overheated lungs. She battled the hurt from the boiled blood pumping through her thin, pulsating arteries. And even more cutting, she battled the hurt from the voices inside her highly electrified brain. Voices that pummeled her with jabs of ridicule and scorn. Voices that bobbed and weaved around her every move with taunts of failure and defeat. You don't have what it takes to make this hill, she heard, like it poked a right uppercut, catching her on the chin. Somebody like you can't do this, was like a left hook swung to the side of her face. Give up. Throw in the towel. Go home where you belong, you amateur, she heard, and it hit her square in the solar plexus.

Anyone battered by this stinging physical and mental assault would give up, would throw in the towel, and would go home. But Sarah wasn't just anyone. Besides, to her, this wasn't anything new. She had faced this familiar opponent, oh, so many times before, as far back as she could remember. In fact, taking on a new challenge without carrying around the cynical excess baggage of her adversary just wouldn't feel right. To Sarah, it was almost laughable, how her antagonist thought he could use the same failed strategies of past defeats to score a TKO and take away her title. Sarah wondered when he'd realize that she had an arsenal of weaponry that she could deploy to defeat, not only this challenger but any other hapless palooka that came along and tried to steal her champion-of-the-whole-wide-world crown, and she wasn't afraid to use them. She knew she had in her corner Poppy Tom and Hollie. She had her feather and her poem. She had the determined never-give-up-the-fight blood of her Grandma Jennie flowing through her veins. And she hadn't even reached into her pack of ammunition yet. She knew too, what feint she would use to subdue the belligerent boxer on tonight's ticket and put him down for the count.

But this wasn't going to be a rough and tumble, toe-to-toe slugfest. Why should she expend all that energy? Why add more lacerations and gashes to the already disfigured and almost unrecognizable battleground that was her enemy's face when she didn't have to? No, her strategy was simple. In fact, it was right out there for all to see. But to her rival, his punch-drunk mind couldn't comprehend it, his swollen shut eyes couldn't see it, and his cauliflower ears couldn't hear it. It was hiding in plain sight, and he was oblivious to it.

Prudently, Sarah chose to tap into the enormous power, infinite energy, and supreme dominance of the pure calm surrender that she could feel surrounding and protecting her and all living things at this time of day. It was this same calm surrender, this hushed limitless energy, that told that massive white hot sun in the western sky to set tonight and to smoothly and gently rise in the eastern sky tomorrow morning. It's that same energy that tells the acorn, the size of a nickel, that someday it will become a giant among giants just by lying there, and sure enough...it does. And it's that same energy that Grandma Jennie used to subdue her burdens and ward off her challengers.

Time, patience, and kind, gentle persuasion can move mountain ranges and can save them, too. Sarah was choosing not to fight fire with fire or waste her precious energy by unnecessarily annihilating her unworthy enemy. No, she was simply doing what Poppy Tom suggested. She became one with nature's rhythm, and in so doing, very efficiently, she also became one with the power that drives the entire universe. No foe could withstand the shock and awe of such awesome authority.

So, once again, as she left her enemy squirming on the ground and eating her dust, she ascended to the top of the rise with her dignity, confidence, and undefeated champion-of-the-whole-wide-world title still intact.

Poppy Tom and Hollie silently celebrated Sarah's victory and eagerly awaited her reaction when she collected her purse by viewing the amazing sight before her. So, they were very surprised when Sarah, instead of rushing to look up and receive her prize, turned completely around to gaze at the hard-won path behind her. They didn't realize that Sarah needed to get a visual of another one of her battle-scarred proving grounds. She needed to get that image, clearly and precisely implanted, as she said, right behind her eyes so she could see it anytime she needed to. Because she *knew* she needed to. This image would get deposited in the high-yield account with other past victories, where it would build compound interest of strength, confidence, and a sense of purpose and pay dividends of love, compassion, and generosity to friend and foe alike. She knew she could pull from these hard-earned and well-deserved funds to finance the next mission in which she'd inevitably be called upon to engage.

So now, with a photocopy of her latest achievement securely tucked away in the "Sarah's Vault of Past Achievements," she could, with a gladdened heart and soul, begin to enjoy the wondrous things this night had in store, which she did just by looking up. For now, the sun that had hit her squinting eyes with a wall of silvery light during her ascent had now dropped down behind the mountains at the far horizon and was bathing the mountains in front of her with stripes of a white, orange, and yellow glow.

Sarah, with a peaceful whisper, said, "Look Poppy, look how pretty those mountains are. The sun's painting them, and they look just like candy corn. To me, they look like candy corn soldiers standing at attention, watching over us and this pretty place."

Poppy Tom, hearing Sarah speak, understood she was out of her doing-battle mode and had changed into her time-to-get-this-show-on-the-road mode and, he looked up to view Sarah's fascination. Then he responded softly, saying, "Wow Sarah, they do! They really do. Good job using your imagination. That's a great comparison. But you're sure taking your time turning around and looking down at the brook. I would think you'd be eager to see the…"

"I'm going to turn around soon, like almost now, Pops," Sarah interrupted and said quietly. "But you know, I'm in the calm of nature's rhythm. No rush, just hush."

Poppy Tom raised his hands up, gesturing to Sarah that she made an excellent point, and he was proud of her poise and composure, then moved his hands in the direction of the brook, gesturing, whenever you're ready.

Just then Hollie's head urgently sprang up and turned in the direction of the path they had just taken to get here.

Poppy Tom and Sarah followed Hollie's stare and saw Cecilia, Justin, and JJ working their way toward them.

Cecilia gave an acknowledging wave and then raised a pointer finger to her lips, signaling that they've come in support and know to be quiet.

Poppy Tom gave them the okay signal and then turned to see Sarah with a huge smile on her face from unexpectedly seeing her family arriving here as opposed to meeting them later on at Grandma Jennie's wall. She then finally turned in the direction of the brook. Sarah's rooting section just increased by one hundred and fifty percent.

Because Poppy Tom was standing behind Sarah, he couldn't see the expression on her face as she viewed the magnificent scene before her. He just heard the faint gasp of air being sucked into her now cooled-down lungs by her amazed reaction. He saw her head slowly moving left and right, up and down, and all around in the same fashion a person wearing a 3-D headset does to follow the illusion they think they're surrounded by. What Sarah saw was pretty much like that, except this was not an illusion. What Sarah was experiencing was real, and it absolutely captivated her.

After a while, Sarah turned her head to look at Poppy Tom, Hollie, and then, down to her mother, father, and brother, who were now standing at the bottom of the rise. After a calm, settling pause, Sarah said in a soft whisper, "It looks like it's snowing upside down, Poppy. It looks like a million glittery snowflakes are floating up instead of floating down." Then her head turned slowly back to resume its gentle rotation.

Poppy Tom nodded in agreement and quietly said, "That's your inspired imagination making another great comparison, Sarah. That's a hatch in all its glory, and that's exactly what it looks like."

What Sarah called glittery snowflakes floating up instead of down are just what Poppy Tom told her they were, Pale Evening Duns, countless ones, doing their ritualistic dance of celebration right before their eyes. Their tiny, almost transparent forms flitted and fluttered on the cool, calm air above the brook, above the place of their birth. And that was why they celebrated. For just moments before, their slight, delicate bodies were held in bondage by a crusty outer shell that kept them weighted to the bottom of the brook, where they crawled between the dark crevices and bucked its forceful currents. Now, by nothing short of a miracle, they defied gravity and glided serendipitously on up currents of flighty freedom.

"Sarah, you just perfectly described what you're seeing," Poppy Tom said quietly. "I would be very interested to have you describe for me what you're feeling."

Sarah's eyes stayed transfixed on this wondrous display and after a long, contemplative pause, she answered in a whisper, "Happy, Poppy. I feel happy, like all these flying fly snowflakes are tickling my whole body and giving me a whole bunch of happy goose bumps. But most of all, Pops, looking at them, I feel love."

Poppy Tom again had reason to nod his head and said, ever so softly and slowly because of the profound words just spoken by his granddaughter, "I'd say they feel the same way. You know how reflection works, my dear."

So, just as Sarah's initial ascent of the rise signaled H-hour, her initial descent from it signaled zero hour. She knew the closer she got to the brook, the more invisible she needed to become. She stressed over every minute noise she unintentionally made, like the small stone that was jarred loose by the front left leg of her walker and rolled about a foot and a half down the slope, which sounded to her like a landslide of massive proportions. She thought the sound of a small twig snapping under her right foot bounced and echoed off every tree and every mountain within a five-mile radius. So, she was tremendously relieved and fantastically amazed when she settled in behind a perfectly located bush at the brook's edge and peeked out upon its surface to see, for the very first time in her life, abundant numbers of sleek, shimmering brook trout quietly and methodically rising like so many graceful, aquatic dancers performing in a highly choreographed, synchronized swimming competition.

Sarah's eyes couldn't open wide enough to take in all there was for her to see, let alone feel, about what she was witnessing. But the one thing that did come through loud and clear was a reinforcement of her admiration for Mother Nature and all her incredible creations. She believed she was witnessing the full depth and breadth of Mother Nature's grand design. She believed that until—WOOSH, WOOSH, SPLASH! WOOSH, WOOSH, WOOSH!!! SCREEEECH, SCREEEECH, SCREEEECH!!!—a majestic bald eagle swooped down not twenty feet below her and plucked a plump, juicy trout from the brook. Then, as if to show off, it flew with the trout flailing in its talons about eight feet over Sarah's head, showering her, Poppy Tom, and Hollie with water.

Sarah yelled out, "Whoa," as she ducked down. Then, after getting wet, turned toward the eagle winging away from his snatch and dash, and yelled, "Hey you!" as she shook the water off her face, hat, and shoulders. This turn allowed her to see Poppy Tom and Hollie, who were just as wet as she was, doing their versions of shaking off their unexpected shower. Sarah and Poppy Tom, seeing each other soaked, caused them to go into a fit of laughter. They turned to see Cecilia, Justin, and JJ rolling on the ground in hysterics at the top of the rise.

After a few moments of their shared hilarity, Sarah took stock of what just occurred and said to Poppy Tom in a disappointed voice, "Poppy, that big ol' mean bird just stole a nice, pretty brook trout and got us all wet. That made me holler at him and now we're not all hushed and quiet anymore. Look, all the nice rising trout went away."

Poppy Tom, still laughing, tried to compose himself, seeing Sarah becoming upset, then said, "Oh, Sarah, honey, you might not think so right now, but what we just experienced was a very special and rare event. That big ol' mean bird that you hollered at is an American Bald Eagle and just so happens to be the national emblem of our great country. No doubt that poor brook trout isn't too happy, but that eagle is doing nothing more than fulfilling its role as an apex predator. Meaning, it's at the top of the food chain for this beautiful and completely intact ecosystem. It feeds upon these brook trout just as these brook trout feed upon the Duns. It's all part of Mother Nature's intricate web of life. I believe you can understand that, sweetheart."

Sarah pondered Poppy Tom's message for a moment, then said reluctantly, "Well, I suppose so, Poppy."

With that, Poppy Tom said, "I'm glad we put your jacket on before. Here, let me brush you off," as he proceeded to brush the few remaining droplets of water off Sarah's wind and waterproof jacket. "You're lucky.

Your lucky hat kept your head dry. So, it looks like you're no worse for wear," as he waved an all's well to Cecilia, Justin, and JJ, who had now regained their composure and sent a signal back that they're happy that all's well after witnessing this comical and quite unique experience.

"What are we going to do now, Pops? I was trying to be all hushed and stuff, but now all the brook trout got scared away."

"We're going to do what every successful corps of discoverers and avid adventurers has done throughout the ages when faced with a setback, Sarah. We'll brush ourselves off, just like we're doing, do an assessment of lessons learned from our experience, and then forge ahead, undaunted. You might view what just occurred as a negative, bad thing, but I view it as a tremendous, positive, good thing."

"I know, Pops, but I still feel...Help me to see it as a positive good thing, like my poem tells me to do," Sarah sincerely requested.

"Okay, Sarah," Poppy Tom began, "you might not be aware, but there was a time not all that long ago, when the American Bald Eagle, our national emblem and a magnificent bird of prey, was close to becoming extinct. That means all of them would have all passed away. There would have been no more of these amazing eagles living anywhere in the world. Can you imagine what a tragedy that would have been, dear girl? Thank goodness, by the gallant effort of so many organizations and people, like your Grandma Jennie, this species of eagle has been saved. Even so, they're still quite rare. Not many people can say they've ever even seen a bald eagle in person, let alone seen one so close up like we just did. Heck, not only did it give us a shower, we felt the wind under its mighty wings. I'd say, that's a big deal for a nine-year-old girl to say she experienced. Wouldn't you?"

"I sure would, Grandpoppser," Sarah said with realization and understanding in her voice, "but I'm ten now, Poppy."

"Oh, sorry, right ten. I don't know why I keep getting the years mixed up...And you know, too, not only did that eagle allow us to witness nature in all its raw, unrestrained beauty, it reminded us of something very important. Something we were forgetting to do, and that is to have fun. I think that eagle saw us taking ourselves and what we came here for way too seriously and decided to shake things up a bit.

It gave us a good reason to laugh, and any day you can laugh is a day to be treasured. And, that's a positive, good thing, if you ask me, Sarah."

"Yup, it sure is. Thank you for helping me see the good in getting a shower from our new baldy eagle friend, Poppser."

"That's okay, sweetie. I believe you would've come around to seeing the good in all this after you had a chance to think about it a bit. By the way, it's bald eagle not baldy eagle, American Bald Eagle."

"Right, Poppy, an American Balding Eagle."

Poppy Tom began to correct Sarah again, "No, no, not..."

When Sarah interrupted him and said, "Does this mean we're done fishing for tonight, Poppy? All this noise and commotion made all the trout go away."

"Well, it really didn't make them go away," said Poppy Tom. "It just put them down. But it does mean they won't be rising anymore tonight, here. That doesn't mean they won't be rising upstream. And that's just where we're headed. So, no, we're not done. Heck, we're just getting started. Onward and upward, Dancing Eagle."

"Dancing Eagle? Who are you calling? Are you calling me? Sarah asked confused.

"Yup, Dancing Eagle," Poppy Tom said, laughing. "Hey, the way you just danced around. Dancing Cloud danced around like that, and she made it rain on her crops. You danced around like that, and you made it rain on you. Oh, yeah, Dancing Eagle, that's your new name alright."

"Okay, Dancing Poppy and Dancing Hollie," said Sarah, making the point that she wasn't the only one doing the shake-the-shower shimmy. All three Dancing Eagles got another good laugh that added to the fun, and overall, what would become good memories of this night's foray.

"So, let's head that-a-way," Poppy Tom directed. "North, as the crow, well, as the eagle flies."

"Okay, Pops. We're all brushed off, so we can go foraging ahead."

"Not *foraging* ahead, *forging*," Poppy Tom began to correct Sarah when she interrupted him.

"Shush, shush, shush, now Poppy. It's time to get all hushed again.

You guys follow me."

On that directive, Poppy Tom turned to Cecilia, Justin, and JJ and waved them on, so they knew to follow, paralleling them along the top of the rise.

Sarah stealthily and wisely led the two members of her corps of discoverers around a wiry patch of brambles, through a fragrant stand of black birch trees, and over rock left bare thousands of years ago by a retreating glacier and a spot that became a meeting place for Mr. Nate's ancestors they called Council Flat. So, it was only fitting that Sarah looked down and saw on the ancient surface of this rock and between a few remaining droplets of water, a feather left like a calling card from none other than their new eagle friend.

Sarah, seeing this feather, whispered excitedly to Poppy Tom, "Hey, Poppy, look, a big feather. The eagle must have dropped it. Let's take it and keep it as a souvo...as a souvy...as a really good thing to keep."

Poppy Tom looked down and saw the feather, then raised a shaking finger to Sarah and said quietly, "No, Granddaughter, here's what we need to do. We won't be touching that feather, we can't. We're going to leave that precious feather right where it is. Tomorrow, we'll pay another visit to Mr. Nate and let him know about our encounter with the eagle and about finding this feather. Here's why. In Mr. Nate's incredible culture, the eagle is a highly sacred being. They believe eagles have a special connection to the heavens because they fly so high up in the sky. So, their feathers are sacred, too. To Mr. Nate and his people, this feather symbolizes wonderful things like honor, trust, wisdom, strength, freedom, and a whole bunch of other great things. Mr. Nate will really appreciate us telling him so he can retrieve this special gift from his brother or sister eagle, according to the customs and ways of his ancestors."

"Mr. Nate and all his ancestor people sure have a lot of good brothers and sisters," confirmed Sarah in a quiet, contemplative voice while gazing reverently down at the feather. "Trees and eagles..."

"He sure...they sure do girl," Poppy Tom replied softly. "They sure know how to love, protect, appreciate, and be one with all of nature.

Something our culture needs to do. You should know, besides wanting to let Mr. Nate know about that feather, we couldn't take that feather if we wanted to."

"Why not, Pops?"

"There are laws on the books that make the taking and possession of that feather illegal," Poppy Tom whispered.

"How come? I don't understand. What does that mean, Poppy?"

"It's like I said before, Sarah, about all the organizations and people that saved the eagle from going extinct. Well, laws were put in place to protect them, too. A whole big list of birds that were endangered are now protected by these laws. Not only eagles, but owls, like good Ol' Scowl, red-tailed hawks, and a whole bunch of other beautiful birds are on that list. The law says folks like us can't take or have in our possession a feather or nests or eggs or anything else from these birds on the list. We can be fined if we do. That means paying money for breaking the rules. But, Mr. Nate can. He has a permit that allows him and other Native Americans to take and possess these special things because, as I've said, these special things play such an important role in their customs and beliefs.

"I guess I should let you in on a little secret. That red-tailed hawk feather in your hat...well, it's not really a red-tailed hawk feather. It's symbolic of one. It's really a feather from a bird called a ruffed grouse. Their tail feathers are kind of similar in size and shape to the tail feather of a red-tailed hawk. The law doesn't allow Mr. Nate to give away red-tailed hawk feathers to anyone who's not a family or tribal member, as I understand it. When Mr. Nate finds ruffed grouse tail feathers, he first freezes them to remove any germs and bacteria. Then, he actually paints and seals them to look just like red-tailed hawk feathers. And he sure does a great job of it. They carry the same power, hold the same secrets, and glow just as beautifully as the real ones. He stores them all in a nice cedar-lined box that he had me make for him a long time ago. I just figured I'd throw that little tidbit of information in there for ya."

Poppy Tom saw by the look on Sarah's face that she was seriously processing all this data and gave her the time and space to allow her to do that. He was very interested to know what she would say about this and, even more so, to know how she would feel about it.

After a time, Sarah said quietly and contemplatively, "Cool, Pops, I'm glad you told me about this. I'm glad we have good ol' Mr. Nate and all his ancestor people looking after all the pretty special birds and all their feathers and stuff and that there are laws that help them do that. And you know, Pops, as long as Mr. Nate made my feather symbolic and all the feathers we gave to all my friends were symbolic, it's like they are really real, anyway. I know because all my soldier friends, when they came to my class that time, they gave us medals like the ones they have, but they really weren't the really real kind of medals. But they said they were symbolic of the ones they had and were just as good and made my classmates and me just as good soldiers as they were. Besides, you know, I color feathers and give them to my friends in the hospital and that's like those feathers are symbolic, too. So, it's like all my color-picture red-tailed hawk feathers are really real, too. Just like my real poem, Pops. I make copies of my real first one and give them to my friends, and those poems have the same power and happy message. No difference. I think I feel as long as the person making something symbolic is doing it out of love for the person they want to give that something to, that love makes it just like the real thing. Love does a lot of good things, you know, Poppy. This is really cool stuff. Thank you for telling me. Now, let's get *foraging* ahead again before it gets too late."

"Sarah, you keep saying…," Poppy Tom began to say, when again Sarah cut in and said…

"Shush, Poppy, its hush time again. Now come on, let's go."

"You stay right down there, eagle feather," she commanded, "so Mr. Nate can find you."

"Hey, Poppy, how can we keep our secret fishing spot a secret if we tell Mr. Nate where the feather is?"

"Hey, Granddaughter," Poppy Tom said quietly and with a slight laugh, "how do you think I found out about this spot in the first place?"

"Mr. Nate, told you abo…," Sarah began to say.

Then Poppy Tom interjected and confirmed softly, "Mr. Nate told me about it. Yes, he did."

Then Poppy Tom turned and waved his arm to signal it was time for Cecilia, Justin, and JJ to follow along again and then turned back to see Sarah already striding ahead. He then looked down and waved to Hollie, signaling her to follow Sarah, as he stood pat for a few moments to gaze intently at the back of his forging-ahead, undaunted granddaughter. His eyes rose as he said a prayer to the heavens—the same heavens where maybe that eagle is soaring to by now—offering thanks for giving him and his Jennie such an amazing granddaughter.

He also prayed for the heavens to continue to provide her with the strength and fortitude she needs to continue to overcome her burdens, because her latest examination and tests showed the beginnings of a curvature of her spine, a condition called scoliosis. It's just that Sarah didn't know that yet. Coincidently, Sarah's friend, Emily, was showing the same developing spine condition. Going forward, they would need each other's happy, love, and love-light shining support more than ever. He also prayed that the heavens help him to be there for Sarah in body, soul, and mind for as long as she needed him to be. Down deep, it was the mind aspect of things that had him scared out of his skin, but he can't, no...he won't...let on...Then the sounds, SCREEEECH, SCREEEECH, SCREEEECH, from high above were heard!

Poppy Tom whispered to Sarah, "Hold up Dancing Eagle." When he got to her, he motioned that he wanted to give Sarah her rod as opposed to him carrying it. He proceeded to slip the butt end of her fly rod into a loop that hung at the bottom of her fishing vest and attached the middle section of the rod to a strap on the upper part of her vest that set her rod in an upright position, allowing her to carry it hands-free. He whispered ever so softly, "You have everything you need now—tackle and knowledge—to make this happen. I'll be hanging back. When you get a trout on and are getting ready to land it, then I'll come and assist. It's all you." He kissed her on the cheek and motioned for her to venture forth. As he turned to walk back, he waved to Sarah's rooting section on the top of the rise that she was about to fly solo. Even Hollie dropped back to allow Sarah an open stage to perform.

CHAPTER 22

From where Sarah now stood, she could see the brook and tell that the hatch was not as heavy as it was before. She whispered back to Poppy Tom saying, "Hey, Pops, there aren't as many flies hatching."

Sarah's statement caused Poppy Tom to stop and turn and creep back to her, then he said quietly, "Right, the hatch is winding down. So are the rises. But listen, you're looking for just one rising trout to cast to. Know this, the bigger the trout the smaller the ripple. The trout you see coming up out of the water are, most of the time, the smaller ones. The bigger guys hang out alone and keep a pool all to themselves and barely break the surface when they take a fly. But understand, the bigger the trout, the wiser they are, too. They're very hard to fool. But that's where the true one-on-one competition resides." Then, Poppy Tom pointed ahead, signaling Sarah to move on as he stood fast with Hollie sitting next to him as Sarah resumed her mission.

He could see from his vantage point that Sarah continually scanned the area before her, looking for a route to the brook that would conceal her movements and quiet her steps. She tread further upstream, passing sections of the brook that, to her, didn't meet the right criteria for presenting a fly. Something a seasoned fly-fisher would do. Then Poppy Tom saw her pause, scan a little more, and then point a confident finger, gesturing, that in her opinion, this was the best spot for her to cast her fly. That was Sarah's opinion. Poppy Tom had a different opinion. He saw what she saw when it came to the numerous trout rising in this particular pool, but he also saw the low-hanging branches from a gnarly old hemlock tree, acting as a canopy above the rising trout that had a way of reaching out and snagging the most expertly presented fly. There were a few slight windows of opportunity to finesse a fly between those rickety old branches, but its success would require an almost miraculous cast. But this was Sarah's show, and if this was where she wanted to perform her act, then so be it.

Sarah settled the feet of her walker into the soft gravel along the stream bank, balanced herself so she could stand unaided, then proceeded to dislodge her rod from its strap, loosen the fly from its eye on the rod, and begin her smooth, delicate casting just like an expert. It was as if she was one with the rod and the rod was one with her. With each forward motion, the fly got closer and closer to the place where she desired it to fall. She thought, okay one more forward cast and the fly will be out to the spot where that chubby trout kept rising. I just need to time it right. Okay good, let it fall...*rrright*...now. Sarah made an absolutely perfect cast and hooked a big, fat, juicy...hemlock tree branch right in the kisser. Sarah stood dumbfounded by what just occurred. She had no clue what to do in this situation, so she did what she knew she could do whenever faced with a challenge and that's turn to the ever-present and always-has-the-answer-and-ready-to-help Poppy Tom, the answer man himself.

Poppy Tom saw this coming from a mile away but didn't reveal that to Sarah. He raised a pointer finger to her, meaning for her to stay put and that he and Hollie were on the way.

Sarah said in an anxious, disappointing whisper, "Poppy, I don't know what happened but that big ol' branch just jumped out and..."

Then Poppy Tom cut in and said, "Hey, that happens to the best of them. If I had a dime for how many branches I've caught in my lifetime, I'd have a whole bunch of dimes and a whole bunch of branches."

"Now what, Pops?" Sarah asked in a low downtrodden voice.

"I need to grab your line and try to pull it free." Poppy Tom did so and was successful in freeing the line with the hook still intact, but the commotion sent all the rising trout in this pool down to depths unknown.

Sarah stood with a saddened look on her face for a few moments and then shook off her depression and said in a low but upbeat voice, "Time to go *foraging* ahead again Pops."

"Okay Sarah, good. I don't mean to put too much pressure on you, but we're starting to run out of time, daylight, and brook. I think you might have one more shot at this tonight and that's it. It's going to be a do or...win or lose proposition."

"Got it, Poppsey. I'll get moving, and I'll get this done," Sarah allowed Poppy Tom and Hollie time to move back away from the brook, then turned to see her mother, father, and brother still faithfully peering down at her from the cheap seats up on the rise. She reapplied the hook to the eye and reattached the rod in the same manner that Poppy Tom did. Then she stood still for a few moments to take a few deep breaths to calm her nerves and got herself back to that all-important and almost psychological camouflaging calm surrender to the rhythm of the night.

Her head was the first to move as she glanced upstream hoping there was a place that would still offer her all she needed to make one more cast, but thought she'd at least be heading in the direction that would get her back to more familiar territory and closer to the entrance to the Dark Woods. It was a place they all needed to go to anyway before they could get to Grandma Jennie's wall. She closed her eyes in prayer, asking the spirits of Mr. Nate's ancestors and her new brother and sister eagle if they wouldn't mind making her feather's luck and guidance shine a little extra glowy on her now. So, with all the preliminaries out of the way, she grasped her walker's handles in her clammy little hands and off she went, in Sarah speak, *foraging* ahead.

It's as if her eyes had tunnel vision as she glared intently at the surface of each pool she came upon, a surface that was becoming blacker and more nondescript with each passing moment, impeding her ability to see the telltale ripples from any rising trout that were now almost nonexistent, coinciding with the almost nonexistent hatch. She felt with each stealthy stride her chances of making another cast tonight, let alone actually landing a trout, were slipping away. When, as she followed the curvature of the brook around a thick stand of willows, to her delight, a perfect pool for casting was revealed. She squinted her tired but now hopeful eyes across its flat, inky surface looking for the slightest crinkle. But none appeared. From here, she allowed her eyes to pan the area more upstream in the hope that another perfect pool complete with a perfect rising trout might be there. She came away realizing that she was coming up close to the spot where she hooked a trout on her very first try, way back when she was seven. This means she was close to the Dark Woods and running out of perfect pool, perfect rising trout possibility options. Her head began to turn back to Poppy Tom and Hollie to signal that she thought they were pretty much coming to the end of the night's effort. When, out of the corner of her eye, she thought she saw the slightest little break in the near pool's surface that made her head spring back to look in its direction. "Was that a rise I just saw?" Sarah asked herself, as her now anxious thoughts pondered. "Come on, let it be one," she invoked, as her eyes tried to will a rise to appear.

Then right in the exact spot where her eyes happened to be peering she saw the smallest dimple on the surface and, at the exact same second, as a confirmation of how attuned and intimate Sarah had become with her surroundings, actually heard the faint sucking sound a trout makes when it takes in a fly. Immediately, in her mind, she heard the words spoken by her experienced and learned grandfather when he told her how the big guys barely break the surface and how they keep a pool all to themselves and immediately knew, without a doubt, this was one of those trout! Talk about tunnel vision. A laser couldn't have had more focus than Sarah's eyes as another rise confirmed the trout's presence and her mind shifted into high gear, planning out her strategic approach to this big guy's lair.

It was all systems go as she slowly and quietly snuck her way closer to the brook where an old decayed, blown-down white pine provided her with the perfect cover to set up behind. She used the cushioning effect of a sizeable tuft of grass found there to kneel on. It was the same native species of grass she helped Poppy Tom plant at that compromised section of brook further downstream, on her maiden voyage years before and one whose roots reached wide and deep into the soil to protect the brook's bank from erosion. Her strategy in kneeling was to lower the angle of her cast, a lesson learned to help her avoid hooking another one of those numerous hemlocks standing sentinel over this bruiser's den. Sarah moved her walker off to her left side, unsheathed her rod like a fencer unsheathing her foil, and freed her barbless fly from the eye. She turned to Poppy Tom to give him a confident nod, who returned the gesture, and then turned back and began to cast. Sarah directed her vapored breaths to slow down and harmonize with her smooth, delicate casts. She directed her casts to harmonize with the smooth, delicate rises of the trout, whose rises harmonized to the smooth, delicate dance of the few remaining Pale Evening Duns, as they harmonized with the smooth, delicate current of the brook that harmonized to the smooth, gentle rhythm of the night that harmonized with the smooth, gentle beatings of Sarah's heart.

Forward and back her fly glided until she felt it was at the point to allow the fly to fall in line with and ahead of the rising trout, which at this point she felt it was. The fly landed gently on the water and floated unencumbered toward its mark, making Sarah's cast a perfect one. Just as her offering was about to sail over the trout's dinner table, a live Dun cut in and settled just ahead of Sarah's fly, and the trout was glad to take that instead. This caused Sarah's now second-in-line fly to bounce unwittingly and unscathed over the rise's risk-free ripples.

"Okay, that was only my first cast," she thought and retrieved her line and began to cast again. And, again she made a perfect cast. With the absence of any live Duns looking to spoil her party, she thought this should be it. When sure enough, her almost X-ray eyes saw the slightest dimple a hair's width away from her floating fly, causing her to pull up quickly on her rod and set the hook. All she hooked was air. The loose, limp fly tumbling back to her said she literally pulled the hook right out of the fish's mouth before it had a chance to gobble it up. Luckily for her, the trout didn't feel a thing and just figured that particular Dun must have been given some sort of super, secret energy potion or something because of the way it just jettisoned itself out from the jaws of destruction.

Sarah, now feeling that this could very well be the last cast of this fast-darkening night, readied her rod in her hand like a conductor readies a baton when she's about to direct an ensemble of musicians, and then initiated the play by casting.

While so doing, in her mind she took stock of all of the night's lessons and experiences. She felt, whether she landed a trout or not, she'd consider tonight's expedition to be a resounding success. After all, she was spending the highest quality of quality time with her Poppy Tom and Hollie, whom she loved so very much and whose love got reflected back to her in the same measure and maybe even a little bit more. She was pleasantly surprised by seeing her mother, father, and brother, who came all the way out here to show their support for her and to show how much they love her, too. She felt there was success in knowing that she had their support and love, not only for tonight's adventure, but for always and forever, and that got reflected back to them from her, as well.

She saw good Ol' Mister Scowl the Owl keeping a watchful eye over that pretty little fawn while she was sleeping when he really didn't have to and told them it was time for them to leave when the mommy deer was calling her baby to wake up and come home. She learned from Poppy Tom how Mother Nature designed those bright spots on all her fawns so they'd stay safe and him telling her to become one with nature's rhythm, a rhythm and calmness she was able to feel for herself, way down deep inside. Seeing the excitement on her grandfather's face and the spring in his step—a memory that would last behind her eyes forever—when he returned to her and Hollie in the Dark Woods with the news that a hatch was in full swing and the trout were loving it, seeing his joyous face gave Sarah tick-a-ly, wick-a-ly giggles throughout her entire body. She knew her grandfather and knew the excitement on his face was there only because he liked seeing her be successful and happy in everything she did. This was all for his granddaughter and having her win. That's what her grand, grandfather, was all about.

She knew tonight was a success for the satisfaction she felt way down deep in her heart and soul from the victories she won by meeting tonight's challenges head on and reaping the rewards. She knew how hard she had to fight to get to the top of that rise, a dress rehearsal for when the day came when she would have to fight, just like her

Grandmother Jennie did, to get to the top of The Mountain of Singing Trees, knowing, once there, the rewards would be worth the effort. And how right she was. The candy corn, sun-painted soldier mountains that filled her eyes with delight left such an impression that they would become the subject of her next painting in art class. Turning and seeing a hatch of Pale Evening Duns, countless ones, looking like glittery snowflakes floating up instead of down and feeling their love, took her breath away. Seeing the surface of the brook alive with rising trout and having a majestic Bald Eagle shower her with water and feeling his mighty wind on her face gave her an experience few human beings would ever have and drove home to her the magnitude, immensity, and intricate balance of Mother Nature's grand wonders, wisdom, wildness, and wow. The hearty laugh session that ensued between her and all her loved ones, and the fun resulting from this encounter, made tonight a success in itself, let alone adding in, her earning herself another nickname.

Success came from finding a single feather left from that majestic eagle, discovering all the power, energy, and inspiration contained within, and learning of the respect and reverence that are awarded to it by an entire culture of people who are truly one in body, mind, and spirit with what that feather symbolizes and to that flying-high-enough-to-touch-the-heavens feather-bearer and torchbearer raptorial bird. Understanding how this culture of people serves as an example of how all cultures should be, act, and feel today toward, not only this amazing creature, but every single solitary animal, plant, drop of water, molecule of air, and each other, with whom we share this incredible and glorious planet. She learned that no living thing, not a single one of Mother Nature's personally designed and delicately painted creations, should ever come close to becoming endangered, let alone extinct.

An outpouring of love can make some things symbolic, such as a feather or a medal, but there isn't enough love in the entire universe to symbolize the raw power and magnificence of everything from a real live screeching eagle to the awe-inspiring beauty of a breeching brook trout and blue whale to the quiet, peaceful radiance of an innocently sleeping white-tailed fawn, if they were gone.

Besides, after all is said and done, she already wet a line and was secure in knowing she'd get another line on the post. But as for Sarah, on this night of discovery and truth, trial and error, victory and defeat, and love and life, it could be said that she had been taught enough, coached enough, victorious enough, and loved enough to become smart enough, wise enough, mature enough and loving enough to realize tonight's expedition has indeed been a resounding success.

So, when her fly, cruising upright and proud like a sailing vessel of old in command of the world's oceans, suddenly vanished right before her eyes, she realized tonight's fishing expedition might not be ending quite yet and that she just might be on the verge of even more success, adventure, and discovery.

Immediately, Sarah was back in business mode but now knew to resist the urge to pull up abruptly on the rod to set the hook until she felt pressure from the other end. Everything in fishing and in life comes down to feel, she realized. That's it, there's pressure, set the hook, and smack, the contest of champions has begun!

Like hitting a switch, the solid, successful setting of the hook kicked off a chain reaction of highly charged energy that pulsated back and forth through the line, making each opposite-end opponent feel like they'd become fused to the opposite ends of a highly electrified rod of lightning. Instantly, telepathically and telegraphically they could feel and understand their opposing views on the rules of engagement, that each side was determined to impose its rules and demands on the other and win an enormous victory in this, what had already become a war of attrition.

It was back to tunnel vision for Sarah's laser-focused eyes and highly attuned mind as they raced back and forth and forth and back between tracking the fast, darting line at the point that it entered the water's surface, circumnavigating the entire pool and to the erratic gyrations of her rod from the extremely strong tugging of the trout, as she struggled to keep the proper bend. So focused and attuned was she that she was totally oblivious to her crowd of faithful fans going wild from their locations right behind home plate to all the way up in the bleachers. To her, it couldn't be any other way. For how this trout was fighting, she needed to stay zeroed in to the duel. No way could she let her guard down. Not for one iota of a second. Sarah felt coming at her, loud and clear, through the taut, dictating fibers of the line, the overwhelming power and immense capabilities being unleashed by her adversary now that she had disrupted his leisurely feast from within his own personal banquet hall. She knew he was big, and she knew he was strong, and who knows, maybe there were two monster brookies hanging out in this pool. Maybe Poppy Tom was wrong for once, and this giant didn't keep this pool all to himself. Maybe he just might be a guy that doesn't play by the rules. Maybe he has another giant brook trout friend that he lets hang out here, and they made one of those pact deals that whenever some girly girl comes around and tries messing with one of them, the other one comes to the rescue and together they show this girly girl who's boss. But even if that were true, the math still didn't equate. One strong giant trout fights hard; two strong giant trout fight twice as hard. Okay, fine. But how come it felt to Sarah like she'd hooked onto a runaway freight train and had all to do to hang on? She could sure use some type of potion, special, secret, or otherwise. Something to help her level the playing field. She was so totally shocked and completely amazed by the sheer force and utter determination of whoever and whatever was hanging on to that little fly that she questioned why, of all times, it had to be tied onto one of those darn barbie hooks!

The battle raged. Each side jockeyed for position, probing the enemy's flanks and looking for a weakness to take the advantage, like in a game of chess being played out by two opposing armies on a grand chess board of water and turf, mountain and blackening sky. Sarah was thankful for the cushion of grasses that her knees had now melded themselves into from the back pressure from all this pulling. But the old, decayed blowdown that provided her the cover to successfully make her cast in the first place had decided to crumble totally into itself from the pressure of Sarah's body leaning against it for leverage and acting as a stop, leaving her feeling exposed, off balance, and vulnerable. She fast came to the realization that, as of right now anyway, her enemy had the advantage and was winning the fight. But she knew, too, that it was way too early in the contest to make any judgments on who the winner would be. She wished her opponent would reveal himself to her, like she, although unintentionally, revealed herself to him. That would tell her so much. His size. If he was wearing a weighted suit of armor. Did he have propellers for a tail and rudders for fins?

She could hear the line cry with agony from the tension being applied to it as this duel of titans continued. The thin, overtaxed line, the feeble hook, the way-too-much bend in her rod, her sore arms, the typical pain in her back whenever she exerted herself like this, then she realized she'd never really exerted herself quite like this before— and a different pain in her back that she hadn't ever felt—had her questioning why. All that opened a second front of sabotage operations assaulting her self-confidence and resolve. Sarah's concern now was in knowing that the line was sending these signals of anxiety directly back to her enemy's intelligence-gathering center and would be used in a psychological warfare capacity against her.

"Battle, enemy, fight, pain, hey, wait a second," Sarah thought. "No! No! This isn't right. What's going on? What am I doing? What am I thinking? What am I feeling? I'm looking at this as a bad fighting thing. I've gotten totally out of nature's calm surrender and rhythms. And that's wrong. I'm not seeing this as a good experience thing, when it is. This is a great experience and accomplishment, too," she realized. "A wonderful, happy memory experience."

Just then, in the behind-her-eyes thoughts, she was taken back to her first time fly-fishing, when the brook trout took her fly and she heard her grandfather's excited voice coaching her, saying, "You feel him tugging? That's the fun part, feeling him tugging is the fun part, Sarah. Just stay calm and play him, play him nice, and that tugging you're feeling is his wildness, Granddaughter."

"Right," Sarah believed. "This is supposed to be play, and play is supposed to be fun. And it is. This is *sooo* much fun. Feeling him tugging is *reeeally* the fun part. I'm supposed to be playing the trout like we're playing a game. Like we're playing a game together and having fun. Just like real good friends are supposed to play. Each one wishing the other one wins the game but not making it too easy for them or letting them know that's what the other one is doing. That's right, I feel this brook trout and all the brook trout are my friends, and I'm theirs. I feel they taught and gave me so much and want me to win, but want me to earn it and appreciate it, too. Doing that will make us become even closer friends."

Sarah, by hearing her grandfather's voice coming from way back behind her eyes and welling up from the deep-down beatings of her good, happy heart and applying her treasuring-each-moment-of-every-treasured-day mantra, and what was now becoming the habit-forming idea of always looking for the good in every experience, caused Sarah to do an immediate self-correction, allowing her to go from a place of agitation, confrontation, and strife to a happy, calm-surrendering place of mutual admiration, respect, and fun. It's a place she'd worked and strived for, for so long, just as she, her Poppy Tom, and Hollie; her mother, father, and brother; all her smiling-people friends; and all of her Mother Nature friends wished her to have and feel.

So, too, the out-of-sync, static-y, battle-the-enemy-in-a-fight-to-the-finish-line vibrations that were stinging these rivals and causing them to accelerate hostilities got replaced by a truce of silky smooth strands of happy, magic touches of love vibrations. Each transformed the tug-of-war, weapon-of-war line to what it was always meant to be and what Poppy Tom knew it to be all along, that being an olive branch line of peace, goodwill, and harmony that reaches out and hugs each player from totally different worlds in a warm embrace of yellow peace rose–scented, cuddling bonds of brotherhood and sisterhood. These are the very same cuddling bonds that exist between all living things and have been so venerated by native cultures over millennia of sunsets and sunrises, droughts and floods, butterfly effects, and eagle screeches.

The benefits of this joyous role reversal were immediately felt by both now willing and happy participants. For the tugging line, the bending rod, and the barbless hook became merely instruments of necessity that bonded the players together. Just like the way a race saddle bonds a jockey to the back of her championship thoroughbred, melding rider and horse into one elegant expression of positive energetic eloquence.

The release of the pressure-cooker mind games Sarah was unnecessarily playing allowed her the luxury to actually turn her head away from the darting line for a moment to glance back up and check on the happenings and whereabouts of her gallery of glad gawkers. To her surprise, they were all now standing together, except for Hollie, who was sitting and wagging her tail so quickly that it appeared it might fly off, not an arm's length behind her. Sarah was so engrossed in this momentous occasion that she didn't even realize they were all right there. Sarah's smile reached the outer limits of its capacity, and the glow on her face lit up the dusk when she saw the glorious smiles and even a few happy tears glistening back down at her.

So, for Sarah, at this very second, with the barbless hook doing its job, the fun wildness tugging coming from her allied brook trout friend, having the bend in the rod just right, and being surrounded by her most loved and loving family, she thought life couldn't get any better...until...

She detected the slightest change in the good vibes coming through the line. They were still good vibes, but because of Sarah's highly developed sense for things, she felt something different about them. To her, it was as if she could feel the sound of a drumroll, like the feeling that something big was about to happen. Then, just as her eyes zoomed back to refocus on the darting line, she saw to her amazement, the trout breeching the surface of the water in a spectacular show of its magnificence and agility. As if on cue, Sarah and everyone else, including Hollie, let out a loud, astonished, "WOW!" As well they should, or...as WOW, they should.

For even in the fading light, even in that split second they witnessed the trout breeching, its incredible beauty and majesty were revealed. JJ and Justin looked at Poppy Tom, Hollie, and Cecilia with a stare of awe and amazement on their faces as they stared back at them with a see-we-told-you-guys-so look on their faces. It was only Sarah, whose stare remained transfixed, almost hypnotized, on the breeching trout, and only she knew why. For in that split second, the trout's eye made contact with Sarah's and peered deeply into her wide open, shining-like-bright-spots-in-the-gathering-dusk eyes and into her wide open, glowing-like-a-welcoming-beacon-of-love soul.

Also in that split second, messages of friendship, familiarity, and camaraderie were exchanged between the two, an exchange with its passage of time that went totally undetected by Sarah's audience.

The brook trout hit the send button with words like, "Hi, Sarah, remember me? I'm the very same brook trout that took your fly when you came and visited here your very first time fly-fishing. We were both a lot younger then. I was happy to hear from our friend Ol' Mister Scowl the Owl's evening report that you were headed my way. So, I was looking forward to seeing you again. I'm so happy to see that the gift I gave you on our first play date was received and has helped you."

Sarah shockingly replied, "You're the same...you knew I was coming? I mean, oh...uh...hi there. But how did Scowl...? Uh, thank you for saying you were looking forward to seeing me again. Oh, yes, I remember you. Of course, I do, and your gift. Your beautiful gift has helped me so much. It's helped me and a whole bunch of my friends, too. Look, I'm not using a chair anymore. See, I can walk now. That's how much your beautiful gift has helped me to be strong and to fight to free myself of my burdens. It's a special gift that you gave me and one that I love and will treasure always. Thank you very much. Oh, this is so...wonderful! I'm so happy and surprised to see you...and to be talking? But...but how can this be? I mean, we're talking. How can we be talking?"

"Oh, Sarah," the brook trout answered, "I do see how well you can walk. And it's so very pleasing to see, my dear girl. You're thanking me for my gift to you, Sarah, but you don't need to be thanking me. I was only returning the favor for the gift you gave me."

"You were only returning the favor, for the gift I gave you? What gift did I give you?"

"You gave me the amazing gift of your love, Sarah. Don't you know?" asked the brook trout.

"My love?" Sarah asked. "I know I love you...Very much I do. But what gift of love? I don't remember a gift."

"Oh, Sarah, you show your love for me in so many ways, and each time you do you give me a gift, a very precious gift," the brook trout began, "like when you restored the bank of my brook. Remember, so many years back? That was your first time ever seeing my brook, Sarah. Your wonderful grandfather had explained to you how fishing is a privilege and making repairs to the brook would earn you the right to enter into my home. Sarah, you went right to work. You actually came out of your chair and got down on your hands and knees and worked so hard, right alongside your wonderful Poppy Tom and Hollie to make those repairs. That was a very generous show of your love, Sarah, and therefore, a very generous gift. If you don't remember how hard you worked, just look at your picture."

"My picture...what pic...? You mean the picture my Poppy Tom took of me and Hollie after he taught me how to cast? The one hanging in my room?"

Yup, that picture," answered the brook trout.

"But we repaired the brook the afternoon before that picture was taken," Sarah stated. "So, I don't understand what the...what does the picture show...?"

"Well, you might not remember, but you wore the same jeans fly-fishing that you wore repairing my brook the afternoon before. Look at the knees on those jeans," the brook trout directed. "Look at your knees in that picture, and you'll see how muddy they were from your kneeling. I can't imagine kneeling like that was very comfortable or easy for you, Sarah. But yet, you did it."

"My Poppy Tom told me we needed to fix the brook so the water would stay nice and clean and cold, so all you pretty brook trout can stay happy and healthy. So, I did it. I didn't mind. I always want you and all your pretty brook trout friends and your pretty home to stay happy and healthy all the time and forever."

"I know that you feel that way, Sarah, and so do all of my brook trout friends, along with all the many amazing creatures that share our beautiful home. We all thank you for willingly working so hard to keep our home such a beautiful, happy, and healthy place. We know how much you love it here, Sarah. And how much you love all of Mother Nature's creations. We know it, but even more important, we can feel it. Way down deep in our hearts and souls we can feel your love-light, sweet girl. So, we all thank you from the bottom of those same hearts and souls that are happy and healthy because of you.

"You're very special to us, Sarah. So, you see, my gift to you was only returning the wonderful gift that you gave and continue to give to all of us. My wish is that the gift I gave you back then continues giving and serving you well, precious friend."

"Oh, you're welcome and tell all your brook trout friends and wonderful creature friends that they're welcome, too. And because I keep your precious gift right behind my eyes and down deep in my heart, it will always be there to help and guide me for all my *whooole* life."

"I certainly will pass on your message, young lady of our planet's people population. However, the gift of your love and desire to help us didn't stop with you restoring my brook. We were all well aware of your concern for our health and well-being when your Poppy Tom informed you that we were in distress due to a drought one year and flooding the next. We know how you enjoy giving Lightning and Thunder and their foal, Raindrop, sweet treats, and how well you built all those healthy and beautiful birdhouses that so many pretty birds joyfully raise their young in. The list of you showing the gift of your love to all of Mother Nature's creations goes on and on, Sarah. We feel your love-light shining on all of us just the way we felt the glorious love-light shining on us from your beautiful Grandmother Jennie."

"My Grandma Jennie, you knew my Grandma Jennie?"

"I knew of her, Sarah, my dear. Your grandmother's a famous hero to us all," the brook trout stated. "If it wasn't for her fighting like she did to protect our home, in spite of her burdens, all you see here would have been gone, including me. Oh yes, your grandmother is a famous hero to us, just as big a hero to us as your Poppy Tom, your mother,

Mr. Nate, and all his ancestors, including Dancing Cloud and her three sisters, even all the wonderful organic farmers that so lovingly respect our environment and the Riveras, too."

"Oh my, you know all those great people?" Sarah questioned.

"Of course, I do, Sarah. You're on your way to becoming just as famous a hero to us as all of those great and glorious people. We just hope you can feel our love-light being reflected back to you in the same measure that you shine your love-light on us."

"Oh yes, I can, my brook trout buddy! I can feel the love coming from way down deep inside of all your hearts and souls and coming into me and going all the way down deep into my heart and soul and that makes me feel all tick-a-ly with happy goose bumps. Just like I felt before when I saw all those beautiful Duns hatching. Thank you, brook trout friend for all your love, and please thank all of your Mother Nature creation friends for all their love, too. I'm happy to know we have all the same great heroes, my great friend who lives in the beautiful bubbly brook."

"On my own behalf and on behalf of all my friends, we say, you're welcome," the brook trout confirmed. And I'm happy we have the same great heroes, too.

"Sarah, you asked me before, how can this be? How can we talk? How can we connect like this when we're so very different in so many ways? And on the surface, that's true. I have fins and you have feet. I live surrounded by water, and you live surrounded by air. But in reality, my sister, we're the same. That's because we have one thing in common. And it's that one thing that connects and unites us and all living things together forever. Do you know what that one thing is and how it acts as a bond and connection between us? I truly believe you do know, my sweet young lady, and I would be very interested in having you tell me."

From her kneeling and soon-to-become worshipping position, Sarah thought long and hard about the answer to what was perhaps the most profound question she'd ever been asked before. Her mind flooded with thoughts and ideas of things she thought just might be right. She resisted the urge to blurt them out, however. That would be like setting the hook too soon and only hooking air. As a result of tonight's trials and tribulations and successes and achievements, Sarah became wise enough to know to apply the same poise and composure that allowed her to align with the all-powerful and all-encompassing calm surrender and rhythm of the night before taking on any worthy endeavor of which this is one. So, to implement this approach, Sarah took a few calming breathes, closed her eyes, and allowed her mind to clear itself of what she was thinking, so she could allow her mind to search for the all-important what it was she was feeling. She knew the true answer wouldn't come from the thoughts within her beautiful, caring mind but from deep down inside her loving, compassionate heart. So, she, with assuredness and dash, steered a course to that now familiar happy-beatings place thinking she'd find the answer waiting for her neatly stacked on a shelf in a cupboard clearly marked in big bold letters, "ANSWERS TO PROFOUND QUESTIONS FOUND HERE."

But not so fast. She didn't know it yet, but as wonderful and amazing and loving and compassionate as Sarah's heart and every single one of its precious beatings were, the answer to this most profound question would not be found there. But she was close. She opened the cupboard door to snatch up the prize only to find that the cupboard was bare. She stood dumbfounded and dismayed, seeing the sure bet of relying on her one hundred percent always-dependable-for-everything-and-anything heart, alas…was failing to pay off and had left her, in this case, high and dry, momentarily. She did what she now knew to do when faced with a setback, and that was to forge, or as she knew it to be, forage ahead undaunted. So, with the swiftness, dexterity, and finesse of a champion race car driver, she shifted into high gear, put the pedal to the metal, and steered a course into, what was for her, an uncharted speedway but one that had, interestingly enough, a surprisingly familiar feel. She sped through the finish line past the waving checkered flag and pulled up to the grandstand to see a glimmering door of gold that beckoned her with a song of peace and joy to open and enter into to receive her Sprint

Cup Trophy. Sarah, of course, strode confidently through its golden façade to find a deep, shining, serene chasm of a place and one that immediately filled her entire being with the same familiar peace and calmness on the inside that she felt surrounding her on the outside and inside by the calm surrender of the night. She realized this beautiful, immense yet close, warm, and inviting place harbored not only the answer to this profound question but answers to questions that have been asked about by generations and even answers to questions that were never asked before.

BING! BING, BING!!! Sarah chose the right curtain, and from behind its golden tapestry, the profound answer to this profound question was revealed. Sarah, with undaunted passion and confidence, dared to go beyond a familiar place, beyond the comfort zone of her happily beating heart and discovered a bright, shiny place the size of the entire universe right within her very soul. It was a place oozing with love and light and euphoric abandon, not only for her but for all living things. It was the place where happiness and harmony were manufactured, a wonderful and amazing place that had been there always and would always be there. It existed over the river, just beyond the beatings of our hearts, and through the woods to be found right down deep in our heart of hearts. It was the place where all the countless and absolutely phenomenal heartbeats that had ever beat originated from in the first place, and where all the countless heartbeats that still have yet to beat were eagerly awaiting their turn.

Sarah, basking in the glow reflecting off yet another shimmering trophy for winning another race and making another discovery, especially one so profound, answered so very proudly and confidently to her brook trout friend when she said, "Yes, I know what that one thing is and how it acts as a connection between us!"

"Tell me, my sweet sister," the brook trout said with anticipation and admiration.

"Yes, we are so very different you and me," she began, "but we do have one thing in common. And you're right, it's this one thing that connects and unites us and all things together forever. And that one thing is...another drumroll please...we all come from the same exact place. It's that quiet, mystery place that seems so way far away but is really close by, just behind our eyes and right beyond the beatings of our hearts.

"It's that big, wide open, happy place where the rose gets its beauty and pretty smell and keeps it smelling pretty even after it's cut from the vine, and a smell that can come to somebody even when they're asleep. It's the place that whispers to the caterpillar that it's time she turns into a butterfly and then whispers to the butterfly what pretty colors she's going to be painted with. It's where red-tailed hawk feathers get all their glowy and magic powers, and it's the place that gives a brook trout like you or a kid like me and even a grown-up like our hero, Grandma Jennie, the will to fight to free ourselves of our burdens and the will to fight with kind, gentle, persuasion to protect things we know are good. Then, it gives us the power and strength we need to win that fight. It's where lightning gets its crack and thunder gets its boom. It's how raindrops make things green and rainbows make things sing. It's the place where happy smiles come from and chase away tears. Discovery cures that help people, and Mother Nature's creations fly out from this place and get caught in smiling people's minds, and then fly out from there and make more smiles. But the biggest, most important thing of all is, it's the very place that all the good and never the bad lives and love floats eternal on cottony clouds of white, deep within a pretty blueberry sky over everyone and everything, and wraps around their hearts and souls like a warm, soft, cuddly blanket. It's that always-there, never-having-to-sleep, or need-any-potions-to-make-it-strong love that comes from this wonderful place and jumps into our beating, happy hearts. Love, that's the most important thing that connects and unites us forever, brookie buddy."

"Correct, my fine, young human being friend," the brook trout stated enthusiastically! "You couldn't have answered my question any better. I'm not surprised. It's love, pure and simple. It comes from, as you say, that mystery place that's really right behind our eyes and just beyond the beatings of our hearts and pours forth in such abundance that no one thing should ever be made to feel that there isn't enough of this love to go around. It's the place where we all, in spirit, lived together as one in happiness and harmony. Until that moment when, with the unbridled power and might of a million lightning bolts and at the same time, with the gentleness of a butterfly kiss or the softness of a baby's breath, it created me to become a pretty brook trout and you to become a pretty young girl. And now we meet again in this pretty place where there's absolutely no reason for us not to continue to live as one in happiness and harmony, just like we're doing now, a shining example to all, until the day when we're summoned to return back to that amazing mystery place to live together as one in spirit, my sweet soulmate sister.

"You know, Sarah, I would say we had a very good talk and as the expression goes, covered a lot of ground. Well, ground in your case, water in mine. We had a very fun time playing our game together and bonding like we did. This will be a night I know I'll treasure forever. All this good talk and fun have really tired me out. What do you say we think about finishing up playing our game? We can always meet again and play our fun game and have another good happy chat."

"Oh, brookie friend, I love love. I'm so happy you helped me discover the place where love is made and to know that it comes from right inside our heart of hearts. It makes me feel so happy, and it makes you and me be friends together forever and to love each other so much. You know, I treasure tonight, too, and I'm getting kinda tired myself. So, we can stop playing now if you want to, but I would sure look forward to playing our fun game again and chatting some more, real soon."

"Sounds good, my special person friend," said the brook trout. "So, okay, here's what I'll do. I'll ease up on my tugging and swim in close to you at the edge of the brook. That will tell your wonderful grandfather that our playing is winding down and to come and assist you with things, something I know he's been looking forward to doing for a long time. I'm very eager to show off my pretty looks to everyone."

"Oh, we saw how pretty you are already, brook trout," Sarah said.

"When you jumped out of the water, we saw how beautiful Mother Nature made you."

"Ah, that was nothing," the brook trout corrected. "Wait until your Poppy Tom gives you a close-up view. Then, you'll really see how talented an artist Mother Nature is."

"Oh, I can't wait," Sarah said excitedly.

Just as the brook trout said, he eased up on his tugging, allowing Sarah to reel in the slackening line until the trout nestled itself facing upstream in a placid little cove at the edge of the brook directly in front of Sarah's playing position.

Poppy Tom's excited voice and his repeated jumping up and down along with the hoots and hollers, yelps and barks, and claps and hugs from the rest of the gallery, hailed Sarah's accomplishment and awakened her from the dreamlike, reflective place she just shared with the brook trout to the celebratory reality of the moment.

Poppy Tom eventually composed himself to a point, but while still breathing heavily and full of excitement, said to Sarah, "Congratulations Dancing Eagle! You did it! You played him to a standstill! Look, look at the size of him! He's a beauty! A real beauty! I was getting worried you were running out of time and space. But no. You did it! And how!"

At the same time, Cecilia hugged her daughter affectionately and told her, too, she did an amazing job and she was so very happy and proud of her. As did Justin, who was thoroughly enjoying this entire night's experience and thrilled to see his daughter having so much fun, while Hollie devotedly rubbed her head along Sarah's back, like the good caregiver she was, helping to relieve the pain she intuitively knew Sarah was feeling there.

And JJ said to his sister, "Nice goin', Sarah, but I could do that too, you know."

"Okay, Sarah, time to get to the business of viewing your trout and then releasing him unharmed back to his home," Poppy Tom directed.

"I've been looking forward to this moment for a long time. Something tells me you have, too."

"Oh, yes, Poppy, I sure have. I and my brook trout friend know... uh...I mean, I know you have been, too, Poppy."

"Sarah, or is it Dancing Eagle? I think I just might know how that nickname came about," said Cecilia as she looked shrewdly at her daughter and father. "You've been kneeling for a long time. We need to get you to sit. Come on, let's get you better situated for this wonderful event, one we're all looking forward to witnessing."

"I'm okay, Mommy," Sarah said.

Then Justin interjected and said, "Yes, Sarah, come on now, let's get you sitting. I'll help you, sweetheart."

"I'll help, too, I guess," said JJ.

Poppy Tom allowed a few seconds for Justin and JJ to help Sarah get comfortable sitting on the tuft of grass that served her so well. Then with everyone ready for the ceremonious brook trout viewing and releasing, Poppy Tom slowly and quietly took the few steps to the edge of the brook, where he reverently knelt down before the trout and began his proper-way-to-release-a-trout instruction.

"Sarah, you're making this very easy for me. You have him in the perfect spot facing upstream. This enables the current of the brook to flow through his gills, allowing him to breathe and regain his strength. Just great. So, the very first thing I do before touching the trout is wet my hands. You don't ever want to touch a fish with dry hands. They have a special layer on their scales that protect them from infection. If we go and handle them roughly and with dry hands, we could remove that protective layer and they might get sick, and we wouldn't want that."

"No, we wouldn't," Sarah confirmed.

Then she whispered to JJ saying, "JJ, Mother Nature gives the trout that protective layer and a whole bunch of good things."

JJ looked at his sister in wide-eyed wonderment and then all around, looking for this Mother Nature lady Sarah referred to.

"Now, I'm going to follow the line down to the trout's mouth with my wet right hand and, at the same time, gently cradle the fish in my left hand while still keeping him under the water. Understand, if we wanted to release him right away, I would simply remove the hook and allow him to swim away, never even taking him out of the water. But because we want to view him up close, once I get to the end of the line, I smoothly raise the trout out of the water like this and...Oh, my goodness, he's a big one," Poppy Tom said with an exaggerated strain in his voice and with a few chuckles. "I think you caught the granddaddy of granddaddies here, Sarah. Then while holding him gently, see, with no squeezing or anything, I remove the hook just like this. Ah, see, see how easily the barbless hook pulls out. Perfect."

With the trout now free from the hook and cradled in Poppy Tom's tender hands, he turned to Sarah and, while still kneeling, leaned forward and extended his arms out over the collapsed blowdown, and presented Sarah with a close-up view of her hard-earned prize.

Looks of awe, silent approving head nods and gestures of complete admiration for this beautiful sight signaled how thoroughly captivating Sarah and all her fellow viewers were by seeing this amazing creature up close. Even Cecilia, who had witnessed this before, knew she could never get enough of such a beautiful image.

Cecilia called out, "Let me get a quick picture of the successful fisher girl and her trusty teachers with that beautiful brookie. Come on, Hollie, swing around and get in the shot." Hollie proudly pranced around and wound in between Sarah and Poppy Tom and acted as the background for the trout that Cecilia centered into the photo. Then said, "Perfect, that's almost a carbon copy of the picture of me with my first trout.

"Remember, Daddy? Mommy took that picture of us a long time ago."

"I do, Ce," Poppy Tom said, as he quickly became choked up. "You didn't find...your picture...did you?"

"I sure did, Dad, just tonight, just before we headed out. I found it right where Mommy kept all...Uh, I'm going to get them both enlarged and keep a set at home and give you a set too, Dad."

"Oh, how wonderful," Poppy Tom said emotionally. "Please do. I'd love it."

Then he said in a hushed but excited voice to Sarah, "Look

sweetheart, see how pretty he is?"

"Oh my, Poppy, he is, he's really beautiful. He looked beautiful when he jumped before, but he's even more beautiful now."

"Hey, listen Dancing Eagle," Poppy Tom said, "you keep calling this trout a he and guess what, you're right, it is a he! Do you see how his lower jaw turns up at the end? That's called a hooked jaw. That's a trait of a male trout. Only the males have that hooked jaw. The female's lower jaw is straight. Now, look what else. See his fins, see how the leading edges of those fins have white stripes, then black stripes above them and then all a deep red up from there? These three incredible colors on his fins, white, black, and red are characteristic of the brook trout species. That same deep red on his upper fins continues up and around his belly and becomes an even more vibrant red during the fall spawning season. That's when they...umm...when the mommies lay their eggs.

"Now Sarah, what I'm really eager for you to see are the details of his spots. Look very closely at all his beautiful spots. Especially those distinctive, well you're the artist here, but I'd say vermillion red spots with pretty azure blue halos around them sprinkled all over his body. Can you believe how intricate they are?"

"Oh, Poppy, I see them. They're amazing!"

"To me, guys," Poppy Tom said contemplatively, "I feel it's like Mother Nature went above and beyond in her design of the brook trout by sprinkling in those beautiful, intricately colored spots. I mean, the brook trout would be beautiful without them, but she wanted to make the brook trout extra special and incredibly beautiful. And, she did. It's like, I might have told you, Sarah, I can imagine Mother Nature sitting at her easel with a fine paint brush in her hand and a palette of amazing colors delicately painting those beautiful vermillion red spots with the azure blue halos on her special creation that is the brook trout. Look how all these bright spots shine. Even in low light, see how all these spots shine so brightly, just like little neon lights."

"I can, Poppsey, I sure can. Mother Nature is the best artist ever."

Justin and JJ added in their approvals, while JJ continued looking around for this mystery lady with the paint brush he kept hearing about.

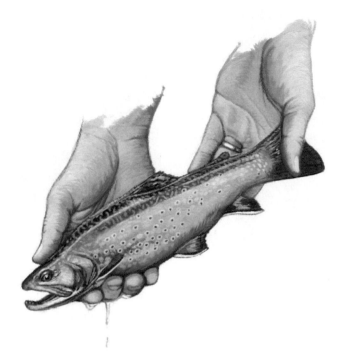

"Now, really quickly, I want to show you guys one more amazing thing about the brook trout before we place him back. Look closely at the top of his back. See how the background color up there is this deep, dark green color, and then there are all those squiggly shaped lines in a lighter, brighter, green color intermixed throughout? There's a name that describes those type of shaped lines. They're called uh, veric... vermicu...vermiculations! Anyway, that dark green background with all those squiggly light green lines combine to make a camouflage design on the trout's back. See what I mean? It's like the camouflage look on the army T-shirts Mrs. Gracie and Paula Jean wear. Can you see that?"

Just then, JJ interrupted and asked excitedly, "Jubee Jean, when can we go see Jubee...?"

Justin said, "Not now JJ," as all went back to answering Poppy Tom's question by nodding their heads in agreement.

Sarah said, "Yes, Poppy. That's Mother Nature giving her brook trout something that protects them. You know, like the bright spots on the fawn we saw before."

"You saw a fawn before?" Cecilia asked, as Poppy Tom interrupted her.

"Right, Sarah, right, I get that. Mother Nature puts this design of camouflaging on the backs of the brook trout to protect them. The eagle we saw before was able to take that trout because he came up out of the water and exposed himself. That's why the big guys and girls get to be big. They know to barely break the surface when feeding. So, as long as the trout stays pretty much below the surface, he doesn't have to be afraid because of how well he blends into the background of the bottom of the brook. It's a perfect camouflage, again, a testament to Mother Nature's design." Poppy Tom turned back toward the brook and said, "But here's the thing that gets me. Here's what I just don't understand. The brook trout isn't capable of seeing its own back. Just like we can't see ours. So, it's not capable of seeing the camouflaging. Yet, he knows somehow, someway, that the camouflaging is there and that he's safe. It's a complete mystery to me as to how he knows that."

Without skipping a beat, Sarah stated, "Oh, I know how he knows, Pops."

Poppy Tom was leaning and just about to release Sarah's trout but stopped short when he heard Sarah's statement and turned back around to her as did everyone else, and asked, somewhat surprised and a little mystified, "You know how he knows, Sarah?"

"Yup, I sure do," Sarah answered with all the confidence in the world.

Poppy Tom said with a pronounced, questioning look on his face, "Wait a second, let me release your trout here and then you can enlighten me, uh, us. Now see, I just get him close to the water, and yup, there he goes!"

And just before the trout's head entered the water, his eye connected back with Sarah's and gave her an acknowledging wink and a saluting smile. Then, unharmed and joyfully he dove back into the clean, cold, dissolved oxygen-rich waters of his home, thanks to a couple of his favorite heroes, where he'd spend the night safe and content below the undercut bank of his exclusive pool, nestled between the tangled roots of an ancient hemlock, to watch, just like his connected-to-the-light-

and-life friend, Sarah, tonight's entertaining and contemplative shower of meteors.

Okay, maybe if Sarah kept this stuff up, its cumulative effect just might be enough to get the trees to sing for her. At the very least, this gave Mother Nature reason to keep them well-tuned.

"Well, gang," Poppy Tom said with a strain in his voice as he struggled to stand from his kneeling position. "Oh, yeah, the old knees aren't what they used to be. Ohh, wow, phew." Then after a pause to stretch and rub his legs a bit, he said, "That was one fantastic adventure. Sarah, I mean, Dancing Eagle, you really earned your line tonight!"

Everyone clapped in praise of Sarah's efforts and accomplishments, as Poppy Tom continued, "Let's regroup now and prepare for tonight's next adventure. The fast-approaching darkness is letting us know we're a little behind schedule. No worries though. I have our headlamps right here in my..."

Cecilia interrupted and said, "Oh, Dad, you know what? I happen to have them in my backpack."

"You do, Cecilia? How did they get...? Did you take them out of my backpack?"

"Oh, uh...yes, yes I did, exactly right, Dad. I took them out of your backpack and put them in mine. I just felt that you had enough to carry. I hope you don't mind."

"Oh, no. But you didn't have to...," Poppy Tom began. "Hey, as long as someone has them. Well, let's get them distributed then. The Dark Woods is really going to be living up to its reputation of being dark as we make our way through there tonight. That's for sure. Oh, hey, did I put...I hope I put the batteries in...?"

"Yup, yup, I, uh...you had the batteries in them, Dad. No worries."

"Oh, thank goodness," said Poppy Tom. "For a second there, I thought maybe I forgot. Hey, they wouldn't have been much good to us without the batteries," he said with a nervous laugh. "Okay, so go ahead and hand them out, Ce. While you're doing that, I'd like to hear from my astute granddaughter how the brook trout knows he has that camouflaging on his back."

"Oh, okay, Poppy, but it's a long story," Sarah confided. "But don't worry, he knows. Everything knows everything it needs to know, Pops. Everything just has to be real quiet and listen and do what it hears and feels it's guided to do from way down deep inside, just like the caterpillar, Poppy. If the caterpillar wasn't quiet and didn't listen and do stuff like that, there wouldn't ever be any butterflies. Yup, Pops, everything knows everything and just has to do the right and good thing, and everything will always turn out right and good. It's kinda like my beautiful poem, Poppy. It really comes down to love. Love makes all this good stuff happen and has all the answers. You know everything, too, Pops. You just didn't remem…you just had to be reminded, that's all. I didn't know I knew this until my brook trout friend, uh…Oh, well, that's my answer to your question, Poppsey. Grandma Jennie knows even more about this kind of stuff. You can ask her later when we're by her wall, if you want."

The hushed, still reaction from Poppy Tom and the rest of his family as they absorbed and pondered the deeply profound statement just uttered by his granddaughter, aligned and joined as one with the hushed, still, deepening, darkening night, leaving Poppy Tom's only means of reply to be a drooping of the edges of his mouth, a slight head nod, and the words, "Tonight the student became the teacher and the teacher became the student."

With that, this corps of newly enlightened discoverers, led by the keen, light sensitive eyes of their faithful guide, Hollie, ventured forth toward the total darkness of the Dark Woods. Each one is a part of this merry band, yet each one is alone in thought with only the beams of light from headlamps piercing the shadows of their minds as they seek answers to a flurry of new questions spawned by Sarah's answer.

And as they left Poppy Tom's secret fishing spot just as they had found it and to the gently streaking, luminescent fireflies, the quick, silent aerobatic bats, and to the cheerful chorus of a choir of nocturnal life forms led by the dictating tempo of Spring Peepers, the first performers in an ensemble cast of shooting stars danced across the eastern sky. Each star carried on its fiery tail even more questions to ponder by their soon-to-be-watching audience.

So, just as an undaunted discoverer takes another grueling, slippery step higher up the rise, to her delight, she is rewarded with the answer she seeks, but soon realizes that from this new, shining-place vantage point, even more questions emerge.

She knows, it's only by making another grueling, slippery step higher will she be rewarded with another answer. It's in that all-knowing, all-powerful, all-loving voice, that, if this discoverer allows herself to be quiet enough to hear and feel, she will be given the faith and fortitude to take that one more grueling, slippery step higher, burdens and all, to be justly rewarded. Keep taking that one step higher, no matter how grueling or slippery. Keep discovering, and keep seeking answers, because that gives a reason for our lungs to take another breath and our heart to make another beat. And it's somewhere in that split second, yet infinite time and space between that next breath and that next heartbeat that love kicks in and takes over and guarantees to that undaunted seeker of the light and the life and the way and the truth, that the effort to discover will forever be rewarded.

For love, like a massive, never-needing-batteries headlamp, illuminates the dark and shines the full spectrum of the light of enlightenment and morality right down to the very depths of our soul, giving us the answer! Then suddenly, from the depths of the deep, Dark Woods, come the sounds, hoot...hoot, hoot, hoot...hoot!

CHAPTER 23

Cecilia was the first to approach, congratulate, and thank Hollie, who sat wiggling with excitement with her back to Grandma Jennie's wall, for so safely and skillfully guiding them through the dark to their desired destination. And as the balance of this fun-loving troupe arrived, they each took a turn doing the same, causing their individual beams of light to converge as one around them and Holly, their trustworthy and richly cherished, four-legged member of the family.

This same convergence of light illuminated this buoyant band's secluded celebration of accomplishment and camaraderie, and softly washed upon Grandma Jennie's steadfast limestone wall and off the trunks of the trees of the primordial forest that this wall had so diligently and successfully protected for all these years. It created in the vast darkness for this eager audience, a naturally structured amphitheater complete with orchestra seating for the pleasure of viewing the highly anticipated meteor shower extravaganza.

And as was always the case, Poppy Tom, with eagerness, levity, and insight, directed the group on what to do and where to go next, as he said, "Okay gang, pick a stump and make yourselves comfortable. I'm seeing that the show has already begun! Shut off your headlamps and allow your eyes to adjust to the dark. Look up and east and prepare to be amazed!"

On that directive, Cecilia, Justin, and JJ scrambled for a stump in the same way a group of participants scrambled for a seat in a highly competitive game of musical chairs. In contrast, Sarah, left the pack and shuffled slowly to a stump at the leading edge of the field, furthest away from Grandma Jennie's wall, looking up the entire time. Poppy Tom settled on a stump right up against the wall itself, allowing him the ability to use the wall as a backrest. Hollie curled herself between his feet and laid down.

No sooner did Justin settle himself on his stump when he asked, true to form, "What do we have to snack on?"

"Already?" asked Cecilia. "We just sat down. Popcorn, I brought us bags of popcorn."

"Here, JJ, hand out these bags please. Your father is getting restless already."

"Okay, Mommy."

"Popcorn, no candy?" Justin questioned.

"Popcorn! You still have strawberry shortcake to burn off, remember?" Cecilia replied sternly.

"Yes, but we walked all the way through the Dark Woods and all along the brook and back," he quickly responded.

"Popcorn! Take it or leave it!"

"Okay, popcorn sounds good to me," Justin agreed because he felt he had to. All chuckled at the expense of Justin's and Cecilia's comical exchange.

When JJ worked his way back to Poppy Tom to give him his bag of popcorn, he asked, "Poppy, can I sit next to you, please?"

"Sure lad," Poppy Tom answered happily as he quickly slid over to give JJ room to sit down.

Hearing this, Cecilia glanced behind her through the dark and smiled, feeling her son's loving desire to sit by his grandfather and seeing her father's thrilled, spontaneous reaction. This scene caused Cecilia to close her eyes tightly so as to implant this low-light image in the file of her mind along with tonight's other joyous memories.

JJ excitedly sat next to his grandfather and proceeded to tuck his feet under Hollie's heat-generating body to warm up his toes from the chill of the night that was fast surrounding him and the rest of his family. Poppy Tom helped JJ's cause by zipping up his jacket, and then wrapped his warm, loving arm around his grandson.

This made JJ feel cozy, safe, and content and gave him the inspiration to look up into his grandfather's kind, loving face and ask him a few important questions. "Poppy, when can I go? When will you take me fry-fishing, too?"

"Ho, ho, ho," Poppy Tom chuckled, like Santa being tickled on his roly-poly belly, and then very sincerely answered JJ's understandable question, by first asking, "So help remind your ol' grandpop. How old is my big, number one grandson now anyway?"

JJ answered silently by flashing his hand and proudly displaying five stout fingers.

"My goodness, five already?" Poppy Tom asked in an exaggerated, disbelieving, and surprised voice.

"Yup, Poppy," JJ answered haughtily.

"Well then, that means in just two short years I'll be taking my terrific grandson fly-fishing. Not *fry-fishing*, JJ. Fly with an ell. You'll be seven by then. That's the magic number, you know!"

"That long, Poppy?"

"Oh, believe you me, those two years will zip by. I know you might not think so, but don't worry, we'll be heading out to go *FLY*-fishing before you know it."

"I suppose," JJ agreed, reluctantly. "Do you think, I mean, Poppy, when you take me, do you think I'll be just as good as Sarah? Maybe even better, maybe?"

"You'll be just as good. Hey, don't forget who'll be teaching you there, buddy of mine. But really, Grandson, you should never worry about being better than someone else. All you need to strive for is being the best *you* can be at something *you* enjoy doing."

"Just like hammering, right, Poppy? I really love to hammer things, and I'm the best hammer guy I can be."

"You're so right! Great example!"

"Sure," JJ said, "hammering, painting signs...I'm the best I can be at all those things I really love to do. Poppy Tom, when can you teach me how to curve things?"

"Curve things, curve things…?" Poppy Tom questioned and contemplated. Then he understood and said, "Oh, you mean carve things. You want me to teach you how to carve things, Grandson?"

"Yes, Poppy. Can you teach me how? Just as good as you, Poppy. We can go in Poppy's Shoppy and you can teach me. Just me and you."

"Gee, well, hmmm, I don't know. I really haven't thought of that…," Poppy Tom pondered. "We'd have to take care. Knives and chisels are sharp tools. But you know what, I can. We'll wear our gloves and eye protection. Yup, why not, JJ? I have a nice soft piece of Basswood we can use. We'll carve, uh…I'll teach you how to carve a flute. That was the first thing my father taught me how to carve," as Poppy Tom took a moment to calm his emotions. "Just us guys. You've got yourself a deal, my good man. How about we do a pinky swear to seal the deal?"

"Let's shake hands instead, Poppy," JJ said in a voice deeper than normal to make himself sound older. "That's the way big guys like us do it!"

"Handshake it is," Poppy Tom excitedly agreed, as he looked down at his grandson in admiration and pride and realized that JJ was no longer a toddler and that time was truly marching on. He added, "Here lad, let me open up that bag of popcorn for you."

Just then, Cecilia and Justin let out a loud, simultaneous gasp and said, "Look, here they come!" as they pointed up to the night sky.

"Oh yeah, right on cue," Poppy Tom announced as he and JJ looked up. "There were a few earlier. I don't know if you happened to spot them. But now they'll be coming more regularly, and we have a ringside seat. Look how bright the stars are shining. Bright spots in the sky. And those shooting stars. Perfect night for viewing this, guys. If anybody has any wishes to make, these are the stars you'll want to make those wishes upon."

"I have a wish, Poppy," JJ said excitedly. "I wish upon that star right there, to go visit Jubee Jean! I want to…"

"Oh, no JJ," replied his mom. "You're not supposed to say your wish out loud. You know, like when you make a wish when you blow out the candles on your birthday cake. You just say it to yourself."

"Does this mean, my wish won't come true, Mommy? Can I take it back?"

Poppy Tom jumped in and said, "Oh, no, don't worry, JJ. You must have picked a special star to make your wish upon because your wish will be coming true on Saturday!"

"It will?" JJ asked, surprised. Cecilia and Justin turned back around to hear more.

"Yes, it will!" Poppy Tom confirmed. "I was waiting until tonight to let you all know. We're going to be attending a very special event at Happy Horizons Horse Farm on Saturday."

"Are we, Dad?" Cecilia asked.

"Oh, we sure are. Here's the deal. You hearing this, Sarah?"

"Yup, I'm hearing, Pops," Sarah replied without turning around, keeping her gaze transfixed on the display of shooting stars. "Happy Horizons Horse Farm is known for special events."

"Yes, very true," Poppy Tom agreed. "So, here's what's taking place. We'll head over to Gracie's first, around 2 p.m."

JJ clapped his hands in pleasure, knowing it would be then that he'd be seeing Jubee Jean and having his wish come true.

As Poppy Tom continued, "When we get there, I want you all to see how much the trees have grown. You know, the trees you kids planted. Those trees have really taken off."

Again, JJ clapped his hands as Cecilia and Justin joined him.

"You'll also see the nice family of bluebirds that occupy Paula Jean's birdhouse," Poppy Tom informed.

"Can we bring Jubee Jean another one, Poppy?" JJ asked.

"Another birdhouse? I guess we can arrange that, JJ. We can put one together between now and then. Why not? Hey, I'll teach you how to do the carvings on it. How's that sound?"

JJ's two thumbs-ups and high five to his grandfather confirmed his approval.

Justin turned toward Sarah and asked, "You okay, Sarah? You keep…"

Sarah answered, "I'm just fine, Daddy, thank you."

"So anyway," Poppy Tom continued, "here's the deal. I have some very interesting news to share. Gracie's husband, uh, you know…," as Poppy Tom snapped his fingers to try to come up with his name.

"Louis, Dad. Gracie's husband's name is Louis," Cecilia reminded him. "Remember, right?"

"Oh, yes, right, of course, Louis. Well, listen to this. You guys don't know. You don't know what happened."

"What happened, Dad? Is Louis okay?" Justin asked concerned.

"Louis is okay and so is the person he rescued from a burning car!"

"What?" Justin asked, as Cecilia and JJ looked on shocked by what they just heard. Even Sarah turned around by what was just mentioned.

"Yes, guys, this was an amazing thing," Poppy Tom stated. "Our Louis saved a life! A young girl, Elizabeth Hawley. You remember the Hawleys, Cecilia, I believe?"

"Sure, Dad. I recall that name."

"Well she, she was a relatively new driver," Poppy Tom said. "It was a dark, foggy night, down by the old quarry. You know, the road is really winding down there, Ce. An animal, I forget what kind they said, jumped out. The poor kid tried to avoid hitting the animal and went off the road, right into some of those huge slabs of stone left from the quarry. Well, luckily for Elizabeth, Louis was on duty that night and just so happened to be passing by. He witnessed the whole thing. He saw the car catch on fire with Elizabeth trapped inside. Louis, without hesitation and regard for his own safety, pulled Elizabeth from the burning car."

"I can't believe what I'm hearing," Justin stated.

"Me neither," said Cecilia.

"Oh, yeah, it was nothing short of a miracle," said Poppy Tom. "If Louis didn't happen by, God forbid."

"So, this year's special event at Happy Horizons, to your point Sarah, is that there's going to be a big shindig in honor of Louis," Poppy Tom happily informed. "That's a party, kids. A shindig is another name for a party. The mayor is going to be there and even some folks from the state house. Think about this, guys. We know Gracie is a hero, right? And now, so is her husband. What amazing people. So, we're going to meet them at their house and leave from…"

Cecilia asked, "Was everyone okay, Daddy?"

"Listen, yes, just a few minor burns on Elizabeth's legs and a few minor burns on Louis' hands," he answered. "It could have been so much worse. I don't even want to think about it. The Riveras have the whole thing planned out. All our organic farmer friends will be there with all their fine products. Food galore, I'm hearing.

"Justin, you'll be happy to know that Louis is making a big platter of those sweet hush puppy battered zucchini flowers you love so much."

"Oh, really...? I'm in heaven just thinking about those," Justin said in a satisfied voice. "This is really shaping up to be a great shindig."

Poppy Tom said, "Hey kids, pony rides and all. Wait 'til you see how big Raindrop has gotten."

"We saw Raindrop before. When we went through...," Justin began to mention, as Cecilia quieted him down.

"Oh, that's right, you all went through the corral. Right, right," Poppy Tom continued, "and, wait 'til you see how well Paula Jean rides Rainbow. She's become quite the expert, you know. I shouldn't spoil the surprise, but Gracie...No, you know what? I won't say. You'll be surprised on Saturday.

"Hey, Sarah, you still with us?" Poppy Tom asked, through the dark.

"Oh, yes, Poppy, don't worry, I'm here! Sounds wonderful."

"Oh, okay, good to hear. I understand there are a few more surprises in store."

"What are they?" Sarah and Cecilia called out together.

"I don't know," replied Poppy Tom. "The Riveras just said that there will be a bunch of surprises for us, too, when we get there. It was the Riveras that asked us to arrive together with Louis, Gracie, and Paula Jean."

"What do you think the Riveras mean, Daddy?" asked Cecilia. Then she, Sarah, Justin, JJ, Poppy Tom, and Hollie turned their soul-searching gazes to the meteor shower that was in full swing above them. Silence settled over them as each viewer pondered the shindig they were all now looking forward to attending on Saturday and what surprises could possibly be in store, thanks to Poppy Tom's sharing of the news and to the amazing stellar shindig they were experiencing overhead.

For JJ, his mind raced with excitement at the thought of seeing Jubee Jean and his wish coming true, and how proud he'll be showing off what a big boy he is now and what a great job he did carving her new birdhouse. He was also thinking about what the carvings should say, and at the same time, he reached his hands high in the air trying to catch a shooting star as it zipped by. He was thinking that those stars were right within his reach and that all wishes could come true, even if you made the mistake of saying your wish out loud. It's a thought and exercise he was only right in thinking he could achieve tonight and a thought and exercise he should strive for and apply for the rest of his life, as should any wishful star gazer. For every star is within reach and every star holds wishes just waiting to be granted. All one must do is keep reaching for the stars, make that wish, and believe. Think about all those countless bright-spot stars and all those bright-spot-star wishes zipping around our incredible universe just waiting to be granted. Reach! Wish! Believe! Repeat!

For Justin, except for feeling a little disappointed by the fact that he zipped through his bag of popcorn faster than any one of those shooting stars and wondered if Cecilia brought any extras but didn't know how to ask her, his mind, like JJ's, raced with excitement, too. Excitement, but more so, wonder, contentment, and bliss. He privately and personally thanked every star he saw, shooting or otherwise, for being, what he considered to be on this special night, his very own lucky stars. For he was wise enough to know that, except for craving a little more popcorn, life didn't get much better than this. And he was totally humbled by it and so very thankful for it. He, like his son, reached his hand high into the night sky trying to catch a shooting star, but not for the obvious reasons. His idea was to catch a shooting star and stop it dead in its tracks, and maybe if he could do that, he could stop time dead in its tracks, too. Making moments like right now, and now, and now, last forever. He realized he had absolutely no wishes he could possibly make, for all his wishes had already come true, thereby making for himself, the ultimate in realizations. And just maybe, somewhere out there, in our universe or another, a star is born in celebration of Justin's profound realization, complete with a fresh new wish.

Cecilia chose a different angle to begin her time of reflection and contemplation by, instead of looking up, spinning around one hundred and eighty degrees on her stump, hitting the on button of her headlamp and scanning the length of her mother's wall to check on the progress her father had made in restoring it. This caused Poppy Tom and JJ to raise their hands to cover their eyes from the surprise jolt of light that hit them straight on as the beam passed before them. "Oh, sorry guys," Cecilia said, as she quickly shut off the lamp.

"What'd ya do that for? Yeah, Mommy, how come you shined your light on us?" Poppy Tom and JJ asked, bewildered.

"I didn't mean to shine the light right on you guys. I just wanted to see my mother's wall. Wow, Dad, you've made great progress," as she stood and walked almost trancelike through the dark toward the wall. Once there, she turned on her light again, stood solemnly before the wall for a moment, and then slowly and quietly began making repairs.

"Ce, what are you...?" Justin asked. Then he silenced himself because he realized what she was doing and understood why, as did Poppy Tom, Sarah, and even JJ and Hollie. They all left her to her quiet, restorative effort and tribute.

Cecilia used each picking up and placing of a stone as a means of communication, remembrance, and thanks to her beloved gone-from-her-world-but-not-from-her-heart-and-soul mother. She worked back through the archives of her memory to envision the proud, happy face of her mother as she snapped the picture of her with her first trout along with her father and pretty Polly on that long-ago thrilling night, and how, afterward, they all merrily roasted marshmallows in celebration on this very same spot. Her mother never let on that she was in discomfort the entire time.

Cecilia picked up an extra big rock and struggled placing it back in the wall, attempting to duplicate the same pain and struggle her mother experienced in her determined effort to save this place and to thank her for so selflessly doing so. If she hadn't, she knew Sarah wouldn't have been able to have those same thrilling experiences or would any others in her family. So much would have been lost, and how sad that would've been. So, she thanked her mother by setting the stone in the wall, just right, for this and all the incredible things her amazing mother did for her throughout her entire life, including tonight. Feeling weary from her labor, Cecilia stood quietly before the wall, satisfied with her efforts. She then turned off the lamp and allowed the dark, cold air to surround her as she gratifyingly wiped her damp, soiled hands. She allowed her gaze to rise up past the solid, stoic trunks of the majestic trees and their mighty blackened branches to see and, because of how well attuned and ensconced she was in the moment, actually hear a shooting star jettisoning through the heavens. She smiled softly and whispered to herself, "Hi, Mom, it's nice to see you and be here with you again. I love you, always. I know you know that." Then she turned to walk silently back to her stump.

Poppy Tom sat comfortably on his moss-cushioned stump and found the folds of the stone in the wall a perfect support for his fatigued back. However, the cold of the night had begun to be absorbed by the stone and was working its way through his buffalo plaid wool jacket and into his bones. He wouldn't consider moving if the chill became too much because, for one, that would disturb JJ, who had warmly snuggled himself tightly against him and fallen fast asleep, and two, separating himself from his connection with the wall would sever his imagined reconnection with his Jennie. Poppy Tom just allowed his head to swivel enough to follow Cecilia back to her stump and to follow the stars as they shot across the sky, taking stock of this magical night, his blessings, his life, and the life and well-being of his most treasured family. Thoughts of thanks, praise, and gratitude flowed from his mind and those he sent directly to the clusters of stars shining brightly above him, asking them to send his message of thanks, praise, and gratitude to the Creator of those stars and the sky and universe and all that is seen and unseen because that is what that still, small voice—the one Sarah reminded him of tonight—was guiding him to do. And after a time of quiet thought and reflection about his Jennie and what she would have to say and feel about Sarah's answer and all of tonight's joys, Poppy Tom said softly and quietly, "I'm reminded of something your mother once said while looking up at the stars one night, Ce."

"What's that, Dad?

"She said," Poppy Tom began to choke up. "If during…," he stopped to clear his throat and then continued, "if during your darkest night, you fail to look for the bright spots, you'll never see the stars," he said, as he became emotional.

"So true, Mom, so true," Cecilia whispered, while gazing up, as she too became emotional.

Sarah was sitting on her stump at the head of her stargazing, night-dreaming, and love-generating family, where she could focus on the infinite expanse of the universe to cast all of her thoughts, feelings, emotions, and contemplations upon. For tonight, a star was born, not in the far reaches of the Milky Way, but on the cool, rich, terra firma of our earth. And every shooting star above, every dew-kissed blade of grass below, and every beating heart in-between knew it, felt it, and celebrated it. Sarah, on this night of nights, by her undaunted determination, compassion, and kind, loving innocence, smoothly cast her fly upon the clean, cold waters of life and landed the biggest prize of all. And that—exploding like ten million billion supernovas illuminating every black hole in the universe with a blinding white light prize—was unconditional, unbridled, and unlimited love, of which she gently harnessed and cradled in her hands. Then, she tenderly unhooked and compassionately released it, unharmed, back into infinity where it could again be landed by the next successful, smooth, delicate caster.

From the multitudes, she picked a certain shooting star to make her wish upon. But Sarah, being Sarah, didn't make a wish that would benefit only her. Of course, not. Sarah's wish was for the benefit of all creation. So, she gazed long and reflectively into the endless, glinting canopy above, slowly closed her eyes, took a deep cleansing breath, turned her meditations inward, and heard a pure, alluring canticle emanating from the shining chancel deep within her heart of hearts, compelling her to prayerfully and introspectively make her wish.

Sarah's Wish

Whether you're a fish or a fly
Or a rainbow in the sky.

Whether you climb the highest rise
Way up in the air
With the help of two or four strong legs
Or the use of a chair.

Our fins and wings
And multicolored things,
Our toes and tails
And someone who needs wheels,
Shouldn't keep us apart
But together they should bring,
For only in happiness and harmony
Can we hear those amazing trees sing.

So, let's close our eyes and imagine a place
Not so far away,
Where it's always good and never bad
Each and every day.

Where I love you and you love me
And together we will see,
That finding this place
beyond the beatings of our hearts
Is truly our biggest
Discovery!

And in hearing this, that single star, chosen by Sarah from the multitude of shooting stars, mystifyingly halted its rapid ascent across the heavens to stand in awe and respect for the honor of the task it had just been given. Then, it blasted off again, to carry this message of love, hope, and benevolence to every corner of the universe for everyone and everything to receive.

A tear of joy and reverence fell from Sarah's eye and landed on a piece of moss that made its happy home at the base of the stump that tonight acted as a throne for the Princess of Humanity to sit upon and make a wish. As the gently streaking, luminescent fireflies, the quick, silent aerobatic bats, and the cheerful chorus of that choir of nocturnal life forms, led by the dictating tempo of Spring Peepers, joined with all those performers in that ensemble cast of shooting stars dancing across the eastern sky in a spectacular display of the hushed, calm surrender in the harmonious rhythm of the night.

CHAPTER 24

Just like little kites, the family of bluebirds occupying Paula Jean's original birdhouse chirpily swooped and fluttered through the balmy Saturday afternoon air and shared the news among their feathered brethren that another newly carved, healthy home just became available in their comfy neighborhood. Meanwhile, a handsome hawk circled overhead. The sun, high in the blueberry sky, shining brightly upon it, caused its red tail feathers to glimmer and glow with stunning majesty and grace, revealing the secrets held deep within them to any curious seeker of secrets waiting to unfold. The object of this hawk's attention was the small convoy of vehicles leaving the scene below and heading in the direction of Happy Horizons Horse Farm. The hawk followed overhead, gliding effortlessly on up currents of positive energy being generated by this kindly caravan.

A psychedelically painted caterpillar slinking along the raked-out mortar joint of the Happy Horizons Horse Farm's bluestone columned portico had a ringside seat to the hero's welcome awaiting Louis and his family, and to their surprise, Sarah and her family as they arrived.

A plump little field mouse scurried for cover when the striking up of Elizabeth Hawley's former high school marching band's boisterous, celebratory percussions disrupted its peaceful cuddle.

A bluebottle fly maneuvered around the twirling of a baton pirouetting in the air as it made its way from its delicacy-abundant home in the horse stable to the vision-of-loveliness table overflowing with other abundant delicacies. All were well-nurtured, organically grown, and proudly picked fresh from the chemical-free, nutrient-rich soils of this fertile valley.

A dainty ladybug rested comfortably between a few remaining droplets of dew on the petal of a daisy growing in a bed with other daisies and wildflowers that today so beautifully bordered the walkway to the award presentation stand. This ladybug, along with a few bumblebees and dragonflies prancing among the fragrant flowers, had vision capable enough to detect the tiny multicolored prism effect of the rainbows glistening from the tears of joy streaming down the face of Elizabeth and her family and from the eyes of Louis and his family as Louis received his Life Saving Award medal from his State's Lieutenant Governor, as other dignitaries and crowds of supporters stood in honor and ovation.

An intricately painted butterfly dipped and glided around the now-seated crowd as they listened intently to Elizabeth's speech of gratitude and praise to Louis, who without hesitation, risked his own life to save her very own, young life. The butterfly decided to settle upon the pale pink-tinted papers held in the highly skilled and therapeutic hands of Dr. Miss Nicole, who gazed down on this perfect picture of creation and smiled adoringly. These papers held the words of a speech she would be giving shortly in gratitude and praise of her prize patient, Sarah. Sarah, by selflessly making those late-night calls to her friends in need and by sharing her sacred, benevolent poem and her sacred, wonder-inspiring feather, her caring compassion, and love for her fellow human beings, helped to treat, beyond any medications or injections, so many who were present here today and who would stand on their own, straight and tall, and applaud Sarah for her goodness and love. One of them is Emily, who now held hands with and sat on Sarah's left, and another is Paula Jean, who now held hands with and sat on Sarah's right. Paula Jean's other hand rested on Hollie's shoulder and held JJ's hand, whose ear-to-ear grin could only come when a wish upon a star comes true!

Dr. Miss Nicole went on to state that Sarah's poem and feather and their kind and good messages of love, inspiration, and strength were now offered to all the children upon their arrival to her hospital.

"Sarah Nightingale's Happy Medicine," they call it. Sarah, the light of the world, shines her light even when she's not there, but its reflection comes back to her in the same measure, just the same.

A buzzing honeybee clung to the bright, bold red stripes of the American Flag that waved lightly in the warm air and proudly decorated Mrs. Gracie's wheelchair. The American flag also donned the arm patches of varying branches of military members in attendance, and a small one was held by Mrs. Bari who was proudly sitting next to her best-of-America's-best-personified disabled veteran son, Sergeant Afraz Bari. Sergeant Bari, with the help of his new legs, would stand along with his friend and comrade in arms, Sergeant Sanchez, and many others when a high-ranking U.S. Army official presented Sarah with a real, authentic, not just symbolic, Civilian Award for Humanitarian Service. This award was well deserved for the good Sarah did in directly helping Paula Jean and Mrs. Gracie and by the good she and her poem, feather, and method of giving love and compassion that had been passed on and helped and continued to help other children of wounded veterans to cope with their burdens. This therapy is referred to as "Sarah's Casts of Love" when it is provided.

Defying gravity, a carpenter ant tracked upside down along the underside of the legs of the podium that Kate, Mr. Nate's daughter, stood behind as she made Sarah, because of Sarah's veneration, connection, and stewardship of nature, a full, official member of their tribe. This permitted Kate, whose real name was actually Spring Song, because she was born on a beautiful morning in spring and her mother swore, while giving birth, she heard the trees from The Mountain of Singing Trees sing out loud, to legally and by proper ancient custom, provide Sarah with a sacred eagle feather. This feather was the very same one Sarah discovered just the other day. This initiation and sacred offering allowed Spring Song to also provide Sarah with—because of Poppy Tom's description of her encounter with the eagle—her official Indian name of Dancing Eagle. All the members of Sarah's newly acquired tribe, festooned in all their fine regalia, sang out their traditional songs and danced to the beat of drums and flutes in celebration of their newly honored member as other young members of the tribe rode, with thunderous rumbles, their ponies bareback around the applauding crowd, encircling their celebration in a halo of dust that rose high into the profoundly deep blueberry sky.

A glittery snowflake look-a-like Pale Evening Dun, tiny and almost transparent, flashed serendipitously through the settling dust as young Sal, the son of the late Sal and now co-owner with his cousin Al Jr., of Sal's and Al's Pipes and Valves, called Poppy Tom, who shyly obliged, up to the podium and presented him with two long, narrow cedar boxes. Poppy Tom, surprised by all this and holding the boxes, was at a loss as to what to do next. All called out to him to open the boxes. Poppy Tom stood, and holding a box in each hand, signaled comically that he didn't have a free hand to open them. Young Sal, seeing Poppy Tom's dilemma, gladly took one of the boxes back, freeing up Poppy Tom's hands, allowing him to open the one box he was now holding. Nestled between the folds of its green velvet lining was one of Poppy Tom's father's rare and completely restored precious bamboo fly rods. Some of the folks in the audience, because of the vantage point from their seats, couldn't see what was inside the box, but could see very clearly that whatever it was had Poppy Tom crying profuse tears of tremendous joy.

Poppy Tom, struggling to speak, blurted out, "This is my father's fly rod."

Young Sal opened the other box for Poppy Tom, revealing the other rod and happily showed it off to the loud applause of the audience. Poppy Tom fell to one knee while literally hugging the box he was holding and continued to say as loudly as he could, "My father's rods, my father's rods!"

All were now standing and clapping raucously in support of Poppy Tom's joyous, heartfelt, and genuinely emotional reaction. After a while, Young Sal bent down to hug and comfort Poppy Tom, and then helped him to stand. Poppy Tom looked long and deep into Young Sal's' eyes and asked, "How did you get these? After all these years, how did you get these, and why are you giving them back to me? I had to sell…," as the tears and crying overtook his ability to speak, only leaving him the ability to shake his head in disbelief.

"Mr. Tom wants to know how I acquired these rods and why I'm giving them to him, Young Sal called out to the audience. "Well, that's easy. My father, Sal, and my Uncle Al, God rest their souls, purchased these exquisite rods from Mr. Tom a long time ago. Their wish was for me and my cousin Al, who is sitting right there, to someday return these rods to their rightful owner. Today, we make good on their wish."

Again, the entire crowd stood in loud ovation. "Mr. Tom," Young Sal said, "you are a pillar of our community. You do so much for all of us, and you mean so much to all of us. We know how much you're loved by your family, and we want you and your family to know how much you're loved by all of us. You're truly the rightful owner of these beautiful fly rods and may they represent to you the love, admiration, and respect we have for you, and may you in good health and luck cherish them for many years to come." Another thunderous standing ovation rose up from the valley floor and echoed off the surrounding mountains as Poppy Tom graciously accepted his amazing gifts and thanked all from the bottom of his heart. Reflections of love spanned the generations.

The partaking of delicious food, refreshing drinks, pony rides, and the coming together of people from all walks of life and all kinds of circumstances, some needing love and comforted by those providing it, defined the balance of the day's festivities.

Our Supergirl Fly, Paula Jean, rode Rainbow alongside, and just as instinctively and expertly as the young members of Sarah's newly acquired tribe, even though she never had a lesson. And to the surprise of everyone because of the apparatus built by Mr. Miguel, Gracie sat astride the accommodating back of the beautiful Lightning and rode alongside her daughter as could anyone else with special needs on this fine day of reverence, recognition, and showering of love, if they so desired.

And so, with the last of the bright spots from the night's celebratory fireworks fading in the eastern sky, a majestic red-tailed hawk sailed over the now cool, darkened, mist-shrouded meadows of Happy Horizons Horse Farm. The hawk triumphantly winged his way back to his ancestral nest in the mountains beyond, as one of his handsome, all-powerful tail feathers became dislodged and lazily waved and wobbled its way down to rest upon the now sacred ground below, officially ending this day's enchanting shindig but yet guaranteeing future ones.

SARAH AT ELEVEN

KEEP ON

SARAH AT TWELVE

KEEPIN' ON

SARAH AT FORTY

MOUNTAINS
IN THE DISTANCE

CHAPTER 25

"Come on, Sarah, hurry! I'll get your luggage later," JJ shouted as he stretched to hold out an open umbrella and at the same time tried to keep the cabin door open for his sister.

"No Mollie, stay!" he commanded. "You'll get all wet! Oh, too late."

"Hi, Mollie, how's my girl?" Sarah said cheerfully as she set her walker aside and bent down to hug and pet the welcoming Mollie as the rain came pouring down. "You wanted to come out to help me, I know, just like your mommy and grand-mommy used to do. You're such a good girl. Yes, yes you are! Okay, okay, I know you're excited to see me. I'm just as excited to see you, too, sweetie. Come on now, let's get inside before we both get drenched. Let's go lady girl," Sarah said as she slapped the side of her leg, regrasped her walker, and with her head leaning forward, trudged toward the cover of JJ's open umbrella.

"Oh, Sair, you're soaked," said JJ as he embraced and kissed his beloved and missed sister. "Juubs went for some towels."

"Yeah, here I am, Sair. Here, dry yourself off. Great to see you, Sis. Wow, what rain! It doesn't seem to want to let up," Paula Jean said to her sister-in-law as they both lovingly hugged and kissed each other. Paula Jean proceeded to help dry off Sarah and her walker.

"Come here you, so I can dry you off," JJ called out to Mollie. "You couldn't wait for Sarah to come in. I know you."

"Give me a minute here ladies," JJ said, "and then I'll get us a nice fire going. Sarah, we hope you're hungry. We have..."

Sarah interrupted her brother and said, "I am hungry, yes. Thanks, Jay. But I can't wait to see my new niece. Where is she? That has to be the first thing I do. Let me get dried off. Oh, I'm so sorry I couldn't have gotten here sooner, you guys. When our parents were all here."

"She's sleeping, Sair," Paula Jean informed. "Safe, sound, and contented in Pop's cradle. You're dried off enough. Come on, I'll take you to meet Little Jennie, our new Light of the World."

"Hold on one second. Let me finish getting this fire going. I want to go, too," said the proud poppa, JJ. "I can't wait for you to see our new little girl, Sis. And I want you to see something else. I carved a few yellow peace roses into Pop's cradle."

"Oh really? How wonderful, Jay. How about Little Tommy? He must be sleeping, too, I presume?"

"Yes, yes, Sarah. He tried staying awake in the worst way but ended up conking out. I carried him to bed. You know he's using Mommy's bed now."

"He's that big already?"

"He sure is," Paula Jean said proudly. "He wants you to go in..."

"Oh, don't worry, a team of wild horses couldn't keep me from seeing my sleeping prince. I miss him so...I miss seeing you all *sooo* much," said Sarah with eyes moistened with joy and reminiscences.

"We miss you, too. We're all so happy you're here, Sis," said Paula Jean, also with teary eyes and genuine love. Then, she hugged and kissed Sarah again, more like a true blood sister than a sister-in-law, understandably so.

Paula Jean and JJ quietly escorted Sarah to the half-closed door of their bedroom, where they then stood aside to let Sarah walk in first. Sarah left her walker at the door of the cozy, amber-lit bedroom and proceeded to slowly, silently, and with some effort and discomfort (which she tried to conceal), moved toward the cradle that rested at the foot of the bed.

"Oh...my...she's an absolute angel," Sarah said in a breathy, worshipping whisper as she peered inside and reverently knelt on both knees alongside Poppy Tom's sun-dance yellow painted cradle that, after all these years, continued to so ably shelter such precious cargo—a resounding testament to the skilled, devoted hands that crafted it. Aunt Sarah leaned in and gently kissed the round, rosy red cheek of her peacefully sleeping niece. "She's a vision of loveliness, you two, just like Mom and Dad said she was. God bless you both. God bless your darling little girl and Little Tommy, too. Please may He bless you all and keep you safe, happy, and healthy always. I love you all so very much," she said, as silvery, chubby tears trickled from her eyes.

After allowing Sarah a few moments to thoroughly absorb the vision before her, a vision he knew she would keep forever in her floor-to-ceiling and wall-to-wall stuffed memory bank with other treasured memories from her rich, treasured life, JJ reached down with both hands and helped his sister to rise. He offered her his bent arm, which Sarah accepted. Then brother and sister, employing soft footfalls, followed Paula Jean from the delicately baby-lotion-scented sanctuary of the bedroom to the open hearth of the rustic, fieldstone-veneered fireplace alive with extra-spicy, flamenco dancing flames.

JJ uncoiled Sarah's arm from his, then intertwined it with Paula Jean's. He whispered, "You two warm up by the fire. I'll get you your walker, Sair, and then I'll go out and grab your luggage. I'm sure you're wanting to freshen up. After that we can eat. Juubs prepared us a nice frittata and a salad of fresh fennel, onions, and beets. I baked a lemon meringue pie for dessert just in case there's any sweet tooth candidates in attendance tonight," as he let out a muted, sly laugh. "They're all Grandma Jennie's recipes, of course."

"Thank you. That sounds just wonderful, JJ. I can't wait. I know there's a trick to making that lemon meringue pie. I'm sure it will be delicious. I'm sure everything will be. Hey, I think I still qualify as one of those sweet tooth candidates," she said, as she raised and waved a self-nominating hand. "No, check that, I know I do," as Sarah, JJ, and Paula Jean had a good wholesome, more on the inside than outside laugh, keeping the noise level low.

After swallowing the last bite of her second piece of lemon meringue pie, Sarah wiped her mouth with her napkin, pushed herself away from the table, leaned back in her chair, and said satisfyingly, "Oh, I'm about to bust! Guys, that was an absolutely delicious dinner."

"Paula, the flavor those wild mushrooms gave to your frittata was amazing.

"And JJ, you have the baking of a lemon meringue pie down pat, brother. So light and airy, with a delicate, flaky crust. Excellent job."

"Thanks, Sis," Paula Jean responded. "We're glad you enjoyed it. You know, it's just a matter of following Grandma Jennie's timeless, neatly written recipes."

"Jubee's right, Sair," JJ added. "But, I think there's a little something else, too. There's a secret key ingredient written neatly between the lines of each of Gram's recipes, and that's oodles and oodles of love. That's what makes everything turn out so extra good."

Paula Jean nodded and said, "Can't agree with you more, Jubee."

Sarah nodded, too, and said, "Oh, so true, Jay. You know, I have to say, you both do such a wonderful job. I mean, I love coming here, you know. I get to see all of you and relive all the great memories," as she looked around fondly at the room. "You both do an incredible job of taking such great care of this place and keeping all the priceless memories and traditions alive. I see how beautiful everything is kept, but even more important, I feel the love, guys. I feel the same strong feelings of love that I felt so many years ago when Grams and Pops and Hollie were here. They're just as strong today. It's truly amazing and glorious for me to see, but even more so, for me to feel and experience. I can't thank you enough for that. You both need to be commended. Really, thank you! To me, it's like Grandma Jennie is still there in the kitchen cooking; Poppy Tom is sitting in his chair by the table telling us a great story; and Hollie is either resting at his feet or by yours, JJ, or mine. Look, just like Mollie is doing to me now, keeping my toes nice and toasty.

"JJ, an example of this is you carving Grandma's yellow peace roses into Pop's cradle. What a wonderful, loving tribute to our grandparents. What made you think of doing that?"

"Oh, thank you, Sarah. Let's just say the idea came to me one night."

"Juber, if there's anyone, anyone in the world you can share your experience with, it's your sister, Sarah," Paula Jean stated, almost laughing by the obviousness of the idea.

"Oh, yeah, I suppose you're right, Juub."

"What?" Sarah asked. "What do you have to share, Jay?"

"Well Sis, it's a little...Uh, I'll just tell you," JJ began. "You know how difficult this pregnancy was for us, you know, for Paula. It was at the time when...oh, we were very scared, Sair," as JJ's voice became labored. "There was a chance we could have lost our...God helped us...," he said, as he began to cry. "We prayed, Sair, we prayed a lot. But thank God, God helped us and saved our baby. Paula Jean went full term, and Little Jennie was born, and she's healthy and...," he said, as his emotions prevented him from speaking further and he wiped away his tears with his napkin.

After pausing to compose himself, JJ continued. "It was one night during that very scary time, Sis. We'd go to bed and try to sleep, but the sleep wouldn't come. But this one night, I don't know, I guess I did fall asleep because I had this dream. But it was like I was still awake, too. I don't know, but anyway, in the dream this very vivid aroma of newly cut wood came over me. You know, like the smell in Pop's Shop. I could smell this aroma, and at the same time, this beautiful, peaceful feeling came over me and I saw Poppy Tom, just as plain as day, Sair. He was standing by his workbench carving something into his cradle and looking directly at me with this awesome smile on his face. You know that smile, Sarah."

Sarah nodded with a warm, understanding smile on her face.

"Well then, this is all happening...quickly, like all dreamy," JJ said. "Then, I mean it, Sis, this wonderful aroma of Grandma's roses came over me, too. It was like I felt my whole body inflate with this incredible feeling of peace and euphoria. See, Sair, I never really knew Grandma. She passed when I was very young, so I don't have the memories of her like you do. But I know about her roses and how she used to come to you while you slept, and I knew right then and there that it was her coming to me, too. She and Poppy Tom both. They both came to me in my dream, Sarah. We had the cradle all made up, because we knew we were having a girl and we knew we were going to be naming her Jennifer. But at that time, we were very scared we might not be using...

Well, having this dream and vividly feeling their presence—so beautiful and loving—made me know that we would be using that cradle and that all I had to do was carve those roses, just how Poppy Tom taught me how to carve, and all would be fine. That's how, Sair, that's how I came to carve those roses. Now Little Jennie, our true light-of-the-world miracle baby is here, sleeping soundly in that cradle...Paula's fine...," as more tears fell from JJ's, Sarah's, and Paula Jean's eyes.

Paula Jean rose and began to collect the soiled dishes from the table and said in a subdued voice, "You two continue to chat, I'll start cleaning up."

"Are you sure, Juub?" JJ asked.

"Sure, I'm sure. This won't take me long. Why don't you guys go sit by the fire and when I'm done I'll come and join you?"

"Okay, Hon, thank you."

JJ placed another log on the fire. Once seated in the comfortable chairs facing the fireplace and feeling he had allowed enough time to transpire with small talk, JJ got down to the business of asking Sarah what was, for him, a burning question. "So, tell me, Sarah, are you still thinking about taking on that journey of yours? I'm wondering if maybe...?"

As Sarah asked, "If maybe I've changed my mind?"

"Yeah, sure, you can change your mind. Why not, Sis? You don't have to do this now," JJ stated, trying to make his sister know that it was okay for her to change her mind.

"Thank you for asking, JJ. But no. I'm not *thinking* I'm taking this journey. I *know* I'm taking this journey." After a quick laugh, Sarah said, "Heck, down in my heart of hearts, I'm already there."

"Okay, Sarah, I know you. I know you've made up your mind, and nothing or nobody's going to change that. But are you still set on going this alone?"

"As long as you and Paula Jean are still allowing me to take Mollie, I won't be alone," Sarah said almost jokingly, as Mollie's head sprang up at the mention of her name and she peered at Sarah then back to JJ, as if she was waiting to hear their answer.

"Of course. You know we'll...It's not about us allowing...Mollie's going with you. That's a definite." Mollie rested her head back down on her front legs feeling relieved by JJ's reply. "Of course, she is," JJ confirmed with a tinge of frustration in his voice. "But why can't I…? Let me join you, Sis. What's so bad about that? I think I should be there to…You know, we've been having a lot of rain. And it's not supposed to be letting up…It's a long, tough…"

Again, Sarah interrupted her brother and said, "Thank you, JJ. I know you want to be there for me, but this is something I need to do on my own. You know, I've had this goal for so…ever since Poppy Tom told me about Grandma Jennie's line. The time has come for me to climb…"

Paula Jean, now that she had finished cleaning up from dinner and was standing behind her husband's chair rubbing his shoulders to help him relax, interrupted Sarah and said, "You go, girl. Mollie will be good company."

JJ turned around and glared at his wife with a surprised, questioning look on his face.

Paula Jean continued, "You go get your line, Sarah, and hear those glorious trees sing!"

Sarah looked happily into Paula Jean's bright, loving eyes and smiled acknowledgingly, while nodding slowly.

JJ glared intently into the fire with a slight frown on his face while shaking his head slowly and in a reluctant, disappointed tone, asked, "When are you planning on leaving?"

"I'm figuring the day after tomorrow," answered Sarah. "Tomorrow, I'm looking forward to spending some quality time with my handsome nephew and beautiful new niece, and checking to see if any repairs to the brook are needed. With all this rain, I'm thinking there will be. Then, I'll stop by Kate's Baits before heading out to Pop's secret fishing spot. You know guys, you have to wet a line, to get a line. From there it will be off to Grandma Jennie's wall. I'd like to finish up that painting I've been working on that shows the wall all joined together, just how Poppy Tom was working to get it to be when he…you know.

"The next morning I'll be looking forward to being awakened bright and early to the sweet music of ol' Brewster the Rooster IV. You know, a long time ago someone very wise told me the day would come when I'd find the coarse crowing of that bird to be music to my ears. Turns out that person was right, as usual. I'll have myself a good hearty breakfast, and then Mollie and I will hit the trail.

"Please don't be upset with me, brother. We'll be fine. I'll make sure we're back in plenty of time for the big shindig at Happy Horizons. I wouldn't miss that for the world. I'm so looking forward to seeing everyone again, Mom and Dad, Gracie and Louis, the Riveras, everyone.

"Listen guys, I think it's time for me to sneak in, steal a kiss from Little Tommy, and hit the hay." With the support of her walker, Sarah rose from her chair, walked toward her brother, who was still staring at the fire, and whispered, "Good night, sleep tight, and know, I know, I'm loved by both of you with all of your might." Then she bent down and kissed JJ on the cheek and then looked at Paula Jean, winked, and kissed her goodnight, too.

As Sarah worked herself a few steps away, she heard her brother say, "I can at least be with you tomorrow when you go fly-fishing. I can use another line, too, you know. And I'll be the one making you that hearty breakfast before you hit the trail."

"I was expecting you to," said Sarah, as she looked back to see her brother's head slowly shaking as the flames in the fireplace flickered out.

CHAPTER 26

JJ sat in an agitated state at his desk in Pop's Shop, the place he earned his living expertly fabricating quality custom wood furniture for a continuously growing number of distinguished clients. He should be diligently working away at the many projects he had in production, so as not to be falling more behind on their promised dates of completion. Instead, he closely studied the never-completed birdhouse he was holding in his hands. He noted the almost invisible precision of the mitered cuts. He saw the painstaking effort that was needed to align the grain of each cut at the corners just right, so the finished product would appear to be made from one solid piece of wood. The concealed hinge and its companion hatch were cut into the surface of the birdhouse so perfectly that it looked like they grew there as a natural part of the tree. But JJ has held this birdhouse so many times over the years that he knew every intricate detail of its framework. He had even become intimate with its everlasting aroma. He, too, knew who this particular birdhouse was being built for and where it was going to be placed, and why it was never completed or made it to its final destination.

Many years ago, the Riveras lovingly adopted a young girl by the name of Alamea, who was born in Laos. In America, unlike in Laos, the soil bears forth rich treasures like the ones Dancing Cloud and her sisters danced and played for, and from which the local organic growers reap rewards and so generously share those rewards with their grateful neighbors. It was from deep within these rich, treasured soils that came the stability and nourishment, allowing the giant trees to stand and grow, which protected the brook, the air, and an entirely still intact ecosystem.

In Laos, there weren't any of those rich treasures that provided stability, nutrition, and life. Buried beneath the scorched earth of Laos lay anything but treasures and nothing but unexploded bombs. And when children like Alamea innocently danced and played like Dancing Cloud, as they do and should, sometimes they kicked up more than dust. Sometimes they kicked up one of those harbingers of destruction. Alamea was a victim of one of those buried nontreasures and lost a leg. Now sitting right on the top of a fencepost in view of Alamea's bedroom and overlooking the green, serene hills of Happy Horizons Horse Farm was the birdhouse that so many years ago, JJ, Sarah, and Paula Jean helped to build. It duplicated the one Poppy Tom had begun to build for Alamea before the ever-loving engine of his heart, which powered that pair of compassionate, masterful hands, stopped beating. And like the birds that live joyfully in their safe, free-of-strife birdhouse, conceived and prototyped by Poppy Tom, then constructed, following that precisely made model, by the empathic hands of JJ, Sarah, and Paula Jean, these birds could fly with unbridled abandon. So, too, did Alamea, for her adoptive home was safe and free of strife, and like the birds, Alamea flew with unbridled abandon on the backs of trusty, therapeutic horses that she, like Paula Jean, took to riding instinctively. In the land of her birth, Alamea lost one leg. In her home in America, on every horse Alamea rode she gained four more legs, giving her a total of five.

Today, Alamea and Paula Jean co-manage the extensive workings of Happy Horizons Horse Farm, which specializes in equine therapy for children and adults with physical and mental disabilities. Victoria and Miguel took Happy Horizons in that direction on that day long ago when Paula Jean first rode Rainbow and Miguel designed the apparatus that gave Gracie the ability to ride Lightning.

The Riveras now spent much of their time tending to the three such facilities they began in their native country of Panama, leaving the day-to-day operations of Happy Horizons to the trusty hands and golden hearts of Alamea and Paula Jean. Grandma Jennie's rose-scented message that appeared to the cuddly dreaming Sarah on an enchanted evening so many years ago continued to pay dividends locally and on an international basis. Like Sarah, and so many others, the Riveras would not only be back to the farm and in attendance for the upcoming shindig, they wouldn't miss it for the world.

JJ held in his hands this never-completed birdhouse, an artifact that to the unknowing eye would appear to represent a project started and lazily left undone. He was one of a few who knew this birdhouse's true legacy, its true worth, and its true love, along with the guidance and life lessons this birdhouse still imparted.

For on this cold, dark rainy night, JJ was hoping for solace to come winging out of the hinged hatch of this avian sanctuary. He was trying to convince himself that the spirit of his grandfather that so lovingly and devoutly molded the object he humbly held and so lovingly and devoutly molded and influenced his sister enough so that on this third night of her journey, with a cold rain coming down in buckets, the life lessons taught to Sarah by Poppy Tom were guiding her, fortifying her, and keeping her safe.

For JJ, the idea of Sarah being out on a remote mountain trail under adverse weather conditions with only Mollie and Sarah's excess baggage of challenges to support her was almost too much for him to bear. He knew he should have insisted on going with her. Not taking "no" for an answer. If ever anything bad were to happen to Sarah, he would never forgive himself. "God forbid," he thought to himself.

He fought his desire to race over to Happy Horizons, saddle up Ebony, and head out to locate Sarah and bring her and Mollie home. He could do that easily enough. It was Ivory that was about to foal. Ebony didn't have to be there. But JJ knew his sister and knew she wouldn't want him to come to her assistance. That would mean in some way Sarah's burdens won and she would not be deserving of accomplishing her goal and earning the treasured prize of a carved line next to that of her hero, Grandma Jennie. JJ knew that's what this was all about. After all these years, it was still about the no-limits-to-what-she-can-do

Sarah. It was about her taking on a challenge head on and on her own. It was about Sarah being strong and brave and fighting to free herself of her burdens. And when her burdens became stronger, as they had on so many occasions, she fought using the same ingrained, fail-safe strategy that served her so well throughout these many years. It was a strategy imparted on Sarah by sparkling, rhymed words beautifully written on a piece of paper; by a promise of love to be there for her every step of the way and to lead her by the hand to a bright, new shiny place; and by a glowy red, sacred feather and a soulmate friend with fins offering her new worlds to discover, secrets to unfold, and the ability to tug and shake with all of her might to hurl her burdens aside and remain free to continue making smooth delicate casts.

So, JJ knew he couldn't go. He must stay and fight his own battle with his own burdens of anxiety and concern for his sister. He would pray hard to God, just like he did when Paula Jean and Little Jennie were in trouble. He'd pray hard to the spirit of his grandparents. He'd ask them to watch over Sarah, to keep her safe, and once again provide Sarah with the strength and bravery she needed to win what was the greatest challenge of the biggest battle over the strongest, most imposing burdens she'd ever had to face in her entire life.

JJ rose from his chair, which had been Poppy Tom's. He droopily walked past the old plywood workbench that still held the shavings of wood and a few drips of sun-dance yellow paint left from JJ's recent embellishments to Pop's cradle along with so much more. He headed to the corner of the shop that displayed a fitting memorial honoring Poppy Tom. It consisted of numerous pictures hanging on the wall, some in black and white that dated back to when Poppy Tom was young, crafting Cecilia's cradle and her big-girl bed, to another one from a little later on of Jennie and him standing proudly before her new, prized kitchen cabinets, to all the way up to the time when Poppy Tom, Sarah, and JJ worked in the shop for the first time together, launching JJ's *hammentering* career. They had just hung the imaginatively colorful "Pop's Shop" sign—painted by JJ—above the door. That sign still hangs there today.

Ceremoniously arranged on the benchtop were many of Poppy

Tom's hand tools, including hammers, planes, chisels, Phillips-head screwdrivers, and even his gloves and safety glasses, all getting a well-earned rest from years of faithful service. These treasured icons sat framed on each side by Poppy Tom's father's glass-encased, precious and rare bamboo fly rods. These fly rods stood like sentinels at attention, paying homage to a national hero.

And as JJ droopily walked, he prayed. As he stood before the memorial, he prayed. As he placed the birdhouse back in its place of reverence at the center of the memorial, he prayed as a cold rain came down in buckets, echoing off the metal roof of Pop's Shop.

CHAPTER 27

The same cold rain came down in buckets, hitting the tops of the giant trees whose sweepingly wide branches acted as an umbrella, so by the time the moisture reached the rainfly on the tent of the soundly sleeping Sarah, it was nothing more than an all-encompassing mist. She was dry in her tent, even though it hadn't stopped pouring since she began her journey almost four days ago. She was warm, snuggled tightly in her sleeping bag but mainly because of Mollie's heat-generating body pressed tightly against her, providing Sarah with soothing relief from the deep-seated ache emanating from every bone and muscle in her body. And, she slept in peace knowing that, with the coming, fog-shrouded dawn, she'd undauntedly begin the last leg of her long and arduous journey.

As Sarah so soundly slept, she dreamed. Her dreams poured forth from the very depths of her soul, swirling and whirling, vivid and rich, during the deep meditative state of her pure, recharging-while-in-slumber mind. Her eyes darted and dashed from behind the curtain of her sleep-laden eyelids. They strove to follow and engage, not only the in-living-color images flashing before them, but also the sounds, scents, and most important, the feelings that jettisoned past them.

There were images of Sarah as a young girl, kneeling in the slick, dark brown mud along the bank of the brook as she obligingly followed her grandfather's direction, diligently doing the right and good thing of repairing the brook's compromised condition. In the dream, Sarah's eyes followed the prettily painted butterflies as they fluttered past. She could hear the birds merrily chirping and the cool breeze fanning through the trees. She could even smell the fresh wildflower fragrance in the air and the rich loam of the earth as she planted her allotment of restorative grasses. And most important, she could feel the gratified, tickling feeling of satisfaction that came when one, as an integral part of a committed team, appraised a successfully completed, highly beneficial exercise.

In another image that just zipped by, Sarah heard the crude cacklings of ol' Brewster the Rooster that jarred her awake and made her feel like pulling the covers over her head until the inviting aroma of pancakes, hot off the griddle, catapulted her from her bed.

As another image went by, she felt the fear and dread in her stomach again, the same as when she saw, for the very first time, the entrance to the Dark Woods guarded by that old ogre of an owl Scowl. However, instantaneously she was able to turn those feelings into the magical sensation she felt when she discovered—thanks to her ever-enlightening, ever-supportive, ever-promise-keeping grandfather—what a unique and fascinating place the Dark Woods really was and how Ol' Scowl's perfect-owl smile lit up the dark.

Images and feelings continued to parade past Sarah's grandstand-viewing mind. There were images of Sarah visiting the crying young Emily in the darkness of her hospital room and in the darkness of her brooding heart and having Emily imagine them having fun ice skating together; of turning Emily's sadness tears to happiness smiles and supplanting her nightmares of despair and trepidation to sugary, sweet dreams of fantasy, possibility, and hopefulness; and of making Emily a friend for life along with Emily's life partner, Jasmine, an expert gymnast, and their two adopted special needs children, Sabrina and Simone.

Sarah felt dizzy by the images of her zipping around the kitchen table playing Supergirl Fly with Mrs. Gracie and of launching the reunion, restoration, and repairs to the wounded minds, bodies, and souls of a beautiful brave mother and her beautiful innocent child.

Sarah felt the purity and innocence from the images of her looking into the bright, whole-new-world-to-discover eyes of the then yet-to-be-named Raindrop. She remembered gently petting her silky, smooth coat and hugging her adoringly. She felt the love coming back to her in the same measure when Paula Jean rode Rainbow and Sarah saw the tears of joy streaming down the face of Mrs. Gracie as a brilliant rainbow framed all in a serene, heavenlike scene.

Like a slide show, images continued to scroll by, like the vibrant red of a luscious strawberry sitting in contrast and atop an overindulgent portion of ice cream and whipped cream on a golden, sweet tooth–satisfying piece of shortcake.

In the next image, Sarah experienced again the reassuring, confidence-building sensation of Poppy Tom's gentle arm over her shoulder and his wise and guiding finger pointing as he revealed to her all the secrets and wonders of nature in the form of a peacefully sleeping fawn. She felt the warmth come over her as Poppy Tom helped her with her jacket, protecting her from the cold, and she felt and sensed from the very depths of her soul the all-encompassing, hushed calm surrender and rhythm of the night.

The next image she saw was one she'd never forget. It was of the thrill and excitement on Poppy Tom's face as he reported back to Sarah and Hollie about the hatch being in full swing and the brook trout loving it. She remembered understanding his excitement as she successfully battled her foe and claimed her victory at the top of the rise, then seeing her family and the love and support they offered her by being there, and then witnessing countless Pale Evening Duns doing their ritualistic dance of freedom and the brook trout doing theirs.

From the splash and dash of an eagle to the mysteries of its sacred feather to the private journey with a special finned friend to a captivating faraway but really close-by place, discovering the golden-fleeced inner sanctum of her soul, which held the answer.

The images kept flowing, taking her now to the future. Sarah saw herself at Happy Horizons, standing at the podium in front of a crowd of admirers and all the smiling people at the upcoming shindig. Sarah received her awards of recognition for years of faithful service in the fields of medicine and environmental sciences, thus fulfilling the goals she set for herself as a young child to help humanity and Mother Nature alike.

Humanity benefited through her unflinching efforts to help those and their families with the devastating effects of Alzheimer's, which led her to discover a cure. Sarah experienced the effects of this, firsthand, when this dreaded condition overtook the glorious mind of her treasured grandfather, taking away his memory but never his brilliant and miraculous shining light of love. She witnessed the tears and sadness of those close to her and so many others, and vowed to turn this around and become their happy. And she did! No young grandchild or child would have to stand by helplessly and watch as their hero grandparent, parent, or loved one slowly fade away ever again. Sarah's "I'll Be With You Every Step of the Way" therapies were helping millions in the U.S. alone.

Sarah's unyielding dedication and earnestness in preserving Mother Nature and all her amazing creations took the environmental sciences field by storm. At a young age, Sarah learned of, experienced, and fell in love with the intricate balance and beauty of the natural world of which, she understood, we're all a part. She also learned how the members of a tribe, of which she was made a member, and other proud indigenous cultures from around the world followed the wise ways and customs of their ancestors to love, respect, preserve, and live as one with all of nature. She followed their example and the example set forth by her hero, Grandma Jennie, using kind, gentle persuasion to inspire those who had the power to destroy nature to realize that there is more value in protecting it. As a result, enormous tracts of land, coral reefs, and oceans, along with their fragile ecosystems, which had been destroyed by years of pollution, deforestation, and ignorance, had been restored with ongoing efforts to restore others. Also, vast areas of wilderness throughout the world that were at risk of being destroyed were now forever protected. And here, too, there were ongoing efforts to protect even more. "Sarah's Bright Shiny World" was the name given to this global effort for restoring ecosystems, and "Leave It as You Found It" was the name given to the protection and preservation of wilderness areas around the world, all in the name of what's right and good.

Poppy Tom's prediction to the inquiring Sarah many years ago when she asked about her discovering a cure so children wouldn't be born with what she was born with, a condition called spinal muscular atrophy (SMA type 2), came true. Poppy Tom told Sarah that many wonderful people were working so very hard to find a cure, and sure enough their hard work paid off and a cure was found, making those wonderful people the happy to so many that were sad. With this goal of Sarah's already accomplished by others, she went out there, like others of her generation, and searched for another way to help children in need. She chose to "discover a cure" for the millions of unfortunate children in our own country that don't get enough to eat.

Sarah knew she was born with burdens and had to fight, and must continue to fight to overcome her burdens. But as challenging as her burdens were, she knew that there was one thing she was never burdened with, and that was an empty stomach. She knew how blessed she was to sit at a table surrounded by loved ones, where food was always abundant and provided not only sustenance for her body and the bodies of her family and friends, it also provided sustenance for their very souls.

Sarah recognized how many children didn't get enough to eat, yet fresh, satisfying food was being wasted at a shameful and alarming rate. Sarah began a program called "Poppy's Piece of Pie," which took perfectly good nutritious food from so many sources that were sinfully sending this valuable commodity to waste facilities and redirected that life-sustaining food to myriad distribution centers, where it was safely stored and promptly and efficiently made available for free to those in need. As a result, the number of children going to bed hungry has been drastically reduced.

Sarah wouldn't rest until she knew there was not a single child in our entire country who lacked enough to eat. "Poppy's Piece of Pie" programs were now springing up in other countries around the world. Sarah knows a sad child couldn't ever be made happy and healthy or able to properly study and learn their lessons if they were hungry. Fill the bellies of hungry children and watch the sadness go away and see their happy, healthy, smart smiles appear. What an amazing gift that is.

On a cool, shooting starry night long ago, Sarah made a wish upon a star for the benefit of all creation. She didn't just sit back and wait and hope for that wish to come true. She went out there and worked to *make* that wish come true, and all of creation benefited.

Another image appears. This one was of Sarah standing at the podium giving her acceptance speech at the upcoming shindig. She mentioned that she had been asked by people on numerous occasions how someone with her challenges could accomplish all that she had. Many expected her answer to reference her scholarships, her many high-level degrees, and her important contacts and resources. Sarah's answer was always the same and left the inquiring person questioning, when she said, "I always first thank the person for their question and then go on to answer that I was able to accomplish all that I have because a long time ago a very special couple loved me enough to write me a poem, and one of those very special people loved me enough to take me fishing. In short, it was because I was loved. And then I would ask them a question. What challenges?"

So, it's no surprise that the image bringing up the rear of this cavalcade of images parading across Sarah's slumbering mind carried with it a distinct aroma of newly cut wood. This aroma mixed pleasantly with the aroma of yellow peace roses that Sarah had been detecting since her first night on the trail. The dreamlike image Sarah was now seeing was of her Grandmother Jennie sitting at the chair of her desk with a fancy fountain pen in hand, diligently writing away. Standing proudly behind her was a radiantly smiling Poppy Tom. His dazzlingly bright eyes looked directly into Sarah's, making her feel as safe, secure, confident, and loved now, as he made her feel when she was a young girl. Poppy Tom motioned with his two hands for Sarah to turn her attention to her grandmother to see what she was about to do. Grandma Jennie, smiling just as radiantly as Poppy Tom, placed her pen down, raised, and turned the fanciful piece of parchment paper toward Sarah, giving her a view of its message. Sarah clearly saw written across the pretty paper's surface in beautiful, flowing letters the words, *Find the Hinge*. And then, the dreamy, tingly feeling image faded away.

With this dream-world communication complete, Sarah softly awoke. As if mentally connected to Sarah, so did Mollie. Sarah blinked to dislodge the sleep from her eyes and tried to focus in on the darkened yellow tent liner above her. But the liner acted more like a screen than a shelter as the images of her dreams continued to play before her, even though she was awake, especially the image of Poppy Tom and Grandma Jennie with their radiant smiles and the words Grandma Jennie so artistically scribed on her stationery. This gave Sarah the ability, now that she was gaining more of an awakened state to contemplate and meditate on the image's true meaning.

Sarah was confident the writing said, *Find the Hinge*, and knew from past experience with writings and messages coming to her via a dream, she didn't need to understand their true meanings immediately. Sarah was secure in knowing that somehow, someway, the true meanings would be revealed. It was just a matter of time. The prospect of that added to her excitement and anticipation on a day when her excitement and anticipation high-octane gas tank was already full and overflowing.

So, because of her stiffened and aching body, Sarah wormed, rolled, and shimmied like a caterpillar to free herself from her cocoon-like sleeping bag. She began the day just like a newly transformed butterfly stretching its wings, preparing for a flight of fancy that she had visualized herself taking on, for most of her life.

Mollie sat at the ready while Sarah performed her ritualistic preflight checks. She took her poem from her pocket, the very same one she discovered waiting for her by her place setting on that gloriously bright, shining morning so many years ago. It was the morning, it could be said, Sarah's journey of discovery, self-discovery, enlightenment, and love began. It had been a journey that brought her to this very spot and one that, if the heavens allow, Sarah just might be bringing to fulfillment today. She kissed the now laminated declaration of love poem and raised it high in the predawn, moisture-laden air in a gesture of thanks and praise to the memory of her grandparents' spirits. Then she placed the poem back in its location-of-reverence pocket, securing it with the zipper.

Next on her checklist was removing her lucky hat to make sure her new, authentic red-tailed hawk feather—the one she purposely went by Kate's Baits to pick up—was in its proper place and securely held there by the hat's band. This too Sarah kissed, then waved the hat high in the air as a gesture of thanks to her brother and sister hawk for their precious gift. Then she asked her feathered siblings to bestow upon this feather an extra secret potion of power, guidance, and courage that would provide her with the strength, direction, and bravery she'd need to win this climactic battle over her burdens and accomplish her goal. Sarah now placed her lucky hat back on her head, just so, and concluded her preflight checks with a prayer of gratitude for the gift and promise of another treasured day. With that, she threw on her backpack, stood straight and tall, even though it hurt, and took a few deep energizing breaths.

With undaunted determination and will, Sarah grasped the handles of her walker and began what was an almost vertical assent to the fog-veiled summit of The Mountain of Singing Trees with the being-there-for-Sarah-every-step-of-the-way Mollie at her side.

CHAPTER 28

Two and a half hours into her approach to the summit, Sarah found herself on all fours gasping for breath and her walker lying on her backpack off to the side. She expected to reach the summit about an hour and forty-five minutes ago. Right now, she didn't think she could go any further. Sarah's body screamed in pain. All the operations, all the reconstructive surgeries, all the fighting she'd done pushing herself through the physical therapies over all these many years, nothing could compare to the indescribable fire coming from, not only inside her body but—what was insane— even from outside of her body. Sarah was actually experiencing pain coming from places she didn't even have a body. Unable to withstand the agony any longer, she collapsed face down on the ground.

Mollie was beside herself, intuitively sensing the extreme pain and distress Sarah was in. Instinctively, she knew even a gentle nudge, and slight massaging with her nose along Sarah's back would cause her discomfort. But Mollie couldn't just let Sarah lie there like this. She knew Sarah was breathing but not the way she should. Mollie decided to do the heroic thing, although painful for Sarah. She positioned her head in such a way, dug in, and after a few tries, successfully pushed Sarah over onto her back. Sarah screamed out in misery and passed out, which wasn't necessarily a bad thing.

Sarah's flat-on-her-back position and unconscious state allowed her breathing to become more even and relaxed. The cool ground and cushioning effect of years of accumulated forest litter under Sarah's body tempered the pain and provided her with some relief. The heavy mist that saturated the air caressed Sarah's face and provided her with a facial of fresh moisture, cooling down her overheated condition. Mollie could sense Sarah had become more stable. She wanted to do more but feared if she tried nudging her too much, the pain would become unbearable.

Mollie's high level of concern had her pacing anxious loops around the prone and vulnerable Sarah, when suddenly there was a loud crashing racket coming from up above that startled her. Mollie quickly looked up and saw a large darkened object swooping down through the trees right toward her. Her first instinct was to protect Sarah. She spun on a dime to face the oncoming threat. Within a split second, Mollie jumped with bared teeth to strike at the assailant but missed clean, giving the attacker a clear path to assault the face of the defenseless Sarah. As if in slow motion, Mollie fell away, helplessly watching as Sarah was about to be harmed, when by the grace of the spirits of the forest, she was relieved to see the aggressor, just when it was close enough to strike, do nothing more than fan Sarah's face with a soggy wave of air from its mighty wings. Then with the swiftness of a rocket, it took off straight up, and before Mollie could regain her balance, the attacker circled back and repeated its measured course with another one of its specialty soggy waves to Sarah's face. By now, through some means of collie-to-phantom-flier communications, a clear understanding of the mission of these swooping sorties was divulged. A majestic bald eagle, brother to the incapacitated Sarah, knowing, like all the creatures of the forest, that his blood sister was here and sensing she was in jeopardy, came flying to Sarah's rescue. And after about his fifth dive, the quakes of cool air to Sarah's face appeared to have had the desired effect, because Sarah began to waken.

Not sure if it was caused by the volumes of air being moved by the herculean wings of her flying-to-the-rescue blood brother eagle or by divine providence, but as Sarah awakened, the dense fog surrounding the scene began to clear and hints of a blueberry sky peaked through the clouds. Sarah's eyes blinked as she regained her bearings. They blinked to adjust to the rays of sun that played hopscotch with the clouds and near impenetrable canopy above, and they blinked as a natural reaction to the slobbering licks to her face by the overly enthusiastic and incredibly relieved Mollie.

Sarah felt totally refreshed but confused. She felt fine and wondered why she was lying here flat on her back, until she tried to move. Then she remembered and wished she could forget. Okay, so now what? Mollie tried to let Sarah know that she could use her for support. Heck, Mollie would let Sarah ride her to the summit, although that would be unrealistic. Sarah just stayed there, motionless. Mollie wondered why. Sarah's guardian bald eagle continued to swoop by. He knew Sarah had awoken, and he too questioned why she remained still. They thought she wasn't doing anything, but they were wrong. Sarah was doing a lot. They just couldn't tell.

Sarah understood the pain that caused her to lie there presented a setback to her journey. She was just doing what every successful corps of discoverers and avid adventurers had done throughout the ages when faced with a setback, except Sarah was doing it lying down. She was eventually going to do an assessment of lessons learned from her experience, brush herself off, and without ever thinking about quitting, continue to forge ahead. She just needed to take a few more minutes before doing so. While resting, she thought about what just occurred and looked for the good in this experience. Sarah wasn't sure of the exact details but was aware that Mollie and her fly-by brother eagle were there for her when she needed them. So that was a good thing. If she wasn't lying here looking up, she probably would've missed seeing the bazillion tiny rainbows dancing through the mist every time a ray of sunshine snuck through the clouds and canopy above. Hey right, the canopy. She decided to take this opportunity to thank the canopy for shielding her like a gigantic hat from that cold rain that came down in buckets for days on end—another good thing or two. And there was one more good thing to be found in Sarah lying here in the middle of nowhere flat on her back. And that was the fact that she was lying on what she perceived to be sacred ground. It was sacred because she knew her Grandma Jennie coursed this very same trail on her way to the summit to hear the trees sing. Her grandmother may have stepped, or very possibly crawled, right where she was lying, so many years ago. So, for Sarah, lying on this ground made sacred by her grandmother allowed her to draw Grandma Jennie's spirit, energy, strength, and determination from it, and bestowed upon Sarah the most special, top secret, super turbocharged…well, we know the rest. This gave her the energy she needed to continue on, which was another really good thing.

With her batteries charged, Sarah brushed herself off, collected her belongings, and did an all-important target system lock onto that all-knowing, all-powerful, all-loving voice emanating from the depths of her soul. This guaranteed that each grueling step forward and upward would bring her closer to her reward. With this assurance, Sarah continued her march to the summit, which was starting to become more visible through the disappearing mist. Mollie jumped, yelped, and wiggled in celebration as brother eagle swooped and dove around them in freedom-ringing support while continuing with his signature fanning, piercingly screeching the entire time.

CHAPTER 29

Sarah thought she caught glimpses of what she believed was the famed old dead hollow tree that bore her grandmother's initial and treasured carved line, but it was still a long way off. As she moved closer, the wind picked up. At first, she thought the wind was blowing the fog away. But really the wind was blowing the fog back in and it had a cold, foreboding bite to it. She paused to put on her warmer coat and decided to put on her gloves as well, because the temperature was dropping rapidly. Sarah thought she had just a little further to go. Mollie respectfully hung back. She knew this was Sarah's show and only she should claim the summit first and alone. Sarah was forced to do a dead-reckoning toward where she thought the old dead tree was, because right now, the summit was socked in solid with fog and she was striding blindly. Sarah knew she was close, because she felt the ground level beneath her feet. But she couldn't believe she came all this way and couldn't see the tree, let alone the view of all her grandmother saved. She thought if she didn't walk right into the tree she could very well pass it by and begin descending the other side of the mountain.

Sarah, sensing dangerous conditions were developing, heeded the sound advice given to her years ago by Poppy Tom and stopped dead in her tracks to make an assessment of her situation. She turned in the direction she thought she took to get to where she was, hoping to see something that looked familiar. No such luck. Sarah came to the stark realization that she and Mollie were exposed and alone on the top of this mountain, surrounded by a dense, bone-chilling fog. Sarah made a wise judgment call and sat right down on a rock scrubbed clean by passing glaciers, eons of drenching rains, and screaming winds that could rip the hair from your scalp, like the one she was experiencing now. Mollie came in close, and Sarah wrapped her arms around Mollie's warm body.

Through the howling wind, through fog thick enough you'd need a chainsaw to cut it, brother eagle's screeches could still be heard. These screeches acted as a benevolent siren's song of safe harbor and sense of assurance for the wayward Sarah and Mollie stranded on their frigid, desolate island in the storm. Sarah had a frightening thought that her walker had blown away and may have fallen down the other side of the mountain. In desperation, she frantically reached in all directions, even over her head thinking her walker had somehow levitated and was twisting around in a funnel cloud above her. To her relief, her flailing arms struck pay dirt and she felt her walker just off to her side and behind her. She grabbed its nearest leg and swung the walker toward her. About halfway through the swing, the walker hit a tree. Sarah, thinking the tree could provide them with some protection, dragged herself toward it, with one arm clutched around the walker and the other clenched around Mollie. She set her backpack-armored body tight against the base of the tree. She kept one arm tightly wrapped around her walker so as not to lose it. She pulled her hood snuggly over her head and tried to wrap her entire body around Mollie. And there they sat to wait out the storm with the faithful screeches of brother eagle barely being heard.

It was hard to imagine that with the wind screaming and the temperature falling Sarah was able to fall asleep. But she did and a bit later was actually awakened by the quiet that prevailed and the warm rays of the sun roving over her still-chilled and stiffened body. Mollie, too, stirred from her slumber. Once again, Sarah had to blink to regain her bearings. She blinked to allow her eyes to adjust from her sleep and mostly to the sun when it happened to hit her eyes straight on. Sarah and Mollie had thankfully passed through the darkness of the storm and now basked in the warmth of a bright, sunshiny world. This gave Sarah a refreshing burst of energy and feeling of renewal. She declared to herself and Mollie, "Enough of this blinking, enough of this lying around business, it's time to get casting!"

Yes, it caused Sarah excruciating pain to rise to her feet, but she did it anyway. She couldn't stand as straight and tall as she'd like but didn't let that reality deter her, because she realized it was all worth it. For, as promised, from this shining vantage-point place in the sky that Sarah strived so long and hard to get to, her reward was received when she peered out over the entire expanse of all that her Grandma Jennie saved and was totally captivated and amazed by the incredible beauty and grandeur of Mother Nature's magnificent masterpiece.

Tears flowed from Sarah's eyes even before the valve operator on duty down in the "Make Sarah's Eyes Tear Department" received the go ahead to open the flood gates. If Grandma Jennie was Sarah's hero before, which she was, they would have to invent a new title for what Grandma Jennie was to Sarah now. And as if to show off even more, Mother Nature gave every droplet of moisture clinging to every branch, leaf, and pine needle that froze during that sudden drop in temperature, the signal to begin to melt. All these droplets of melting ice, infinite in number, fell like rain and glistened like countless rainbows from the reflection of the sun until they all blended into one. Sarah and Mollie stood surrounded and hypnotized at the sight of this kaleidoscope of a wall of glistening, countless rainbows. In this dreamy, trancelike state, Sarah again detected the hint of roses and the smell of newly cut wood in the air and was reminded of the words written by her Grandmother,

"Find the Hinge!"

Just then Sarah remembered the tree and shook herself free from her spell. She spun around, still clutching her walker and banged it into something hard. She looked up and saw the tree and, staring her right in her face, was a carved letter "J" and right below that, one single line, both looking like they were carved yesterday.

Sarah let out a loud holler and said, "Mollie, it's the tree!" Mollie bounced in excitement. "We didn't even realize it, but it was right behind us. It sheltered us from the storm, and we didn't even know it!"

Just then, something caught Sarah's eye. Above Grandma Jennie's initial, Sarah saw something glinting. She moved in to get a closer look and was astonished to see screwed into the tree was a hinge. "The Hinge!" she shouted with excitement as the realization of the moment hit home. Instantly, her throat went dry, causing her to swallow hard. Goose bumps careened across her entire body, and the tears began to flow once again. Sarah dropped her head down and swayed it slowly as she tried to absorb the magnitude of the situation. Then she realized she stood in a halo of luminous light and was communicating directly with the very souls of her grandparents. She could sense them both smiling radiantly down upon her, knowing their message, which was transcending heaven and earth, was being received and understood. Sarah raised her head up, looking worshipingly into the blue rapture above and with her emotions on high, shouted out as loud as she could, "Grandma Jennie and Poppy Tom, look, I found the hinge!"

Sarah now excitedly turned her attention back to the hinge and examined it closely. With her trembling hand, she gently wiped years of debris off its tarnished surface in the same manner an archeologist would do when first discovering a rare artifact. Sarah noticed the hinge was attached to a hatch in the same manner Poppy Tom used to build his birdhouses, so the hatch could easily be lifted to clean out the nest. Because of the highly decayed state of the hatch, Sarah wisely used both hands to carefully open it. This revealed to her the opening to the hollow of the tree. Sarah sensed there was something waiting for her inside. She timidly reached down into the hole and felt something smooth and circular. Something like a bottle. Mollie sat in utter suspense. Sarah, with an intense, questioning look on her face, slowly lifted the mystery object out of the hollow of the tree. Sure enough, it was a bottle. Sarah gingerly wiped the bottle clean, exposing its intricately cut crystal surface. This exposed the bottle to the sun for the first time in who knows how long, causing it to spring to life with reflections of shimmering light and a dazzling dance of color. It was like the bottle was celebrating its freedom as a genie would do after being unleashed from years of confinement inside his dark, damp lamp.

Sarah was utterly mystified by this beautiful object and by this totally unexpected experience that had turned her journey of discovery and accomplishment into a hunt for buried treasure. Sarah cradled her precious find in her arms and shimmied around to again face Grandma Jennie's perfectly preserved piece of heaven on earth, leaving her walker behind. She wanted to face in the same direction she felt her Grandmother Jennie was facing when she heard the trees sing their glorious song. And Sarah felt this was an awesome direction to be facing when she opened the bottle and removed the rolled piece of paper she spied neatly tied with a pretty pink ribbon resting at the bottle's base. Sarah spun the highly corroded top to open it and was surprised as to how easily it unwound. Sarah the seeker didn't realize it, but bee's wax deftly applied to the threads of the top of the bottle by the guiding finger of a long-ago hider was the reason why. She daintily lifted the rolled paper from the bottle and immediately recognized the pretty pink ribbon. Sarah knew this ribbon belonged to her Grandma Jennie. She could still picture this roll of ribbon sitting on Grandma Jennie's desk, next to her sewing kit, alongside her pens and pretty stationery.

Grandma Jennie used this ribbon to tie bouquets of roses she would cut from her garden along the fence and gift to her friends. She used it to decorate Cecilia's pigtails when she was a little girl, and Cecilia used this same ribbon to decorate Sarah's. There was still enough of this very same ribbon sitting on Grandma Jennie's desk for Paula Jean to use to decorate Little Jennie's pigtails when the time comes.

Sarah tucked the bottle under her arm so she could untie the ribbon and unravel the paper, but she felt unbalanced and was afraid she might drop the ornate, heirloom bottle and it would break. Sarah decided to play it safe and carefully set the vessel down on the ground. She stood back up as straight and tall as she could and readied herself to do the unveiling. Sarah took a couple of deep breaths and with jittery hands untied the ribbon, uncoiled the wonderful feeling parchment paper, and saw, exquisitely scribed across its face, this beautiful poem.

To the Light of the World

We knew built on the power of love,
You would climb this mountain high above.

To gaze upon worlds shiny and new
Because of discoveries made by you.

We saw the benevolent good that you had
And a happy so bright that makes everyone glad.

So we say to you, our fine granddaughter dear,
Who so bravely fought your burdens fair,

Stand straight and tall and know you've won,
As these amazing trees sing out gloriously to your rising sun!

Keep on making smooth delicate casts,
And all of life's joys forever will last.

All of creation knows that is true
And knows there are No Limits to what you can do.

For your love-light shines on all to see
And ours back to you for eternity.

Words do not exist and never will to describe the significance of the spectacularly inspiring poem Sarah had just read or for how incredibly wonderful it made her feel. Thrilling emotions beyond emotions flooded into every pore at the very core of her being like a tidal wave of biblical proportions. Of all the amazing and precious gifts Grandma Jennie and Poppy Tom had so generously furnished Sarah with, throughout her entire life, nothing could compare to this ultimate precious gift that they had bestowed upon her today. And Sarah knew it, and even more important, she could feel it and was, beyond words, grateful for it.

Love. Love, in all its glory and magnificence, when so graciously and unselfishly bequeathed cannot help but have this desired effect on all that it embraces. Love is the answer, my friends. If there ever was a question, *love* is the answer.

Grandma Jennie and Poppy Tom knew that all along, and dedicated their entire lives and beyond to provide their granddaughter, Sarah, with the love, guidance, and wherewithal she would need to remain strong in body and soul to make that shining-like-a-thousand-million suns discovery for herself. They knew it wouldn't be easy for Sarah but also knew it would be well worth her effort.

Many years ago, along the bank of a brook, Sarah learned where love is manufactured and where the answer lies. Today, standing on the top of this remote mountaintop and looking out at the result of Mother Nature's unimaginable creative love, Sarah discovered her hard-earned and well-deserved reward neatly tied and hiding at the bottom of an elegantly crafted, brightly shining, crystal bequest. Sarah's reward for all the love, good, happy, charity, and grace she so willingly gave, despite her many burdens, along with all there is and ever was, is that SARAH IS THE ANSWER and always and forever shall be. What an amazing gift it is and one that was received in such an incredible way by the amazing Sarah from her miraculous, dedicated, and cherished grandparents. It's a gift that fills her with feelings of absolute peace, gratitude, and love divine.

Perhaps by some special means of communication between the spirits of Mollie's ancestors, she seemed to have known all along that Sarah was going to be rewarded with this unique and special gift. For she literally bowed before Sarah in a sign of respect and then joyously jumped up and bathed Sarah's face with congratulatory kisses. Sarah enjoyed every one of Mollie's soaking smooches, immensely.

Not to be outdone, brother eagle flying overhead screeched loudly to get Sarah's and Mollie's attention. They looked up and were astonished to see an incredibly vibrant rainbow, being unfurled from the golden talons of Sarah's high-flying blood brother eagle, across the bright, penetratingly deep blueberry sky.

With the stage now set and right on cue, Mother Nature struck up her choir of majestic trees in thunderous, wondrous, inspiring song, honoring, as she did for only a select few, her heroine, Sarah, for all her epic efforts to repair and protect so much of Mother Nature's artistically designed and intricately fashioned creations of absolute genius. Mollie didn't hear a thing but could see by the look on Sarah's face that Sarah was hearing their glorious song and that this hymn of reverence and veneration filled Sarah's heart and soul with feelings of impassioned love and euphoric bliss.

Using Poppy Tom's ol' pocket knife, which was as sharp as the first day he acquired it, Sarah put the finishing touches on the carvings of her initial "S" and her one line of triumph and achievement on the old dead hollow tree, right next to Grandma Jennie's. She looked beyond The Mountain of Singing Trees and saw an even higher mountain in the distance. Sarah pocketed Poppy Tom's knife right next to her two treasured poems, secured her transcending-time-and-space bottle into her backpack, grasped the handles of her walker, and, because there are no limits to what she can do, began striding toward that mountain in the distance with Mollie at her side.

After a few gamely paces, Sarah stopped and, after some wise reflection, said to Mollie, "You know, girl, I think we'll have to discover that mountain another time, we have a shindig to go to."

As a big red ball of a sun set in the western sky, brother eagle floated lazily on cushiony up currents of love over ground made sacred by his blood sister, Sarah, and the kindred spirits of her hero grandparents. With the exception of a few carvings in an old dead hollow tree, Sarah and Mollie believed they've left this sacred ground exactly as they had found it. But brother eagle knew differently. His eagle eyes were keen enough to see etched upon this sacred ground's surface the markings left from Sarah's walker and Sarah's and Mollie's footprints. And he also saw, what is invisible to the human eye, the footprints left by the spirits of the loving, guiding, and eternally dedicated Grandma Jennie and Poppy Tom leading the pack!

Every step of the way Sarah, every step of the way.

Then, from the depths of this deep, dark primordial forest, whispering to the hushed calm surrender in the harmonious rhythm of the night came the callings...hoot...hoot, hoot, hoot...hoot! When translated from perfect smiling owl-speak to the perfectly aligned-with-the-powers-of-the-entire-universe human-speak, means, love...love, love, love...love!

THE END

RESOURCES

Petri, R.L., Fly-Fishing, *Encyclopædia Britannica*, 2008; https://www.britannica.com/topic/fly-fishing#ref980173

Wulff, Lee, *Handbook of Freshwater Fishing*, J.P. Lippincott Co., Philadelphia, 1939.

MDA, Spinal Muscular Atrophy Type 2 (intermediate SMA), web page, Muscular Dystrophy Australia, North Melbourne; accessed 8/12/16; https://www.mda.org.au/disorders/spinal-muscular-atrophy-an-overview/

ABOUT THE AUTHOR

(Photo Credit: Rigoglioso Photography, www.paigerigoglioso.com)

Jeffrey J. Antonucci followed in the footsteps of his father, uncle, and grandfather, all master tradesmen, by working in construction as a bricklayer. It wasn't until the idea for this story came to Jeff, as he tells it, like a slideshow before his eyes, that he ever even thought of writing, what would become, this novel.

Up until that point, Jeff's writings consisted of small personal pieces and poems for family members and friends. In addition, for the time he was employed as a senior facilities manager for a European corporation, Jeff composed email communications that were creative and fun to read yet conveyed information that was pertinent to the safety and well-being of the four-hundred plus people that worked at that facility.

Jeff attributes his ability to write this story, which speaks to the infinite power of love, to the love and devotion given to him by his incredible parents, Sarah and Thomas, to his four brothers and their beautiful families, to all of his extended family, and to so many friends that, to Jeff, are like family, too. He also attributes it to the immense love, support, and unflinching commitment given to Jeff by his wonderful and amazing wife and children, and their little dog, for not only this endeavor, but for always and forever.

It's mentioned in this story that, when the gift of love is given, it gets reflected back to the giver in the same measure and all bask in its glow. Jeff knows he has been gifted with such love and is eternally grateful to the heavens above for that. Jeff's desire now is to give each precious word of this story as little gifts of love to the reader, which in turn, gets reflected back in the same measure, allowing all to bask in its glow.

www.jeffantonucci.com